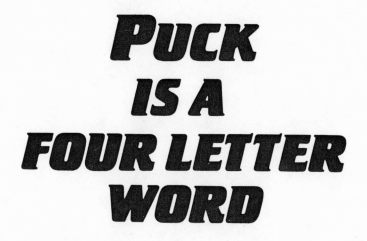

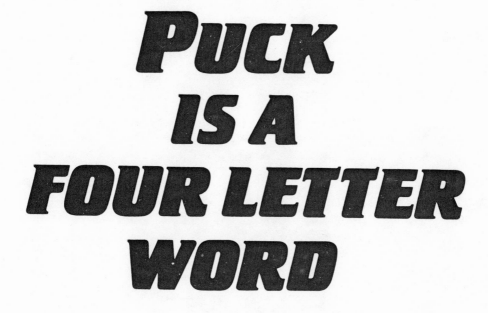

PUCK IS A FOUR LETTER WORD

Frank Orr

William Morrow and Company, Inc.

New York   *1983*

Library of Congress Cataloging in Publication Data

Orr, Frank.
  Puck is a four letter word.

  I. Title.
PS3565.R69P8   1983   813'.54   83-5459
ISBN 0-688-02478-5

Printed in the United States of America

First U.S. Edition

1 2 3 4 5 6 7 8 9 10

To Harold Ballard
He very badly wants to have his name on a winner.
This might be his only hope.

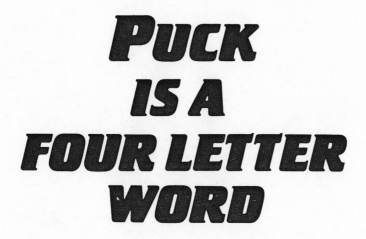

~1~
The
Off-Season

Introduction

So what's a farmer named Willie Mulligan doing writing a book on hockey? Or a book on anything?

Simple. A New York publisher's big cash advance induced my decision to "go literary," as my pal Hartley Laidlaw said.

The publisher was grabbed by the wonderful sport of hockey last spring when he saw his first game. A friend took him to a New York Rangers' playoff match when they won their first Stanley Cup since Christ was a choirboy, beating me and the marvelous Montreal Canadiens in the final to end our Cup-streak at six.

The Rangers really bought the Cup. They paid huge sums to several top National Hockey League free agents, like the Yankees in baseball. So in a way I guess I had a hand in the Rangers' win. I was vice-president of the NHL Players' Association when we had that big battle with the owners two years ago. Hartley Laidlaw, star center for the Maple Leafs, was our president, and he and I were the most militant players. We led hockey's only strike. After a six-week delay in the season, the NHL team owners, a group with more oddballs than the Harper Valley PTA, caved in on unlimited free agency. Or so we thought.

Until then, when a player's contract expired and he changed clubs as a free agent, his new team compensated his former one with players, cash or draft choices, subject to binding arbitration. Really, players had little freedom.

After much bitterness, we got free agency but the bloody owners made a secret agreement not to sign free agent players. They didn't want guys moving for deals with long rows of zeroes. The Rangers, though, owned by a huge multinational conglomerate with a finger in every money pie in the world, broke the agreement, signed five all-stars as free agents and also worked a nifty deal to land two great players from the Soviet Union. After that, it was just a matter of time before the Cup ended up in New York.

The Rangers' victory drove nutty all the weirdos, drunks, junkies, hoods and six-figure guys who go to games in Madison Square Garden. The publisher got all excited, too, and decided the "definitive" hockey book was needed.

I am the author because of an interview I did for a TV network during the strike. The publisher was impressed by the insightful, handsome, articulate young man picketing the NHL's headquarters in New York, wearing a sign that said: THE NHL OWNERS SUCK. NO FREE AGENCY. NO SHOOT THE PUCK.

Actually, I was the second choice. When the TV crew came to film the bit, our president, H. Laidlaw, was in the rack with a strikers' groupie. In New York, every group has groupies.

In my big-league TV presentation, the six pickets, the lowest paid earning $167,500 per season, appeared to be galley slaves, unable to obtain the freedom to earn enough to buy groceries for their families.

Right away, the publisher figured I was his man. He wanted an inside look at hockey with "all the warts" left on. I told him it would be more accurate to say "with all the crabs left on" because the outbreak of warts in the NHL was in 1948, while crabs were an epidemic last season. A sure-thing in Chicago was likely the main distributor, though some born-again Christians who caught the little devils insisted a toilet seat in the Fabulous Forum in Los Angeles was the culprit.

"How strong do you want this book?" I asked.

"You have a college degree and you led a successful strike," he said. "Give us a hard-hitting, inside look at your game. How about a diary on the ordeals of the great Canadiens through your eyes? Pull no punches! Throw the puck in and chase it! Place the old biscuit in the basket! Shoot and score!"

A small hitch did arise after the ink was dry on the contract, however: This book is about Willie Mulligan, but not Willie Mulligan, great star of the Montreal Canadiens.

During the strike, a couple of owners told Hartley and me: "We'll get you smartasses somewhere along the line." They did. When the NHL expanded to twenty-four teams by adding one in Cleveland, the noted labor agitators were not protected by the Toronto Maple Leafs and Montreal Canadiens. They were claimed by the Cleveland Big Green.

So that's how a guy who's spending the early part of his adult life in short pants and long stockings, chasing a hunk of rubber across a frozen pond, trying to shoot it past a man covered in mattresses guarding a fishnet stretched out on some pipes, came to write this book.

Here it is, the humble NHL beginnings of the Cleveland Big Green, the dumbest-ass name ever for a team, and a few months in the life of Willie Mulligan.

June 15 (morning)

Noon or some ridiculous hour and the phone rings in my Holiday Inn suite ($135 per day, U.S.) on the island of Grenada. It clatters a dozen times before my head unravels to answer it.

I am on vacation, all expenses paid (no hookers or VD treatment), the owners' Christmas gift to Montreal Canadien players. Had they known we would lose the Stanley Cup to the New York Rangers, the gift would have been a bus tour of Trois-Rivières.

The Stanley Cup, the National Hockey League's big prize! If the Canadiens don't win it, Montrealers feel like the folks in England did when the barbarians took the Holy Grail away from the Crusaders.

When the Rangers beat us in seventh game overtime, the Forum fans cried. French-Canadians on the team did, too.

You needed a boat in our dressing room. The frogs (a euphemism for French-Canadians) won't be able to take a leak this summer without hearing: "Hey, der! How come de Canad-ee-en no win da Cup dis year?"

Losing it shouldn't be such a big deal. The team won the last six years. I have five Cup rings and while I'm not big on the rah-rah, win-one-for-the-Rocket, schoolboy stuff, to wear the *blue-blanc-rouge* is very special.

That six guys are in the press box or on the farm team eager to take your job is an inspiration, too.

The final ended June 8th because the NHL had twenty of twenty-three teams in the playoffs. I stayed in town for a club wipeout at Henri Richard's pub, then hauled my tired ass to Grenada.

I checked and picked a spot with no players or chance of recognition. My luck lasted six hours. I was at the bar last night with a Chivas 'cap when a guy said: "Aren't you Willie Mulligan?"

I almost said: "Shit, no! I'm Otto Schmiddlapp, an exchange student from East Germany." But I was trapped. The man is from Toronto and I got the story of his life. He had been in Granada two days with his wife and daughter, who has just graduated from college. Soon, he and "the missus" will be off on a cruise, leaving daughter on the island.

He asked me to join them as a fellow-Canadian.

The missus is a blue-rinser, a blonde but blue-tinted in certain light. His name is Ralph and he fights gray hair with a color rinse he combs in and the gray disappears so slowly that "even your best friends don't notice." Friends do notice your hair has a strange reddish tinge, however.

Ralph, the only man in the world who could belong to Rotary, Kiwanis, Kinsmen, Lions, Masons, Orange Lodge, Knights of Columbus and B'nai B'rith at the same time, introduced me as "Willie Mulligan, the great star of the Montreal Canadiens," then gave his old lady a head-jerk. She lifted her ample backside over one chair so the Canadiens' star could sit beside only daughter, a brunette knockout outfitted with all-star jars.

Her caliber of chest once inspired Hartley Laidlaw to say: "If she's a winger, she stays behind the play or her boobs are offside."

Her name is Clarice. We exchanged nods and Ralph took over, telling us why the Rangers won—that they did what any good business would do and that's win, and that "they showed those commies how things are done" by getting the Soviet players.

Ralph bought drinks and prattled, then gave the missus an elbow in the ribs worth a major for a deliberate attempt to injure. "You young folks stay. We're on a yacht early and need our sleep."

When they left, only daughter switched to Scotch, which she drank very well. She's a physiotherapist with a master's degree, and starts a job with a Toronto hospital after vacation.

Clarice was on the defensive because of the way old loud-mouth shanghaied me from the bar, but I told her not to feel obligated to stay. I was a little light on sociability anyway because every time I turned my head I felt a sharp pain, courtesy of a Rangers' Russian who gave me a cross-check on the neck when the sneaky commie knew the ref couldn't see it. I'll spear that red first chance I get next season.

"I'll finish my drink," she said. "Sorry to tell you I'm not very big on jocks."

I replied that I wasn't too large on chiropractors, and Clarice boiled, pointing out the large difference between chiropractors and physiotherapists, but who could expect some dumb football player to know it? I cleverly informed her of the large difference between football and hockey players, but why should some bone-cruncher realize it?

She laughed, I turned my head and the pain bit again.

"You always make faces like a little kid who's stubbed his toe?"

I explained about the Russian and she placed her hand on my neck with a grip that would squeeze the juice out of a hockey puck.

"I might not know about hockey but I know a little about sore necks," she said, starting to massage.

At first, it hurt like hell, more than the pain, then started to feel good. That broke the ice and we chattered away like long-lost relatives. Eventually, a Chivas-front moved in.

"Let's go to your room and I'll fix it for you, just to show you I haven't wasted six years," she suggested.

Well, Clarice fixed my neck and, with some persuasion from the slick center, my entire anatomy, before the night melted into Caribbean dawn. I promised her a job as physio for a hockey team, which would have a long injury list.

When the stinking phone rings, I feel around for Clarice but she's gone like summer wages. I finally locate the phone which, I think, is slightly smaller than Clarice, under the bed.

"This is your old pal, Heavy Hung! I'm in jail for the trick with the camel and need bail," the voice says, loudly.

No way Hartley Laidlaw could find me. "You asshole! Even if you could find me, you'd never waste money on a call. Is this collect?"

"It's not trivial," he says. "Besides, your mother can't keep a secret when torture is applied." His voice goes serious and he says: "The rotten piss-pots did it to us."

"Who's done what to whom?"

"Sounds like the limerick about the queer and the lesbian," he laughs. "We wondered how they would shaft the John L. Lewis and Jimmy Hoffa of hockey labor? Well, they found a way. Welcome to the Cleveland what-the-fuck's-their-names!"

If lightning strikes me, it will be fun compared to this moment.

"The expansion draft was this morning and we were claimed by the team with the funny name."

It's so absurd that I laugh.

"A man laughs when he's told he's about to be castrated or hears the death sentence. I don't phone in prime time for a joke."

"It's impossible. The Leafs wouldn't leave you unprotected and the Canadiens need me."

"Noble thoughts, lad! They said they'd get us and 'get' day is here. Oh, is it here! I can't believe the crap they spouted.

Your owner said they wanted to make the new team competitive and the Leafs used the same caliber of junk."

"Cleveland! It's impossible."

"Very possible, chum," Hartley says. "Gotta run! Have a neat holiday, new teammate. It might be the last time you'll show your ugly face in public."

June 15 (evening)

After my chat with Hartley, I resume my holiday—several cold Banks beer beside the pool and a daylight examination of Clarice in a bathing suit made from two fried eggs and a cork.

Hartley, a good guitar picker, once had a great idea for a country song, titled *I Never Went to Bed with an Ugly Woman but I've Sure Woke Up with a Few*. It doesn't apply to Clarice.

Clarice has a brilliant idea: her room because the sun is making her amorous. She's an all-purpose lady because both the sun and the moon rev her engines. She's like a left winger who can score forty-five and backcheck, too. But when you're shit at and hit, enthusiasm is difficult, even for Clarice's all-star frame. The bottom has dropped out of my world but she's not sympathetic.

"Does it matter which team pays you all that money to chase a dumb puck?" she says.

I tell her that the difference between doing it for the Canadiens and the Big Green is the same as the difference between sheep dung and sherbert. She concludes I'm as much fun as a good flood and, in all her splendor, walks off to the beach. The next time I see her, she's on a catamaran with a college kid who has muscles in his hair.

A profound thought: dirty, rotten, no good son-of-a-bitch! The Cleveland Big Green! Everyone in the NHL laughed when that won a Name The Team contest. Contest? My ass!

Big Green Transport is the trucking company owned by Clive Anderson IV, who paid eight million bucks for an expansion franchise in a city where two attempts to make big league hockey work already went tits up.

The NHL wanted a twenty-fourth team to have four, six-team divisions and Clive Eye-Vee, as he's known, was the only millionaire who didn't know better. His eight big ones earned really nifty privileges. Each NHL team protected twenty skaters and three goalies for the expansion draft to stock the Green, who drafted one unprotected body from each club.

What a bonanza of talent in the twenty-first skater and fourth goalie on most teams! "Screw-all but guys who are small but slow, big but dumb, jerk-offs, drinkers, wife-beaters, dopers, stick-men, chickens and a batch of frogs," as Hartley perceptively noted.

Then the NHL board tried a bunco by trying to keep the Green out of this year's entry draft, the one source of players from Canadian junior, U.S. college and European hockey. They not only pooped on Anderson's doorstep; they wanted to ring the bell and ask for toilet paper.

But Clive IV told the NHL: No draft picks, no eight million. The NHL understood that and the Big Green drafted first.

Clive IV won points there but not many for his appointments to the team's executive. He named Clive V (Clive-Five) as president, Gerald (Gee-One) as vice-president and Peter Edmunds as director of hockey operations and general manager.

Edmunds was a fine winger as a player, but as a GM and coach, he could screw up a hand job. Somehow, he kept getting hired, first as the coach of three teams that sagged, then GM of two teams that sagged.

Edmunds is a paunchy, back-slapping gladhander, a super bullshit artist. He always had a windy explanation for his bad teams in which everyone else was to blame. Obviously, he can talk the nuts off an iron bridge when it comes to convincing owners to hire him, and he earns good press because he hangs out with the writers and is fast to add a tab to an expense account.

A Canadien who played on one of Pete's teams made a comment I think of 867 times today: "In judging hockey talent, Pete couldn't pick his mother out of a gang of aborigines."

By mid-afternoon, the Big Green, tropical sun and cold suds make it time to head home. I want to find out what's going on. I call Canada and after two hours, I get my mother on a line that passes through a food processor. My ma is fine but, beyond that, it's garble.

Home means flying to Barbados on the local airline, the only one with Gideon bibles in the seat pockets, then on to Toronto. The airline books me home in two days, claiming nothing else is available for two weeks, which is a crock because the islands aren't busy in June.

I hit the hotel disco after a wet dinner and Clarice is boogeying her lucious buns off with the beach boy, a big, blond, corn-fed college football tight end. I regret being rude to her today because Clarice would have made me cope with reality. Or made me think of it less.

June 16

The final day of my vacation, a royal brown-off. I forgot the sun is brutal here and now have a healthy sunburn. Last night only cold beer inspired sleep.

How fast life changes! One night, the Canadiens' star shares his sheets with the gorgeous Clarice. The next, it's Big Green and sunburn.

I bundle up for my morning excursion. Walking on a beach, watching the waves, is a fine place to contemplate life's vagaries.

I make a deal with myself: no getting my shorts in a knot until I know the facts. Maybe Clive Eye-Vee will write me a new contract to make me rich. Fat chance! They'll cut my salary and shorten the deal. I remind poor me: no whining, self-pity or contemplating suicide.

Besides, the Big Green has to take my contract, which is super, even by today's inflated NHL standards. Before the free agency guff, I negotiated a long-term deal. I should say that my agent, Brock Prendergast, known to his clients as "Ten Percent," convinced the Canadiens that I am simply the world's greatest player, an outlook I share.

I was twenty-four and just off my best NHL season—47 goals, 55 assists plus 15 goals in the playoffs—when we won the third of the six Cups. I signed a six-year contract plus an option season with a team that loves one-year deals to keep the men hungry. It paid me $180,000 that first season plus a $10,000 annual increase over the six years.

Although the Canadiens don't like individual bonus clauses, I had one worth ten grand for 35 goals plus $1,000 per goal over that figure. I cashed it twice, including a nifty twenty grand for 45 goals.

I'll earn $220,000 next season from the Green, and something I didn't think of earlier brightens my day magnificently —I'll be paid in U.S. funds. The difference in value between the Canadian and U.S. dollar will give me a raise of $40,000 and I'll avoid the wallet-killer Quebec taxes, too.

That will help finish remodeling the house on the lower two hundred acres of Shoot-The-Puck Farm, the most beautiful and best operated agricultural set-up in the world, situated near the metropolis of Mount Everest, Ontario.

Mount Everest is a Hall Of Fame name for a hometown. I waited six years to use my socko line about it, and a New York television guy finally gave me the chance in an interview. He had a five-line bio sheet, all he knew about me or hockey.

"Your hometown sounds interesting," he said. "Why would anyone live in a place called Mount Everest?"

"Because it's there," I dead-panned.

He browned me off by sticking to the point.

"Small town, eh?"

"So small the town hooker is a virgin. Mount Everest never grows because when a girl gets pregnant, six guys vanish."

The interview went downhill from that point.

I'm a farmer in the summer; in the winter, I'm a hockey player, although a coach once hinted it was the other way around. He said I handled the puck as if I was using a manure shovel and he bet that I shoveled manure like I had a hockey stick.

When the technocrats talk about how complicated hockey is and use their fancy terms, I sometimes tell them not to forget that hockey was invented to give farmers something to do in the winter.

This is a good time to reveal a few things about myself, about how a humble farm boy became the mighty NHL star, the embodiment of the Canadian dream. (On the silver sands, I have a tape recorder in my beach jacket pocket and a microphone on the lapel, and two old sports with blue hair figure I'm not in the fast lane because I'm talking to myself.)

My name is William Francis Mulligan, about whom a lady writer once wrote: "He's ruggedly handsome with sandy hair and intelligent blue eyes." And I really am from Mount Everest.

Grandfather Mulligan migrated from the old country and settled about a hundred miles from Toronto, cleared the land, fought the mosquitoes and started the family farm.

My father, Charlie Mulligan, and my mother, Bertha, a solid rural Ontario name even though she was a big-city girl, produced three children. There's Little Charlie, thirty-seven now, my partner in the farm; Sandy, thirty, an all-star wise-mouth and a nurse married to Ralph Johnson, whose farm is next to ours; and Willie, twenty-seven, and at the top of his game. The three of us always referred to our parents with the word "big" — Big Bertha, Big Charlie, The Big Pair.

A favorite gag is that I'm from Poverty Line, down a dirt road from Soup Kitchen. Many NHL players are farm and smalltown boys and we play games called "my hometown is so small that..." and "when I was a kid, we were so poor that..."

When we were playing the Rangers in game seven of the Stanley Cup final in New York on national TV, I lined up for a faceoff opposite Lester Franklin, a buddy from the players' association. Lester hails from Peterson's Siding, Saskatchewan, a grain elevator on the rail line plus a combined service station and grocery store with a pool table in the back.

We were waiting for a TV commercial before restarting

the battle and everyone's ass was so tight needles couldn't be pulled out of them with tractors when Lester said: "Geez, were we poor when I was a kid."

"How poor, Lester?" I asked.

"Had a fire in the bathroom; got it out before it reached the house."

The referee laughed, so did I, the other players, too. It was an all-time loony scene, two teams going for the big one, standing around and giggling like idiots.

The Mulligan family wasn't rich but we didn't miss any meals. My mother, from Toronto, met Big Charlie at a dance when visiting cousins in Mount Everest. She always maintained he was funny-looking but sure could polka.

"She was a stuck-up city brat among a bunch of hicks," Big Charlie countered. "Not much to look at but she didn't spit through her teeth like most girls around here."

Big Bertha was a school teacher and her salary helped Big Charlie build up a fine Jersey herd. Now that I've matured a little, I realize I had great parents.

From my father, I learned: "No use getting your shorts in a knot," one of his favorite expressions. He had a little parable to sum up his laid-back philosophy. "An old bull and a young bull are on a hill looking down on a herd of heifers," he told me. "The young bull says: 'Let's run down and jump one of those heifers.' The old bull says: 'Hell, let's walk down and jump 'em all.'"

Big Bertha inspired my talent as a smartass because she's a fine wisemouth, the one person Hartley Laidlaw won't engage in one-upmanship. From Big Bertha, too, comes my love of books, an asset for a pro athlete. After all, we can't spend all our road-time in museums.

A farm with a pond near a village of 350 people with a hockey rink supplies plenty of ice surfaces to skate and play hockey on. And if there's one strong point of my game, it's my skating ability.

An old sportswriter in Toronto once wrote: "Willie Mulligan should have played in the 1930s because he's a river skater all the way." I asked what he meant and he said: "A guy who moves like he never took his skates off when he was a kid so skáting isn't work for him."

That was me.

I remember when Hartley found out I was from Mount Everest, he asked how one passed the time in a small town.

"We had three forms of recreation," I said. "The ball park, the hockey rink and Sheila Symons."

"I've watched you operate in both areas," he said. "Obviously you spent more time on the hockey rink than you did on Sheila."

I was often tempted but never did explore Sheila's charms. Ralph Johnson, my brother-in-law, lost his virtue at fifteen to Sheila in the evergreens near the ball park and she extorted twenty cents a week from him for three months by threatening to tell everyone that he had "a little wee pecker."

So Hartley was right about the rink. On the farm was a marshy area, known as the frog pond, that was a natural skating rink. The wind, deflected by the bush, kept the pond free of snow and when it was cold enough we had a place to skate. The local kids gathered there to play games six hours long with scores like 321 to 197.

Little Charlie was the only goalie in town and, one season, he played for the midget, juvenile and junior clubs, plus the men's team, the Mount Everest Climbers. He should be in the Guinness Book Of Records: One Saturday, he played goal in six games.

Little Charlie might have made it in pro hockey but, as he says now, "I didn't burn to do it the way you did." He wanted to farm, and in grade eleven he walked out of history class, hiked home and told Big Charlie he was ready to go to work. Big Bertha almost had a hernia because she had visions of him as a veterinarian.

Last summer when we were building a fence, Little Charlie said: "If I had stayed in school, know what I'd be doing today? I'd be in this dumb-ass hay-field with my useless hockey-playing brother, stretching a fence."

Little Charlie played for the Climbers until last year, and they had a big night for him at the arena when he hung up his pads, featuring an oldtimers' game with many guys from the twenty-two years when Charlie was the team's one goalie playing against the current edition. The rink was packed to the crappers.

I got permission from the Canadiens to take three team-mates with me. Hartley and three Maple Leafs came, too, although we couldn't play in the game because of the risk of injury.

The pros sneaked into town, dressed in oldtimers' uniforms in Wally Kelly's hardware store across the street from the rink and rode in Wally's truck to the back door. When the one spotlight was on Little Charlie during the anthem, we slipped into the oldtimers' line. When the lights went up and the people spotted the NHL players, the place went berserk.

Little Charlie and I skated to center and hugged each other. He cried and Big Bertha and Sandy, standing in the penalty box, bawled like babies. So did I.

"You no-good sucker," my brother said. "You probably bet a C-note on the oldtimers and brought those ringers to make sure you won."

The NHL players had a penalty-shot contest against Little Charlie. Laidlaw said he didn't try to win because first prize was a night in a hay mow with the best-looking chick in Mount Everest and self-abuse was preferable. But Hartley was still a big hit because he brought a box of frozen horse turds. His father, who owns race horses, had a stablehand gather up some road apples, freeze them solid and pack them in dry ice.

When his turn came in the contest, Hartley took a little box to center and grabbed the microphone. "So the Mulligan boys will have the hockey pucks they've used all their lives, I brought a few," he said, dumping the horse balls on the ice.

He stickhandled a road apple in on goal and the place went nuts.

Hartley achieved in that one night in Mount Everest a feat I didn't accomplish in a lifetime: He got together with Sheila Symons in the biblical sense.

After introducing almost an entire generation of area lads to the finer things in life, Sheila had married Mad Jim

Dawes, who drove a transport for Waldorf Feed and Grain. Mad Jim is the meanest, biggest dude in the county (he still wears a duck-ass haircut) and no one ever dared hint that his lovely wife wasn't as pure as the driven snow in her younger days.

On Little Charlie's night, Mad Jim departed early to drive a load of hog concentrate to Windsor. At a post-game reception, Sheila, who never was real fanatical about being married, went after Hartley like a cow at a salt lick.

They disappeared for an hour. Hartley claimed the nice thing about slipping around in a small town was no taxi-fare to the chick's place when the urge to mingle struck. "My boy, by not combining with Sheila in your youth, you missed half the education your hometown offered."

I suggested that he wouldn't be so smug when Sheila conned him for a couple of hundred bucks a week by threatening to tell everyone in the NHL that he had "a little wee pecker." Even worse, she might turn Mad Jim loose on him.

"No danger of that," he said. "Tonight was the highlight of the lady's life. She got to do it with a real star. Come to think of it, so did I."

I don't think Little Charlie is correct that I burned to be a pro hockey player. Like most Canadian boys with skates, I fantasized about it and, on the frog pond, I was Gordie Howe and Bobby Hull. We were saturated with Maple Leaf and Canadien games on TV and radio but the Boston Bruins were my team, even though my dad said Bruins weren't worth a crap since Milt Schmidt retired.

Although a good hockey player in a small town had much ice time, there was a drawback: few good coaches. Mostly, we just played. Wally Kelly, the hardware magnate, coached the teams, if you can call it that, but about all the hockey Wally knew was that a team needed a goalie and five skaters on the ice. His favorite instruction was: "Stick the assholes." Come to think of it, a few pro coaches I've seen didn't know much more.

At fourteen came my big hockey break. Old Doc Martin, who practiced in Mount Everest for forty-five years and had delivered every kid I ever knew, died. After a long hunt, a new doctor was found.

George Bradshaw was fresh out of medical school. People often said Skinny George might be a horseshit doctor but he sure knew a lot about sports. He played college hockey at McGill and was a fitness nut, Mount Everest's first jogger. He was single — most females in the county suddenly developed a disorder, mostly gynecological — and while his practice was large, he seemed to have lots of spare time and a large amount of rink-rat in him.

Mount Everest's kids' teams played in a local league against towns in the area. That year, when Wally Kelly figured there were enough players for a good midget team, he entered the Mount Everest Royals in the Ontario Minor Hockey Association midget C series. (The OMHA runs minor hockey in the province, the midget age-group is for lads up to sixteen and the "C" category designates the population of towns that compete in it.)

When Wally called a tryout camp, like every kid in the township I packed my equipment to go.

"Just where are you off to, young man?" Big Bertha asked.

"Into town to play hockey," I replied as if the only creature who wouldn't know that was a retarded jackrabbit.

"That's what you think. You're too young to play on a team for that silly dope, Wally Kelly. Grade ten is an important high school year for you, and you won't have time for all those games."

I was dejected by this turn of events so I went to Big Charlie, who always understood. But he had a viewpoint similar to my mother's, so I did the only thing a guy could do in that situation — I went to my room and bawled. Fortunately, Little Charlie came to my rescue, although I didn't really like his approach.

"Every kid is going to the practices," he said. "Willie is too young and not good enough so after three or four workouts, they'll send him home. Let him go! It's better than having him sulking around here like a sick dog."

To my mother's chagrin, I made the team, the only kid on it who wasn't sixteen. I was a good-sized lad and farm work and playing ball all summer had me in good shape. And I was a fair river skater, even at that age.

The second night of camp, Doc Bradshaw watched the chaos of Wally trying to organize forty kids into a practice session. Little Charlie and the Doc asked Wally if he needed any help.

Wally conceded that he could use someone "to drop a few pucks on faceoffs," and before long, he had competition for the head coaching job. Wally never gave up the title, although he did name himself general manager and head coach. Doc Bradshaw knew his stuff and very soon he was in charge, diplomatically, of course. Little Charlie never had a title but he worked with the goalies and helped the Doc coach the Royals.

Big Bertha threw a large snit about it and turned her formidable tongue loose on Little Charlie. "You horse's ass," she steamed. "That child is in grade ten and you guaranteed he wouldn't play for that team. Now William's head is so full of hockey that he'll probably fail at school."

A deal was struck between the Royals' star center and his ma. I could play if I had good marks, did my homework and didn't neglect my farm chores. I never worked as hard in my life. To win a Stanley Cup was a breeze compared to that year.

But I'll never have a finer season if I play until I'm ninety-five. The team had a few kids who could play, though not many, and the Doc was a fine coach. After I became a pro, I told him he should forget medicine and become a teacher of hockey fundamentals.

When the frog pond froze, the Royals often practiced and played shinny there. The Doc's station wagon would roll across the fields, the players he could find would pile out and we'd play.

Not even a Stanley Cup in Montreal where the Canadiens are a religion matches what happens in a small Canadian community with a good hockey team. The Royals improved slowly and so did I, playing against kids two years older and, in many cases, bigger and stronger. By the time the provincial playdowns started in February, we were a splendid team. The Doc convinced us that we lacked individual stars to make much noise but working as a team we'd have a chance.

At any level of hockey, a team that can move the puck out of its own end well is ahead of most opponents. The Royals moved it about as well as any club I've ever seen.

I'm not bragging; by February, I was the Royals' best player. I had the base of good skating ability and the Doc and I spent hours on the frog pond, working on the other skills. In all my hockey since that glorious winter, no coach taught anything the Doc didn't cover.

He taught me to pass the puck both ways, to make a fake that froze an opponent in his tracks and to fade off and attract opponents to create holes for my linemates. He told me to forget the slap shot and wrist the puck, and to use my backhand, a skill just about gone from the game. We worked on faceoffs constantly.

The team won the district title and the thing gained momentum. The old rink was packed for every game and no other subject was discussed in the township for two months. When we played a road game, a caravan of cars and pick-ups would leave Mount Everest and head for the other town.

We won twenty-five games in six playoff rounds to collect the Ontario midget C title. I scored 38 goals in the playoffs, including the title-winner in overtime.

Thirteen years later, local folks still talk about "when we won 'er all." There's a big team picture in the rink and Royals' players are still a little special around the town. I attended a minor hockey dinner in Mount Everest after one of the Canadiens' Stanley Cup victories and was introduced as "Willie Mulligan, the leading scorer on that midget team."

Big Bertha gave up and went to the games after a time. When one team had a big, strong kid checking me man-to-man (boy-to-boy?) and beating on me a little, she offered a little advice: "Why do you let that jerk push you around? Don't you know how to slash and spear?"

We lost the opener in that series at home, mainly because I couldn't do anything with that big goof sticking to me. The next game was in the other team's rink in eastern Ontario and when we lined up for the opening faceoff, my shadow issued a warning: "Okay, ace, your hot-shot days are over. I'll be three inches from your ass all night."

In the first period, he "japped" me—hockey's expression for a sneak attack from behind—with a cross-check on the back of the neck. I wasn't notably brave and I've always been more of a lover than a fighter, but when I saw the kid laughing and heard the people cheering him, I went after him.

In hockey fights, the element of surprise is a big factor and my antagonist wasn't ready. I hit him with a right in the face and felt sick when his nose bled. I socked him four or five more times and it felt good. That was one of maybe a half-dozen fights I've had in hockey, but he didn't bother me after it.

In an interview when I became a pro, I was asked for my view on fighting in hockey. I replied: "I don't like seeing blood on the ice, especially when it's mine."

The next season, most players from the championship team were too old for midget hockey and our club wasn't very strong. But I had a chance to play a great deal and I improved as a player.

Because of Big Bertha's work with me, by the time I was sixteen I was well along in high school. My mother wanted me to make some sort of career decision and the idea of being a pro hockey player had never crossed my mind. I said I wanted to be a farmer, and she looked at the ceiling and said: "Oh, Lord! Not another one!"

But then the Junior B coach in Waldorf, a town of 3,000 near Mount Everest, invited me to a tryout camp. Junior B is a good level of hockey. There's Major Junior at the top, where most NHL players are produced, Tier Two, then Junior B. The Big Pair opposed the idea because the Waldorf team played a heavy schedule, practiced daily and the town was twelve miles away.

Once again, Little Charlie, who was married by then, came to my rescue. "Let him go!" he said. "He's got his driver's license now and he can take the half-ton. He might be a hot-shot in Mount Everest but Junior B is very good hockey. If he makes it, I'll bite the ass-end out of a Jersey."

"Charles, I've heard before that William (she always uses our full names) isn't good enough," my mother said. "Oh, I give up! If he doesn't go, he'll sulk and it's one way to keep him interested in school."

To this day, I remind Little Charlie that he hasn't chewed the ass-end out of that Jersey yet.

I made the Waldorf Rangers and although the club didn't have a very good season, I did, scoring 55 goals and 60 assists in 48 games. But I missed Doc Bradshaw and I didn't have much time to skate on the frog pond.

It seemed I lived five months in that old Chevy pick-up truck. Most days, I'd leave school at four and drive to Waldorf for a workout at five, often cutting a class for a road game. I'd rush home to help the two Charlies milk the sixty cows, then came the books and bed to be up before six to milk those bloody cows again. I never had time for girls, just hockey, Jerseys and books. Hartley used to say: "Mulligan never dated a girl until he was in his twenties, and even then he was surprised she didn't have four boobs and give twenty gallons of milk."

That June, the Toronto Marlboros made me a first-round choice in the Ontario Major Junior League's midget draft of players sixteen years old.

Big Bertha boiled when she found out about the draft. "They can just pick you and you have to play for them. That's interference with your human rights because they remove freedom of choice. That's the end of it and, Charles, don't try any manure about William going to the Marlboros' camp for a few practices because he won't be good enough to make it. He's sixteen with a runny nose and he's not leaving home."

A long chat with Big Charlie convinced me I should finish high school before leaving the nest, even though I was excited about the Marlies, who play in Maple Leaf Gardens and have produced more NHL players than any other junior team. The Marlie people were shocked that I turned down the chance to play for them. They worked on Big Bertha with promises that my education wouldn't be interrupted, but she was abrasive and firm.

I had a few anxiety attacks about not going, especially when two other Waldorf players went to Major Junior camps. Big Charlie supplied some peace: "Son, when you make a decision, stick to it. Don't get your shorts in a big old knot about what you might have done."

Big Bertha was in ecstasy when I decided not to play in Waldorf again. The people in the area couldn't understand why I didn't move to Toronto or why I wasn't going to play Junior B. Many figured it was Big Bertha's influence. She was regarded with awe in the community, and although she had lived there for thirty years, she was a bit of an outsider. She was always "that woman from Toronto Charlie Mulligan married."

I was picking my grade thirteen courses when Big Bertha got on my case again about what I wanted to do with my life and to take this or that to be a doctor or lawyer.

"But I want to be a farmer just as I've always wanted to be a farmer," I said.

"I always hoped one of my sons would be a doctor or lawyer."

"What's wrong with being a farmer? It's a good life."

Big Bertha gave a sigh that sounded like a hammermill being shut down and said: "I give up! But if you're going to be a farmer, why don't you study in college how to do it right?"

I agreed to apply to the University of Guelph and study to be a hay-kicker.

When the Mount Everest Climbers started workouts in September, I went along with Little Charlie. The Climbers played two games and practiced once every week, a leisurely approach to the game. The hockey was very physical and, at times, very violent, but it was great fun. I learned to keep my head up because if I didn't, some farmer would knock it off.

I studied hard in the first term and when I earned first-class honors in the Christmas exams, I rejoined the Waldorf Junior B team. Big Bertha had a small fit when I made the announcement.

Luckily, the fickle finger of fate pried her off my back.

When Doc Bradshaw and I were skating on the frog pond after Christmas, he asked about my future. I told him I planned to study for a degree in agriculture and play a little college hockey. A week later, the hockey coach at Cornell University in New York state, a friend of the Doc's, called to ask if a recruiter could talk to me about attending that school to play hockey.

I figured an Ivy League college man would be one hockey person Big Bertha wouldn't regard as if he had a social disease. He won her over when he talked of the world-famous agriculture school there. Because Cornell is Ivy League, it doesn't offer full athletic scholarships, but if I agreed to go there, I would receive a grant-in-aid which amounted to the same thing.

I visited Cornell, saw a college hockey game, explored the school and placed the wraps on my future for the next four years by signing a letter of intent to attend Cornell. When I told Big Bertha, she gave me a hug that inflicted more damage than any hit I've ever had on a hockey rink.

So at seventeen, I moved to Ithaca, N.Y. I was very lonely at first, being away from home for the first time. I missed The Big Pair, Little Charlie, Sandy, Doc Bradshaw, even the Jerseys, and was especially homesick for the frog pond. But there I was, learning to be a farmer with animal husbandry and dairy science as majors.

The four years at Cornell were a wonderful time in my life, except for one event. I did well in my studies and loved the college atmosphere. And the college hockey, a very high caliber, was great fun. The coaches were excellent, the practice-to-game ratio ideal. The team played forty games, mostly on weekends, plus a couple of tournaments and had unlimited time for workouts. I played well and earned All-American nominations in my last two years.

The bad part of the four years came early in my sophomore term when Big Charlie died. He and Little Charlie, harvesting corn, were resting on the back gate of a wagon, when my dad fell over, on his way to the big dairy farm upstairs in a second with a massive heart attack.

I wanted to leave school and help Little Charlie run the farm but he and Big Bertha said the operation was big enough to afford a hired man. Besides, they said, I needed the degree to help turn the Mulligan spread into the best farm in the world.

It was a lonely winter for me, being away at a time like that, but I stuck it out.

After my junior year at Cornell when I was nineteen, the NHL included "underage" players in its entry draft because some lawyer threatened to sue the league for denying his eighteen-year-old client the right to earn a living in hockey. On the third round of the draft, the Canadiens' general manager announced: "The Canadiens claim William Mulligan, center, from Cornell University."

I realize I've been walking up and down the sand for three hours and the tape is almost full. And who appears all by her lonesome but Clarice, wearing a bikini that's even briefer than yesterday's. I've seen more cotton in an aspirin bottle.

"Has it all driven you whacko?" Clarice says. "You've been walking back and forth up and down this beach talking to yourself. Too much sun or what?"

I show her my little machine and tell her I'm taping a speech for the fall. Then I inquire about old muscles.

"Oh, that dope," she says. "His strongest muscles were between his ears. You were right: There's a big difference between football and hockey players."

I can't think of anything to say but Clarice saves me.

"If you're not in mourning for Montreal and full of Green anxiety, could we walk along the beach, hold hands and get to know each other? I got carried away the other night — it must have been the Scotch — and never did get your name, you little devil!"

"It's Otto Schmiddlapp and holding hands is one of my best skills."

June 17

Air Canada lands at Terrible Terminal Two in Toronto after a scary milk-run hop from Grenada to Barbados (we almost hit a canoe head-on), then the long haul north. Outside customs stand Hartley Laidlaw and the only woman (other than Big Bertha and Sandy) I'll ever truly love, his gorgeous, sexy, super-intelligent, funny wife, Diane.

I once told her I'd crawl through ground glass and chicken-dirt to sniff the exhaust of the truck hauling away her laundry. I still would.

"What's going on?" I say as Diane gives me a hug that rivals Big Bertha's best.

"A new charity project," Hartley says. "We take in refugees with a bleak future in the Big Green."

"Oh, Willie, he's having a colossal anxiety attack and only you can settle him down," Diane says quietly to me.

Fine, but what do I do with my anxiety?

"How did you know I was on this flight?" I ask.

"Hartley figured you'd be home soon after the good news," Diane says. "I called Big Bertha and she said you called but it was like talking to a herd of goats. You did say you were coming home and we checked the airlines."

"It was a good holiday until this jerk ruined it. He got a clear line for the worst news any human ever delivered but I couldn't get one to receive solace from my ma. That confirms what I've told you for years: Tie the can to this downer and come to the hills with me."

"You couldn't afford her," Hartley says. "She just invested more hard-earned loot in another rag shop. That's three now, and I can't go near the models."

"The farmer knows one does not place the fox in the chickenhouse," she says. I've always suspected Diane knows her husband isn't a one-woman man but has a tolerant outlook towards him.

"Can I borrow a limo to get to Mount Everest?" I say.

"Tomorrow is soon enough for your beloved Jerseys," Hartley says. "Tonight, we talk. You're booked into the royal suite at stately Laidlaw manor where we will contemplate life's vicissitudes plus the regal screwing we've just been given."

As should be clear by now, Hartley and Diane are my closest friends, and had it not been for hockey I would have never met either of them in a million years. Hartley is a rich kid from the Rosedale area of Toronto. His pa is a big-wheel corporation lawyer and when we were in the big battle with the NHL owners that led to the strike, his father gave us approximately $2,367,986 worth of free legal advice, at his rates.

He's a marvelous natural athlete, great at all team sports, a scratch handicap golfer, a tennis player of pro potential and a good enough equestrian to be considered for the Canadian international team.

Hartley played very little hockey as a kid (no frog ponds in Rosedale), just a little at the private schools. But at nineteen, he gave the game a whirl. He wrote a letter ("all fiction") to a new Major Junior team in Kingston, Ontario, asking for a tryout. He claimed the motivation was his father's booting him out of the house and the need of room and board for the winter.

He made the team, scored 40 goals and was claimed by the Toronto Maple Leafs on the seventh round of the entry draft. Hartley made the Leafs first crack, too, and as a rookie, he met Diane, daughter of a trillionaire and educated in the world's best schools.

When Hartley married Diane at twenty-one, her parents objected strenuously. He was in his second NHL season after apprenticing at several private schools and colleges.

Her parents are so upper crust that Hartley says "her old man scratches his jacks with one finger in the air." They wanted no part of any hockey player, despite the Rosedale pedigree, and tried to block the romance. But Diane was determined, too, and they eloped in his second NHL season.

"I couldn't help myself," she said at the time. "His inside-outside fake was irresistible."

She was as eager to make it on her own as he was, and anxious not to have her family "yank the strings of my life." No idle rich kid, she studied fashion design in New York and Paris and is now well established as a designer.

Hartley had enough credits from four tries at college to be halfway to a degree. He returned to school in a big way, finished his degree, then went to law school fulltime while playing in the NHL, no easy task. He completed his article year, received his call to the bar and, at twenty-five, was a full-fledged lawyer as well as a hockey star.

Like Sheila Symons, Hartley has never been 100 percent fanatical about his marriage vows. But he says: "Diane brought me uptown. Maybe I can't resist a good body but my heart is her's alone."

We're in Hartley's battered old Chevy on the way to their restored slum house downtown that's six inches wide and a half mile long, and he's prattling about some court case.

"What's the fillibuster, chum?" I say "I'm dying to hear about our plight and you're ranting about some court case. Spill, little man! The Big Green? The draft? Our teammates?"

"You won't like it," Diane says. "You need a little Chivas in your mitt before we tell all."

We ride in silence and I can sense more than a little tension between the Laidlaws. Finally, I blurt out: "Have I landed in the middle of a family disagreement? I haven't noticed love's young dream warmth between you two, so what the hell is going on? I didn't rush 3,000 miles and leave behind the wonderful Clarice to sit in a freezeout between my two best friends."

Hartley sighs like Big Bertha at her best.

"Okay, I apologize," he says. "Diane wants me to hang up my skates and get on with a normal life. She thinks the dirt done thee and me is unforgivable, and that I should concentrate on the law and you on the Jerseys."

"You two have been a credit to the game, you busted your butts off for those teams and you fought for something you believed in," Diane says. "And what's it get you? A kick in the buns! You can give it back to them by not joining their dopey expansion team. You have alternatives."

"An excellent idea, favorite lady," I say. "I've thought

about it a great deal since Hartley called and I have considered telling them to stuff it. Three years from now, I would. But there's Shoot-The-Puck Farm. Little Charlie and I are up to our ears and the way out is to collect this contract. I've got guys working on my house now and, frankly, it would be cheaper to exhume Michelangelo and have him do the ceilings. Little Charlie is all excited about the great bargain he found on some purebred Jersey heifers. They're as expensive as a Diane Laidlaw original design and the bank already owns my ass. I have to go to the Big Green."

"The cold, hard facts of life bounce off this homely broad's skull," Hartley says. "Maybe I have a future as a lawyer but the most I can earn in the next few years is twenty-five Gs. We have three dress shops and the bank has us in the vise, too."

"This mule won't give an inch and get my dad to help us," Diane says. "It's not charity. He'd loan us the money at a good rate, and we could get the bank off our tail and live a normal life."

"Place your hand over your luscious backside until I ask him for anything and you'll have a permanent patch."

"That's the enlightened attitude I'm trying to cope with," Diane says. "I can't leave the business and it's going to be great with lover-boy in Cleveland."

"A half-hour hop across the lake," Hartley shoots back. "Just a minute! Who's Clarice?"

"A lady I met in Grenada," I say. "We walked on the beach a couple times, then I had to leave."

"Willie, I love that farm-boy innocence," Diane snickers. "We walked on the beach! Was it before or after when you walked? When are you going to get married?"

"I'm waiting for you to grow tired of this person here, boot him out and take me in."

"She'd be no good to you, hayseed," Hartley says. "She can't drive a tractor and she can only shoot the bull, not shovel it."

The needle we've carried on for years is ended by arrival at the Laidlaw home. Maybe now I'll hear what has happened to my life.

June 18

A spot on Shoot-The-Puck Farm has always been my special place. In a corner of bush is the highest ground for miles where I'd climb a tree to inspect the countryside. Big Bertha and I walked there on Sunday afternoons. In the summer, we'd take our books and read; in the fall, we'd pick beech nuts for the Christmas candy.

When I have some heavy thinking to do, I head for that spot. When I've been in scoring slumps, I've wished I could go there for an hour, then goals would go in.

After a wet, windy night with the Laidlaws, I'm ready for some time there. When Hartley drives me home early in the morning, we have the quiets from the Chivas we inhaled.

Big Bertha is on a bus tour of great ragweed patches or something and Little Charlie is at a cattle sale, undoubtedly spending my playoff bonus on Jersey heifers. I'm happy to have solitude to sit by myself, watch a few clouds form and sort out five hours of Laidlaw talk.

I check around because I haven't been here since Christmas. Little Charlie has the place in tip-top condition. He's a good farmer and I'm not bad myself. Our empire is 650 acres, 150 head of purebred Jerseys, 100 of them milkers, modern facilities with milking parlors and pressurized silos ($45,000 a pop) and much expensive equipment. It's the result of Big Charlie's building the basic farm, Little Charlie's ambition and business sense, my good contracts and a willing bank manager.

Hartley has put together a folder of newspaper clips on the expansion draft and the reaction of the Big Green and our previous teams. I take it to my special spot.

I think back two years when we settled the players' association strike and, after thirty-five hours of nonstop bargaining, wore down the owners to agree to total free agency with no compensation. We didn't know of the owners' secret agreement to grant free agency on the understanding no club would sign a free agent. Their plan was to offer no contract to a free agent that was larger than his club's deal.

After the press conferences, the NHLPA executive, led

by president Laidlaw, vice-president Mulligan and our executive-director Walter Enright, had a victory dinner.

During the celebration, Hartley and I were on our way to the whizzer when we met the two team owners most strongly opposed to free agency, both slightly hammered.

"There's the two smartass shit-heads who caused the trouble," slurred one.

"I goddam near kicked in my TV when you two were so arrogant with all those jokes about it," the other guy said.

"Great to be held in high esteem by such distinguished citizens," I said.

"It's reassuring that our league is in such great hands," added Hartley.

"Laugh it up, you piss-pots," said owner A. "I'll make you a promise: We'll fry your asses before this is over. I'll give you credit: You stuck to your goddam guns. If it hadn't been for you two, the jerks in your association would have folded like wet toilet paper. Remember, though, that down the road we'll fix your wagons bloody good."

We laughed it off as booze talk. When the Rangers broke the agreement and signed five all-stars, it caused a big uproar and we started to get darts again.

"Mulligan, you're about to pay a big price for being a union militant," said an NHL owner after a game.

"Will the hit-man break my legs or throw me in the lake tied to a juke-box?"

"You'll wish that's what we had done to you," he said.

Last night, Hartley informed me that after the Leafs lost in the playoff quarter-final, the owner had told him it was his last game in blue-and-white. There was a lot of trade-talk, so he figured the owner was giving him that. He never thought about the expansion draft.

Under the beech tree, I read newspaper clips, especially one when the protected lists were released the night before the expansion draft.

Two top National League centers are available to the Cleveland Big Green in the expansion draft to stock the new team.

Hartley Laidlaw of the Toronto Maple Leafs and Willie Mulligan of the Montreal Canadiens are not on their teams' protected lists of 20 skaters and three goaltenders.

"The new team should be competitive quickly and for the good of the NHL, we decided to protect a young player and make Mulligan available," a Canadien spokesman said.

The Maple Leafs denied that Laidlaw's leadership of the players' strike for free agency had any influence on the decision not to protect him.

"Laidlaw's play declined last season and we protected a young player instead of him," a Leaf official said.

Some decline! Hartley led the team in scoring last season with 46 goals, one fewer than in the previous term.

The expansion draft list should be in a black folder. In the draft, the Big Green claimed one player from each of the twenty-three teams. Players who had not completed their third pro season were exempt to keep the Green out of any club's young-player storeroom.

The draft list would make a buzzard puke.

GOAL: Joe Badgly, Minnesota; Marc-Luc Radisson, Quebec; Rollie Regan, Washington.

DEFENSE: Jean-Pierre Marcotte, Los Angeles; Walter Simpson, Detroit; Marty McNeil, St. Louis; Rejean Labroche, Hamilton; Hector Ankorn, Calgary; Lester Franklin, Rangers; George Johnson, Vancouver; Miroslav Kardek, Edmonton.

CENTER: Hartley Laidlaw, Toronto; Willie Mulligan, Montreal; Rene Racine, Islanders; Salvatore Mancino, Buffalo.

LEFT WING: Paul Byers, Philadelphia; Guy Lacombe, San Diego; Harry Li, San Francisco; Jim Sanders, Winnipeg.

RIGHT WING: Hugh Long, Chicago; Pete McFatridge, New Jersey; Serge Lapierre, Boston; Brooker Duncan, Hartford.

When I finished reading it, I accused Hartley of printing the list as a joke. "That team couldn't beat the Mount Everest Climbers. It's the weirdest collection of humanity in history."

"When I read it," Hartley smiled, "I cried for the first time since my daddy took my sports car away, after he got it down from the tree where I had parked it."

"Have they named a coach?"

"The illustrious Peter Edmunds claims he's screening candidates. He won't hire anyone smarter than he is and the only creature in that category is a retarded ape."

"I hope he's looking for a coach in one of two places—the Canadian Psychiatric Association or the American Kennel Club."

Few players on the list were in the NHL last season. Most were in the minors with mediocre records.

"Read Edmunds' comments on it," Hartley said. "An air sickness bag is beside your chair."

Edmund is quoted: "We have the best roster of any NHL expansion team. There's considerable potential there. What new team ever had quality players like Laidlaw and Mulligan? We're grateful to the NHL for making them available. They're winners who will be the leaders on our club."

"Moses Mulligan, our leader!" Hartley said, raising his hands in praise.

"On that rat pack, it'd be like Moses trying to lead a pack of winos up the real Mount Everest," I replied.

Reading over the folder again, I try to detect some hope and decide Diane was right—we should get out and continue life as civilians. But I hear a Jersey bawl in the distance and think about the trucks hauling the herd away when we go bankrupt.

Some true beauties, magnificent loonies, are on that draft list. The goalies are an unusual trio. Joe (Barf) Badgly's main claim to fame is throwing up, before games, between periods, and once under his mask during a scramble when he almost drowned before he could smother the puck. Marc-Luc Radisson is five-foot-four and has a great catching hand but he's hopeless with the other parts of his body. Rollie (Red-Light)

Regan earned his nickname from two sources—all the goals he surrenders and being caught in a raid on a whorehouse in Atlanta.

Edmunds is quoted as saying he likes the international flavor of our roster—the interesting combination of many schools of hockey philosophy.

Sure. The Big Green has Harry (Hi) Li, the NHL's only Chinese player. The San Francisco team had him to appeal to the large Chinese population there. The Chinese are as interested in hockey as Diane's father is in poverty. Hartley always figured that to appeal to a big minority in San Francisco, they should have had four fags on defense and a transvestite on the wing.

Salvatore (Little Sal) Mancino, known as the "Italian Stallion," can skate like the wind but can't execute a single move above half speed. His father is Big Sal Mancino, a mobster deported when Sal, Jr. was fifteen and a good midget player in Toronto. Little Sal was a star with the Italian national team when the Sabres imported him. One coach claimed the Italian Stallion nickname was wrong and that it should be "The Dago Donkey."

Miro Kardek, a defenseman from Czechoslovakia, was thirty-two when he defected four years ago. He hid in a truckload of sheep going across the border to Austria. He wasn't after political freedom; he just wanted to get away from his old lady and six kids. He's built like a dump truck and about as agile.

Brooker Duncan is one of the few blacks in the NHL. He's nicknamed "Midnight." He's tougher than pig shit and slower than molasses in January. Brooker is thirty-four, was married when he was seventeen and has seven kids. Lester Franklin told me Brooker beat the crap out of him when they were lined up for a faceoff and Lester said: "Midnight, I always wondered why if you black dudes have such a natural sense of rhythm, how come you got so many kids?"

The NHL has produced a new divisional arrangement, schedule and playoff set-up on reaching its goal of twenty-four teams in four, six-team divisions.

After losing large amounts of money in Pittsburgh and Denver, those teams became the San Diego Freeway and the New Jersey Devils. Then expansion teams were added in Hamilton and San Francisco three years ago.

The league looks like this for next season.

ALLAN EAGLESON CONFERENCE. *West Division*. Vancouver Canucks, Edmonton Oilers, Calgary Flames, Los Angeles Kings, San Diego Freeway, San Francisco Wharfs; *Central Division*. Chicago Black Hawks, Minnesota North Stars, Winnipeg Jets, Detroit Red Wings, St. Louis Blues, Washington Capitals.

JOHN ZIEGLER CONFERENCE. *North Division*. Montreal Canadiens, Quebec Nordiques, Hartford Whalers, Boston Bruins, Toronto Maple Leafs, Hamilton Steelers; *East Division*. Philadelphia Flyers, New York Rangers, New York Islanders, New Jersey Devils, Buffalo Sabres, Cleveland Big Green.

The first executive-director of the NHL Players' Association, Eagleson is now leader of the Opposition in the Canadian Parliament. Ziegler was a good NHL president for a few years until he threw in the old expense account and went off to the hills to chase his dream of writing mystery novels.

Teams will play an eight-four game unbalanced schedule, six against each club in their division for thirty, three against the other eighteen teams for fifty-four. Four extra games over the previous eighty means a five percent raise for all players, courtesy of the collective bargaining agreement.

The top five teams in each division qualify for the playoffs. The NHLPA wanted only eight, twelve at the most, in the playoffs, which are almost as long as the season.

"Isn't it going to be wonderful?" I said to Hartley.

"At least the entry draft in two weeks will give the Green some young players."

"Surely Edmunds will draft Jimmy Miller."

"I don't think even he can screw that up," Hartley said.

Miller, a seventeen-year-old left winger, produced 110 goals and 135 assists for the Sudbury Wolves last season and is called the best prospect in the past twenty years.

Apparently, Edmunds says he has a few tricks up his sleeve in regards to other talent, though as Hartley says: "That guy will be lucky if he has his arms up his sleeves."

I lean back against the beech tree and look at the sky where fluffy clouds float against the blue.

"Why me, Lord? Why me?"

I fully expect that a big voice will answer: "Because you piss me off, Mulligan!"

June 20

A couple of days on my land has my head partially straight. No one mentions hockey, the Big Green or the expansion draft. Little Charlie and I inspect the 650 acres to show, he says, that "I'm not frittering away your hockey bucks." Little Charlie never has wasted a dime and he has our Jersey herd producing lovely milk at full blast.

Shoot-The-Puck Farm is a name Big Bertha produced. When Little Charlie and I became partners, we needed a name for our enterprise. Sandy suggested "The Belly Acres." Because we sold our bull and moved into artificial insemination, I tried "No-Bull Farm." After joking about a name for an hour, Big Bertha said: "The only thing that ever mattered around here was hockey so why not call it 'Slap-Shot Farm,' or maybe 'Shoot-The-Puck Farm.'"

The work is rolling on my house. It's on the last two hundred acres we added, a good buy because the barn had burned on it. We didn't need barn space, just land. Everyone suspected that the barn was struck by "Italian Lightning" when the old bachelor farmer, "Weird Walter" Walker, heaved a match into a hay mow.

Diane Laidlaw had had the idea to remodel by building a new house inside the old stone walls. It will be beautiful when finished but it might be the end of me when I pay for it.

Tonight, Big Bertha has her annual "Welcome Home, Willie" dinner for "my little goal hunter home from the hills." The spread is breathtaking in its scope and variety. I've conducted expensive research into the best eating spots in North

America—Le Perroquet in Chicago, The Fish Market in Philly, Tony's in St. Louis, St. Amable in Montreal, Winston's in Toronto—and they could all take lessons from the Big B.

The famly is there—Little Charlie, his wife Nadine and their two daughters; Sandy and Ralph, who have no kids because she's a career gal, director of nursing at Waldorf Hospital; a few aunts and uncles; and Doc Bradshaw, who's semi-family.

The family isn't wild about it but my ma always includes Aunt Jessie and Uncle Clyde, Big Charlie's oldest brother who farms, if you can call it that, in the next township. The term "hayseed" was invented for them because their whole scene is out of the hills of Oklahoma in the 1930s.

Jessie and Clyde had ten kids, eight of them daughters with big chests and small morals. Five, in Mount Everest vernacular, "got themselves knocked up" as teenagers.

Every year, Uncle Clyde puts the bite on me for "a wee loan to tide me over a rough spot." His pitch is always the same: "You're doin' so well playin' that hockey, William, and things are a little rough with Jessie needin' the doctors."

According to him, Aunt Jessie has had two hysterectomies, an appendectomy, a tonsilectomy, new false teeth and four root canals in the past five years.

The first year, I loaned him $500 and he bought their first television set. The next year, he cornered me again, but Sandy tipped me off that he wanted the money to add a tape recorder to his home entertainment center. If he wanted the money to install a flush toilet in the house, I would have produced.

This afternoon, Little Charlie and I perch on our one rail fence, along the back lane to the bush.

"Wanna talk about it?" he says.

"Yeah. I can do it now."

"Sure did a number on you and ol' Hartley, didn't they? I couldn't believe it when you guys weren't protected. It's all anyone around here talked about because you being a Canadien is such big stuff in our humble village. How did the owners get the Leafs and the Canadiens to agree to shaft you two? He was the Leafs' top scorer."

"The good-lookin' kid had his best all-round season, too. Hartley was third in all-star center voting and I was fourth.

"Hartley canvassed all his sources to try to find out what the payoff is. The best we can do is that the owners wanted the Big Green to stay out of the entry draft this year but were told to stick it in their backsides. The Canadiens had first pick because of a trade for the New Jersey Devils' first rounder this year or next, whenever they choose. If the Green doesn't draft, the Canadiens get Jimmy Miller.

"We figure the payoff is that the Green picks first and takes Miller, unless Pete Edmunds is really a dunce. The Leafs and Canadiens name the players they want and the other clubs won't claim them."

"They sacrifice two top players, just to get even for free agency," Little Charlie says. "Has it hurt the NHL that much?"

"Until the Rangers broke the agreement, no trouble! In fact, the owners were gloating over their accomplishment in really giving us zip. Gaston Beaupre (my left winger with the Canadiens) went shopping as a free agent, thinking he would get maybe $400,000 a year. He talked seriously to two teams but they offered him only $240,000, $5,000 less than the Canadiens' offer. He was the first big guy to try the market and you know how good he is! His offers confirmed the secret deal."

"How did they stay so quiet about it? If the players' association could prove they have a secret deal, you could take them to court."

"We couldn't find airtight proof. The NHL board is a disparate group of men who don't get along very well, but on that agreement, they're tighter than a bull's ass in fly time."

"Why did the Rangers break the agreement?"

"The Rangers are owned by a multi-national company. If they lose a little money on the Rangers, it's tax writeoff, but the big poobahs of that company are winners and the Rangers hadn't won the Cup since before Big Bertha got her first corset.

"When the Rangers signed those guys, the guns went on us and, brother, someone is a good shot. When the Rangers landed the two Russians, the other owners thought of a firing squad for Laidlaw and me, even though we weren't to blame for that."

"What's the real story on the commies?" he says and I tell him, incredible as it seems.

Ever since the Soviet Union's national and club teams started whipping the NHL on hockey rinks, NHL teams have tried to get the Soviets (that's their correct name but NHL people call them "those fuckin' Russians") to defect like those ballet dancers who are always going through the Iron Curtain. They figured that if the Swedish and Finnish players (sixty in the league now) and dozen Czech defectors can be that good, then the Soviets would be prized possessions.

Several NHL teams tried shady deals to get the Soviets when they were on North American tours. They offered big bags of loot which the comrades could have used on their tours to load up with blue jeans, stereo tapes of decadent western rock music, windshield wipers and sparkplugs, which they can't buy in the USSR, porno videotapes, plus a few dollars for ten-buck hooks, something a few Ruskies have snared on their tours.

But the Soviet tours always included a few "advisors," dour guys in shiny dark suits. Everyone knew they were KGB, along to make certain none of the lads went over the fence.

The Rangers decided a couple of Soviets would help them and they used the old smarts and money to land Valeri Dinkov, an incredible defenseman, and Sergei Pukov, maybe the best right winger in the world.

A company in the conglomerate controlled much of the world's laxative and sanitary napkin market. By unusual (or was it?) coincidence, the factories in the USSR that produced laxative and sanitary pads exploded. There were some hints that the CIA was behind the blast.

The Soviets were in a bad way. Constipation is a big deal over there because of the godawful food and the whole country was walking on tip-toes. The government encouraged pregnancy and offered free hysterectomies.

Eventually, the Soviets approached the company that owned the Rangers to try to solve their problem. The Yanks said, sure, you get all the laxative and sanitary pads you need at a good price but remember how commerce works. You arrange for Dinkov and Pukov to "defect" to the USA and not be worried about their grandparents ending up in the Gulag Archipelago.

The Soviets didn't want to lose the two players but everyone there was red in the face, and not from too much vodka, and the women were sick and tired of trying to make tampons out of yesterday's copy of Pravda. So the Soviets went for the deal.

Dinkov and Pukov, their wives and kids, were granted visas, passports and a few Yankee bucks for a holiday on the French Riviera. They should have smelled a rat but they didn't ask any questions. Their previous summer vacations were spent at push-up camp.

The Ranger guys just happened to be there, too, and convinced Pukov and Dinkov to shift their act to New York, where they became big NHL stars.

The Ranger players like Pukov and Dinkov, especially after they convinced the Soviets that it wasn't western decadence to take a shower now and then. Lester Franklin was a Ranger last season and he told me: "Them two Russians smelled like a buzzard's crotch until they started to use deodorant, something Soviets do only on Lenin's birthday."

"Too bad the Big Green couldn't get a half dozen Ruskies," Little Charlie says. "From the look of that line-up, you won't knock anyone's dick in the dirt."

"Five guys with their skates on the right feet will be a help," I say.

June 21

Two telephone chats with whackos and a whacko chat with my mother highlight this day.

I'm back in my farmer routine, up at 5:15 a.m. to help our herdsman milk the one hundred Jerseys. The hired hand is the one sane guy in the operation. We pay him $22,000 a year plus a free house on a written contract. Hartley thinks that's a better deal than he has. "Good hours, no road trips and better smelling creatures than the ones I hang around with."

My habits drive some roomies nuts in hockey season because I'm up very early on the road to indulge in one of life's joys, a leisurely breakfast. I usually hit the lobby by 7 a.m., buy newspapers, and find a quiet corner of the coffee shop with plenty of coffee and no conversation.

Big Bertha, who lives alone in "The Big House" where we all grew up, is happy to have her boy around because she says it's no fun to cook for herself. I finish milking at 8:30, hungry enough to eat a moose. Her breakfasts are terrific but there are no papers and no escape from conversation.

Annually, Big Bertha conducts an exploration of my social life, and it's time this morning.

"Did you have much snow in Montreal?"

"A record fall," I reply. "I was glad I lived within walking distance of the Forum."

"You live in the same place?" she says, knowing her Sunday night letters have had the same address for four years.

"Yeah, of course, it's a good apartment. I'm sorry to give it up."

"Living alone isn't much fun. I've had it for a few years and I don't like it very much."

"Find yourself a dirty old man. You're not a bad looking old broad and you could fatten him up."

Big Bertha snorts: "One dirty old man was enough for me. Besides, my case isn't under discussion here."

"Is anyone's case under discussion?"

"Well, your's is, sort of," she smiles. "Find a special lady yet?"

"A dozen different ones lived in this year but they only stay two weeks because all I talk about is my mommy's great cooking. Besides, I've met only three women I would marry— you, Sandy and Diane. You're trouble; Sandy and Diane are spoken for. I have high hopes, though, that Diane will see the error of her ways and I'll carry her away."

Diane and Big Bertha are great pals. When the pressures of her job get to Diane, she calls Big Bertha and drives to the farm for dinner.

"I admire your taste, if not your intentions," she says. "Diane is a rare one and I so enjoy her visits. Maybe you should take out a contract on Hartley."

"Wanna make a couple of hundred bucks?"

"Don't change the subject," she says. "Your house will be finished soon and it's time you found a lady to share it with."

"You sound like Diane," I shoot back. "Soon, you'll pick a bride for me."

"The subject has been discussed," she smiles.

I'm saved by the phone, person-to-person from Chicago.

"Is that Willie Mulligan?" a female voice says.

"Yes," I reply and know I should hang up.

The voice raises almost to a scream. "It's really Willie Mulligan?"

"The one and only."

"I'm lucky to get you and I hope you don't think I'm being forward, but I didn't know what else to do."

"Ma'am, what's this all about?" I say coldly.

"Don't hang up: I'm not some nut," she replies. "I read in a magazine where you helped some bad kids in Montreal. Well, I have a fifteen-year-old son who's not really bad, just misdirected. He's interested in farming, so could he come to your farm for the summer and work? You wouldn't have to pay him, just some spending money. If you just send me a plane ticket, he'll be there right away."

"We have all the help we need," I say and hang up.

The ideas people have about pro athletes never cease to amaze me. I've had probably two dozen calls and letters over the years like that. Three years ago, a national magazine writer and photographer from New York came to the farm and did a big story and picture layout on me. A full-scale color photo had me haying minus a shirt, and while my battered body doesn't turn Arnold Schwarzenegger green with envy, it isn't exactly dump city, either.

Large amounts of mail from ladies contained interesting

suggestions on things they would like to do with and to my body, and soon after the story appeared, two teenage boys hitch-hiked to Mount Everest from New York, ready to work on the farm for the summer.

The inevitable arrives today and I place a call to my new employers. A girl answers with "Home Of The Big Green" and I have a large urge to retire.

I ask for Mr. Edmunds and the girl says: "Can I tell him who's calling?" I reply: "Willie Mulligan." I'm on ignore for what seems like five minutes, then she says: "Mr. Hannigan, can I tell Mr. Edmunds what this concerns?"

I almost tell her I'm breeding stooges and want him to stand at stud. "Miss, the name is Mulligan; the first name, Willie. I'm a hockey player, once of the Montreal Canadiens. I'm reporting for duty. Tell him that's what it concerns."

"Just a moment, please," she sighs.

In another two minutes, a male voice says: "This is Peter Edmunds. Can I help you?"

"Praise to heavens! This is Willie Mulligan."

"Willie boy, terrific to hear from you!" the very loud voice says. "The girl on our board isn't very swift but she's got a tremendous chest. She said a Mr. Hannigan wanted to talk to me. I guess you Irishmen all look alike." Edmunds guffaws at the depth of his wit. "Hey, old buddy, how's it going? I called just after the draft but you were on a holiday. Welcome to the Big Green! You're going to be a driver of it. You know, we were overjoyed to claim you in the draft. Hartley Laidlaw, too. I understand you boys know each other. Now, what can I do for you?"

I try to think of a good answer, hoping he'll tell me why I called. "Nothing in particular; I thought I'd check in and see if you had traded me back to the Canadiens yet."

"Are you kidding? We're busier than a one-legged man in an ass-kicking contest around here. Starting a team from scratch is a big job but we have the people with the itch to do it."

Edmunds guffaws again and an old Grenadian thought runs through my head: dirty, rotten, no-good son-of-a-bitch.

"Our office staff is organized now, we're kicking off our season ticket sales campaign and, my boy, I'm glad you called. I want a few players to come here in a couple of weeks, you and Laidlaw especially, for a media luncheon to launch our ticket campaign."

"What appearance money are you paying?" I ask.

Pete's service club heartiness disappears quickly. "What in hell are you talking about, appearance money?" he snarls. "I never heard anything like it. We're trying to make our team a success and you ask about goddam appearance money. Surely you're joking."

If I'm going to have a confrontation with him sooner or later, it might as well be right now.

"It's customary for NHL teams to pay players for off-season appearances on behalf of the club," I say in a professorial tone. "It's part of the collective bargaining agreement. The obligation the player has for promotions at no fee are spelled out very carefully. So are the ones for which he's entitled to compensation."

"Shove your collective bargaining agreement up your ass. I don't need any lectures on how to conduct my business. That goddam agreement and union are ruining the game. You won't take a crap unless you're paid for it. When I played, we did things to boost the game and never thought about pay.

"We just want a few players here to help get some publicity. I've heard you're a smartass loud-mouth with a bad attitude, but I'll whip your ass into shape and that goddam wisemouth Laidlaw's, too."

"If anyone told you that I, quote, have a bad attitude, unquote, they're full of shit," I steam. "I work my butt off for the team that pays my salary. I cooperate with the media, I get involved with charities and I do promotional stuff. But I worked hard to get that agreement with the dumb-cunt owners, and I don't ask for anything to which I'm not entitled.

"If this farce is to have a chance, let's get things straight. I didn't ask to be claimed in the expansion draft. When I was, I thought of, first, suicide, and second, retirement from hockey.

"Your team was able to get me and Hartley because some dopey owners didn't realize that slavery ended with the Civil War. I may come to you on the end of a shaft but that doesn't mean I have my hat in my hand.

"So I suggest you read the collective bargaining agreement—the words aren't too big—and find out the rights the players have. That way we can save aggravation."

"Just a minute! Don't go off half-cocked!" Edmunds says. "Our show here is more first class than anything you've ever seen. I know all about the agreement but is it too much for you to come here to get things rolling? Of course, we'll pay you. Do you think we're cheap?"

"Let's get this off on the right foot," I say. "Have you hired a coach yet?"

"I'm interviewing candidates but don't worry, we'll get the best possible man for the job," he says. "Besides, it's none of your business. All you have to do is play hockey."

"Is there any chance of you trading me soon, like yesterday?"

"Sorry, buddy," Edmunds says. "For openers, we want you on our team. Secondly, and I'll deny I ever told you, we agreed not to trade you or Laidlaw for three years before they would leave you unprotected. The Leafs and Canadiens don't want you two on a contender. Dear fellow, you're stuck with us."

June 23

The NHL entry draft is conducted via a conference phone hook-up today, not live in the Montreal Forum as it has been in the past few years.

The thought runs through my head that the girl in Pete Edmunds' office screws up the phone hook-up completely. When the NHL president calls to ask for Edmunds' draft selections, she says: "Can I tell Mr. Edmunds what this concerns?" She puts the prez on hold, tells Edmunds a guy from the NAACP is on the line and the team winds up with no draft picks.

Film on the evening news shows the Green's brain brigade round a table, with Edmunds at the speaker phone. I recognize Clive Anderson IV, who looks as if he had a two-quart breakfast and could be face down before the first round is complete.

When Edmunds makes the first draft pick, it's pure bull.

"The NHL's newest team, the Cleveland Big Green, has a wonderful honor in making the first entry draft selection and we take enormous pride in choosing hockey's next super-star, left winger Jimmy Miller from the Sudbury Wolves," he crows.

In an interview, Edmund makes the hill Jimmy Miller must climb a little steeper. When asked if Miller can earn a job, even though he won't be eighteen until December, Edmunds has a look of righteous indignation. "Not only will Jimmy Miller make the Big Green but he will be the top rookie in the NHL."

Miller and his agent, Williard (Weasel) Webb, are interviewed. Weasel is the most despised man in hockey, a little worm of whom Hartley once said: "He's got rubber pockets so he can steal soup."

Miller looks like a pleasant, gawky nine year old who hasn't had a square meal in three weeks. The kid's answers are unbelievable, and that his agent hasn't coached him confirms viewpoints about Weasel.

"Are you happy to be the first player picked in the entry draft, Jimmy?"

"Well, yeah, sorta," Jimmy stammers. "The first draft choice gets the most money."

"Are you pleased you were selected by the Big Green?"

"No, because it's an expansion team that won't be any good for a long time and Cleveland is a bit of a dump, isn't it?" he says in a little kid's voice. "I wanted to be a Montreal Canadien and I thought they'd made a deal for me. I wouldn't have minded the New York Rangers either, because of the endorsement stuff there."

"Don't you have a better chance to make it with an expansion team?"

Jimmy looks at him as if he had asked: Can you find your ass with one hand?

"I can be a regular on any NHL club."

"How big are you, Jimmy?"

The kid looks embarrassed: "I'm five-eleven and 160, but I'll end up at least six-two and 195. My dad's that big and he was my size at my age."

"With your size and age, won't the tough guys give you a rough time?"

"Junior goons didn't bother me and they won't in the NHL, either. If they do, I'll spear them. But if the team is smart, they'll have guys to protect me."

Hartley is on the phone when the interview ends. "You like our boy soprano?"

"If they show the interview in Cleveland, it will give Edmunds a heart attack. But it makes it tough for the kid. If we have any fans, they'll be on his ass."

"It will be expensive to move that kid around," Hartley adds. "He'll travel on the plane but they'll need one of Clive Five's Big Green sixteen-wheelers to carry his balls."

On the second round, the Green selects Joel Reid, a defenseman who's six-foot-six and weighs 235 pounds, from the Medicine Hat juniors. Last season, Reid played 36 games and had no goals, three assists, 789 minutes in penalties and three paternity suits. He was suspended for another thirty games for various capers—spearing a linesman, choking an opponent half-dead and biting a lady on the ear when she leaned into the penalty box and beat on him with her shoe. He pleaded self-defense.

I figure they must have found him high in the Rockies, stretched out on a tree limb, ears flat back, over the path to the watering hole and waiting to pounce on his lunch. He's the sort of guy you wouldn't want to share a swimming pool with if you were bleeding.

The entry draft now is peppered with European names. The Green's third-rounder is Anders Nilsson, a center from

Sweden, and on the fourth, they claim Ilko Mikkolainen, a right winger from Finland.

On the fifth round, it's Pierre Lambert, a defenseman from Sherbrooke juniors. Pierre had 156 points and a minus-78, which indicates some defensive deficiencies.

Edmunds announces he will make a little history on round six and it's hilarious. "For the first time in the NHL draft, from the great country of Poland," he says into the phone speaker, "the Big Green selects center Firpo... Sibbie...Firpo...oh, hell, I'll spell it."

The name is Firpo Zybysadoskowski.

When it's all over, Hartley's on the phone again. "I can't wait to see them put old Firpo's name on his sweater. They'll start it below the elbow of his left arm, across the back and down the other arm."

"We'll just call him 'The Big Zed.'"

"This is going to be an interesting season," Hartley says. "Now, excuse me, please. I'm going to get drunk."

July 6

Our haying operation has been rolling smoothly because of good weather and no equipment breakdowns and I have agreed, after Edmunds called four times, to attend the Big Green's colossal kickoff luncheon.

There's no way I would miss it but Edmunds' act browned me off. I'm not the only one who reacted that way to him, either. Hartley and the other players who have called me all talked about the same problems.

Lester Franklin called at 2 a.m. from Saskatchewan—he was half gunned and forgot the two-hour time difference—and cried on my shoulder after a talk with Edmunds.

"That turd Edmunds wants me to carry the puck this season and if I can't, I won't make the team," Lester said. He's strictly a defensive defenseman, slow with stone-hands, and he's happy to work in the team's own zone. "Shit, Willie, you know I'd be an all-star if the game wasn't played with a puck. But if they want me to rush a lot, I'll be in the minors."

I tried to reassure him that he'd have a job.

Edmunds told Hartley that part of the deal for us was that we couldn't be on the players' association executive (our terms ended the year after the strike) and couldn't be the Green's player rep or the team captain. I decided Firpo will have my vote as captain and rep.

Hartley and I take the early flight from Toronto to Cleveland today and Edmunds asks us to bring Jimmy Miller along. Miller flew to Toronto last night from Timmins and stayed at the Laidlaw residence.

Socially, my summer has been zilch because the selection of ladies around Mount Everest is rather slim. If I'm seen with a local belle, everyone knows it in five minutes and assumes I'm either bedding her or wedding her. I did meet Sheila Dawes (nee Symons) who asked if Hartley would be around this summer. She also offered to call me when Mad Jim is on a long haul to drop in for a drink, but I told her I was going on safari in Africa.

Being a robust farm boy, I find celibacy isn't healthy to the psyche, so I spent half an hour one night tracking down Clarice in Toronto. She agreed it would be a great idea if we could have dinner when I pass through on my way to Cleveland.

As a result of dinner with Clarice, who is looking absolutely sensational, I barely make the 8:30 flight. Hartley leaves a seat for me and Jimmy is between us.

"You look like something that was ordered and didn't come," Hartley says. "I have an idea what happened though. You couldn't allow the great Laidlaw to have an edge with Sheila."

"I became re-acquainted with Clarice."

"I'll bet you showed slides of your summer vacation," he smiles. "Jimmy Miller, this is our illustrious teammate, William Mulligan, who's not to be trusted with money or women."

I shake hands with a black-haired teenager in a light-brown, three-piece suit.

"I can't believe I'm between you two guys," he says.

"You've been my heroes since I was a little kid. When I tell my friends I stayed at Hartley's house, they won't believe it. Willie, you should see Hartley's wife, Diane. If I ever get married, I want my wife to be just like her."

"Jimmy, your taste in ladies is impeccable," I say. "I've seen Mrs. Laidlaw and you're right, she is better than a poke in the eye with a sharp stick."

Air Canada's breakfast is the usual high quality, although I don't think scrambled eggs should glow in the dark. But the coffee is black and strong and I decide to live.

"What's happening today?" Jimmy asks. "My folks told me just to be myself all the time but I'm a little scared about this."

"It's a luncheon to get publicity for the team," Hartley explains. "They're having some players and the people from the newspapers, television and radio. They plan to announce the coach of the team."

"Will I have to make a speech?"

"Just a few words, if anything," I say. "You'll be interviewed a few times because you're number one draft."

"Sportswriters from all over called me. When I got sick of it, I told my mom to tell them I wasn't around. The day of the draft, I was on national TV."

"I saw that interview," Hartley says.

"What did you think? Did I do good?"

"It's none of my business, Jimmy, but can I say something?" I say. "It's great to be frank but be careful what you say about the team paying your salary and the city where you earn it."

"But I didn't want to play in Cleveland, I wanted to play for the Canadiens and they said they had a deal with the Big Green for the first draft pick. I shouldn't have said those things, eh?"

"Handling the media is something you have to work out for yourself," Hartley says. "For me, the best approach is straight up. The writers and electronic guys can be a nuisance but I look on them as part of the job. The odd asshole is trying to make a name for himself by always knocking but, mostly, they're guys trying to make a living just like us. Cooperate and they'll usually be in our corner. Give them a hard time, they get on your case and the fans and management follow."

"You shouldn't have said you didn't want to play in Cleveland or that it's a bit of a dump," I say. "But, it's done so carry on today like it didn't happen. Have a couple of yarns ready when you're interviewed. If they ask about it today, tell them your mother wanted you to be a Canadien so she could watch you on TV."

The kid gets very downcast: "I screwed up, eh? I must be really stupid."

"Wrong on both counts," Hartley says. "It was an awful jolt to Willie and me not to be protected in the draft. Had we said what we really felt, our names would be mud. You gave an honest reaction and no one can dump on you for that. Just don't lean on it any more."

I change the subject because Jimmy looks ready to drop into a deep depression. "Do you have a girlfriend?"

"Yeah, in Sudbury, but she's just sixteen so it's nothing permanent," he replies. "Hockey players get lots of broads, eh?"

Hartley has an "okay, wise guy, what do we tell the kid about that?" look on his face.

"Many people hang around the hockey scene, groupies included, but you must be careful about them," I say. "People try to attach themselves to players because of the celebrity thing. Most are looking for something and they use you any way they can. Finding friends can be tough because you can't figure out if it's the person you are or what you do that attracts them."

"One of Laidlaw's laws is: Don't loan money to anyone," Hartley says. "You'll have some money now and people will try to get it into their hands."

"I know about groupies," Jimmy says, proudly. "We loved the trips to Ottawa, even though it was a long bus ride. There were twin sisters there who would get on the bus and give head to the whole team in about ten minutes. One guy told the coach they were his cousins. Another time, three of us joined the mile-high club on a flight from Sudbury to Toronto."

Hartley smiles: "Two questions: Why do you want to turn pro and can I go back to junior?"

"Have you signed your contract yet?" I ask.

"Mr. Edmunds and my agent worked it out but it isn't going to be announced until today. I got..."

Hartley cuts him off: "More advice for what it's worth— Never discuss your contract with anyone, especially teammates. For instance, if Willie found out I'm getting twice as much as he makes, he won't be my pal for long."

"I sure have a lot to learn," Jimmy sighs.

"Only in some areas," I say.

In Cleveland, two men are waiting, one, tall, skinny and nervous, wearing glasses as thick as beer bottles, the other a short, chubby guy.

"I'm Barry Bascom, the director of public relations for the Big Green, and this is our trainer, Harry Tatum," the tall one says. "Welcome to Cleveland. We'll take you to the Coliseum for the lunch and press conference."

The bright green limousine carries the Big Green's insignia, which bears a startling resemblance to the emblem of the Big Green Transport Company.

The Coliseum is in Richfield, Ohio, twenty miles south of the city, a magnificent building with 18,544 seats. Drive south on the interstate through open country and it's in the middle of a field.

We try to pick the brain of Barry Bascom, whose nickname is "Beady," short for "Beady-Eyes."

"What are they announcing today?"

"Oh, several important features."

When he doesn't continue, I say: "What features?"

"Some important appointments with the Big Green,"

"Aw, give us a little hint," Hartley says.

"Hey guys, I only work here. I'm not to tell a soul a single thing."

"Barry, old boy, we're not souls; we work here, too," I say. "We going to be brothers in the Green so let's scratch each other's backs. Tell us what's being announced and we'll go to some horseshit banquet to save your ass."

Hartley digs me in the ribs with his elbow: "Well, shucks, William, we don't want Barry to get heck from Mr. Edmunds, do we?"

"Aw, heck, no! I bet Mr. Edmunds isn't purty when he's mad. But maybe old Barry could tell us which illustrious players will be there. Then we won't be overwhelmed in the company of important luminaries."

"I guess I could tell you that. But don't tell Mr. Edmunds. Rollie Regan, Pete McFatridge, Salvatore Mancino and Harry Li will be present plus you three."

"That's exciting, Barry," I say. "We're happy to be present."

When Jimmy wants to see the inside of the Coliseum, we go down the ramp to ice level. I played here against the old Barons and the place was as empty for the games as it is at 10:30 a.m.

Jimmy stares at the mountain of seats and the two tiers of private boxes up near the roof. "It's the biggest place I've ever seen. Can we fill it for our games?"

I'm about to say "that's up to you, kid," when Beady takes over. "Mr Anderson's surveys before he made the commitment to underwrite the Big Green revealed good hockey interest in this market area."

"Yeah, but is anyone interested in paying to see a game?" I say. "One time I was here, and to save time, they introduced the fans to the players, instead of the players to the fans."

"The response of potential purchasers to our season ticket packages is strong," Bascom says.

"No accounting for people's tastes," Hartley mumbles.

"What do you mean by that?" Beady says.

"Just kidding, fella."

"Prior to the press conference, the Andersons and Mr. Edmunds wish to meet you three in the offices," Bascom says.

I check out the receptionist who Edmunds claims has colossal lungs. She's nineteen and cute but she couldn't fill half a Clarice bra with both of her's. I have doubts about Edmunds' judgment on anything.

In a plush board room, we meet Clive Eye-Vee, Clive-

Five, Gee-One and Edmunds. Clive IV is a florid, chubby man with a glass of booze in his hand. "Great to meet you and see what I got for eight million," he roars. "Don't tell me. That's Hartley Laidlaw and Willie Mulligan and this young fellow must be Jimmy Miller."

My Big Green days start promisingly when Clive Eye-Vee extends his hand and his drink is still in it. I can't resist and take the drink from him. "Thank you, Mr. Anderson, I don't usually drink this early but I'll make an exception today."

Edmunds grimaces and shakes his head; Anderson roars with laughter.

"Son-of-a-bitch!" he says, loudly. "I like you, Willie."

Clive-Five is a well-tanned, easy-going sort of guy and Gerald (Gee-One)—his son, fourteen, is Gee-Two—is nervous, pale and quiet.

"I hope we all have plenty of laughs this winter," Clive-Five says. "A big job is ahead and we're counting on you three to help with a big part of it."

"Absolutely correct, Junior," Pete Edmunds says. "These are the crown jewels of our collection. Can I get you fellows a drink or coffee?"

Edmunds wears a three-piecer he must have bought when he was playing. The vest buttons are under stress and I see a headline: FIRST DRAFT PICK KILLED BY FLYING BUTTON.

Hartley and I have coffee and Jimmy, as comfortable as if he had landed on the moon minus a space suit, has a soft drink.

The hour around the table is very pleasant. Clive IV consumes a lake of Scotch but never seems any drunker. Clive-Five (the family calls him Junior) is a loose cat and, although he seems to be the brains of the outfit, Gee-One says very little. Edmunds concentrates on buttering up the Andersons.

"My father, my brother and I are not experts in hockey," Clive-Five says. "That's why we hired Peter to run the operation. We won't be interfering owners, just very interested ones. Peter assures us we have a good chance to be competitive quickly and having you three is a big reason for our optimism."

"Yes, sir, Junior!" Edmunds enthuses. "These are quality hockey players and people. Willie and Hartley have been all-stars (Hartley has, I haven't) and Jimmy is the best prospect in a long time."

"What are our chances, Willie?" Clive Eye-Vee asks.

I hesitate, not knowing if I should pour butter on him or say what I feel. I compromise. "Building a competitive team takes time, a few seasons to find the right ingredients and patience from those in charge. I think we can be modestly respectable but we'll hardly be world-beaters from the start. But with the right coaching and good effort, we should improve as the season goes along."

Hartley congratulates me later for giving them what they want to hear without telling them anything.

When we move into the auditorium for the press conference, the room is packed and ten television interview areas with lights are set up. I feel like I should announce that I accept the presidential nomination. We parade to a raised platform with Rollie Regan, Pete McFatridge, Harry Li and Sal Mancino.

When Clive-Five introduces the players, the reaction of those in the room, mostly media people, is a typical smattering of applause.

Clive-Five continues: "Here's our general manager, Peter Edmunds, who has some important announcements."

Edmunds walks to the podium, waving like he's won the heavyweight title.

"A big day for us, the chance to meet our friends in the media and give you some news," he says. "I know you've been looking forward to meeting the men you'll cover all winter."

"Until they find out ol' Peter never told the truth about anything in his life," says Pete McFatridge.

"I have a very big announcement to make," Edmunds continues. "I'd like you to meet the coaches of the Big Green. First, our head coach, the man we're certain will guide our team to the top very quickly, Andy Jackson, and his assistant coach, Sammy Sparks."

Hartley says the color drained out of my face "like a thermometer stuck up a polar bear's ass."

Andy Jackson! Beyond belief! Jackson coached three teams in the NHL with little success and is regarded as a cementhead. He's in the Hall of Fame as a player, a tough winger noted both for scoring goals and carving people with his stick.

"Shoot me and put me out of my misery," says McFatridge. "He's the biggest fuck-up ever. Played for Jackson in Atlanta and he doesn't have an answer for hello. Runs the worst practices in history but thinks he's a genius."

Sammy Sparks played in the minors for ten years and coached several seasons in junior hockey, where his teams were often in trouble for goon tactics.

Jackson, who's five-foot-nine and hard as nails at forty-seven, turns to the players on the platform like Sammy Davis, Jr. asking his orchestra to take a bow.

"It will be a pleasure for me to coach quality players like this on the Big Green and for you to watch them," Jackson says, in a raspy voice produced by a spear in the throat during a stick fight.

"It's wonderful to be in Cleveland with its great sports tradition, and we'll do our best to add to it. This is a class organization and I'm pleased to be part of it. The Andersons are great owners and in Peter Edmunds we have a very experienced general manager. I ask only one thing of my players: total effort."

The remainder of the day is a semi-fog of a dozen TV interviews and two dozen radio tapes. The questions, and the answers, are almost the same in all of them.

Yes, it was a bit of a shock when the Canadiens didn't protect me. No, I'm not bitter, because I had a great stay in Montreal. I don't know if the strike was the reason I wasn't protected; ask the Canadiens about it. Yes, there's potential on the team but it will take time. Yes, if everything I've heard about Jimmy Miller is correct, he'll be a fine NHL player. Yes, Andy Jackson and Sammy Sparks will do a good job as coaches. No, I'm not married. Yes, I am a farmer in the summer.

When the electronic guys have their way with me, I'm approached by a very beautiful girl in her mid-twenties.

"Willie, I'm Jennifer Brown from the Cleveland Dispatch," she says. "I'm the hockey beat person for my paper. I hope you don't have Andy Jackson's hang-up about lady writers. He says no damned broad is going to get into his dressing room."

"I have no hang-ups about any writer, except those who don't try to understand the game or who dangle their participles," I say. "We went through that bull about lady writers in the players' association and most teams agreed to complete access for them.

"Though I confess it was a bit of a shock to a naive farm boy to confront a lady journalist for the first time when I was starkers. The Canadiens were one of the last holdouts against allowing females in the room. I was drying my face when a woman's voice said: 'Willie, did you really deflect that puck into the net?'

"I dropped the towel on the floor and tried to cover up with my hands. Someone kicked the towel away so I stood up, looked her in the eye and said: 'Yes, ma'am, the puck hit me on the ass and went in.'"

Jennifer laughs: "What did the lady do?"

"She bore me resentment and three children."

"Could we go to a quiet corner and chat?" she says.

"Of course, but could I first grab a wee dram of good Scotch? All this talk has me a tad dry. What can I get you?"

"Scotch and water would be fine," she says.

Finding a quiet spot in a room where everyone is talking baseball and football is impossible so I suggest the arena seats. Jennifer is more than a little different from most sportswriters, so I get the first question off: "How did you get to be a sportswriter?"

"As a kid in Minnesota, I went to North Star games," she replied. "I studied journalism at the University of Wisconsin and covered hockey for the school paper. I worked for a small paper back home on everything from rape to high school football, then my husband was moved here.

"I got a job on the night sports desk at the Dispatch because I could edit copy. When the hockey team landed, I went after the beat because I want to write. The sports editor was reluctant to give it to me because two guys were itching for it, but the editor-in-chief had a little pressure on him to give a female a major beat. If I don't do a socko job on it, I'll be back on the desk."

"So you're married."

"To a chemical engineer," she smiles. "Does it matter?"

"He's a lucky man. What sort of sportswriter do you want to be?"

"Hey, fella, who's the interviewer here?" she says. "Mostly, a good one, a writer who is honest, who tells about the people in the game and can dig out a story."

"Ask away!"

"Didn't you give the TV and radio guys tailored stuff?" she says. "When Jackson was named as coach, you looked as if you were told you had a terminal illness. The forced optimism is getting to me and nobody tells it straight. Outside of you, Hartley and the kid, isn't this team a crock?"

"Ask an easy one!" I say. "I have to be careful. If I tell you what I feel and you write it, where does it put me? If I lay on the company line, you'll think I'm a phoney baloney. Jennifer, I don't know how to operate. When you say you're under pressure to hold the beat, I'm wary that you're looking for every edge.

"I think I understand your job and try to cooperate with a little smartass talk and a few funny lines. But I was burned a couple of times by writers I trusted with off-the-record stuff. That made me cautious."

"You're a live one, Mulligan!" she smiles. "And I was going to ask if shoot-and-chase hockey was the best approach."

"I'll bet you were."

"I keep the off-the-record stuff right there," she says. "I'm no dilettante chick looking for a kick. I'm not a raving feminist and I'm no pecker-checker who wants to ogle the genitalia of athletes. I'm serious about this job. If word gets out I can't be trusted, I'm dead."

"Okay, let's talk off the record first. The Andersons got stuck with a bad deal, a real bunco job. If teams had protected sixteen skaters and two goalies in the draft, we might have had a modestly competitive roster. But with twenty and three plus the exemption for young players, there wasn't much available."

"What about Mulligan and Laidlaw, the labor militants?" she smiles.

"You said it; I didn't. Let's just say I would be equally happy to be a Montreal Canadien as I am to be a Big Green today."

"Then the team is going to be really lousy?"

"We're a long shot for the Stanley Cup," I reply. "But some strange things happen with expansion teams. The Atlanta Flames were a good example of one that had a surprising first year with sixty-five points. Others have been hopeless. Accidentally, the right chemistry happens, a coach gets every guy to play at his peak, all sorts of things. Or it can work the other way."

For some reason, I tell her about the Mount Everest Royals, Doc Bradshaw, Wally Kelly and all.

"Can the kids' team stuff be on the record? Maybe a story about the little team that didn't know the meaning of the word can't?"

"There were many words we didn't know the meaning of," I smile. "Of course, use it, if it's any good."

"How about this approach? The man with the new team reflecting on the boy with the new team, what it accomplished and how."

I'm very open with her, although we jump on and off the record more times than a stereo needle in an earthquake. When it's all over, she thanks me for trusting her and says she'll mail the article. If she's betrayed a single confidence, I'm to tell her about it.

When we head back to the madhouse, she says: "One

more thing. What do you know about Jimmy Miller?"

"I've never seen him play," I say. "All indications are that he's very gifted."

"Not as a hockey player; what sort of kid is he?"

"He seems like a naive, shy, seventeen-year-old kid. I sort of like him."

"Guess what the naive kid said to me?" Jennifer says with a wide grin. "I interviewed him and he seems about as deep as most his age. He told me he wants to continue his education, especially after talking with you and Hartley and finding out you have college degrees. Then he said he had a question for me: Was I in the mile-high club?"

I laugh: "What did you tell the little bugger?"

"I acted as if I didn't know what he meant. Then the little punk said that the first time I made a trip with the team, he'd make certain I got a membership."

July 7

Maybe the date is correct. Right now I'm not certain. Every so often, I drink a little Chivas to relax and become so relaxed I have trouble standing up.

I'm in a bar in downtown Cleveland. Red-Light Regan deep-sixes it under the table. Harry (Hi) Li prattles away in Chinese, Little Sal Mancino threatens to have his Uncle Vito break the waiter's legs if the service doesn't improve and Hartley lays lawyer charm on a big dude who wants to punch out Jimmy Miller for making a pass at his wife.

Jimmy doesn't drink booze, but something in the cola here affects a teenager's libido. He's made a move on every female in the joint. That kid would diddle a rock-pile if he thought there was a snake in it.

Last night and today, the Big Green takes its stars through a heavy series of personal appearances to beat the drum for the team. I never knew there were that many shopping centers and department stores in the world, yet alone in Cleveland, Ohio.

I've noticed Gee-One Anderson doesn't say much when his father and brother are around but he's the brains of the Big Green's ownership. He should know what he's doing with degrees in business, marketing and economics.

Last night, the team hosted a dinner for Cleveland's business leaders, heavies in their fields who were at the dinner as a business obligation to the Andersons (who wouldn't mind if they bought season's tickets). I shared a table with Gerald, two bank presidents, a city councillor and the head of a rubber company in Akron. The Andersons cut no corners because the groceries were in a photo-finish with a Big Bertha spread.

One banker told me Gerald's marketing has been responsible for the Big Green Trucking Company's success. "He used saturation advertising to an extent that if anyone in this area thinks of moving anything by truck, from local delivery to coast-to-coast transport of liquid chemicals, he thinks Big Green. If anyone can make hockey work here, he's the man."

When Gerald told them about Shoot-The-Puck Farm, their reaction was one I've often encountered. Maybe I'm a little paranoid about it but often when I meet people outside of sport, I feel I'm regarded as just a jock, maybe not too bright, and the result is perfunctory chit-chat. When I first encountered the crack about the long summer vacation hockey players have, it burned my ass no end.

I thought I had learned to be cool about it but when Gerald mentioned the farm, a banker browned me off royally.

"What do you have, a ten-acre country place where you can retire?"

"Not quite," I replied, with some bite in my voice. "I have a degree in animal husbandry and dairy science from Cornell University, 650 acres of prime Ontario farmland, 163 pure-bred Jersey cattle with 100 of them milkers, and a few hundred thousand worth of equipment. Starting from scratch, the outlay would be at least three million dollars."

There was a — what do they call it — pregnant pause at the table and the banker chuckled, "I apologize for being patronizing."

"A common mistake about athletes, sir. I apologize for reacting the way I did."

They grilled me about the farm, its financing and the return on capital investment. The rubber man noted the makes and models of our tractors because his company has an experimental tire and needs to test it. If he sends us the tires he promises in exchange for a detailed check on them, we'll save eight grand.

Hartley went through the same jock-talk until the men at his table discovered he's a lawyer. He met the main man at a big law firm here who offered to talk to Hartley about spending time as a researcher in his firm.

In the bar we invade, no one cares about such high-tone, distinguished chaps. When we make the last appearance in a sporting goods department, sign the last autograph and do the last interview with a TV sportscaster, Hartley, Jimmy and me plus Li, McFatridge, Regan and Mancino decide to get to know each other.

Jimmy has promised his mother he won't drink booze until he's twenty-one (he doesn't see anything wrong in smoking the occasional joint) but he concentrates on every female he sees.

"Kids sure have changed since I was a junior," says McFatridge, who's thirty-three and is known as Pete The Cheat because he knows every shortcut to make hockey easier. There's no commodity yet invented on which Pete can't get a better price.

The joke goes that, during stoppages in play, The Cheat pulls up his sweater sleeve and shows his latest line of watches, at a good price, of course. The Cheat was the best junior in Canada fourteen years ago, but he's played for six NHL teams. He claims to have been a future consideration or the player to be named later more often than any man alive.

"When I came out of junior, all I thought about was getting enough money to buy a car," Pete says. "I didn't know what poontang was until I was twenty-five."

"Bullshit, Cheat!" Li says. "You were married in junior."

"That's what I mean: I was married so I didn't know what poontang was." Pete has visited the wedding well four times but is "between engagements" now.

"Waddaya think of our team here?" slurs Regan, an Olympic caliber beer drinker. "I think we'll surprise a few people this winter."

"Red-Light, you must know something the rest of us don't," Hartley says.

"You played for Andy Jackson, Pete?" I ask.

"He's got all the style of a horse turd," McFatridge replies. "All he ever talks about is knocking guys' cocks off. You guys will hear one expression until you could puke. His pre-game preparation usually is: 'Stick the assholes.'"

They should have hired Wally Kelly as coach.

Just then, Red-Light descends slowly to the floor and Jimmy muses that all the women in the place "must be butches" because they haven't fallen for his youthful, albeit undeveloped, charm.

"We'd better get Red-Light and the sex symbol to bed," Hartley says.

"Yeah, and me too," I say. "It's back to the hay tomorrow and I'll need my strength."

"Hey, I've always heard that doing it in a hay mow is fun," Jimmy says. "Any horny farmer's daughters around where you live, Willie?"

July 23

Little Charlie, our herdsman and I have every third Sunday free of labor and it's my day off. Some sleep-in! I'm awake at 5:30 a.m. even though I spent a debauched Mount Everest Saturday night of euchre with Big Bertha, Doc Bradshaw and Millie, the wife the Big B picked out for him a few years back. The Doc and Big B stripped $17 each from Millie and me.

Writer's Note: Euchre is a card game popular in the rural outposts of the country. None of your big city games such as bridge or backgammon for us farm folk.

I get up, walk around a little, have a coffee and go back to bed. I'm just having a dream in which a barefoot Jimmy Miller, pants in his hand and shorts on his head like a turban, runs down a street, chased by a mean dude with a shotgun, when Big Bertha pounds on my door at 8:45. She says a lady is on the phone.

I stagger to the kitchen, two-thirds asleep, drop the phone twice and say: "Yeahhh." Big B loiters behind the kitchen door.

"Morning, starshine! Sorry to disturb your beauty sleep because I know how badly you need it," the cheery voice says. It's Clarice.

"How are you?" is the best I can produce.

"Terrific," she says. "Willie, I have a super idea but if it's not possible, 'no' is all I need. I took delivery of a bright-red, super-keen Corvette yesterday and I want to show it off. Could I come up and see the farm?"

"Oh, terrific!"

"See you in a couple of hours," she says and hangs up.

Too late, I'm awake. And when Big Bertha sweeps into the room from behind the door, I figure I've done something nuts.

"Who was that, William?"

"A fan who wants to see the farm."

"Oh, that's unusual. You seemed to know the fan's name. What was it . . . Clarence?"

"I should have slammed the door on your nose, the way you threatened to do with Sandy and me when we used to listen there. The name is Clarice."

"Who's Clarice, dear?"

"A girl."

"Oh, that's interesting. A girl?" she counters.

"A female-type girl with standard equipment. She's from Toronto, I met her in Grenada and she's driving up to see the farm."

"Good heavens! I don't have a thing ready for supper," Big Bertha exclaims.

"I don't even see anything ready for breakfast."

I read the paper over breakfast and the steam builds up in my ma. Finally, she blurts it out. "You really can be a horse's bum sometimes. A girl calls you up early in the morning, tells you she's coming to see you and you toss it off with: 'I met her in Grenada.'"

"She's a nice lady and I had dinner with her once in Toronto this summer." That's a numerical fib because I have seen a fair bit of Clarice this summer, what with several trips to Toronto on the excuse of meetings with my agent, personal appearances, a visit with Hartley and a couple of concerts.

In addition to being very beautiful, Clarice is a bright, interesting lady who's deeply involved in her career as a physiotherapist, working mainly with crippled children. I spent an afternoon at the hospital as visiting hockey star and the kids were super, although one little smarty just had to ask: "Do you know Hartley Laidlaw of the Maple Leafs? He's my favorite player."

Why is a man of twenty-seven so secretive with his mother about his romances and reluctant to have a splendid lady visit his home? Mainly, my mother is very concerned about my not being married and trying to produce her first grandson. Clarice is the first female friend to visit the farm in more than three years.

On the three previous occasions, Big Bertha took an instant dislike to my ladies and conducted a grilling that lacked only a stool, a spotlight and a length of hose.

"It's been a long time since you brought a friend here, William," she says. "I guess the last one was that bird-brained stewardess with the skinny legs and no behind who turned up her nose at the smell of a little honest cow poop. What was her name? Denise? Bernice?"

I figured the big romance of my life was on until the stew encountered the Big B. After one meeting, passion quickly turned to warmth and then to ice-box time.

"Don't try any third-degree with this one," I say. "She might spit in your eye."

"I like her already. Do I have to feed her, though?"

"I surrender. You can feed her the evening meal if you don't go berserk and if she's still speaking to you."

After breakfast, I wander outside to get my head straight. I have bad vibes about the day but how do you tell your mother, when she's as strong as the Big B, how to behave? Big Bertha is sixty-eight years old and the finest green-thumb in the township. Her flower garden around the big house and yard is a blast of color. Bus tours stop frequently to inspect it.

From the front porch, I can look out over the garden and see a stretch of road a car travels to the farm from the county line that runs into Mount Everest. I sit there to read the paper and watch for Clarice's 'Vette.

After a while my ma joins me on the porch. "You haven't watched the road since you and Sandy sneaked smokes when Charles and I went to town."

We'd sit on the front steps and smoke, then destroy the evidence when we saw the car coming along the road. I shake my head: "How in hell did you know that?"

"Why else would you two smell of toothpaste and soap in the middle of the afternoon? You buried the butts in the front flower bed behind the marigolds."

"What other little scams do you know about?" I ask.

"I have a very good idea why you're half-blind," she smirks. "A bright red car just drove along the road and you missed it. That your new fan?"

"The lady's new Corvette might be as spectacular as she is."

"I should wear sun glasses to face all this big-city dazzle," she smiles.

A small rocketship with an open sun roof wheels into the yard. It indeed is a dazzler but pales by the vision who emerges from the driver's seat. Splendiferous is the only word for Clarice.

She wears what she calls her "new shit-kicker outfit"—designer jeans that show off her magnificent bottom magnificently, cowboy boots with high heels and a checked shirt worth at least three hundred bucks. Her sun glasses are roughly the size of dinner plates and the Grenada tan has been perfected.

"Lady! You look terrific!" I say. "If my straight-laced mother wasn't peering out from behind the curtains, I'd chase you into the haystack."

"I suppose you'll use the excuse that you don't have a haystack," Clarice says. "Some farm, buddy! Where's the rustic down-at-the-heels, rural slum you're always talking about? I've never seen a lawn and flowers like those in my life."

"How did you find the place? You hung up before I could give you directions."

"I didn't want to give you the chance to change your mind," Clarice beams. "Mount Everest is on the map, you know. In fact, you told me you put it there yourself. So I just asked at a service station if they knew where Mr. Wonderful lived and they sent me right here."

I think Clarice is about to place a large embrace on me so I say: "Shake hands; I'll explain later." Clarice looks puzzled but extends her hand.

Clarice peers around the huge kitchen, a real farm number with a fireplace at one end and a beamed ceiling.

"My whole apartment isn't as big as this kitchen," she exclaims.

Big Bertha sweeps in and all my fears are substantiated.

"My second son is a bit slow but I never thought he had queer tendencies, despite the way hockey players hug each other," she says. "I couldn't believe the handshake. You're Clarice and you're lovely. If my dim son here lacks the manners to give you a hug of welcome to our home, well, I'll make up for it."

I almost wet the floor when the Big B gives Clarice a rib-cracker, just like they're old buddies. I'm double-teamed on this one when Clarice hugs her back and says: "Hey, you're beautiful yourself, Mrs. Mulligan."

"I hate to tell you this, Mrs. M. but your son obviously has played too much hockey without a helmet," Clarice says. "He said he'd explain the handshake later."

"I don't remember dropping him on his head." Big Bertha says. "His brother and sister are quite normal. William, why don't you read your old press clippings while Clarice and I inspect the garden."

I phone the area's only decent eating spot, the Inn-On-The-Pond at Waldorf, for a lunch reservation. An old chopping mill converted into a restaurant, Little Charlie and Doc Bradshaw own most of it, a silent partnership that no one, except me, knows about. The Doc wanted me to take a piece of the action but my agent, Ten Percent Prendergast, who thinks Canada Savings Bonds are a big gamble, talked me out of it. Little Charlie had to scrounge up the money but it's like an annuity for him.

I don't like going there on a Sunday because of the recognition factor, but it's the only spot within forty miles that isn't a slop-chute. The first time I phone, I fake a voice and am told rather hautily that the Inn has been booked solid for two weeks. I phone again and say: "It's Willie Mulligan. Do you have a spot for two for lunch?"

"Of course, Willie," the lady says. "It's lovely on the terrace over the pond."

"Then I married William's father and moved into this house, which was much smaller then," Big Bertha is saying as they come into the kitchen. "William, you never told me that Clarice knows all about flowers."

"I didn't know it was among her many talents," I say. "We'd better head for the groceries soon, Clarice. You'll come with us, of course, mother."

"Oh, no," she says. "I have things to do and you two have much to talk about, I'm sure. Clarice, if you'd like to freshen up, it's at the top of the stairs."

When Clarice is out of the room, Big Bertha says: "William, that girl has far more than standard equipment. A physiotherapist and she's just gorgeous! You've only been to see her once? What a laugh!"

"Do you have nose trouble today?"

"I didn't pry into your business, I just assumed you would see that one as often as you could."

"Well, a couple of times," I say, wishing to Harry Li that Clarice would hurry.

"I hope you don't mind, Mrs. M. but I had a little snoop upstairs and those hand-made quilts on the beds are super," Clarice says.

"My dear, I'll do one for you," she beams. "Me and the girls have quilting bees in the winter."

I better get Clarice out of there before they're planning the trousseau.

"You'll stay for supper, Clarice?" Big B says.

"Oh, I'd love to, if it's okay with Willie," Clarice replies. "But please don't go to any trouble."

"I want you to stay, even if it's not okay with William," my mother says. "If it isn't, I hope he runs away from home. And I'll go to a big heap of trouble if I feel like it."

"Want me to drive?" I say when we reach the 'Vette.

"No way, buster," Clarice says. "No hockey player or anyone else is going to drive this beauty for the first 25,000 miles."

"Did you get the family history in one walk?"

"Parts of it," she says. "Your mother did mention that you didn't bring many lady friends home and she told me something you've never mentioned, that you're having a house remodeled. I have a suspicion that she wonders why her baby isn't married at such an advanced age."

"My ma talks too much sometimes. I haven't brought many ladies home because a couple of times I did, Big Bertha conducted a reign of terror that the PLO could envy. I'm having a house fixed up because I plan to live here when I rejoin the real world. Yes, my mother would love if I were married and all settled down."

"You're a rarity, Clarice, because the Big B liked you right away. Maybe she thinks time is running out for me and it's any-port-in-the-storm time."

"Thanks, chum!" Clarice says, faking petulance. "So I'm any old port in the storm. Willie, don't be intimidated! I'm not on any husband hunt. I just finished six years of tough college, a doctorate looms on my horizon and I'm a long way from any center aisle. That doesn't mean I don't think you're a cute little fella. Sorta cuddly, too."

"You have my vote, too, kid," I say. "Do you want to have lunch or pull into a farmer's hayfield and play patty-cake?"

"Your offer is tempting," she laughs. "But I'm a growing girl and I need my groceries."

"I knew that your yearning for my beautiful young body would wane," I say. "I'm getting tired of being treated like a sex object and it's reassuring to know that you really like me for my mind."

"The body attracted me, the mind will keep me," she says.

I don't mind the recognition that goes with being a hockey player in Canada, especially one who has played on a high-profile team like the Canadiens. As Hartley says, it's when all the brats ignore you that you should hang up the old blades for good. This time, though, it's too much.

The man who runs the Inn, Herman Sheldrick, greets us effusively: "Willie, where have you been? We haven't seen you all summer! What a beautiful friend you have! I have a table on the terrace where you can have some peace and quiet."

Herman does nothing to insure peace and quiet. He parades us through the main dining room and across the terrace. I'm spotted immediately but Clarice, in all her splendor, is a showstopper. Several farmers almost drown in their soup, trying to get a good look at her.

The room goes quiet and I hear loud whispers: "There's Willie Mulligan!" and "Who's the girl with him; I've never seen her around here!" and "Wow! What a great lookin' lady!"

Many there are folks I know and it's: "Hey, Willie, howya doin'?" and one guy says: "Yea, Big Green!" I hear a male voice say: "I didn't know Willie ran around with girls who are physically deformed."

When we reach the table, I know how Columbus felt when he reached North America. The terrace extends out above the mill pond and overlooks the mill race and a little waterfall.

"You're a popular little devil!" Clarice says.

"It's not the hockey star in this entry who's so popular," I reply. "These simple country folk don't often see sights like you in your new outfit."

We have about five minutes of peace, just enough time to order a jar of cold and white. The autograph hunt always begins the same way. A mother brings the reluctant kid part-way, gives him a shove and says in a stage whisper: "Oh, go ahead and ask him; he won't mind."

The first one is a boy about five and after his mother launches him, he comes slowly towards our table as if he's on his way to the dentist. "Mistah Muwigan, can a pwease hab you autogwaph?" he says, looking at the floor.

I sign his paper, ruffle his hair and send him on his way. That starts it and for the next half hour, I sign pieces of paper, cigarette packages, church programs and even a dollar bill for every kid in the place. The adults, of course, want autographs for grandchildren, nieces, nephews and the kid next door. One woman breaks up Clarice when she requests an autograph for her grandson and when I ask his name, she replies: "Susan."

Folks I've known all my life stop at the table and there's plenty of: "How's your hay crop?," "We could use a little rain for the corn," "How's your mother?" and "Do you think you'll like your new team?"

Many people talk to me while staring at Clarice, who leans back against the terrace railing, wine glass in hand, placing the buttons of her shirt under maximum stress.

Finally, the autograph habit of the entire township is gratified and we get around to ordering lunch. The wine is already warm.

"Is it always like that?" Clarice says. "If it is, I'm glad I'm a nobody."

"You're a celebrity in this area right now. Big Bertha has had some phone calls already from old friends who just want to chat, and in their second sentence they ask who Willie's new friend is."

"Does all the attention bother you?" she asks.

"Sometimes, but these are the folks I've known all my life," I say. "To make it in the NHL, especially with the Canadiens, is just about the biggest thing in the world for someone from an area like this."

"It's easy to tell they're very proud of you," she says. "You have a nice way with people, especially kids."

"I look on it as part of hockey, like pulled groins and the charley horse. There's no use getting my shorts in a knot about it."

This isn't the first time a few Willie-knockers are present when I'm receiving a little adulation from the folks at home. Mostly, it's friendly needling but, today, it's nasty.

Herb (Sludge) Symons, Fast Sheila's brother, is seated three tables behind us with two buddies, probably still half-gunned from Saturday night. Sludge was the class-bully in public school, and for a couple of years he beat the crap out of me every week for the sport of it, then threatened to cut my nuts off if I told anyone. Sludge grew up from a little turd into a big one.

A grubby-looking man with a beer-gut, he lives about half the time on pogey (unemployment insurance) and is renowned for his beer capacity and for missing support payments for this three kids.

Clarice and I are on the paté when Sludge, with a voice between a fog horn and a moose in the rut, cranks it up. "Let's go somewhere with no friggin' celebrities to cause a stampede," Sludge bellows.

The best reaction is to ignore it totally.

"We'll see how good the hot-shot stud is when he doesn't have the Canadiens to carry him."

His pals "shhh" and others tell him to be quiet.

"Obviously a close personal friend of your's," Clarice says.

"That's Sludge Symons, an old classmate, and he pounded me any time he wanted to," I say. "You know what? He could do it again. Ignore him and he'll go away."

Sludge isn't about to vanish: "Maybe the great Mulligan got the shaft but he's over the hill. They'll replace him easy."

The reaction is a little louder this time and Sludge is quiet for a couple of minutes. I'm just starting to relax when away he goes again!

"She ain't such a hot looker," he roars. "I'll bet them things have that stuff in 'em, what do you call it, silicone?"

Now I'm no fighter, but Sludge has gone too far. When I start to get up, Clarice grabs my arm. "You can fight him only if you agree with that statement."

Herman, the head man, tells Sludge to be quiet or leave. We dine in peace, although I'm about as comfortable as a skunk at a garden party.

We're having coffee when Clarice excuses herself and does a head-turning walk across the terrace. All of a sudden, I hear a shout and a splash and look down to see enlarging circles in the water fifteen feet below. Sludge Symons' head emerges in the mill pond, his arms flailing about.

Applause breaks out, Clarice is gone and when I get to the table, Sludge's pals are guffawing uproariously.

"Willie, you ain't seen nothin' like it," one snorts. "Sludge is leanin' against the railin' when your lady walks past and he reaches up and pinches one of 'er boobs. She says: 'They're real, ass-face,' grabs the front leg of the chair and tips ol' Sludge, chair and all, over the railin' and into the pond like the drip from a tall cow's ass. Willie, goddamedest thing you ever saw!"

When I go in to pay the bill, Herman apologizes profusely (he, too, says it's the goddamedest thing he ever saw) and refuses to take payment. Clarice emerges from the ladies' room, appearing oblivious to the sensation she's created.

"Why were you worried about that sleaze, Willie?" she smiles. "He's not so tough."

My favorite musician, Oscar Peterson, is on the stereo in the 'Vette and, for a time, we listen to the man do it better than anyone can to that Steinway. Hartley claims we have some genes mixed up. He's big city and likes country music, I'm country and like big city jazz.

Finally, Clarice says: "You're very serious."

"Everyone says it's the goddamedest thing they ever saw. Cripes, lady, you'll be fabled in these parts."

"I hope I didn't embarrass you, Willie, but I can't stand some turkey grabbing at me like that. Besides, he didn't smell too good and he needed a bath."

I laugh at the looniness of the whole scene.

"Please don't tell your mother," Clarice says.

"I can guarantee Big Bertha knew before Sludge hit the water. Word travels fast around here."

"Then I better go home right now," Clarice says. "How can I face your mom after that? Oh, Willie, I'm so ashamed. What will she think of me?"

"Big Bertha will think it's the goddamedest thing and want to adopt you on the spot," I say. "Don't worry! It will never be mentioned."

I give Clarice the tour of the farm. We see my house and the Jersey herd and we walk the fields and lanes, winding up in my special spot in the bush under the beech tree.

"You're the first female I ever brought here, other than Sandy and Big Bertha," I say.

"I always wanted to explore virgin territory," says Clarice, unbuttoning her shirt. "I'll find out how Jacques Cartier felt when he planted the first flag."

"The birds, the squirrels and the farmer's sons around here are very naive. You want to corrupt them?"

"There's only one squirrel to corrupt," she smiles as the cowboy boots stand beside the beech tree.

"But what if the earth moves and knocks over my mother's favorite tree?"

The designer jeans with the fancy stitching go over a limb.

"Get your bum over here or do you want to end up with Sludge?" she says.

What can a fella who doesn't swim well do when faced with such a threat?

It's four when we return to the Big House and Big Bertha is on the screened-in patio, overlooking the garden. Now, my ma is a staunch church-lady, a leading light in just about every organization in the area, all of which regard demon rum as a major curse. But she likes a "wee nip" now and then. Johnny

Walker Red on the rocks is her favorite, and when on her "mental health visits," Diane Laidlaw always brings a crock. Big Bertha, in her Sunday best, has a wee nip in her hand.

"Have a pleasant lunch?" she says.

"Oh, yes, the mill is gorgeous and the food, too," Clarice says. "Then Willie showed me around the farm. I just love this place."

"It can have that affect on you," Big Bertha says. "When I first married Charles, it seemed quiet and lonely at first. Now, it's the city I don't like very much."

I fetch the drinks, wine for Clarice and Scotch for me.

"I think we'll just eat out here around six, buffet style, if that's okay," my mother says.

Just then, Sandy and her husband Ralph appear.

"We were just out for a little drive and thought we'd see how you were; we didn't know you had company," Sandy says. Interesting, considering she spent Saturday making pickles at the Big House, and they're dressed pretty fancy for a little Sunday drive.

I introduce Clarice as "a friend from Toronto."

"Willie, you never mentioned any friend named Clarice," Sandy gushes.

"I just met her this afternoon," I say.

Sandy sits beside Clarice and blows the cover story. "You're a physiotherapist, eh?" is her opener.

I'm about to open the guns on that when Little Charlie, Nadine and their two girls, Marty and Joey (short for Martha and Joanna) appear. The girls are very special to me and they're on my knee in a flash.

"We were just out for a little drive and thought we'd drop in to see how you were," Nadine says.

"Mother, it's heartening your offspring are so concerned about your welfare, especially when they all saw you yesterday," I say. "Could a dread disease have struck and inspired all this concern?"

"I saw that space-ship in the yard and figured our momma might be under seige by the Martians," Little Charlie snickers. "Clarice, I envy you. I always wanted a 'Vette but I had to buy a tractor instead."

"My family amazes me," I say. "Incredible how they're on a first-name basis with someone they've never seen."

Millie and Doc Bradshaw show next and they, too, are just out for a drive and drop in to see the Big B.

"She's the same old bag she was when you left at 12:30 a.m.," I say.

By then, Clarice is playing Frisbee on the lawn with Joey and Marty.

"Willie, Clarice is sensational," Sandy says. "Where have you been hiding her and what happpened at the Inn today?"

"Yeah, what went on there?" Nadine adds. "It's all over the township."

"Clarice heaved Sludge Symons into the pond when he touched her as she walked past his table," Big Bertha says. "I wish she'd drowned that ass. Anyone mentions it, and I'll have their guts for garters."

"Wally Kelly says it's the goddamedest thing he ever saw," Little Charlie says.

"How could Wally say that; he wasn't there," I say. "But I'll agree: It was the goddamedest thing they ever saw."

"What's the goddamedest thing they ever saw?" a new voice says and I can't believe it. Hartley Laidlaw, holding two liters of wine by the neck, and Diane, with a jar of J-W Red, come up the steps.

"I've got it," I say. "You were out for a little hundred-mile drive and decided to see how Big Bertha is doing."

"How did you guess?" Hartley says. "Where's the all-star chick? That her with the girls?"

Well, the party is superb. Big Bertha lays on a spread that's truly awesome, the white and cold flows freely, and eventually, I don't even mind that my ma has summoned the family for what I call The Clarice Summit.

Clarice charms their pants off and fits in like she's been around for years. Marty and Joey don't move more than six inches away from her.

"Is there anyone you didn't invite to see Willie's lady?" I ask the Big B when we're in the kitchen alone.

"Some, but they weren't home," she smiles. "When they hear what they missed, they'll pee their pants. You're not mad at me, are you, William? It's a big event when my baby brings home a girl who isn't an air-head."

"A great party, mother," I say. "I might bring home a new lady every week."

"You allow that one to get away and I'll have *your* guts for garters."

Diane gives me a nod and we take a little walk down towards the barns.

"I like her, Willie," says Diane, who's been even more critical of my ladies than Big Bertha. "She's going to drop in at my shop next week and we'll have lunch."

"She'll never replace you as the number one object of my affection," I say.

"Oh, I hope not. But I have an idea that if we're an entry, I'm not going to be One, but One-A."

Hartley, as always, has a memorable line for the occasion: "If I had known Big Green's lived this way, I would have become one a long time ago."

August 1

This is a day I don't like because I start my serious conditioning program for hockey, a reminder that my time on the farm has slightly more than a month to go before I head back to the hockey wars.

Hartley always said he had no sympathy for my brief off-season because I always played on teams that won the Stanley Cup. Many players gladly would trade places and have the chance to play in May. Next spring, though, I'll be home in early April.

My conditioning program isn't inspired by being out of shape. Working a farm hardens a man's muscles. At thirty-seven, Little Charlie weighs the same as he did at twenty. My weight has been 195 since I was eighteen.

Doing a tough program daily for six weeks builds up stamina and endurance for a long season. Most teams have only four or five days of training camp with full rosters before the first of eleven pre-season games. To show up out of shape is suicide.

The short camp is part of the agreement with the owners I don't like. It leaves no time for two-a-day workouts or teaching sessions. But my suggestion to extend camp to at least thirty days was voted down quickly. The players want the owners to cut the pre-season games to six and use the time for workouts.

The NHL is "kid-crazy" and, at twenty-seven, I'm practically a fossil. Hockey once had a sane order to it. Players were juniors until they were twenty, then were drafted. Maybe it penalized the precocious lad who was ready at nineteen but there weren't many in that category.

The birth of the World Hockey Association in the 1970s to rival the NHL upset the order. Of course, the WHA was great for the players because it pushed salaries sky-high. Were it not for the guys who lost fortunes in the WHA, I wouldn't be earning more than $200,000 a season.

When the WHA signed players as young as seventeen, the NHL did the same and order was upset badly. When the leagues merged, it didn't end. Some agents threatened legal action if the NHL didn't give players of eighteen a chance to earn a living in the game. As a result, teenagers now show up at training camp, a year of Major Junior behind them. A few make it but most return to their junior teams.

The owners discovered that a teenager at $60,000 per season is a better financial proposition than a veteran at $150,000. Suddenly, kids are all over the place and the NHL is offense loony.

Along with smaller contracts, the kids bring young legs to give them an edge in speed and stamina. The older player who has lost a step is in trouble. Experience is fine, but if you can't catch some brat on whom you can use it, you're up shit creek.

Many young players are into the new programs with a

language few NHL oldsters understand. They toss around such phrases as aerobics, anaerobics, oxygen uptake and cardio-vascular build-up. To match the kids in the new programs, the older player must be into a program that builds stamina and endurance more deeply than the younger guy.

"Tougher than dog shit to do an exercise you can't spell for part of your body you didn't know was there," Lester Franklin once said. "When I was a kid, it was so simple. A little jackin' off, a few push-ups and we was ready to go."

My new mate, Brooker Duncan, is thirty-four in the record book but NHL guys claim he's at least four years older than that. Brooker comes from the black ghetto in Halifax and his parents didn't register his arrival.

I got to know Brooker as a player rep and he's the toughest man I've ever met. He still takes a bit of crap about his color, but only from fans. No player in his right mind does anything to get Brooker sore at him. Brooker jokes about his color and people he knows can, too. But if he ever senses legitimate racism in the gags, somebody gets drilled.

Brooker knows the book on conditioning inside out. He's five-foot-ten, weighs 220 pounds and is built like the weight-lifter he is. He told me that when you got seven kids, you have to be strong to get anything to eat.

Brooker was a boxer ("I had a dozen different names," he said) and, in the off-season, he does a little pro wrestling as The Black Panther and runs fitness programs for the YMCA in Halifax.

Although Brooker is slow, he knows how to play the game, seldom placing himself where his lack of speed gets him burned. Brooker goes to every camp with no guarantee of a job because his team (the Green is his sixth NHL club) usually has a hot-shot kid ticketed for his job.

I talked to him last week and he was already into his conditioning program. For him, it's insurance.

"Never been to a camp where I was in the team's plans," he said. "I've started seven seasons in the minors, but eventually, they rediscover the old lad."

"What's the secret?" I asked.

"Hard work!" The kids have a background in fitness programs and the older player in basic good shape hasn't done enough. He needs the stuff that builds stamina and improves the heart and lungs. You can't do it overnight because you need three years in a program to get any real benefit. A couple of wrestlers I got to know a long time ago got me started.

"The important part of the season for me now is September. Man, am I in shape when I hit camp! The day one season ends, I start gettin' ready for the next. I organize a hockey school the last two weeks of August supposedly for kids. Really, it's a good way to get ice time and skate the shit out of myself until camp.

"Few coaches know much about conditionin' and from the first day of camp, I impress them all to hell because I have a jump on everyone else.

"I have another little trick, too. In an exhibition game, if the team's big star or a guy who isn't too brave gets into a beef, I fight his fight for him. Never fails to impress 'em. Remember that doozer I had with the Canadiens three years ago? Saved my job in the NHL."

Brooker was a Chicago Black Hawk at the time and a Canadien medium-range tough guy picked a fight with a Hawk pacifist. Brooker cleaned him and the team's two enforcers.

"Willie, how many guys in the NHL wanna fool with ol' Midnight?" Brooker said. "When a coach is pickin' his roster and he thinks about protection for all the chickens he's got, I've refreshed his memory. Or maybe the team has a new, tough kid so I go the minors. First time the kid gets his clock cleaned, they send for me.

"Another little dodge is that the referees, 'specially guys who've been around, know what's shakin' and when I play bodyguard, the refs understand. I've been third man in and didn't get a game misconduct because the zebra knew the old lad's just tryin' to stay employed."

Game misconducts in exhibition games count in the

three-per-season a player is allowed before he earns an automatic suspension.

Doc Bradshaw cooked up my training program for me. He figures farm labor is part of it and I run, swim or ride a bike four days a week in June and July. Today, I start the heavy load.

This year, I have pleasant company when I start. Clarice, who has been almost adopted by Big Bertha, is a guest for the weekend plus a few off-days. When I hit the kitchen at six this morning, Clarice is at the table, drinking orange juice and wearing a warm-up suit that fits like a second skin.

"What is this?" I stammer.

"You certainly are a cunning linguist in the a.m.," she says. "I'm going to work out with you. I do it every morning anyway and this country air will be an inspiration."

"This is no frivolous little jog I'm on."

"Don't worry, pal, I won't keep on rolling after you poop out," she says.

We do stretching exercises and she really knows how to loosen up that awe-inspiring frame.

"Get the lead out of your ass," she says when we we're working on leg muscles. "You're not stretching anything."

"Stop stretching your tongue if you want to be on the team," I reply.

Three miles is about it for me. I'm surprised at how much of the fine edge I've lost because I haven't really extended in my maintenance runs. Clarice barely works up a sweat, while my suit is soaked.

"I surrender," I gasp. "Your hidden talents always dazzle me."

"Willie, it's my field and I know a thing or two about my body."

"I'd like to find out more," I smile. "Wanna go in the barn for an examination?"

"The blistering pace I set was to control your runaway libido," Clarice says. "Besides, your mother and I are going to pick raspberries after breakfast."

Big Bertha has breakfast on the table.

"How did fatso here bear up?" she says.

"Do you have a whip?" Clarice replies. "I'll need one to get this boy into shape."

August 10

My new master, Andy Jackson, coach of the Big Green, calls today, my first real contact with him. The only person from Cleveland with whom I've had any truck or trade in a month is Jennifer Brown, who sent me a copy of the article she wrote. The lady is right: She can be trusted—and she can write.

Of course, she had a batch of good anecdotes about the Mount Everest Royals on which to base a fine, funny story. She does a nifty sidebar on Jimmy Miller, capturing his chippy arrogance and little kid's awe. I'd only argue one point with her. She says Hartley Laidlaw has "matinee idol good looks." Even Diane says the last person to qualify as a matinee idol is eighty-five years old and Hartley looks like him now.

Last week, a truck wheeled into the farm from the rubber company in Akron with at least $8,000 worth of new tires for our machinery. The tire technician gave Little Charlie and me a lesson in testing the new rubber compound. We are to check the wear and submit a written report.

"L'il brother, you've done it again," Little Charlie said. "The next time, though, try to sit next to a guy who operates a string of whorehouses."

Grain harvest is about finished, the result of ten days of hard work. Today, I'm having the noon meal at Little Charlie's when Jackson calls. Andy doesn't waste time on salutations.

"Mulligan! Andy Jackson!"

"Coach, how are you? Got our play book ready?"

"Not quite, Mulligan," he says in a voice that's mostly snarl. "No use giving play books to a bunch of assholes who can't read and understand them. If they could, we wouldn't have them.

"I called to make certain you're getting your fat ass in shape. I've tried your friend Laidlaw but he's in court on some land deal. If there's anything I need on my goddam hockey team, it's a lawyer. When I did get him, all I heard was a batch of bullshit. Says he's taking ballet lessons to get in shape. What are you doing up there in the sticks? Abusing yourself?"

Something in my conversations with the Big Green brass brings out the smartass. "I'm doing aerobics, anaerobics, isometrics, running eight miles a day, lifting weights and working twenty hours a day on my grain harvest. I gave up jacking off because I'm going to need glasses soon."

"Can't I talk to a player who isn't a dumb asshole?" Jackson rasps. "That dumb coon we drafted says he's mud wrestling with midgets to get in shape. It's sure going to be fun with all you comedians."

"I'm really looking forward to that part of it," I say.

"Let me warn you, Mulligan: I run a camp like nothing you ever saw before," Jackson snaps. "What you went through with that pack of pansies in Montreal will seem like a goddam picnic. You better show up here ready to haul ass. We're having a rookie camp and while I know that your beloved players' association says you wonderful veterans don't have to attend anything so degrading, it wouldn't hurt your cause with me if you were here for it."

"I'll have to check with my attorney, Mr. Laidlaw," I say. "Coach, I'm three pounds under my playing weight. What off-ice training are we going to have?"

"Shove that off-ice garbage up your ass," he says. "No hockey player learns to knock guys on their assholes or to score goals running around a fucking field in short pants. There's one way to get in shape for hockey and that's by skating and playing hockey. Will you have a chance to skate before camp?"

I'm tempted to tell him I'm going to ballet classes with Hartley and I won't be on the ice until camp, but I figure I've smart-assed enough for one day. "I'll be on the ice next week and every day from then on."

"Hope you push it hard, too," Jackson says. "Glad we had this little chat, Mulligan. Just wanted to check up on my boys."

I say the pleasure has been all mine.

August 12

Because a lack of morning papers on the farm means I'm often behind the news, Hartley is my information service. I sit down to breakfast at 8:30 a.m. and he relays anything in the Toronto papers I should know. He says the calls are tax deductible, because his books say he's Bertha Mulligan's lawyer and must consult her on business matters, although she wouldn't have him rake her leaves without a reference.

I'm digging into my grapefruit when he calls. "It's radio station F-A-R-T with sports news for the boondocks."

"Thank heavens! I figured it might be Andy Jackson," I say.

"A charmer, isn't he?" Hartley says.

"I hope you're skating because it's the only way a hockey player can get into shape," I reply.

"I started yesterday. The NHL players in the city rent a rink in the suburbs every morning. The frog pond frozen yet?"

"The ice goes in the Waldorf rink next week, and I'll be at it. The rink manager was my Junior B coach."

"There's a little yarn this morning about our illustrious team," he says. "I'll read it and you will see that Peter Edmunds is indeed leaving no stone unturned in his search for talent."

CLEVELAND — The Cleveland Big Green of the National Hockey League have signed Sven Stinquist, 24, regarded as the best player ever developed in Norway.

Stinquist played for the Norwegian national team last season, scoring four goals and 20 assists in 30 games. Big Green general manager Peter Edmunds met with Stinquist in Oslo this week.

"Stinquist is a mobile defenseman who will fit very well into the style of hockey played in the NHL these days," Edmunds said.

"I scouted him last season and was very impressed with his ability. He has a good chance to earn a position on our team this season."

Edmunds also reached an agreement with the Sports Federation of Poland to allow center Firpo Zybysadoskowski to attend the team's training camp next month. He was a sixth-round draft choice.

A Polish sports official claimed the Cleveland team will send hockey equipment to Poland as part of the deal.

"Where's Norway?" I say.

"Over there somewhere," Hartley says. "Must be a big country because Edmunds couldn't have found it any other way. The Green is reviving the League of Nations. We'll need fourteen interpreters."

"Norway isn't exactly a great hockey power."

"Ah, yes, but Edmunds is missing no bets in his search to make the Big Green into an instant power. Let's give him credit, chum. He's rounding up as many bodies as possible under circumstances not conducive to getting all-stars. If one can actually play in the NHL, it's a bonus for us."

"Edmunds has achieved the GM's Valhalla," I say. "In that equipment deal with the Poles, he's the first guy to trade a few old jock straps for a hockey player."

"I'm off to skate, then I have eight hours in the library on a case," Hartley says. "What's your agenda?"

"To loiter by the pool and have the wench here fetch me drinks," I say. "We should finish the grain harvest today, then Little Charlie and his family will take some vacation."

"One more thing," Hartley says. "The lawyer I met in Cleveland can get me a terrific deal on an apartment downtown, a sublet from an old broad client of his. She spends her winters in Arizona and would like to have two clean-living young fellows live in her luxurious pad. Let's share it for the winter. Diane thinks you would be a good influence on me."

I've thought about where to live in Cleveland because of the arena location. Montreal was ideal with an apartment two blocks from the Forum. In Cleveland, unless I pitch a tent in a field, there's nothing close to the rink.

I've been trying to decide if I should live in the city and

commute to the rink for games and workouts or try one of the communities a few miles away. Also, I've always lived alone, well, most of the time, anyway, and liked it. Hartley is a great friend but I don't know how it will be if we shack up together.

"Think over my little proposition," Hartley says. "I'm a neat, tidy chap who can use a skillet. We can retain the cleaning lady."

"Okay, it sounds good," I say. "I just don't like the idea of the drive to the rink every day."

"We've been spoiled by being able to walk to the office," he says. "But those halcyon days of our youth are gone forever. I'm a downtown guy and I couldn't stand living out in the sticks. Besides, I've already said we'll take it."

August 15

The Waldorf Arena is mine when I skate this morning. Jim Cameron, the rink manager, gives me a key and I'm there at 6 a.m. Next week, Cameron's two sons and a few locals will join me for some shinny but I want the ice to myself today.

Nostalgia grabs me on the twelve-mill drive to Waldorf in a pick-up. I think about the miles I logged playing hockey there. Big Bertha contributes to it this morning at 5:30 when I go past her bedroom and she says: "Do well in school or you can't play in Waldorf. Damn that Charles! He said you'd only last three practices."

I wear a sweat suit and have sticks, hockey gloves, pucks and a thermos of coffee plus two pairs of new skates to break in for training camp. Enough light comes in that I don't need the rink lights on and the place has an empty, eerie quality to it. Every sound is magnified and echoes back. I sit in the penalty box to lace my skates and something happens to me. This is the time I get reflective and introspective about my life and hockey.

Each summer, I dread this day but can't wait for it to come. When I go through my preparation, maintenance work-outs, then serious off-ice training and now skating, each reminds me the season is getting closer. But I'm always tempted to break my schedule and start the on-ice part much earlier.

Hockey means leaving the farm, my home where I have peace, the people I love and care about and the work that will occupy my life to go to an alien place. Even though I spent most of six years in Montreal, I had no real feeling of permanence there. Had I bought a home, it might have been different. But I felt like a transient passing through town—take the money and run.

Hockey means a new place to live, planes, buses, hotel rooms, Sundays on the road (what I dislike the most) and down time that makes me itchy because I could use it on the farm. This winter, I plan to take college courses.

From the first of October on, a part of me aches just about all the time, a twist here, a sprain there, bruises from sticks, elbows, the puck. I'll be whacked by sticks, elbows and, occasionally, fists, drilled into the boards and, once in a while, harpooned.

Hockey means getting dressed for work, going to work and getting dressed for work. I must take more showers in a year than any man alive.

There's the boring repetition of practice, the same drills over and over—breakouts, forechecking, line rushes and speciality units, penalty-killing and power plays. I have been lucky because the Canadiens' coach, Alfie Brisebois, is creative and innovative. We worked on the same systems but Alfie had an endless batch of drills to accomplish the same ends.

The complaints heard most concern the boredom of practice, the same dopey drills, day in, day out, until the players are lobotomized. Line rushes are the biggest bug-bear.

"In San Francisco, we did three-on-nothings, it seemed, an hour at a time," Harry Li once told me. "We'd laugh that if we ever had a three-man breakaway, we'd be ready. In the seventy-fourth game last season, we did and screwed it up. One guy said: 'Hope the coach didn't notice or we'll do three-on-nothings for two hours tomorrow.'"

Hockey is trying to be psyched up for eighty-four games (an impossibility) and compensating for the lack of adrenalin by using your head and playing the game well technically. It's the big surge of emotion in a game, then coming down from it, trying to sleep at 3:30 a.m. when your body aches and you know you must be on a plane at 7:30 or at a workout at 10. That drives more than a few players into booze or pills.

Being reasonably certain of a job with the Canadiens, I missed much of the insecurity many players face daily, the paranoia generated by screwing up and costing the team a goal, being in a slump or injured. Players in a fight for the jobs have anxiety attacks when they miss one shift.

Most coaches do very little to allay that insecurity. In fact, many do all they can to create anxiety. They feel that if a player is certain of his job, his effort is reduced.

I had a partial shoulder separation one season, missed a dozen games and learned what other guys go through. I wasn't going well and neither was the team when I was hurt. A shake-up was rumored to give some good kids the Canadiens had the chance to play. The restlessness I felt in three weeks out made it a miserable time and when a rookie did a good job in my spot, my insecurity expanded. Too soon, I declared myself fit to play, fibbing to the club doctor that I had no pain.

In my first game, I was banged into the boards and felt a dreadful pain in my shoulder. I figured it was separated totally but it was just aggravated. It hurt for the last half of the season but the pain was easier to handle than the insecurity.

When I got home, Doc Bradshaw told me how serious the injury had been and that I was lucky not to have permanent damage. It was the last lie I told a doctor.

I'm lucky, I suppose, because I love to play hockey. That's square one. To do it is fun, great pleasure for me, and I've never had the "love-hate" relationship with the game many players go through.

Hartley insists he doesn't like to play the game, an outlook I hear from others, too. He says it's hard work, he does it only for the money and he can't wait until he's out of it.

We talked about it the night I got back from Grenada and, as always, we were poles apart.

"If it wasn't for those dress shops, I'd be a fulltime lawyer," he said. "If I ever allow Diane to float a loan from her old man, I'll be out fast. Most mornings, I look in the mirror and say: 'And what are you going to be when you grow up, little boy?' It's a little kid's game."

"But you drive hard every time you're on the ice," I said. "You even raise your stick and holler softly when you score a goal. There's no better team guy than you."

"They pay me extraordinarily well so they get all I've got, just as some poor lady who's divorcing her drunken old man and hires me as her lawyer will get all I've got. But if the NHL announced no more pay for players, you'd be at practice tomorrow, kicking the door. You always look like you're ten years old and out on the frog pond for shinny with the farmers."

"Sure, I enjoy hockey but I like the loot, too," I countered. "Minus my fat contract, I wouldn't have those Jerseys and all those acres. Don't make me sound like a retard."

"For you, the money is a bonus. I'm not knocking your attitude or suggesting it's phoney or wrong. Often I wish I were the same. But I didn't get hooked on the game as a kid. At the schools I went to, the games were cricket, tennis, soccer and rugger.

"If I had a choice of sports for a career, I'd pick an individual game—golf, tennis or show jumping. I loved cricket but the future as a pro wasn't bright, even in Rosedale. I really wanted to study music but my father thought it was a sissy idea. We had our first serious split over it."

"We don't play cricket in Mount Everest; it's too tough to keep whites clean of cow manure. Golf and tennis aren't big, either, so we jack off and play hockey. But you like hockey more than you admit. It opens doors for you and, while the game is hardly your way out of the ghetto, it gives you independence from your family and more important, from Diane's lovable old pappy.

"You've made many friends in the game, even though you don't like the close team thing much. You're the rugged individualist type. But don't you have a good feeling when a group of guys get together and accomplish something?"

"Willie, you look at hockey through bleu-blanc-rouge glasses," Hartley said. "The Canadiens' organization distorts a chap's perspective and isolates him from the real world out there. You played on the farm team and won an American League title. Six years with the big team, five Stanley Cups. You were the best owned, best managed and best coached team in the NHL, and any club able to sustain a winning streak that long doesn't have many jerks. You got naked in the shower with some very outstanding men.

"Few players in their entire careers ever get close to a Stanley Cup. In Toronto, we could at least drive to the Hall of Fame and see it. I was a Leaf for seven seasons and the couple of times we got above five hundred, people were dancing on the tabletops.

"They seemed to change coaches every other week, did four major rebuilding jobs on the roster when I was there and, in seven seasons, I had at least 150 different mates. The few of us who survived were fairly close but, mostly, a basic introduction was all I wanted because the guy wouldn't be around long.

"Ask Brooker or Pete The Cheat the joys of the grand old game. They've been around a dozen years and they've been traded so often that Brooker didn't unpack his bag with three teams. Willie, you're the exception. I'm not being nasty, just realistic. You were with the best outfit in the pro sport and it distorts a man's outlook."

"Do you think there was no pressure or insecurity with the Canadiens?" I offered. "The organization was operated ideally but even after my best seasons, I felt I had to win my job at camp the next fall.

"Brooker says it would have been nice to be a Cup-winner but he figured the heat was on the Montreal players more than it was on the raggedy-assed teams."

"Pal, Cleveland will be an eye-opener for you," Hartley continued. "You'll find out how the other half lives."

I reach no definitive conclusions in my assessment until I step on the ice, take a few strides and know what it is that I like so much. Skating is a joyful experience and I wish I were a poetic type who could describe it in flowery terms.

I do some stretching because there's no quicker way to yank a muscle than to over-extend early. I've enjoyed the feeling of freedom in skating from the first time I did it on the frog pond when I was four. It's physically demanding but, for me, jogging is hard work, skating is pleasure.

I move around the ice and the lovely sound of skates biting the ice is very clear. I circle the rink a few times to build my speed, I carry a puck, shoot it against the boards, work fakes on imaginary defenders, cut to the net and score on every try.

For forty-five minutes, I lose myself in it. The old river skater is back.

August 17

I have a delightful conversation with Peter Edmunds when he claims the Big Green won't pay the performance bonuses in my contract because they apply only if I'm a Montreal Cana-dien.

Because my mother is present (Edmunds always calls at noon), I temper my reply, using an expression Moses often employed: "Go forth and multiply." I tell Edmunds I won't argue with him because it would inflict deep bruises on our warm relationship, so I'll turn the matter over to Ten Percent Prendergast.

Edmunds gloats as if it is a huge feat to find a loophole in my contract. He wants me in Clevleand next week to do a promotion, something I readily accept because Hartley and I want to check our apartment. My chat with good ol' Pete ends when I tell him to "blow it out his ass."

When I return to the table to finish lunch, Big Bertha delivers a succinct assessment of my attitude. She calls it "horse crap." "When you talk to anyone from the team, you end up in a fight with them," she says. "Shouldn't you be a little more reasonable?"

"Mother dear! That man told me they weren't going to

honor parts of my contract. What should I do? Congratulate him on his perception?"

"Oh, your agent will sort that out," she replies. "I'd feel better if you tried to get along with these people. It's not their fault you and Hartley weren't protected. You're not a Canadien, you're a Big Green and even though that doesn't sit very well, it's how it is and you should try to make it work.

"Clarice told me that when she met you in Grenada, she thought you would take a walk into the sea over it. Well, I think it's time you got your head straight."

"Two points," I say, knowing I've never won an argument with her but, like a true pro, I keep trying for a tie. "You and Clarice talk too much. In fact, my whole family acts as if we're heading down the center aisle. Well, I have no intention of taking that plunge and neither has she. Clarice is a fine lady but she's twenty-two and three months out of school. She's thinking of a doctorate and getting hitched isn't high in her plans.

"Point two! I've leaned over backwards with Edmunds and Jackson but they're getting on my nerves. I'll do anything I can to make it work but that call makes it a half dozen from Edmunds, first, to ask me to do something, and then a niggling point to create a confrontation.

"If it were just me, I'd worry but he's the same with Hartley. He thinks that the players' association stuff means we're trouble-makers. Before the season goes far, they'll kiss the ground we crawled out of because they'll find out what real trouble is. They have some pros in that department."

When I think I've shot down Big Bertha's argument, she simply voices it again: "If there's nothing to their little nags at you, then you shouldn't react, should you?"

She has a point but I'll never admit it to her.

I call Ten Percent with Edmunds' latest news. "Your contract is tighter than the hubs of hell and he knows it," my agent says. "He's trying to get your goat with these little things. You and Hartley are front-line players and he simply must try to one-up you. Remember that because you two achieved some notoriety in the assocation, a guy like Edmunds, who's run out of pit stops in his distinguished managerial career, feels very insecure with you. I'll give him a call and get back to you."

Edmunds doesn't own the insecurity franchise. I have the player's basic allotment, the feeling that something is amiss, and any indication that all isn't right triggers an anxiety outbreak. All hockey executives and coaches play on it, seldom giving the worker an endorsement that says: "Everthing in your life is under control and you have nothing to worry about."

They drop little hints to fuel your paranoia. Fortunately, the Canadiens didn't indulge much in mind games. For openers, any Rhodes Scholar could figure out the club had quality players itching for a job. And the Canadien management used a direct approach. They would say: "You're playing lousy hockey and if you don't get your ass in gear, you'll play your lousy hockey somewhere else." They meant it and it always worked.

Hartley always laughed at the mind games the Leafs played. In conversation a GM or coach would talk about how well some kid in the minors was going, and Hartley could be sure the player was a center.

Or if things weren't going too well, they'd ask about his health. If he replied that he felt good and why did they ask, they'd say that he didn't seem to have his usual steam.

"One coach who was really great with the 'how ya feelin'?' routine was a fitness loony and a hypochondriac," Hartley told me. "We reversed it on him and for a month almost drove him batty. Every two or three days, we'd ask him: 'You not feelin' well, coach? You look a little pale.' He'd go to the mirror and check. Or: 'You puttin' on weight, coach? Your face looks fatter than usual.' When no one was watching, he'd be on the scales.

"Another time, after he really had a campaign going for a week by hinting at trades about to be made, a couple of us really worked a scam on him. It was a little cruel but the prick deserved it.

"One night in Boston, we saw him in a bar with that sure-thing, the famous Thunder-Thighs. No player would go near her when they heard the coaches and GMs were stabbing her. A couple of days later, he was in his office with the door open and two of us stood around the corner and talked so he could hear.

"I said: 'You didn't screw old Thunder-Thighs when we were in Boston, did you?' and the other guy said: 'Cripes, give me credit for some taste. I wouldn't touch that old bag with a ten-foot-pole. Why do you ask?' I said: 'A Bruin told me she had a heavy dose and a bad outbreak of pant rabbits.' Then we walked away.

"The coach looked downright worried for a month. The trainers told me he swiped a half barrel of blue ointment out of their medicine cabinet."

Fifteen minutes goes by before Ten Percent calls to tell me Edmunds says I must be confused because he never mentioned my bonus clauses.

Sure is fun in the big leagues!

September 8

Dirty, rotten, no-good son-of-a-bitch!

No other way to sum up how I feel on my final day of summer on Shoot-The-Puck Farm. Although I don't have to be in Cleveland for another week, I like to be settled when hockey starts. The team's rookie camp opens tomorrow and I can skate for a few days there.

Yesterday, I had my annual check-up from Doc Bradshaw, including tests to evaluate my physical condition, complete with treadmills, lung capacity apparatus and other Buck Rogers equipment.

Because I've been having trouble getting my heart into it this summer, the Doc's words were music to my ears.

"You're in the best physical condition ever," he said. "I don't know how you could improve. Your bodyfat is perfect, your lungs are tops and you breezed through a heavy stamina test."

"I can't believe it, Doc. I've had no enthusiasm because I've felt like I was getting ready for prison."

"I've noticed a lack of enthusiasm for your new team but it doesn't show in your body. You're in superb shape. You always forget the work you do on the farm, and you are on a very advanced program. You do it easily and you don't feel you're working hard.

"You ran a lot with Clarice and she provided a competitive factor that made you push harder. She could be a fine distance runner, you know. The lady has been very good for you."

"You sound just like my mother," I laughed. Doc Bradshaw is the person to whom I can best relate.

"What are you plans for her?"

"Nothing long range right now. We've had a great summer but that's as far as it goes. Clarice is involved in her career, I'm a little involved with the Big Green so we'll find out if absence makes the heart grow fonder."

"Your family and everyone else is a bit in love with her," the Doc said. "It would break your mother's heart if you and Clarice end whatever you have going."

"Doc, I have absolutely no intention of ending whatever it is I have going with Clarice. My problem is that I don't know what I have going with her."

I've had a hectic two weeks, preparing for the safari to Cleveland. Hartley and I went to Ohio late last month to make an appearance for the team and check out the apartment, which is slightly beyond belief, a two-storey, eight-room condo in the downtown area, complete with fireplaces, a grand piano and expensive furniture.

One of Hartley's endorsement deals is commercials for an auto manufacturer, and even though he's now a Big Green, the company gave him a new contract. At my suggestion, part of his deal is wheels for both of us in Cleveland.

I flew to Montreal, arranged to have my furniture moved to Mount Everest for storage in Sandy's big farmhouse and closed the lease on my flat.

I figured I'd have great pangs of nostalgia and regret over the official end of my association with that city. But it didn't work that way. Because I'm a Canadien no more, I felt as if I had no ties there at all.

I had a long lunch with Alfie Brisebois, the Canadiens' coach with whom I had an excellent relationship.

"Willie, I want ya to know dat I fight like de bitch to keep you here," Alfie said. "I tot it was a crock what dey do to you but der was nuttin' I could do. Da decision was made at da owner level. You were a great player for me, da very best, and I hope dose guys in Cleveland know how lucky dey are to hab you."

Last night, we played "The Annual Goodbye-To-Summer General Piss-up Cup" game at the Waldorf Arena. Little Charlie, Doc Bradshaw, Jim Cameron (the arena manager) and his teenage sons plus other local floaters play a game in which the Mulligan brothers are the goalies and the losers buy the beer.

The beer-bash in the back room at Inn-On-The-Pond was a dandy. The Doc went off the terrace railing into the pond backwards to demonstrate what Clarice did to Sludge Symons, and Little Charlie got superbly smashed.

I took him home and helped Nadine get him to bed while he mumbled about the Mulligan boys switching jobs. He'd go to Montreal to play hockey because he's just as good a goalie as his horse-shit brother.

"Willie, I'm glad you don't leave every week," Nadine said. "It's the only time he gets hammered, although he insisted he wasn't going to this year.

"I get sad, too, but about half as much as Charles does when you leave, and your mom will be down in the dumps for a couple of weeks. Playing hockey means a great deal to you and it's sure done a lot for all of us on this farm. But we'll be happy when you're here all the time. This summer has been especially good because of Clarice. Hope you plan something permanent with her."

If I don't, this family will adopt her anyway.

After my last feed of Big Bertha's groceries, I take my valedictory walk around the farm. This time, though, I'm not alone.

"How can you leave here?" Clarice says. "It's sad that I won't be spending most weekends here, even though Diane and I will pop up a few times to see your mom. Diane doesn't look forward to Hartley being away but we plan a few things to ease the pain of our men being off to war, including trips to the battlefield."

"Leaving ain't easy, lady," I say. "Isn't it amazing what a man will do for two hundred big ones a year?"

~2~
The
Pre-Season

September 12

I discover a shocking fact this morning: Hartley can't poach an egg. He's also an a.m. grump, a man who has a battle to marshal his corpuscles on life's drill square.

About 10 a.m. on our first morning in Cleveland, when he can speak English, he says: "This match certainly wasn't made in heaven. Just don't be cheerful in the morning. It took a year to train Diane not to open her yap in the first two hours of my day, and I hope it won't be the same with you. Can you suppress the urge to be happily philosophical at an hour when people with brains are asleep?"

"I've had my ass hauled out of bed at sun-up since I was twelve to commune with Jerseys," I say. "But I promise to walk on tip-toes across our lush carpets, to rattle no dishes, play no cheery music or speak a word."

Today, I'm up for four hours, jog three miles, have a swim in the pool, read the papers and have breakfast by the time Hartley appears.

"Speak softly and no serious subjects," he says.

"What do you want for breakfast?"

"That's too serious. I'll get it myself."

Hartley's egg-poaching effort is a send-up of The Three Stooges. He places too much water in the pan, drops egg on the stove, burns the toast and produces a soggy mess.

"Oh, shit!" I hear from the kitchen. "It wouldn't have lived anyway; it only has one eye." When I go in he's staring at a blob on his plate. I take it away and prepare breakfast for him.

"Marry me, you talented, sexy little devil," he says.

"No, you told me lies about your skill in the kitchen," I reply. "I have a beneficial trade: I won't talk in the morning and you stay the hell out of my kitchen. Already, I have to cope with an egg-splattered stove."

"Don't be a nag, too."

We locate the necessities of life—a supermarket, a fruit store, a butcher shop, a deli, a laundry, a couple of bars and two or three decent restaurants.

The car company delivers the wheels, a luxury job for Hartley, a compact for me.

"What's this? I thought it was all for one between us," I say. "How come you get the gold mine, and I get the shaft?"

"After spending your life in pick-ups, you just wouldn't be comfortable in a big car," he snickers. "A modest compact is your first step towards limo land."

When we inform the club we won't need hotel rooms for training camp, Andy Jackson raises hell, claiming it shows we think we're better than the other players. I argue that it shows we have a place to live and can save the club unnecessary expense.

"We might promote togetherness by having the team in a group at camp." Jackson says.

"Okay, book us into the hotel," I say.

"Then again, maybe it's a good thing to keep you donkeys separate from the others," Jackson says. "You might organize a strike because the camp oranges aren't sweet enough. Stay in your own place."

We plan to sneak into the arena this afternoon, view the rookie-camp sessions and arrange some skating time. We enter through an employees' entrance, look for a place from where we can watch the workout undetected and settle in seats high in a corner.

One group of rookie-camp players is filing on to the ice in a variety of tattered uniforms. Such camps consist of real rookies drafted this year; young, undrafted players from

junior and college hockey who asked for a tryout; free agent
veterans trying to keep their careers alive; and minor leaguers
who never despair of catching the brass ring.

"There's Brooker Duncan," Hartley says, "What's he
doing here? He could have told them to stuff it."

"Trying to salvage a job and looking for any little edge,
like impressing Jackson."

Jimmy Miller is in this group, too. It's nice to know he
could spare a few minutes from his busy sex life for a little
hockey. I knew he was just a little kid but I didn't think he
looked that young. It's hard to believe he and Brooker play the
same game.

"Ever see a collection to equal this?" Hartley says.

"Guarantees a playoff spot and a run at the Stanley Cup,"
I reply. "Same as all rookie camps. Imagine how many guys
came out of the woodwork and asked for a tryout. Recognize
anyone?"

"A guy named Al Barnes was at Leaf camp about six
times. He's the big defenseman with red hair, skating with
Brooker. Crazier than a loon."

"Couple of guys were in Canadien camps," I say. "That
little guy with jet-black hair in the old red sweater is a pepsi
named Michel Vaillancourt. Great skater, super practice
player, can't do anything in games."

A whistle blows and Andy Jackson and Sammy Sparks
skate onto the ice in green sweat suits. I watched Jackson on
television when I was a kid and he looks the same, as hard as
nails and moving with a swagger.

"Arrogant little shit, isn't he?" Hartley says.

"Looks like a tough dude to tackle, even now. Sammy
looks as if he might have a few shingles flapping."

"Sparks was at Leaf camp as a fairly bright defense prospect when I was a rookie," Hartley says. "I had a hand in his
demise. In an intra-squad game, my line victimized him for six
goals. I saw he couldn't pivot so I dumped passes behind him
all day and he was like a drunk in a revolving door. I hope he's
forgotten about that."

I detect a movement behind us just as a voice booms out:

"Ah, hah! I thought it was you two. The lure of competition too great to resist?"

Peter Edmunds sits down behind us.

"Who do I have to beat out to make this team, Pete?" Hartley says. "Any gems walk in off the street?"

Edmunds laughs: "There's so much talent here, we don't need you guys. More than 400 players wrote or called for a tryout. I'll show you the letters; it's great comedy. It was a big job to make certain we didn't miss a body that might help us. We cut it down to ninety-five and, tomorrow, we'll chop to forty because housing and feeding them is very costly.

"Four or five walk-ons might get contracts because we need forty-five players this season to have a minor league farm team. It'll be rough but we might as well start out right, don't you think?"

Hartley and I both nod.

"What's the farm set-up?" I ask.

"A team we'll run and staff in the Central League at Fort Worth and we need twenty bodies for it. We also have a partial agreement with Port Huron of the International League, and we'll send them a minimum of six players."

"How's young Miller looking?" Hartley says.

"Watch this scrimmage because he's in it. The little bugger is incredible with the puck sometimes. He makes moves at a high level, and the other guys are far behind him. They get in his way, and his frustration shows. When he doesn't have the puck, he hasn't got the faintest idea what to do or the slightest inclination to do anything."

"Sort of a normal seventeen year old," I offer.

"Exactly, and we'll face a tough decision to keep him or return him to junior," he says. "But he's three months short of eighteen and it's tough to keep our expectations realistic."

"I'd say there's more involved than hockey ability, too," Hartley says. "Jimmy has an enormous ego so he won't cheer on his way back to Sudbury. Another year of junior with heavy ice time might be the best thing for him if his attitude is right."

"We might run him back with a gun if he doesn't quit

pestering the secretaries," Edmunds says. "He's after the receptionist with big boobs like a bear after honey."

"I've noticed the lad has active hormones," I say.

"Any chance of a little ice for, say, a half-hour skate?" Hartley asks. "I want to keep my edge."

"Of course. After this group, there's a ninety-minute break. Take as much of it as you like. Let's watch the scrimmage, then the trainers will fix you up with anything you need."

It's a surprise, but none of the abrasiveness I encountered all summer from Edmunds shows today. He's oozing charm, asking what we think of players on the ice.

Jackson drills the players hard, starting with ten minutes of stops and starts, traditional but necessary.

"I have a small favor to ask," Edmunds says. "Our Europeans arrive tomorrow and in the evening, could you come to a little welcome dinner? Beady Bascom, our PR man, went to Poland and completed arrangements for Firpo Zipper-Head, or whatever his name is, to leave for Frankfurt. Anders Nilsson from Sweden, Ilko Mikkolainen from Finland and Sven Stinquist from Norway met them there."

"Of course, we'll be there," Hartley says. "How do the imports and English get along?"

"That's a problem. Firpo speaks only Polish. The Norwegian speaks Norwegian, of course, but is fluent in English, French, German and Russian. The Swede has some English and the Finn doesn't say enough for us to know if he can talk at all."

"How good are they?" I ask.

"Nilsson, the Swede, is a good prospect, very fast but not wild about heavy traffic. The Finn is a find; he skates and handles the puck well. The Norwegian is a gamble. I watched him in the B pool of the world tournament, which isn't great hockey, but it was worth a ticket to have a look at him. He's a lanky guy and I liked his intelligence on the ice, his mobility and passing skill. He's working on his PhD in anthropology and didn't want to come but he can take some courses here if he sticks.

"The Pole is really strong, five-ten and 220 pounds. He can skate forever and isn't afraid. Had he been a Finn or Swede and easy to get, he would have been a first-rounder. The Polish junior coach spoke English and he and I got tanked at the world juniors. When I said I'd like Firpo at our camp, he told me how to do it, starting with a hundred Yankee bucks for him. We don't know until we see him in action but we had to try everything. Hey, watch this!"

On the ice, scrimmage has started and Jimmy Miller moves through the neutral zone with the puck. He skates with a short choppy stride, bent over a little at the waist.

I almost holler "look out" when a player roars at him from the blind side. Jimmy just knows he's there and leans far enough that the check misses him, barely. That sends him one-on-one with Red Barnes, the hacker defenseman, and what happens is difficult to believe. Jimmy skates right at Barnes, the puck close to his skates, and a collision seems unavoidable.

Jimmy drops his left shoulder and fakes to the outside. Barnes makes a forty-five degree turn that way to head him off but no one is there—Jimmy goes left to the inside, an incredible change of direction. Barnes smashes his stick on the ice while Jimmy cuts across the slot and unloads a wrist shot through the other defenseman's legs, over the goalie's shoulder and under the crossbar.

"Tell me I didn't really see that," I say. "Barnes was parted from his ass."

"The kid's done things like that a few times this week," Edmunds says. "But in his own zone, it's disaster. Let's go downstairs."

The Green trainers are Harry Tatum, who has a degree in physiotherapy, and John Hannigan, sixty years of age, a "lifer in linament." Edmunds says that Jackson wanted Hannigan because he's good with equipment and sharpening skates, but coaches like Andy want their man in the dressing room as a spy. We'll be careful not to say anything we don't want Jackson to know post haste, via Hannigan.

"Harry, these two rooks want to skate between sessions," Edmunds says. "Fix 'em up."

"Just sweats; we only want to loosen up. I'm ready to kick ass but Hartley isn't."

"How about a brand-new, still-in-the-box set of Big Green sweats?" Harry smiles. "No tradition in 'em but they're good ones."

"Toss you to see who goes to the car," I say. I've never won a flip from Hartley and I carry in our bags.

The sweat-suits are bright green with white trim and when we're dressing, I have a funny feeling in my gut.

"Thinking the same as me?" Hartley says.

"Sort of official now, isn't it? It's been six years since I wore anything but red, white and blue. Think you'll ever develop great devotion to bright green and white?"

"That first check in U.S. bucks, signed by this organization, will do wonders for my view of these colors."

"How do I look in green and white, Harry?"

"A big mess better than a lot of the dudes who wore the colors this week," Harry says.

"Much crap on the ice?" I ask.

"A few fights and one stick-swinger because guys figure that impresses the coach. On the first day, a couple of young dummies challenged old Brooker but he laughed at them. He's one tough old bugger, and is he in shape! First day in the weight room, he stripped a hundred off the young guys in a bench-press contest."

"Mulligan's first law: Never enter contest with crafty old black man. You have a weight room?"

"I'll show you the set-up," Tatum says. "They gave me a free hand and a blank check to set things up. I hope it meets with your approval."

Harry knows his stuff. He's grabbed large amounts of space for a room with the latest weight-training and fitness testing equipment, another with a sauna and whirlpool, and a carpeted, furnished lounge with a pool table and an old pinball machine.

"You can be my interior decorator, Harry," Hartley says. "It's terrific."

"The Andersons run a good ship and they'll do everything possible to make the players happy. We'll even have a lounge with a bar for your ladies ready by the first game."

"Now, if the players just do something to make the Andersons happy," I say.

The players are coming off the ice and Jimmy spots us.

"Hey, what are you guys doing here?"

"Just settling in. We're going to skate when the ice is resurfaced," Hartley says. "How's it going?"

"Okay, but the coach says I should check more. After I saw you guys, I did a weight program a little and I'm up eight pounds to 164. And I went to summer school and I've got my diploma, just like you."

"Great, man!" I say, shaking his hand.

Jimmy moves close to us and whispers: "I got some stuff lined up for us. Three of 'em, good-lookers, who have an apartment together. Some night, we'll go over, eh?"

"Jimmy, you want me to cheat on my wife?" Hartley says.

"I never thought of that. I guess I'll just take Willie and one of the other guys."

"I never fool around during camp," I say. As he moves away the thought strikes me that if he ever grows a beard, it will be pubic hair.

Hartley and I do some stretching and Harry tells us the ice is ready. We expect the arena to be deserted but all ninety-five rookie camp players are in the seats at one end.

"Can't we just skate in peace and quiet?" Hartley says.

"Pal, everyone wants to see the stars," I smile.

Hartley and I do a few easy circuits of the rink, then Jimmy, wearing his sweat suit, skates out. We tell him to save his strength for his next session, but he says that at least once this week, he wants to be on the ice with "someone who knows how to play the fuckin' game."

"We're stretching it out so don't try to keep pace," Hartley says. "Take it easy or I'll boot your ass off."

An absolutely gorgeous skater, Hartley isn't quite as fast as the old river rat but he's just as agile.

"These nice people paid to get in so let's give 'em a little show, farmer!" Hartley says when we see Edmunds, Jackson and Sparks at the end of the rink.

"Okay, flatout, no breaks, six around each way, five backward crossovers, along-the-line agility and eight sets of stops and starts."

We circle the rink one way, then six the other way, at top speed. We go up and down the middle of the ice backwards, weaving around each other. We run sideways on the toes of our skates back and forth across the blueline in unison like chorus girls, then do stops and starts, using the three lines as boundaries.

We stand at the penalty box and suck some ice.

"You're whacko!" I say. "That was hard work."

"Then why aren't you breathing hard? Summer with a physio obviously tones up the muscles."

"I heard Jackson say: 'Look at those big-wheel assholes, showin' off,'" Jimmy says. "You guys must be in shape."

"You play two-puck, Jimmy?" He smiles and nods. "Okay, let's give 'em a biggie."

For five minutes, the three of us keep two pucks on the move without a flaw as we zip around the center-ice faceoff circle. Jimmy is a wizard with the puck and has some ham in him, too. We pass every way—forehand, backhand, in front, behind our backs, through our legs—and expand the game to three pucks. At the end, the players stand and clap, whistle and cheer loudly. We skate down in front of them in a line and take exaggerated bows.

"Wonderful, just wonderful," Jackson says, his mouth pulled in a hard line, when we come off the ice. "A cute little act for between periods for the people who don't like the real hot dogs."

"Hey, coacher! Good to see you. How's your old snapper?" I say shaking his hand.

"Yeah, great to be here, coach!" Hartley says.

We're saved from further pleasantries by Brooker Duncan, who gives us each a "high-five."

"Super shit, you honkies!" he says. "You need a record of

Sweet Georgia Brown for that circle. I thought the Harlem Globetrotters had discovered hockey."

September 13
"The Big Green's First Annual Welcome The DPs to Ohio Dinner and Polish-Finnish-Swedish-Norwegian Friday The 13th Gala Festival" is an all-time, Hall of Fame and Academy Award whacko night.

The dinner for the Europeans is held at Swingo's Hotel, which has a fine dining room, so Hartley and I deck out in our three-piecers and ride over in his luxury car. Hartley asks Brooker Duncan if he wants to wear a uniform and be our chauffeur, but he says he already has a part-time job as a porter on the train and he's working the ladies' car tonight.

The Green group is around a table in the bar for infield practice before dinner. There's Andy Jackson, Sammy Sparks, Peter Edmunds, Beady Bascom and Clive-Five Anderson, four chaps who look a trifle puzzled and an older, overweight, tough-looking guy.

Sven Stinquist, a tall, slender man with fair hair, wears glasses, smokes a pipe and looks the way a Norwegian candidate for a doctorate in anthropology should look.

Anders Nilsson is a blond, of course, a handsome lad with a rosey complexion like the Swedish kids on posters. "Yaw, Villie and a-Hartley, I know you vrom readink de Hockey Noose for years."

Ilko Mikkolainen stares at his hands, clenched in his lap. When I shake with him, he has a grip like a vise.

Firpo Zybysadoskowski is all muscle and his head seems too small for his massive body. His nose is flattened beyond reclamation. Hartley claims Firpo's face is so flat he could bite a wall. When he smiles, it's like a crack in a pie.

Firpo wears an ill-fitting, somewhat shiny gray suit and his bowling ball shoulders place the seams under stress. He has an aura of enormous power and no Polish jokes will be heard within a half-mile of him in case he understands.

The hardboot between Clive-Five and Firpo is John something-or-other (all consonants, no vowels), who drives a sixteen-wheeler for Big Green Transport. He speaks Polish and is Firpo's interpreter. They hum away in Polish and John says: "Firpo is honored to meet the great NHL stars, Mr. Mulligan and Mr. Laidlaw."

"Tell Firpo we hear good things about him and we welcome him," I say to set off more yabbering after which Firpo nods and shakes our hands again.

Everyone looks at everyone else awkwardly and no one speaks. Finally, the Finn mumbles to the Swede, who speaks in English to John, who talks in Polish to Firpo, who shakes Ilko's hand. Apparently, Ilko remembers Firpo from the world junior championship.

Sitting between Nilsson and Stinquist, I lead off with a beauty: "Did you have a good trip?"

"Yaw, Villie, ve fly on yumbo yet," Nilsson says.

I try not to, but I guess I look puzzled.

"William, when a Scandinavian learns English, some sounds are very difficult for us," Sven says with almost a British accent in his speech. "When Anders says yumbo yet, he means jumbo jet."

I nod. "From your speech, I'd say you spent time in England."

"I studied English in school in Norway, then was an undergraduate at Cambridge. By osmosis, I picked up their inflection."

"You acquired, by something, a splendiferous vocabulary," Hartley says. "So, you're an anthropologist?"

"I'm working on my doctorate and if I stay here, one university has a post-graduate program where I'll do courses," he replies.

"Vat's atro-poop-ogy?" Anders asks. Sammy Sparks guffaws and the Swede's face goes red.

"It's the study of man, his origins and how we got where we are," Sven says. "My thesis is on the development of man's dietary habits."

"There, coach," I say to Jackson. "You can find out why players are the way they are."

"I'll be happy if he can get the puck out of your zone," snarls Jackson, who looks as if he wants to be elsewhere.

Firpo talks to John again: "Firpo wants a drink to make a toast."

No one can decide what to order. I have an urge for a Chivas and rocks but I don't want a scowl from Jackson.

"Scotch on the rocks, a double," Stinquist says and everyone orders booze, except Firpo who has a Coke.

"Firpo ain't against booze but Coke ain't available in Poland," John assures us. "When I visit the old country, all they want is blue jeans and Coke."

When the drinks arrive, Firpo stands and makes a long speech in Polish, shakes hands again, looks very smug, and chug-a-lugs a Coke. "Firpo is very happy to be here and make wonderful new friends," John translates. "He looks forward to learning from distinguished coaches and being on a team with such great players."

Another round primes Clive-Five's pump. "On behalf of the Big Green, I want to welcome everyone to Cleveland," he says. "The team will have an international flavor this season, and we will do everything possible to make the newcomers welcome to this country."

There's a delay in the reaction to his words while John translates it to Firpo and Anders to Ilko. A minute after Clive-Five sits down, there's nodding and smiles around the table.

Hartley leans over: "We need someone to translate into dumb asshole, then Sammy Sparks would know what's being said."

Everyone is inspired to speak as if he were the official representative of his country at a summit meeting on a treaty to ban the slap shot.

Nilsson keeps it short: "Speaking for Sveden, I vant to say, yaw, I'm very happy to be here and I hope I stay," he says to set off some cheers and more Firpo handshakes.

I appoint Hartley to represent Canada but he defers to

Jackson on seniority as a Canadian. Andy has zapped several rye and gingerale's (ugh!) and even shapes his face into what might be called a smile. He says his piece sitting down.

"We're happy you guys are here and you'll have every chance to make our club—now, if you're ready, or in the future, if you develop. Undoubtedly, you've heard I'm a mean bastard. It's true. I guarantee it. We'll work like a bitch at this thing but remember: I don't give a goddam where you're from if you work your ass off..."

Clive-Five cuts him off with applause. "Well said, coach!" Anderson says.

Sven speaks in his precise English: "I have no idea if I can play hockey well enough to be here. In my country, the game is not of such a high caliber as all you men have played. Therefore, it is an honor for a Norwegian to attend the training camp of an NHL team. I will discover quickly if I have enough ability, but it is worth the trip to meet such warm people. Thank you."

Only Finland is to be heard from and Ilko says something to Nilsson. "I only speak small Finnish and Ilko only little Svedish," Anders says. "He say tell you he very happy to be here and vill do best to play good."

More cheers and another toast! Ilko finally smiles, pulls on his Tuborg and nods to everyone.

"What about our illustrious Canadian superstars?" Jackson snarls.

"Absolutely!" Hartley says. "William?"

"You fellows from Europe should realize I'm as apprehensive as you because there's no way to know what will happen in the next nine months. We don't know if the baby we've conceived will be stillborn or healthy. It will be an adventure for us and it's great to have you guys along. Maybe we can surprise a few people, especially ourselves."

Hartley slowly stands and clears his throat. "When the fuck do we eat?" he says and sits to cheers, toasts and a hug from Firpo.

I hope Sven Stinquist, who sits next to me in the dining room, makes the team. He's an interesting man.

"Give me some advice, William," he says. "In Norway, people say the NHL is very rough and players try to harm each other. Is it true?"

"Well, the NHL has changed in the past few years because the Europeans showed they are better at basic skills. These days, there's more emphasis on skating speed, passing, handling the puck and offense than ever before. Sure, it can be very physical, although not as rough or dirty as Europeans think. Some players try to get along on muscle but there's little space for them now. But you can expect to be tested to see how you react to physical stuff. All new players are, but Europeans receive an extra dose because some have trouble handling it."

"What if opponents take liberties with me? I'm not a fighter and I will not hit people with my stick."

"You'll have to return a certain amount. I'm not very tough but, at times, I'm forced to stick up for myself. Most teams have a policeman whose job is to protect his mates from the tough guys."

"Doesn't coach Jackson prefer players who fight?" Sven says. "He told me that Europeans must prove their toughness to him. Isn't his attitude a bit neanderthal: I think fighting with fists has no place in sport. Why do they allow it in professional hockey?"

"Those who run the league want it because they think the fans in the United States like to see fights. They also talk about the safety-valve factor, that if the players can't fight, they'll use their sticks to get rid of frustrations. They see fighting as less dangerous."

Sven looks appalled. "Have the players not objected to that? They are saying that the players are animals who cannot control their emotions and if they can't punch each other, then they must strike with their sticks."

"We've said exactly that but it gets us nowhere. Their reply is: 'Hockey is a man's game and no one is hurt in fights.'"

"But, Willie, isn't their concept of manliness rather strange?"

I throw up my hands: "We've made all those sane, civilized points to the governors many times but we haven't gained an inch. They don't like change. We have to thank the Soviets for the changes in the game, especially the emphasis on skill."

Sven looks like he's having thoughts of packing his bags and heading home, then finally stops staring at his salad and scans the group of screwballs he might have to spend a year with. "What sort of player was coach Jackson and why did he fail in two other coaching positions?"

"Two different players," I reply. "He was very skilled, a fine scorer and a good skater. But he also was regarded as the toughest, meanest man ever to play in the NHL. Opponents avoided him because he was vicious with his stick. He doesn't like the changes because he feels much of the tough stuff is out of the game. Apparently, one reason he failed in other coaching jobs was that he wanted nineteen players with his approach to the game. We're all a little concerned about him. But all you can do, all I can do, is play the way we play."

"I was hoping you would say that," he says.

Jackson and Sparks are well gunned when they leave. Ol' Andy sure can be a charmer when it comes to farewells.

"I want to see you guys on Monday, ready to kick some ass," he says. "This won't be any fuckin' picnic."

The party, which rates as a smashing success, breaks up. Sven finishes his coffee and leaves. Ilko and Anders, who have consumed a large amount of beer, head for their rooms, supporting each other. Big John, the interpreting teamster, asks if he and Firpo can talk to Hartley and me alone. We adjourn to the lobby.

"What's the problem, John?" I ask.

Big John looks embarrassed as Firpo babbles to him.

"This is very difficult for me," he stammers.

"Tell it like the delegate from Poland does," I say.

"Firpo has heard about the NHL in Poland. He's heard things about the way hockey players in North America live and he wonders if they are true."

"What things? Money?" I ask.

Big John looks at the floor: "No, other things."

"What other things?" Hartley says.

"His coach said the reason NHL players are not strong on the ice is that they spend all their time in bed with women," he blurts out. "Firpo wants to know if those stories are true."

"Tell him we screw our silly little heads off," I say.

"NHL teams have a pre-game gang-splash to promote togetherness," Hartley smiles. "It browns off the gays but it helps us relax."

"Yeah, that's why we lost the final to the Rangers," I say. "We had better pre-game bangs than they did but before the seventh game, the Rangers gave our's a big bonus not to show up."

Firpo and John talk away, all smiles and nudges.

"Firpo wants to be like NHL players and he has a favor to ask his fellow athletes," John says.

"We'll do what we can," Hartley says, having a tough time to keep from breaking up.

"This is very...hard for me," John splutters, while Firpo gives him little punches of encouragement in the back. "He... he...he asks a favor."

"Ol' Firp wants to get laid, right, wants to get his ashes hauled and his oil changed," Hartley says.

"Yes, and I feel very silly to tell fine men what he says," John adds, blushing. "I tell him he is very silly man and it is impossible."

"Maybe not!" Hartley says. "Wait here a minute."

Hartley goes to a telephone, his little red book in hand and, in two minutes, he calls to John and Firpo. They chatter away, Hartley gives them a piece of paper and they bolt out the door of the hotel.

"There! I've done my bit for Polish-American relations."

"What did you do to that poor sucker?"

"You know Al Barnes, the red-headed goon," Hartley says. "Big Red is a lousy defenseman but he's a big-league stick-man. He told me about the great act he'd met, a not too bad lady with a little rough mileage on the chassis, but very fond of athletes. She told Red to tell his hockey buddies to drop in and he gave me her name and address. I called her and explained that the Big Green needed a favor because our prize Polish prospect was going to blow up and bust from congealed and coagulated hormones, and she said to send him over and she'd try to help. I said he spoke no English, but she said she didn't want him for a fireside chat anyway."

September 14

Obviously, the Big Green wants the players to have no medical problems. When we arrive at the Coliseum for pre-camp check-ups today, it seems every MD in Ohio is there. It looks like a M.A.S.H. unit, but without Hot-Lips.

Only through the courtesy of the NHL Players' Association will we be probed, poked and prodded today. Our agreement states no player with one year of NHL experience is obligated to engage in any club activity before Sept. 15, not even a doctor placing his cold hands where you don't want them, unless the doctor is a lady.

Last week, Peter Edmunds asked Hartley and me for a favor, although we have no power to grant it. Ol' Pete is the world's leading asker of favors.

"Everyone for the main camp will be here Sunday," Pete said. "Can we do the medicals then, a day early? I'm not trying to violate the precious agreement but we can get the best doctors that day. If you suggest to the players that it's a good idea, they'd agree."

Hartley and I don't agree on the agreement and its observance. I see some niggling points in it and enforcing them creates unnecessary hassles. He feels it should be followed faithfully. So, of course, we disagree on what to tell Pete.

"What's wrong with medicals a day early, unless you plan to catch something Sunday night?" I said. "Guys will be in town, looking for something to do, and we could get camp rolling on Monday. Why not have the medicals and get the equipment fixed up?"

Hartley finally agreed, as long as we made sure management knew it was a special case and that we couldn't guarantee a full turnout a day early. It would be strictly volunteer.

But the entire roster is there when Hartley and I arrive

today, our first chance to see our illustrious new mates in one big, happy group.

Firpo Zybysadoskowski, wearing a T-shirt that makes his upper body look like a bag of boulders, and Big John spot us and wave us around a corner. Firpo shakes our hands four times each.

"Firpo thanks you for your kindness," John says as Firpo pumps my arm until I think water will squirt out my ear.

"Everything okay?" Hartley says.

"Firpo thinks United States is a very fine place. The lady was most hospitable. She even telephoned a friend for me."

Fifty-five players are attending the Green's main camp, the twenty-three from the expansion draft plus thirty-two others from the entry draft, free agents and rookie-camp survivors. The dressing room is buzzing with noise but when Hartley and I walk in, a hush sweeps the place. It's embarrassing.

Booker Duncan notices my discomfort and quietly says: "You guys are stars. Willie, you've been on Cup-winners and Hartley is as well known as any player in the game. You've been forty-goal scorers, all-stars, players' association wheels, things most guys only dream of doin'. Enjoy it! Because when they find out what a pair of assholes you are, they won't speak to you."

I know maybe six guys on the team. When I walk into the room that will be my second home for seven months, I realize fully the major change in my life. For the past six years, my dressing room contained friends, men I cared about and with whom I had been through a great deal. Opening day of the Canadiens' camp was a family reunion, a catch-up on the summer.

"Okay, everyone on their knees; the biggies are here," Pete McFatridge calls out.

"Eat shit, Cheat!" Hartley says. "Merely salute when we pass."

Other than Hartley and Brooker, the player I know best is Lester Franklin, who was the Rangers' player rep for several years. A few folks think Lester is a few bricks shy of a load but he's pure country, a Canadian good ol' boy who talks slow and deliberate in a hayseed jargon all his own.

"Hey, guys, walk the white line," Lester says. "You're goin' to be damned glad these two jerks are around."

"Any race riots or student demonstrations in Peterson's Siding this summer, Lester?" I say.

"Don't knock my hometown, Willie, or I'll pound the poop out of you. I'm a big wheel in Peterson's Siding and that ain't wormy buckwheat, buddy. I added the service station to my empire this summer."

Lester and his father Wilmer own everything worth owning in the Saskatchewan village.

"So how big is your conglomerate now?"

"We got the general store and we widened that sucker for a hardware department," he drawls. "The pool room in the back has four tables now and there's a lunch counter my mother runs. We have the service station, an implement dealership, which is flatter than piss on a plate 'cause of the economy, and we're dickerin' to take over a Chevy dealership from the next little town and move 'er to Peterson. By the way, we dropped the Sidin' part. It's just Peterson now."

"You should call it 'Franklin,'" I say.

"How's the family, Lester?" Hartley says. Lester's wife Margie is a big-league lady and they have three kids.

"Good, back home 'til I find out what's the shit with this team and where I'll be this season," he says. "Hey, Harts, any '57 Chevies in this burg?"

Lester has his own rating system for ladies, based on what he considers to be the greatest cars in history. In a barn near Peterson, Lester has a dozen cars, all collectors' items, totally refurbished and increasing in value every day. Lester rates the 1957 Chevrolet to be the finest auto ever constructed and to call a lady a '57 Chevy is Lester's highest accolade, a "10" to everyone else.

Lester's "poon-rating" is a difficult assignment to grasp. He uses ten auto names, the first five of which are good in receding order—'57 Chevy, '46 Ford, '48 Merc (Mercury), '56 T-Bird and '62 Pontiac. Then come five wheels Lester figures are bummers, running from lousy to disaster—'65 Mustang, '76 Cordoba, '59 Plymouth, '67 Dodge and Edsel (any year).

Lester will spot a lady and say: "She a '46 Ford." Then you know he's impressed. But if she rates a " '67 Dodge," you know Lester feels she should stay indoors.

"Only '59 Plymouths in this town, Lester, although I did spot a '56 T-Bird the other day," Hartley says. "But I'm the wrong dude to ask. I decided long ago to start all over again as a virgin when I moved to a new town."

A dressing room is an interesting study and the Green's quarters quickly become structured. The seven French-Canadians are in one area and the Europeans create their own little sub-division. Sven Stinquist moves from group to group, chatting away.

The guys with the most NHL experience gravitate towards each other—Hartley, me, Brooker, Harry Li, Lester, Pete The Cheat, Marty McNeil, Biff Byers and Barf Badgly. Of course, Jimmy Miller bunks with the vets.

Jimmy gets Hartley and me, his soulmates, aside for a chat. "You guys should have taken my offer on those chicks. Me, Harry Li and Sal Mancino were there last night and things got out of hand."

"Jimmy, promise me something," I say. "For the next three weeks, don't talk about anything but hockey. If I hear you're doing anything else, I'll have your balls for bookends."

"The party's over, Jimmy," Hartley adds. "You don't have enough attention yet to divide it. This will take all you've got."

"Come on. You guys won't be doing that."

"Jimmy, I won't even call my wife until the season starts," Hartley says.

The pre-season schedule is on the bulletin board.

"Cripes, is this a beauty or what?" Brooker says.

Friday, Sept. 19, Buffalo at Lake Placid, N.Y.; Sunday, Sept. 21, Philadelphia at Portland, Maine; Wednesday, Sept. 24, Montreal at Halifax; Thursday, Sept. 25, Montreal at Moncton; Monday, Sept. 29, Winnipeg at Brandon; Tuesday, Sept. 30, Edmonton at Regina; Thursday, Oct. 2, Calgary at Lethbridge; Monday, Oct. 6, Detroit at Toledo; Wednesday,

Oct. 8, Toronto at Kitchener; Friday, Oct. 10, New York Islanders at Erie, Pa.; Saturday, Oct. 11, New York Rangers at Hershey, Pa.

Not one game in a big league rink or one at home. Edmunds obviously figures an exhibition here won't draw. I can't argue with that. I doubt if the regular season will, either.

"The pre-season travel will be the shits," I say. "We fly someplace, then take a bus somewhere else, a tour of small-town North America. The Mount Everest Climbers play better towns than these. I feel a pulled groin coming on."

September 15

And away we go! The big adventure starts and I'm awake at 5 a.m., itching to get at it. The apartment security guard, bribed by the promise of hockey tickets (tickets work better than cash), drops my morning papers outside the door.

Last night, I dined with some players at their hotel near the Coliseum. Hartley had something to do and a rule for co-existence is that we go our own way. He wasn't back when I sacked out at 11:30.

At 6:45, I'm at the kitchen table in my pajamas with coffee and the papers when I detect a movement in the doorway. She's absolutely gorgeous, with very long dark hair, a Hart Trophy body covered only by one of Hartley's shirts, open almost all the way.

"Hi, I'm Darlene," she says, smiling. "You're Willie? What's his name says you'll have coffee ready since you have no cows to milk and he'd like some."

"I was Willie last time I checked, the cups are in the first cupboard and don't tell me old what's his name is awake?"

"He did speak in some language I could semi-under-stand. Nice pad!"

I feel an emotion I can't quite define at sharing my a.m. solitude with this ravishing creature.

"Do I make you uncomfortable?" she says, reaching for a cup as the shirt flies open.

"I had hoped our first meeting would be a little different. Do you come here often?"

"I like you, Willie. I'm a stew, I flew in from Miami last night and fly out again this morning. I bumped into Hartley in the hotel bar and he invited me up for a nightcap. Kinda turned into a morning-cap. Mind if I join you for a coffee? Old thing can wait."

"Join me for a coffee, but please, button that shirt! The sight of you at close quarters might be too much for me."

Darlene is a live one and we're giggling away when Hartley appears, semi-awake. "Thanks for the coffee. Your head has obviously been spun around by the awesome presence of my roomie."

"Our eyes met across this crowded kitchen," Darlene says, "and you know what can happen — some enchanted morning or something like that!"

"Tell the lady, farmer. No. a.m. chatter."

"What a grump!" she says. "Hartley, why didn't you tell me about Willie? I would have brought my friend Susan along."

"Never would have worked. He's in training for the ordeal that starts in three hours."

"That true, Willie?"

"Yes, ma'am, there's no more devoted athlete in the world than me. Celibacy is a must for anyone who seriously wants to be a Big Green."

"Then Hartley won't be your mate this season," Darlene snickers. "Hey, I have to get organized for the next flight. Let's stay in touch and the next time I'm in town, we'll have a drink. I don't know if Susan will be along but I could certainly find someone who would meet your approval, Willie."

Darlene heads for Hartley's bedroom on the upper level.

"Brother, did you turn your oozy charm on or what?" he says. "If I hadn't showed up, you would have been at it in the kitchen sink."

"Wish I'd thought of that," I say. "You sure supply great entertainment. Nice to know you haven't lost your touch as a Green. She's not bad."

"Definitely a '46 Ford," he says. "I had dinner with that lawyer last night and just drifted into the hotel bar. There was

Darlene in all her splendor. She just couldn't help herself, I guess."

"Of course, you fought it like a tiger."

"What was I to do?" he says. "Should I have turned her down and created a scene?"

Darlene is back in the kitchen very quickly. "Give me a call, Hartley. So long, Willie. Good luck at camp. See you soon."

When Hartley returns, I say: "I think I'll tell Jimmy what a hypocrite his main role model is."

"I try so hard to be a good example to the youth of our nation," he grins. "But I needed a little tune-up from this camp. The pressure is really on me because I have to beat out you, Nilsson and Firpo with all those muscles for a job. But I promise you that's it for a month."

"A month or until a '48 Merc crosses your path, whichever comes first."

September 16

Training camp is in its second day and after a check of my body reveals the parts are all there, I debate if strangulation or slashing to death is the best fate for Jimmy Miller.

In a scrimmage, I center a line with Jimmy and Brooker on the wings. A couple of minutes ago, we venture across the blueline and Jimmy wanders into the middle of the ice, a spot I'm handling quite nicely, I feel.

I leave the puck for him and move left, drive towards the goal and holler for it. Jimmy holds it a second too long, then passes the puck behind me. When I reach back for it, the lights go out. Joel Reid hits me head-on, eight dead at the cross roads, and the collision is a mismatch. Reid is the advanced crazy the Green drafted from Medicine Hat juniors and he's the biggest dude I've ever seen in hockey. He's six-foot-six and he says that a weight program has boosted his pounds to 244.

Reid is a baby-faced lad of nineteen who calls everyone "mister." Nothing so far here hints at his past record of violence, although Andy Jackson wants to see it. He's on Reid's back, hollering: "Kick some ass, you big jerk."

The ass he kicks is mine. My shoulders, chest and torso, too. I've never been hit as hard in my life but, like a great trooper, I skate to the bench before I semi-collapse. If the big turkey had used an elbow or stick, folks would be talking about what a great guy I was while walking slow and wearing black.

Bad enough to be sent to wipeout city by some rookie but when my vision clears, I see Jackson and Sparks across the ice, laughing to beat all hell about it.

"You okay, bubba?" Brooker says.

"Unless you're the first black angel, I think so."

"Geez, did he ever hit you!" Jimmy says and the little shit is laughing, too.

I sit for a minute, discover my body has survived the holocaust and take a few deep breaths.

"Better straighten that kid out," Brooker says.

"Jimmy, we gotta have a little chat," I say quietly. "For one thing, stay the fuck on your wing and don't wander around like it's Sunday afternoon in the park. Unless I'm screwing your wife, don't ever give me a pass like that again for no reason."

"Gee, Willie, the coach told me to play like in junior and that's free-flow hockey with no definition of my position," he replies. "You should have let that pass go; you were vulnerable when you reached for it."

"You dumb little turd! Stay on your wing or your career may end this afternoon," I steam. "Push your free-flow hockey up your ass. This isn't a picnic. You try for every pass."

Jimmy looks as if he's going to bawl. "I'm sorry," he says. "Everything happens so fast."

"Kid, you're trying to do too much," Brooker adds. "It's a simple game and you're makin' it difficult. For the the first few days, go up and down your wing and try the basic things. Hey, you got a big bag of tricks but feed 'em to us slowly."

"Yeah, you got twenty years more in this game so keep it simple today," I say. "Stay wide, let us force the play and you come a little late. We'll loosen a little garbage for you. If you lose it in the attacking zone, get out of there fast, pick up the winger on your side and stick with him."

"It ain't a criminal offense to come back in our end for somethin' other than a faceoff, kid," Brooker says. "You step on a mine in the defensive zone one time?"

"Sure," I tell him. "You can't score goals from there but go back deep and don't start up-ice until we have possession of the puck. Stay deep, we can move it with a short pass; exit too soon and we're in trouble."

Jimmy looks as if we're trying to explain Einstein's theory to him. "I wanna learn but on a lot of that stuff, I don't know what you're talking about."

Brooker gives me an elbow and we both laugh.

"We forgot for a minute there, Jim, that you got twenty years to play this game," I say.

A shadow comes across the bench and Joel Reid looks at me from the ice-side of the boards.

"Mr. Mulligan, I didn't hurt you, did I?"

"Joel, forget it and thanks for keeping it clean," I say. "You hit a ton, pardner!"

After the workout, Jennifer Brown is waiting for me. "Ever get hit that hard before?"

"He's a puddytat," I say. "My mother hit me harder than that when I was a kid."

September 17
Impressions after three days of the Big Green's training camp, the boring, repetitive, two-a-day grind of all camps.

Until now, I knew Hartley Laidlaw better as a civilian than as a hockey player. Over the years, I played maybe thirty games against him and saw firsthand what a splendid athlete he is because we often went head-to-head.

Being his roommate for a week, I now think he's a split personality, Jekyll and Hyde.

At most times, he's loose, funny, a keen observer of life's absurdities. In the dressing room, he keeps things relaxed and on the bench between shifts, the quips and little boosts come thick and fast.

The other Laidlaw is 200 by 85 feet, the ice surface, and Hartley's transformation happens when he's on it.

A metamorphosis in two parts occurs the instant his skates touch ice. His look hardens, he never smiles and he shuts out everything when the puck is in play. It's total concentration. When the whistle blows and he's waiting for play to resume, he'll smart-ass, but when the puck is dropped his face has the cold look of a fanatic.

He hounds the puck the way he pursues a '57 Chevy and he always does something smart with it. In skating drills, most guys don't really push but he digs hard. Then he hits the bench and, instantaneously, the other Laidlaw appears, accompanied by laughter.

I ask him about it when we're loafing around the condo. "Hockey is work for me and that ice is my office. When I'm at the office, I work. It isn't pleasure for me as it is for you. It's just friggin' work."

If Brooker Duncan had just twenty percent more natural ability, he'd be an all-star.

He plays the game technically as well as anyone, staying within his limitations, especially his lack of speed. Brooker doesn't skate; he lumbers. He has "hard" hands and passes bounce off his stick. His shot wouldn't break wet toilet paper.

An awesome fist fighter, Brooker is no goon. He never uses his stick on an opponent, he never picks a fight and when he throws a bodycheck, it's clean.

His reputation earns large amounts of space. Few foes ever give him a cheap-shot with the stick, or even risk a bodycheck against him, because it might turn loose his fists.

"They're afraid I might use my mitts," Brooker says. "But if they use their heads, they'd know I never fight without a reason. I'll fight to keep my job or if some guy is workin' over a mate who's little or can't look after himself or if some sucker gets me dirty with his stick."

Brooker talked to his wife Julianne in Halifax last night and for the first time since he turned pro at least fifteen years ago, she and the seven kids, between five and seventeen, plan to remain there.

"The oldest, Brooker Two, has been in eleven different schools," he says. "He's finally comin' good with his studies in his last year of high school, and he has a chance for a hockey scholarship in the States. It wouldn't be fair for him to make a move. Ain't good for me, though, to be without 'em. Love every one of 'em and my old lady, too."

"Brooker, you'll be able to cut loose without the old ball and chain," I smile.

"You know it ain't that way with me, Willie. Hasn't happened yet since I got hitched."

Brooker will take a look at his situation at the end of camp. If he's sent to the minors, he'll retire, return to Halifax, work fulltime for the Y and be a pro wrestler in the Maritimes and New England.

"I have a two-way contract (big reduction in salary for the minors) and at my age, I gotta look where I'm goin'."

"How old are you, Brooker?" I say.

Brooker flashes his big, white-toothed grin. "Tryin' to catch me, eh bubba?" he says. "I'm the same age as my tool, and a little older than my teeth."

Sven Stinquist is the most popular player in camp. In three days, he calls most players by name and he has questioned many about their backgrounds. Because he speaks fluent French, Sven moves into "Frog Hollow," where the French-Canadian players congregate in the room. I speak fair French and spend time there, too.

Several times a day, Sven has a new observation.

"Hockey is much more important to the French-Canadian player than to the English-Canadian," he said yesterday. "They don't try harder, but to be a player in the NHL is a very strong motivation for the Francophone."

"Most French-Canadian players have some resentment

that they cannot play with the Montreal Canadiens or Quebec Nordiques," Sven offers this morning.

I tell him that that outlook is not unique to the French.

"Brooker Duncan is the first black man I have observed closely," Sven says this afternoon. "It surprises me he accepts jokes about his color and makes them himself, all based on stereotypes. I suspect it's a defense mechanism he's developed, although he is very secure in himself, the way Hartley is."

He scores high on people-watching, but it's too early to rate Sven's ability to play in the NHL. He has the basic tools to do it. A fine skater with a long, easy stride, he handles the puck well, passes it beautifully and, while not noticeably aggressive, he doesn't back away from contact.

The Green candidates aren't exactly the USSR nationals with the jets lit but the pace is quicker than he's seen.

"I must establish my own pace and reach comfort with it in the context of this hockey and execute within the boundaries of my capabilities," Sven says. "I will slowly increase my pace, being comfortable with each plateau before I move to the next one."

I think I understand that.

Andy Jackson is on Sven's case nonstop. That Sven never appears bothered by it visibly frustrates the coach.

"Coach Jackson does not want European players," Sven says. "He is convinced we will not fight and we will be useless in his plan, which is to use muscle, not skill. We are here because of Peter Edmunds, not Jackson, and they will disagree on keeping us."

"Not even Jackson will cut a player who can help because of where he was born," I reply.

"Don't be too certain of that. I might change the subject of my doctoral thesis to Andy Jackson. The evolution of a society in which he is the end product would be a fascinating study."

"Title it 'Bastards Are Made, Not Born,'" I say.

Firpo receives a standing ovation today. He has mastered his first English word, although he tends to over-use it. The word, of course, is the hockey player's general reaction to everything: "fuck."

Big John and Firpo babble in Polish and Firp slips in his English acquisition quite often. In all situations on the ice, he hollers it. Hartley suggests a simple "hey" would suffice, and after that, whenever John and Firpo chat both words are prominent. In the next workout, when Firpo wants someone's attention, he yells: "Hey, fuck!"

Hartley describes Firpo as "a large mass of potential, although in what is yet to be determined."

Firp is a powerful skater with some agility. Under a full head of steam he's an awesome sight, about as subtle as a bulldozer. His game is straight lines with no cute tricks.

When Firpo walks past Jackson, his muscles rippling, on his way to the shower, the coach remarks: "Firpo plays like a bull in a china shop," and Harry Li calls out: "Hey, coach! That a racist remark?"

Henry Lamont is nineteen, five-seven and 146 pounds. Off the ice, he wears thick glasses. On the ice, he wears thick glasses behind a wire mask.

Henry is a goalie out of Tier Two junior in Vernon, B.C. He wrote for a tryout and received a rejection slip but came to rookie camp, anyway, bringing his goalie gear in an old car, a five-day drive. Edmunds figured he could be a target for shooting drills. Henry has no technique but he owns an incredible set of reflexes.

"Only thing the little fart does right is stop the puck," Jackson says.

Henry stops pucks the wrong way in rookie camp and he's doing it in the main camp, too. Today, he beats Hartley twice on breakaways and my roomie is perhaps the best in the NHL in that situation.

Henry is also a sadist with the goal-stick on the legs of loiterers around his crease. Today, Joel Reid, almost a foot taller and a hundred pounds heavier than Henry, is planted in front of the net as a diversion on a power play.

When Reid elbows him in the head, Henry scythes him across the back of the legs. Big Joel straight-arms the little squirt into the net and Henry drops his gloves, whips off his mask and glasses and goes after Reid with his fists.

Hilarious is all it is. Blind as a bat minus his specs, Henry swings first at Brooker, then unloads a windmill attack on Reid, who retreats, not knowing what to do with a berserk midget.

"Bite him on the knee, Henry," Pete McFatridge yells.

"Ten bucks says Henry by a TKO," Brooker shouts.

Brooker and I grab Henry, who struggles to get away. "Lemme go, you shit-heads!"

"Simmer down," I say. "Joel is afraid of you."

"Look at him backin' up," Brooker adds.

Henry is far from finished verbally.

"Reid, you retarded cocksucker!" he yells. "Do that again and I'll cut your fuckin' head off."

I'm drying after a shower, close to the open door of Jackson's office, where the coach is with Edmunds.

"Fine bunch we got," Jackson says. "Two old hotdogs and one young one, chickenshit Europeans, half a dozen homesick frogs, guys who can't play and one good goalie who's a half-crazy, cross-eyed dwarf."

Because baseball is in pennant races, football is opening and basketball teams are at camp, media space is slim for the Green. The two papers each have a beat writer around every day but only one columnist has appeared. He writes about the slow sales of Coliseum luxury boxes.

The beat writers are an interesting contrast: Jennifer Brown, young and eager; and Hap Lonsdale, in his mid-fifties with a boozer's face, slow-moving and lazy. Jennifer digs hard for every snippet of news. Hap talks to the coach daily but has yet to talk to a player.

Because the players are accessible in the rink, Jennifer hasn't tested Jackson's dressing room ban.

She quotes me today and it leads to a confrontation with Jackson. The quotes are innocuous but, obviously, Andy is waiting for any excuse to get on my case.

He also has a joust over helmets with Hartley, one of a half-dozen NHL players to work bareheaded. It's a non-issue because Hartley signs a league waiver like all vets who don't wear headgear. Hartley claims he's very confused because the coach says he wishes all players would play bareheaded "the way we did when I played."

Yesterday, I had lunch with Jennifer and she asked my impressions of camp. I gave her bland answers, mainly that I liked the good conditioning and effort but the team will need plenty of patience from all involved. I said several young players looked good and the Europeans showed quite well.

Today, the trainer says Jackson wants to see me.

"What's this shit?" he says, pointing to a paper.

"What are you talking about?"

"You know, the crap you told this broad. She misquote you?"

"No, it's very accurate," I say. "Jennifer is a serious pro at her job. Why do you call it that?"

"What's this junk about patience?" he snarls. "That for my benefit? Think I don't know this mess needs patience? If you think those chickenshit Europeans look good, you can't tell a hockey player from your jacks. And I had a great old goddam laugh over this bullshit where you think these fat turds are in good condition and working hard. What fuckin' camp you been at?"

There is no point in a defense when Jackson is off on a tirade. Besides, I'm not granted the opportunity.

"I wish you arrogant young punks had been around in the six-team days," Jackson sneers. "When I played (his favorite expression), camps were really tough. We kicked ass for a month. Those chickenshit Europeans wouldn't have gone on the ice at gunpoint."

Suddenly, his face goes from a grimace to a smile. "Just wanted to have a chat. Watch what you say to the press, and don't tell that broad anything unless you're screwing her."

As I turn and open the door, he says: "How's things with you? Got any questions?"

"Just one. You must have known the team would be like this. Why did you take the job?"

September 18

The Big Green players act as if tomorrow's game against the Buffalo Sabres at Lake Placid is just another exhibition. But it's much more than that. It's the first game for a new team in those spiffy green and white sweaters, an historic occasion.

We'll make a four-game, seven-day trip to Lake Placid, Portland, Halifax and Moncton and the players, always pessimists, believe the jaunt will be a killer by bus.

But—surprise—Edmunds says it's charter plane all the way. He says he couldn't ask a jet-set guy like Hartley to ride a bus.

Another surprise is that Pete has become downright talkative. "How many guys making the trip?" I ask.

"Around thirty," he replies. "Hell, you two could list our line-up for the opener of the season. Camp is going on the road, at least the guys with a remote chance to be on the NHL roster. The others stay here to work as Fort Worth.

"We're watching the other camps in case they cut loose any bodies we could use to give us some depth. We've tried to buy players because the Andersons will spend to help the team, but any player close to the big league level carries a gigantic price and a fat contract.

"We've had offers for future draft choices. Some packages for our first pick this year were tempting. They would have given us more competent players, but we never considered it because successful expansion clubs are built on draft choices."

"You try to sign any free agents?" I ask.

"How many free agents changed teams this summer?" Edmund says. "Two, both low-ranked players. Despite what the Rangers did, no one else will because we must hold costs down. Besides, the top player doesn't want an expansion team. I talked to three good ones just as a test and they weren't interested at any price."

"Peter, you sound down and we haven't even lost yet," Hartley says. "The kids look okay and getting the Europeans was a wise move."

"Think so? Between us, I'm a little discouraged by what I've seen."

"Hey, Pete! Buck up!" I say. "We'll be okay."

The change in Edmunds since our summer conversations is astonishing, making Hartley and me suspicious.

"I have a hunch," I say. "The Cheat says in Atlanta, Jackson fought the owner and GM all the time and tried to convince the players that tightwad owners and stupid management were the enemy as much as other teams. In Vancouver, he battled the front office, too. Maybe Andy is cutting off the front office here and Pete needs friends. Being Firpo's buddy won't do him much good."

"Interesting theory but it could also be the fact that we're such nice guys," Hartley says. "One question, though: Is Jackson ever going to coach this team? He hasn't told these kids anything!"

"Wrong! He told Joel Reid to boot some ass."

"There've been no hints at the style he wants us to play. It's just line rushes, shots on goal and scrimmage every session. He reacts only when someone is knocked on his ass."

"Maybe he's trying to see what he has before he does anything with it."

Even as I say it, I don't believe it.

Hannigan, the old trainer, says the coach wants to see me. Jackson, in his underwear, is behind the desk with Sammy Sparks.

"Willie, sit down," the coach says. "Have you ever played right wing?"

"A little. Some on left, not much on right."

"You're on right wing tomorrow," he says. "It's not permanent; you're too damned good a center, but a good show would boost everything. The Andersons and a batch of their friends are coming in their private plane.

"The Sabres should use quite a few kids and guys from the minors so I want our best line-up in that game. You with Laidlaw and Jimmy Miller gives us a line that could do something. Miller's a cocky little turd and working with his heroes might help him. Waddaya say?"

Back in the room, I extend my hand to Hartley. "Meet your new right winger."

"I might make this team after all," he says.

"One problem: I've never played a shift on right wing."

"Here's the line-up for tomorrow against Buffalo," Jackson says before the workout. "The goalies are Henry and Red-Light. Defense pairs are Lester and the Norwegian, Reid and Pierre Lambert, Marty McNeil and Miro Kardek. The lines: Laidlaw, Miller and Mulligan; the Swede with the Finn and the Chink; the Polak between Midnight and Biff Byers; Mancino with The Cheat and Frenchy Lacombe."

Center is one thing; the wing is something else. At center, I freelance everywhere. The wing is defined by the boards and the good ones go up and down on a track.

"You'll find out now it ain't all fancy figure skatin'," Brooker says. "Wanna borrow my hard nose?"

At least Jimmy is excited: "Hey, terrific! I can't believe it! Playing on a line with you guys."

"Yeah, well, Jim, you better get the rag out of your ass," Hartley says.

"Why, Hartley? Haven't I been doing good?"

"Sometimes you play as if you had a job locked up and you loaf when you don't have the puck. You have to haul ass every minute and you don't do that."

Jimmy's emotions go up and down like a yo-yo again, and he walks off slowly.

"Aren't you a little rough on him?" I say.

"The kid has good raw talent but he's so immature. No one's telling or teaching him a thing. He gets by on instinct; he doesn't think the game at all and he's lazy. Now Anders Nilsson thinks the game well, has fine skill and hustles. The Finn knows how to play and he works like a bitch. But so far, it's come too easy for Jimmy. Jackson will crap on us if we tell him anything but if somebody doesn't, he'll waste it all."

The new line has little success in the morning, some in the afternoon. The center and left winger are fine; the right winger is pukey, hesitant, slow to forecheck and often offside.

"You're trying to de-program a set of conditioned reflexes," Hartley says.

"Ah, *that*'s what I'm trying to do," I say. "Thanks. I didn't know."

Sven invites Hartley and me to dinner at a Scandinavian restaurant where, he claims, the food is almost as good "as in my ma's kitchen back in Vestervested in Norway." There's no rush until traffic dwindles so Hartley and I loiter in our underwear.

Lester Franklin joins us. "Notice sumpin' different about that Norwegian dude?"

"He speaks English better than I do," I say.

"Really? I can't understand half his words. But that ain't what I mean. Ever see him naked?"

"Watching Norwegian defensemen with their clothes off isn't one of my hobbies," I reply.

"Ol' Sven don't strip in the room," Lester whispers. "Always wraps a towel around hisself before he takes off his jock. Shower's empty before he goes in and he wears a towel on the way."

"So what?" Hartley says.

"I looked and found out why."

"Lester, I know you're a bit screwy but a peeping Tom?" I laugh.

"He's had a Norwegian sex change operation?" Hartley offers.

"Nope. He's just the heaviest hung dude in history," he says. "Couldn't believe it! Guys, his weapon is enormous. Looks like a baby's arm with an apple in its fist. Mustn't want guys needlin' him 'bout it so he ain't showin' it."

"What do you expect him to do, Lester?" Hartley says.

"Walk up to people and say: 'Isn't this a whopper?' Sven's a good guy, so I wouldn't say anything. Maybe he's self-conscious about it."

"Don't worry," Lester says. "But if it was mine, I'd be walkin' down the street backwards with my fly open, trollin' for '48 Mercs."

Hartley and I flip to see who checks it out and I win. When Sven goes to the shower in his towel, Hartley wanders in. When he comes back, I say: "Well?"

"You didn't expect me to see it all in one look, did you?"

"You want a transplant?"

"With my body, it would be like mounting an anti-aircraft gun on a skateboard."

Sven, Hartley and I lounge around the condo with a short Chivas before dinner. Sven seems to have put on his brooding face for the night.

"I am surprised to play tomorrow," he says. "I have not played well enough to be included."

"If that were the criteria," I say, "Five guys would play."

"Who do you think has performed well?"

"The best player in camp is Ilko Mikkolainen," Hartley says. "Then there's Brooker, Anders, Pierre Lambert, although he knows nothing about defense, and Willie."

"Bullshit, I've been horseshit," I say.

"Your language is picturesque and your humility touching, William," Hartley says. "Sven, Willie maintains a very high level, game in, game out. He plays few bad games. But he's never certain he has a job. It's the farmer in him. You know? Plant the crops in the spring, then worry until they grow."

"How do you rate yourself, Hartley?" Sven asks.

"I hate camp and exhibitions. I work hard but only to get into shape. I'm a slow starter every season and I don't have my head into it at all this year."

I figure it's time to nail down the European impressions.

"I am disappointed in many things, perhaps because I expected too much," he replies. "I am surprised at the low skill-level of many players in the basics. I am disappointed it is not an educational experience for the young and new players.

I can't believe no attention is paid to physical conditioning, that there is no land training, no organized weight program.

"The coaches do very little. Coach Jackson only calls the players names about their lack of aggressiveness and coach Sparks seems to have no role at all."

"No skill is why most players are here," Hartley says. "If a good player must do five or six things efficiently, the majority of players here do only two of them. Or they fall into other categories—lazy, drinkers, trouble-causers, drug users, skirt-chasers."

"Why would the team hire a man with as little insight as Jackson?" Sven says, more to heaven than to us.

"At least Peter Edmunds is better than we expected," I say. "But he's from the old school of hockey, too. If he hired an innovative young coach, he'd feel threatened by him. Jackson played minor pro hockey here in the 1950s and maybe Edmunds thought his name would give the team some prestige."

The phone rings and I answer it.

"Willie?" the female voice says.

"In all my splendor."

"It's Darlene. I'm at the airport and my friend Susan is with me. Would you guys like to have a drink, dinner or something?"

"That 'or something' grabs me but we're having dinner with one of the guys. Just a minute. I'll talk to Hartley."

"Willie, don't go. There's a third girl in our crew, so bring your friend along."

"I'll conduct a little poll. You chaps interested in some female companionship? It's Darlene, at the airport with two pals."

Hartley nods; Sven looks puzzled.

"Sure, Darlene, the six of us will have dinner. You like Scandinavian food?"

"Yumpin' Yimminy, yaw!" she says. "We're at the airport hotel. Pick us up in an hour."

"What is this about?" Sven says.

"Our pal Hartley knows many splendid ladies. One,

indeed splendid, is in our town, accompanied by two others, undoubtedly splendid. Perhaps presumptuously, I figured three and three is a good combination."

"Hmm, I suppose that would be nice," Sven says. "But I am very shy with ladies."

"We'll get along fine because I am, too," Hartley shoots back. "It's mad-dog Mulligan we must watch. Can you believe it? The night before a game?"

Susan turns out to be a '46 Ford with parts from a '57 Chevy and, if you can believe it, a farm girl from Iowa. Noreen, the third lady, is, well, a '62 Pontiac but she did take some anthropology minors at UCLA.

Much later, I pass our guest room to get Susan some wine and the door is slightly open. Sven is propped up on the pillows, smoking his pipe, and obviously, research is being conducted into man's dietary habits.

Later, Hartley and I notice a distant gaze in Noreen's eyes, like she had been to the promised land.

Or seen a monster.

September 19

The first game of the wacky, wonderful Cleveland Big Green attracts less than global attention. If folks in Lake Placid, N.Y., had a sense of occasion, more than 1,200 of them would be at the Olympic Arena.

Our Europeans love the ice surface. Ten feet wider than NHL rinks, it's a skater's paradise. "This is more like it," Sven says. "I won't feel like I'm playing in a phone booth."

Jimmy Miller almost misses the plane, a decent feat because we take a bus to the airport and he's on it. When Harry Tatum counts bodies on the plane, no Jimmy! Andy Jackson wants to leave him behind but Hartley and I return to the terminal and find him playing a video game in the bar.

"For crissakes, Jimmy, the coach wants to leave without you," I say.

"Hey, I'm breaking the record on this machine for shooting dinosaurs."

"You'll break the record for fastest fine in a career from a dinosaur," Hartley says.

I take one arm, Hartley the other and we semi-carry him out.

"Coach, he was signing autographs for some fans. He'll have to learn to break away."

"I should nick you $200, Miller," Jackson says. "But because Mulligan is a good liar, I'll let it go."

As always, I'm at the rink early, 3:30 for a game at eight. Brooker, a noted game-day sleeper, is my roomie on this trip. He'll doze to 6:30, walk to the rink and dress quickly.

Harry Tatum checks on personal idiosyncracies so he has a pot of fresh coffee ready for me. We sip and chat.

"Sabres have a batch of rocks. My spy says they got good young ones and some vets are in trouble."

Harry's "spy" is the Buffalo trainer. The trainers know what's going on because information flows on their network. The Buffalo trainer gives Harry an item today, Harry tells the Philly trainer tomorrow in Portland, who tells the Boston trainer Saturday and, by Sunday, the whole league knows. The players are the same on the ice but the trainers have better stuff and don't put each other on the way the skaters do.

Hartley is fabled for bad rumors. TV commercial delays, which players detest, are the time for gossip, mostly junk.

Hartley's specialty is Lester Franklin tales. He says to an opponent who knows Lester: "Hey, Lester's got the crabs bad" or "Margie Franklin tied the can to Lester." By the time it filters back to Lester, he has permanent gonorrhea and Margie has tried to kill him and run away with the kids. Lester quickly launches a counter-attack, telling someone: "Diane caught ol' Hartley screwin' around with a '67 Dodge." I heard that one from a Minnesota North Star when we were paired off during a fight.

Lester figures he'll have an easy year ahead with Hartley as a teammate since he won't have to waste time denying all his bullshit.

Today I find that Harry Tatum and Jackson are knocking heads. The coach thinks Harry allows goldbricking by players on minor injuries. Harry wants to run a land-training program but Jackson blocks it. "Am I training the Montreal Maroons?" Harry says. The Maroons were an NHL team in the 1930s.

The rest of the afternoon I stare at the ice, walk the corridors and check my sticks. Most players shape their sticks with tools and blowtorch, especially the curve in the blade. I'm a traditionalist. I use a straight blade on my gad so I can control the puck and have more use of my backhand.

Around 5:30, the players drift in and my reverie is broken. Four Canadiens played euchre before games but I haven't found the Big Green card players yet.

In my underwear, I do ten minutes of stretch work, then install my equipment, working left to right. It's not superstition, just the way I've always done it.

"Some guys need straightening out," mumbles Hartley, who's very superstitious, when he comes in.

"How are they placing the voodoo on you?"

"The Cheat is bad because he whistles in the room on game-day," he says. "That's the number one no-no. Frenchy Lacombe put his hockey pants on the floor upside down and the Swede's skates are parallel to the bench, not at right angles. If we aren't struck by lightning, it will be a miracle."

As game time gets closer, Henry Lamont bolts to the john and surrenders a day's groceries. "What a relief! I didn't think it was going to happen," Henry says. "Lemme at those sons-of-bitches!"

I'm all emotional the first time I don the Big Green sweater with my world-famous No. 15 on the back. Jimmy creates a hassle over his numeral. He wants No. 8 but it goes to Brooker on seniority. Then he demands 13, which most athletes won't touch, and Jackson turns it down. Jimmy settles on No. 88.

The Big Green's nifty uniforms are a bright, vivid green with a small bit of white trim. There's a "C" on the front that surrounds the Big Green's initials on the background of what appears to be a truck. The NHL tried to block the name and the crest because of the commercial tie-in with Big Green

Transport, but Gee-One Anderson refused to budge.

When we appear on the ice for warm-up, the Andersons and their friends applaud and cheer.

"A snootful of booze does wonders for folks' enthusiasm," Brooker notes.

The Sabres seem to skate faster than we do. A very quick team, their roster is loaded with good players in their early twenties. We try to do a few fancy things, too, just to impress them.

We warm up Red-Light Regan, who plays the second half of the game, and a few guys brown him off by trying to score. Goalies want to handle the puck, not face slap shots.

Then little Henry moves in to the net. I lob an easy wrister on his glove side and I'm turning in the corner when a puck makes a hollow "thunk."

Joel Reid's slapper smacks Henry on the helmet and knocks him flat. Henry jumps to his feet and smashes his stick over the crossbar into a jagged stub three feet long. His mask, helmet and glasses fly over the glass, his blocker to the boards and his catching glove to center.

"Reid, you stupid shit-head!" he hollers. Waving his stick-stub, Henry looks like a duck with a hernia as he pumps his short, padded legs towards Reid at the blueline. Cursing every step, Henry roars at Reid and spears him in the gut with the sharp end of his stick. Reid grimaces and breaks his stick over Henry's shoulder, then takes off towards the Sabres' end of the ice with Henry in hot pursuit.

It's only totally crazy. Joel, who seems to be afraid of little Henry the way an elephant fears a mouse, goes backwards through the Sabres' warm-up with Henry close behind, screaming invective.

Two Sabres try to grab Henry but when he just misses spearing one in the face, they back away. When Joel tries to turn up-ice, he falls into the boards. Henry throws away his lumber and dives on top of him, his little fists pumping at Reid's head.

Several of us skate down the ice—the Sabres are roaring

with laughter — as Joel throws Henry aside and gets to his feet. Henry charges again.

"Fuck off, Henry, before I really get pissed off," Joel yells.

When Henry doesn't, Reid grabs him under the arms and lifts — tosses is a better word — the goalie over the boards and into the seats. Henry lands behind the second row as small boys run for a closer look.

Henry jumps up, climbs over the seats, a difficult task in goal pads, to the penalty box, and skates back to the net. His equipment retrieved, he puts it on and, armed with a new stick, is ready to continue the warm-up.

"Some zoo you guys got," a Sabre says to me.

"Wait until you see us in a game."

"I feel a hamstring comin' on," he says.

"Pukin' doesn't do much for a guy's disposition," Hartley says back in the room. Henry is in the john to chainsmoke two cigarettes while Reid has his stomach taped from the spear.

Brooker just sits on the bench shaking his head. "That's gotta be in the record books. First time anyone slam-dunked a goaltender."

Jackson's opening address won't be engraved on belt buckles. "The Swede's line starts, Norway and Lester on defense. They're fast, so stick the assholes a little."

Much back-slapping and pad-whacking sends us forth for our first game. Henry slaps Reid on the back and says: "Go get 'em, big buddy!"

At the five-second mark, Henry makes a save that he may never equal in his career. A Sabre winger slips in behind Lester, the center gives him a pass and he quickly crosses it to the other winger, wide on Sven and cutting for the net at the top of the circle. Confused by the motion, Henry is past the post on the wrong side when the winger unloads a sure goal, low on his side. But Henry launches a belly-flop across the net and gets the tip of his blocker on it.

"That crazy little fart," says Reid on the bench.

Firpo appears mesmerized with no Big John to interpret and he doesn't move until Brooker points to the ice.

The Green's first score should be a classic, executed with grace, craft and skill. But it's somewhat tacky, just as you would expect.

Brooker and Biff Byers decide it would be fun to go on a little search-and-destroy mission. Biff is a great beer-hall scrapper, not much for violence on the ice but often devastating anywhere with cheap draft and a shit-kicker band wailing away about gloom and my baby up and left me.

The Sabres have five kids on the ice when Brooker and Biff start to ram people. Brooker catches a junior with his head down and simply buries him, then Biff clobbers both the goalie and a defenseman on a swing through the crease.

Now, Firpo sees the fine example of the vets and follows it. A large run at a Sabre misses and he totals the referee.

While this finesse display is on, the puck is ignored, except by Joel Reid. He acquires the rubber at the Sabre line and walks it towards the net. A defenseman moves on him but Joel plunges on, pushing one Sabre, then another and the puck ahead of him. Eventually, the slow-moving pile-up nears the net. Joel, who looks as if he's shoving a car, simply muscles a skater, the goalie and the puck into the net.

The red light goes on and Joel breaks into a dance. The Sabres swarm the referee, who's groggy from his collision with Firpo. They head for a linesman but Joel is there first and whispers: "That don't fuckin' count and you're dead."

Henry skates the length of the ice and hugs Joel. On the bench, I say: "Let's go!" The whole team swarms out to mob Reid. Hell, it isn't every day a team scores the first goal of its history.

The referee has no sense of history, giving us a delay-of-game penalty for leaving the bench. Jackson doesn't, either. He just says: "It'll cost you, Mulligan, for taking these assholes on the ice because of that bullshit goal."

"Will you forget about it if Hartley and I kill the penalty?"

"I'll think about it. Mulligan and Laidlaw to kill it."

We skate hard for two minutes, a long shift in the first game, and the Sabres don't have a shot on goal.

"You're off the hook," Jackson says.

"Gee, thanks coach," I reply.

The Green's first game is a decent effort, although our flaws stand out like a belch in church. We have a little speed in Hartley, me, Anders, Ilko, Firpo and Sal Mancino, but our defense is dead slow, except for Sven and Pierre Lambert.

Jimmy spends much of his time as a spectator. Handling the puck is his strong point, but tonight, he seems to be stickhandling a cement block.

Thanks to Little Henry, our lead stands up through the first period. He flops, dives and scrambles but somehow stops the puck.

The Sabres strike fast early in the second when they pour in three forecheckers. The puck is in our zone much of the time, especially against the Nilsson and Firpo lines, and they score three goals in five minutes. With the lead, the Sabres back off, a common mistake by young teams, and we can move it out and even exert a little pressure.

Halfway in the period, Rollie Regan puts on his mask and gloves and is going on the ice when Jackson roars: "Red-Light, what are you doing?"

"Playing half the game," he says.

"Sit down, Henry goes all the way."

We get one back on a dazzling move by my crafty center. Hartley anticipates a Sabre kid defenseman's pass up the middle and he hops into the gap, intercepts it and slaps a forty-footer over the goalie's shoulder.

I do not want to be a winger. I flounder around because everything is coming at me from different directions than usual. In the third period in our zone, I lose my concentration and react like a center, not a winger. I leave my check, who moves into the hole to give the Sabres a 4-2 lead.

"Mulligan, stay with your man!" Jackson snarls.

The Sabres check us strongly and there isn't an inch of ice on which to move. We're close because of Henry, who doesn't give up or shut up. He hollers nonstop obscenities at us and the Sabres, remarking on my sexual inclinations, the size of my testicles and animals with which I have relations.

In the concluding ten minutes, we're nowhere until the

Europeans go to work. On a faceoff in our zone, I see Sven nod to Nilsson. Anders slides the draw back to Sven and hot-foots it up the middle. Sven doesn't look. He just lofts a pass that hits Anders and the red line coincidentally. Nilsson leaves the Sabre defense behind and finds a low corner.

Our bench comes alive. "Laidlaw's line and go after 'em," Jackson screams.

A dazzler by the ex-Canadien star does it. I get a step down the boards on my checker, who's been crowding me all night. The defenseman lines me up, I fake inside on him, he leans that way and it's all I need to swing outside.

When Hartley hollers, I slide a pass into the slot. The goalie saves on his shot, but Jimmy, drifting in late, snares the rebound, drops it back to his skates, kicks it up to his stick to elude a defender and lifts an easy backhander over the goalie.

"Must have woken him up when I yelled," Hartley smiles.

"Check like shit, you guys," Jackson says. "I'm buying the beer if we tie it."

Ninety seconds to play and Jackson sends out our line, including Jimmy, which is a surprise because he hasn't touched a foreign body all night. Hartley and I skate miles, breaking up plays, and Jimmy contributes a nifty bit of stick-handling to eat up ten seconds.

With twenty seconds to go, my legs feel as if they've gone home. The Sabres mount their last rush, four players in a wave. Two flood down Jimmy's side. But when the puck-carrier swings towards the boards, Jimmy simply picks the puck off his stick with a poke-check and yells "go."

I take off down the boards and halfway between center and the Sabre line, Jimmy places a ninety-foot pass on my stick. The defenseman scrambles to get into position but he doesn't have a chance. The old Mount Everest river skater touches overdrive and starts his cut for the net. The goalie, moving out, gives me space on the far side, where he wants me to shoot. At the faceoff spot, I unload the wrister, high on the short side and place it, if I'm allowed a little vanity about such an important score, right on the old top shelf.

Even Hartley, who seldom gets excited, pounces on me

and the bench empties again. I'm almost blubbering when the announcement is made: "Cleveland goal by No. 15, Willie Mulligan. Assisted by No. 88, Jimmy Miller. Time of goal, 19:58.

Our Stanley Cup triumphs in Montreal didn't produce dressing room bedlam to equal this one. Jackson shakes hands with every player and Peter Edmunds, the Anderson clan and their half-gunned buddies pour in, back-slapping like a pack of kids.

Jennifer Brown seizes the excitement of the moment and enters the dressing room, interviewing everyone on the thrill of it all. Even old Hap Lonsdale talks to a few players, especially Hartley.

"It was milking all those cows, Hap, that gave my winger the wrists for a shot like that."

September 21

Today we move to Portland, Maine, to play the Philadelphia Flyers. An amazing thing has happened: Andy Jackson had a meeting before yesterday's workout and even had a blackboard.

He gave us a basic system of play, a forechecking format and the fundamental breakout plays from our zone. Andy's teaching methods were a little different. He really did growl and he referred to us with such collectives as "you jerks." His system amounted to the basic approach a team needs before it can do anything else. It's the easiest way to play but it needs much discipline to execute properly.

The wingers are important in his system. They do the forechecking and they stay back in our zone on breakouts. One problem: Our wingers aren't noted for their poise.

I'm back at center with Brooker and Jimmy Miller against the Flyers. From our line-up, Jackson anticipates a rough one. The Flyers aren't the pack of yahoos they were in the 1970s when they mugged their way to two Stanley Cups, but they're no barrel of chuckles to play against. They dress several kids, all trying to muscle their way on to the roster, and Jackson counters with his most muscular group. The Europeans, except Sven, sit it out.

Yesterday, Red Barnes, the perennial minor league favorite, was air-lifted in for the game, and has already had an effect on the team without stepping on the ice.

Hartley, Brooker, Harry Tatum and I had dinner and went to a movie last night. Brooker was asleep and I was reading about 12:45 in the morning when Jimmy banged on the door.

"Willie, come on, there's a party in a room Barnes has on another floor," he enthused. "Barnesie found some broads."

Big Red has logged time in every minor league city and retained contacts in most. "Jimmy, you dumb little shit!" I said. "I'm in bed; Brooker is sleeping. Go to bed or Jackson will kick your ass."

"Okay, but you had the chance."

Jimmy supplies the details today. Barnes hauled them to a country-music bar where Jimmy tried to pick up the bartender's wife. Henry Lamont argued with a patron, undoubtedly about USSR foreign policy, and swung a chair, Joel Reid half-killed the poor chap and Biff Byers forced a guy to take a mandatory eight-count because he talked when the band was playing a hurtin' tune.

"We had a great party later," Jimmy says. "The ladies were no hell as lookers (Lester claims there haven't been so many Edsels in one place since the '50s) but they sure were fun. Reid and Lamont are kinky, you know. They had two of 'em in the bathtub at one point. Isn't it great they can get along?"

"Greatest thing in hockey since the invention of the tube-skate," I reply. "A question: Can we work two bar-flies into our line-up?"

But Jimmy can't be stopped. "Red-Light knows some neat games, like man-in-the-crease, goal-mouth pile-up and two-deep forechecking."

I suggest it might be a good idea if he pays as much attention to hockey as he does to important things.

"Aw, Willie, don't you ever think about anything but hockey," he says. "Don't you ever have any fun?"

"You'll have fun back in Sudbury."

"They won't send me back; I'm first draft pick."

"The old coach would farm out his mother. Have fun but use your head. This is your first training camp and, surely, you could give it your full attention."

Having Barnes in the line-up against the Flyers is a wise decision. Although he's a terrible hockey player, Red is an asset to your side in a game that has as much to do with hockey as rape does with a relationship.

The Flyers have a batch of young bozos who look like Joel's cousin, plus a few experienced ones. From the start, it's obvious they plan to welcome Sven to the NHL. They run at him repeatedly and only his agility saves a wipeout. After three shifts, Jackson teams Sven with Barnes.

Nothing unusual happens in the first ten minutes until crazy Henry starts it. A big Flyer rookie runs Sven into the boards and gets a penalty but Henry takes justice into his own hands. He skates out and whacks the guy on the ankles. Another Flyer flattens Henry and that brings Barnes into it.

The kid who gunned Henry has his stick up but Red grabs it with his left hand and punches him on the head with his right. The player who ran Sven walks into a right hand from Barnes and lands on his back.

When things quiet down, the young referee (the NHL tests officials in exhibitions) gives Barnes a major and the same to the two Flyers he's punched.

"That dope in goal and the kid ref got 'em pissd off real good," Brooker says.

"It's going to be a long night," I reply. "They'll gun Sven every chance they get."

"We'll monitor that," Brooker says. "He'll have to handle it sooner or later."

Obviously, our power play has a few bugs. We manage one goal in seven minutes when Hartley tips in Sven's shot, then the Flyers, masters at killing penalties because of all the practice, tie it shorthanded.

A game with the Flyers means your body is aching and racked with pain. They apply the gad in liberal doses to our frames, and through the second period the heat builds up.

Jimmy touches it off by reacting to an innocuous bump by spearing a Flyer. I stand between Jimmy and the guy he's pitch-forked, who has his gloves off. When his first punch misses my head, I grab him and hang on, figuring that will end it. But Big Joel jumps in, blasting with both fists. He's so massive that the Flyer, a fair-sized lad, has no chance.

A Flyer pairs off with me and we move out of the way. Reid is frightening because he's so cold and calculating and he pummels his opponent, obviously enjoying it. Joel lands assorted punches before the linesmen pull him away and he raises his hands like a boxer. He's awarded a game misconduct as third man in.

The Flyers make Jimmy the new object of their affections, although they hand everyone a few shots. Jimmy is hacked, chopped and run at but he skates away from it.

Last season, the NHL's unofficial heavyweight champ was Marv Chambliss, a Flyer defenseman, who was runner-up for top rookie. A talented player, he loves to scrap and is very good at it, although he's accused of picking opponents carefully.

He leads the assault on Jimmy with his stick and body, not fists, and the kid uses it to set up a goal. Jimmy moves on him, then fades off on three rushes and Chambliss takes the bait on the fourth. Jimmy crosses the line, eludes a winger and skates towards Chambliss. Out of range of Chambliss' stick, Jimmy cuts towards the boards, the Flyer lunges at him, Jimmy flips the puck to Brooker in the hole and we're ahead.

Jimmy makes a rookie mistake by watching the pass. Chambliss cross-checks him into the boards and Brooker confronts him: "Do that kid dirt again and you deal with me. Lay off the shit."

The Flyers herd Chambliss to the bench, telling him to take it easy, but on the next shift, Chambliss just misses Brooker's head with an elbow. Brooker skates away.

"All talk, eh, old man?" Chambliss hollers.

"You going to take that crap, Brook?" Jimmy says.

"Jimmy, don't start no shit with that sword," Brooker says. "I ain't goin' to fight your war if you start it yourself."

Chambliss tries Brooker again, a whack across the calves, but my winger skates away once more. Chambliss goes back to working on Jimmy. On a faceoff, the other center and I are heaved out and Jimmy moves in against Chambliss, who jumps the gun, places his stick between Jimmy's legs and flips him. When Jimmy gets up, Chambliss belts him to the ice.

"Okay, son, you want it, you got it," Brooker says and Chambliss grins as he drops his gloves.

It isn't very pretty. Chambliss is four inches taller than Brooker with more reach, but instead of using it to punch long range, he moves in close, right into Brooker's strength.

Brooker throws no punch more than six inches because he has a boxer's experience in close. Chambliss' head snaps back and forth like a high-speed punching bag. To make it worse, he spits in Brooker's face and grabs his hair, which just increases the number of times he is hit.

The officials stay out of it. Chambliss' face is bleeding when Brooker pushes him away and skates to the penalty box.

That ends the nonsense and the remainder of the game is tame. Unfortunately, Red-Light, who plays the second half, blows a long shot and it finishes in a 2-2 tie.

Brooker sits in his underwear for a long time, staring at the floor, saying nothing until there's only Hartley and me left.

"Great fuckin' game, ain't it?" he says. "Jackson had an orgasm because of the fight but never said a thing about the fact I had a goal, an assist and wasn't on for a goal against.

"He hasn't taught one thing to these kids to help 'em play the game and he wants me to give 'em boxing lessons. I almost slugged him. He thinks it's hot shit because I bounce my fists off some young dummie's face a few times. If he hadn't spit on me, I woulda stopped after two punches.

"Maybe I'm too old for this game and what I gotta do to stay in it."

"When word gets around about Chambliss getting it, you won't be bothered any more," I say.

Jimmy walks over and shakes Brooker's hand for a long time. "Thanks, Brooker," Jimmy says. "I learned something tonight. You won't have to save my ass again because I do dumb things."

Brooker places his arm around Jimmy's shoulders. "Kid, you'll be okay, I might even adopt you. One more at our dinner table won't make much difference."

September 26

A day off! When our charter reaches Cleveland at three this morning from Moncton, N.B., Jackson surprises us with: "I don't want to see you jerks until Saturday."

Diane Laidlaw calls early to say she and Clarice will arrive late in the afternoon. Suddenly, my day is brightened.

In the past few days we have played the Canadiens twice, in Halifax and Moncton. Halifax was big nostalgia for me. I spent my first pro season there with the Canadiens' farm team, the Nova Scotia Voyageurs. I renewed old friendships, especially with the family I boarded with that season.

On a free night in Halifax, Hartley, Lester and I went to Brooker's house for dinner. Lester summed it up perfectly: "If they ever made better folks than Brook, Julianne and them seven kids, they've hid 'em away."

I can understand why Brooker will hate a season without them. I've never been in a place with as much love hanging around. Being there it was hard to believe that Midnight was the same guy who gave it to Chambliss.

Julianne told me they've tried to live on half Brooker's salary, no matter how small, and bank the rest for the kids' education. To add a little more to the pot is the main reason Brooker wants to stay. She asked if Brooker would stick and if he'd have to fight a lot. I told her he'd be a regular and while he'd be our cop, who'd be dumb enough to challenge him? She knows he can handle himself but when there's a story of his fights, the kids have a bad time at school about their father being a goon.

"Julianne wouldn't mind if Brooker packed 'er in," Lester said. "That lady is an all-time '57 Chevy. He told her he'd never played with guys like you two and wanted to enjoy it as long as he could."

When the Canadiens danced around their zone in Halifax the Big Green's uniform suddenly felt very shabby. With chewed-up emotions, I stood at our bench and stared at them. Godammit! Those red, white and blue sweaters were almost printed on my skin. Being part of that team meant a great deal to me and I suppose a chunk of me will always be Canadien.

"Bubba, you feelin' like Second-Hand Rose?" Brooker asked.

"I suppose it will always hurt."

"What those suits represent is a little special in this league," he said. "Ain't a guy ever played didn't want to wear one. You were special enough to do it for a long time. Don't ever forget that."

The Canadiens used the game to examine their kids, as usual, a fine crop. They dressed ten veterans, all of whom hollered at me during the warm-up. I chatted briefly with Gaston Beaupre, my buddy and left winger.

"Good batch of kids?"

"They're good but they're not big Willie," he smiled. "Everyone misses you, pal."

It was a good hockey game with a great pace, a big night for the farmer. The Europeans dressed and their speed helped. Hartley once said that every player loves to work against the Canadiens because you had no worry about cheap shots.

To say I didn't want to shove it up the Canadiens' ass is a lie. Not the players, but I wanted to show the front office. And I did.

In the first period, Hartley was stretching for a pass when he was bumped and his groin gave out. He grimaced as if he'd been stabbed. Yank a groin and the pain is terrible. Everyone dreads it in camp because a pulled groin can nag you all season. Hartley's was a moderate pull and he spent the next two days with an ice pack jammed in his crotch.

When Hartley departed, I played every second shift. "Like a man possessed by devils," Sven said—and I had a goal and four assists in a 6-6 tie.

Julianne and the seven Duncan kids were behind our bench and the best thing about the game was that Brooker scored three goals. Only four times in his pro career had he scored even two goals in a game.

After the game, Brooker said: "Bubba, for as long as I live, I'll never forget what you did tonight."

"What are you babbling about, Midnight?"

"Willie, don't bullshit me! You wanted to stick it to 'em but you made it so my kids saw their old man score three against the Canadiens. You coulda had two of 'em yourself but you gave it to me. Thanks!"

We moved to Moncton (back-to-back exhibitions are retarded). The Canadiens don't fool around. Their front-liners all dressed and it was wipeout city. They came at us from all directions plus above and below.

That the final score was only 8-2 is a tribute to Henry Lamont. It was 5-0 in the first twelve minutes and at the end of the first, Lester said: "Now I know what a carrot feels like in a blender."

I expected Jackson to be catatonic but he just said: "I guess they showed us where the bear shit in the buckwheat."

Hartley goes to the rink for a treatment from Harry on his groin, then grabs the ice-pack again.

"It's not as bad as I thought," he says. "When I did it, I figured I had pulled it so far my equipment would fall off."

"How long?"

"A week, ten days, and I'll miss western Canada. I won't play until it's about 120 percent. I did it once before, about the first of November, came back too soon, popped it again and it bugged me all year."

"Hey! I forgot to tell you Diane and Clarice will be here about five."

"Thanks, pal," Hartley says. "I don't see the lady for two weeks and when I do, my crotch is in a cast."

Late at night after a multi-quart dinner, many groin jokes and the Laidlaws' adjournment to the master suite, Oscar is plunking low and Clarice is looking magnificent. It makes a fellow tend to be mellow.

"I miss you, bone-cruncher."

"Wanna retire to Mount E?"

"I have to stick around and see if Jimmy Miller grows up or if Joel Reid eats Henry Lamont. I got a family to raise here."

"Always excuses, farmer," she says. "I suppose you can't carry me up the winding staircase to the bedroom because it would be a bad example to the team's youth."

"You won't tell them, will you?"

October 2

There is little to do on a Thursday night in Lethbridge, Alberta, and boredom, I suppose, inspires the Warp Brothers to go berserk. Harry Li gave Joel Reid and Henry Lamont that nickname on our western tour. The evidence builds on their lunacy, especially as an entry.

Those qualities place them in fine company on this team. If I start to babble incoherently, I won't be surprised.

Reid's father and three brothers were in front of the hotel in Lethbridge when we arrived yesterday. They're all Joel's size and, obviously, his crazies are hereditary. The family has an excavating company in Red Deer, Alta., and as Brooker says: "Bet they dig ditches with bare hands."

Henry started it before we were off the bus: "Wonder who that stupid-lookin' old moose is with those three dumb-ass yahoos?"

"That's Daddy and the boys, you little shit," Joel said, placing Henry in a headlock until he could hardly breathe.

The family reunion was back slaps and punches that would maim normal men. One brother, Elmer, got my autograph: "It's for momma to prove Baby-Joel really is on a team with Willie Mulligan." They call him only Baby-Joel.

Peter Edmunds joins me at breakfast and has chagrin and coffee. Pete is my buddy and I wonder if it's phoney, motivated by Pete being in over his head. Andy Jackson is trouble and he needs a pal.

"What a night!" he sighs.

"A good night in this burg means you're a hell of an operator."

"Not that," he says. "I think I'll tell those crazy Reid's to bury Baby-Joel in a ditch."

"After seeing those wing-dings, I call Baby-Joel 'sir.'. What's up?"

"At 2:30 a.m., the local police called me to get our star draft choice out of jail and the rookie goalie, too," he says. "The old man, the brothers and the two loonies were drunk and in the cells."

I can only laugh. "Let me guess. The cops caught them raping a dump truck, using Henry for a dildo."

"In some goddam beer hall, that little shit-ass Henry needles Baby-Joel and the big loony hauled Henry up above his head," Pete smiles. "Henry was yelling and some guy tried to prevent a murder. The Reid's told him to get lost, but the guy persisted so Joel dropped Henry on him.

"You can guess the rest. The Reid boys clobbered a dozen guys. Henry dropped his glasses and figured Joel was losing a fight. He thought he was chewing the leg off the other guy but his eyes are so bad he almost bit Joel's leg off. He chomped a chunk right out of the calf and it needed a dozen stitches."

I can't help it, I'm laughing hard. "Henry been tested for rabies?"

"There's more," Peter continues. "They were at a table, the only furniture left in one piece, when the cops arrived. It was all settled because the old man will pay the bill for any damage but Henry couldn't keep quiet and said: 'No fuckin' way we're payin' because we didn't start it.' It winds up the cops used their guns to herd them into the paddy-wagon and on the way, Henry and Joel decided it would be a great old joke to take a crap on the wagon floor.

"The cops locked them up but Henry insisted on one call, to me, of course. The police agreed to drop charges if they pay the damages, clean up the wagon and the Reid family, includ-

ing Baby-Joel, leave town. They'll have him in Calgary tomorrow for our flight.

"Willie, those two crazy young bastards will have me in a
mental hospital."

"You can always send them back to junior."

"Jackson wants Reid to give us some muscle and he claims
Henry is our best goalie so far," Edmunds says. "Andy thinks
they're just kids feeling their oats. I think they're psychos. I
knew we wouldn't get much in the drafts but I didn't know
we'd get so little talent and so many nuts."

"Peter, you don't have to answer this question. But why
did you hire Jackson?"

"It wasn't my decision," he says. "I played with Jackson in
Boston for two seasons and we were friends. When I was hired
in Cleveland, he called about the job. My idea was a bright
young coach, but at the NHL meeting in June, Jackson did a
big selling job on the Andersons.

"They don't know shit from paste wax about hockey and
he convinced them the one hope for an expansion team was
discipline, which he could supply, and defensive hockey. They
even bought it that he was still a name in Cleveland.

"Gerald is the brains of the family. The old man is pissed
most of the time and Clive V is interested in little except
chasing broads, getting married and getting divorced. Gee-
One was really upset because they agreed that all the hockey
decisions would be mine, but it was too late because Clive V
had already signed Jackson."

"Jackson giving you much trouble?"

"Keep this to yourself, Willie," he says. "Not bad yet but it
is a big argument over everything. The contract they gave
Jackson gives him the final say in selecting players.

"He has a hard-on for the Europeans. I'm proud of the
job we did in landing them because Europe was picked clean.
Sven, Anders and Ilko are good ones and Firpo, too, down the
road but he's in tough because of the language and change in
lifestyle. Jackson thinks they're gutless and useless. I'm going
to the wall with him on it."

"It'd be a sorry scene without them, especially Sven on

defense," I say, figuring flattery will keep him talking. "Hartley and I say it's a major coup on your part."

"I'm glad to hear that," Edmunds says. "The other night, Jackson told me he's talked to the Ranger GM, a buddy of his, who offered five players, all capable NHLers, for either you or Hartley. He knows we can't trade you two for three years because of the deal with the league, but he says that's bullshit and the Rangers can do what they want."

"Not a word or my ass is a ploughed field, but the Andersons have a half-million dollar bond with the NHL that we won't move you for three years."

"Would you have made that deal, Pete?"

"Would you trade yourself or Laidlaw for a capable NHL goalie, two defensemen and two left wingers, a spot where we're really weak?"

I chuckle: "Maybe I would for Laidlaw but not Mulligan."

"My outlook, too, Willie," he says with a smile.

Our western swing isn't too bad. Monday in Brandon, the Winnipeg Jets dressed a large number of kids and we won, 7-6. Ilko scored four and Nilsson had a goal and four assists, to lock up their jobs.

I should have stayed in the hotel because I just couldn't get cranked up and our line was on for four Jet goals, three when Jimmy forgot about his check.

In Regina, at least a million Franklin's were on hand. Small-town folk are the same all over the world. Drop Lester's relatives into Mount Everest and they would be like natives. Lester took Brooker and me to lunch with the family.

"Lester says you a good farmer, Willie," Lester's pa, Wilmer, said. "You good plain folk who knows about a day's work. Shee-it, Willie, you'd fit right in out in Peterson."

"What about me, Pa Franklin? Think I'd fit in out there?" Brooker asked, flashing his grin.

"Long as you ain't one of them Catholics," Wilmer said. "We don't hold them micks too high out here. Kinda lean heavy on Baptists."

Margie Franklin was close to stripping her gears. "You a Baptist, Brooker?"

"Hell-fire and damnation, I sure am."

"Then I don't know how anyone could tell you from a permanent resident of Peterson," Margie said.

The Edmonton Oilers, a premier club, brought their first-string line-up to Regina. Marc-Luc Radisson played his first game in goal and was outstanding, although we lost, 4-2. Firpo scored one and I sent Jimmy in alone for the other.

We hit Lethbridge to play the Calgary Flames tonight. There's a big lethargy around the team at this stage of training camp on a tiring road trip.

When I go to the coffee shop at three for toast and honey before my early walk to the rink, the Warp Brothers are there.

"Thought they ran you out of town," I say to Joel.

"My daddy says no asshole cop is going to chase the Reid's out of any town," he says. "He ain't scum in Red Deer. He got our member of Parliament this morning and reminded him of a little donation to his election campaign by Reid Excavating. He said his boy is trying to get an NHL job and the cops is interfering with that because some drunks butted in on our family reunion. In a half hour, Jackson told me to get down here."

"How's your leg?" I say.

"Okay, but Henry needs contact lenses to fight in beer halls."

Henry squints through his thick glasses: "The old coach told us to eat 'em raw, didn't he, Willie?"

"How could I miss a game here?" Reid says. "Do they hate me in this town! I'd come in here with the Medicine Hat Tigers and they'd scream for my hide. They had a bunch of little sucks on their team who were scared shitless of me. They'll be here tonight, yellin' for my ass."

I say that I'm looking forward to that.

"Joel knocked up a broad here in a Volks after a game with everyone lookin' for him because he beat up six guys and a bunch of fans," Henry says, obviously in awe. "Ain't that somethin', Willie?"

"Ranks right up there with scoring five goals in a Stanley Cup game."

"Some stink about that," Baby-Joel says. "I'm runnin' through the cars or the posse's goin' to skin me alive and this chick opens the car door and tells me to get in. Didn't take five minutes and I skin my knees and bump my head cause there isn't much room.

"About two months later, her pa shows up in the Hat and tells me his baby has a bun in her oven. I call my dad, he gives the guy a few bucks and tells him to leave his boy alone. Well, the guy keeps the pester on me so my brothers call on him. Elmer, the good-lookin' one, gets carried away and sorta takes the front door off the guy's house and puts him under it. The three of 'em sit on it until he agrees not to bother me. Cripes, I had the draft to worry about without some jerk buggin' me."

I admit that could be a distraction to a fine athlete.

The Calgary Flames, a set team, show us how a big league club works. When we get into their zone, the puck is on the way out and their forwards make life miserable for our defense with quick forechecking.

If Jackson doesn't want Sven Stinquist around, he's found a way to get rid of him: Play him until he collapses and is shipped home to Norway in a box. Sven is our one defenseman who can do something with the puck other than turn it over to the Flames.

A team that checks well renders Jimmy invisible and he drops out of the action early, when Brooker and I are coping quite well with the Flames. Brooker muscles a defenseman off the puck in the corner and feeds me a beauty for the first goal. Then we set up a hole in the defensive alignment on a "pick" play—we should both have interference penalities for the blocks we throw—and Sven moves in to make it 2-0.

But the Flames go to work on our defense, especially Baby-Joel, and score four in a row in the first period. Baby-Joel was right: The fans in Lethbridge really give him a ride and when the Flames pour down his side, victimizing him for two goals on one shift, the crowd laughs at him. I figure

Jackson will sit him because Joel looks as if his gaskets are disintegrating, but he plays every shift.

Jackson yanks Henry and inserts Barf Badgly, who reacts by throwing up three times before the second period starts. Reid teams with Sven in the second and it eases the pressure on him a little.

"A little tip, Joel," Brooker says. "Don't hold the puck. Give it to Sven and let him screw up."

In the third, Reid, under some forechecking pressure, tries to cross the puck to Sven and hits a Flame stick in the slot. It's 8-3.

When Joel bangs his stick on the glass, the fans hoot. I'm behind him skating to the bench and a man in the front row leans over the low glass and heaves a soft drink in his face. Baby-Joel drops a glove, grabs the guy by the hair and pulls him over the glass on to the ice.

Baby-Joel's stick is over the guy's head, ready to descend, when I place a diving tackle on him. Brooker helps the man climb back to his seat.

"You fuckin' asshole, Mulligan," Baby-Joel says, almost foaming at the mouth. "That bastard threw a Coke at me."

"Joel, you can't haul people on to the ice and hit them with your stick, even if they take out their gongs and leak on you."

Halfway through the period, the 6,000 fans are hollering in unison: "We want Reid!" On every change, Baby-Joel stands up but Jackson sends out another pair.

Our bench is cut into the seats and several loudmouths gather above us, giving it to Joel. When one big dude leans over and hollers, Henry gives him a swat across the face with his blocker. The man leans down, grabs Henry's sweater and, aided by two buddies, raises our promising rookie goalie towards the spectator area.

In the milling about on the bench, Baby-Joel charges through with his stick in the air, ready to bingo someone, but all of a sudden, he's out cold on the floor because Brooker pops a short right jab on the point of his chin. The fans drop Henry and everything settles down.

Harry Tatum needs smelling salts to bring Joel around and for the rest of the game, he rubs his chin and wags his jaw, checking for damage.

"Who hit me?" he asks me.

"Geez, Joel, there was so much confusion I didn't see anything," I reply.

After the game, Joel stands in front of Brooker and asks: "Brooker, which fan smacked me? He musta had a club. If I can't find the sonuvabitch, my brothers will."

"No fan hit you, you big dumb turd. It was me," Brooker says and the room goes silent.

"What...what...what did you do that for, you stupid old coon?" Joel rants. "Those guys were going to kill Henry."

"You were about to hit a man on his head with a hockey stick and that can have very serious consequences, although you'd never think of anything that deep. As for Mr. Henry Lamont, why save that little crackpot from being eaten alive? I can't speak for anyone else but I've had it up to my ass with you and Henry and your goddam craziness. What do you think this is, a fuckin' circus? Maybe you two have somethin' to offer this team, but I sure ain't seen it yet."

When Joel turns to walk away, Brooker taps him on the shoulder and says softly: "Ever mention my color again, Joel, that punch on the jaw gonna seem like a love-tap."

October 9

Hartley's groin injury still bugs him. It's not painful but not right. Although Jackson hints that he's sand-bagging, I know Hartley wants to play badly, especially last night in Kitchener against the Maple Leafs.

He makes the trip and in the warm-up, he suddenly departs for the dressing room.

"When I extend, my crotch seems filled with worms in the mating process," he says. "It gets my head, too, because I need a couple of games to have an edge when the season starts. Besides, the way you guys are going, I'm a cinch to be in Fort Worth."

"Good chance," I agree. "Anders and Firpo look good."

"That's a fine reassurance in my hour of need," he says.

The Mulligan clan is on hand at Kitchener, along with Clarice and Diane Laidlaw. I catch up on the news. Big Bertha dominated the Waldorf Fall Fair flower show, although she lost the dahlia class to her arch-rival, Maude Andrews. Sludge Symons is in jail for his tenth impaired driving charge. The corn crop is outstanding. Our Jerseys are winning on the fall fair circuit and Little Charlie feels we have the heifer to win the big show, the Royal Winter Fair in Toronto.

Clarice never has seen me play hockey and I'm hoping to do something sensational to impress her. The first thing I do is get into a fight. The Leafs, too, have a batch of young players and a draftee defenseman, Cam Rooney, earns heavy media attention in Toronto for a good camp. The kid has talent but he's a hot dog.

Early in the game, Brooker carries the puck into the Leaf zone, I swing in behind him and he works a "pick" on Rooney. I use the screen to score. Rooney throws a tantrum but the ref waves him away. Jimmy played against Rooney in junior and it doesn't help when he says: "I see you're still a horse's ass, Cam!"

On the next shift, I drop the puck to Brooker and head for the slot. Rooney thinks "pick" and even though I'm fifteen feet from him, he comes across, gives me the stick in the face and I can feel the skin on my cheek rip.

I drill him a dandy square in the face without taking off my glove. Rooney drops his mitts, so do I and we have a splendid dust-up. I'm bleeding like a stuck pig which, as my loving mother later says, "certainly added to the drama of the occasion."

I'm not Sugar Ray Mulligan but I have a sneaky left with some power in it. Rooney lands a right on my cheek and another on my head that shakes my fine tuning, but I pile up points with the left. One beauty will give him a race track around his eye and he'll have a pregnant lip, too.

Rooney grabs my arms and butts me with his head on the cut cheek. His forehead is covered with blood, which I prefer to donate to the Red Cross. That makes me hotter than a pot of Big Bertha's baked beans. I club him another shot to the face before the linesmen jump in. Brooker has a towel from the bench. My green sweater is mostly red and my cheek aches, with a furrow along it that would win the plowing match.

In the room, Dr. Jay Stanley, who's on the trip, goes to work.

"Hmmm!" he says.

"Doctors always say 'hmmm' before they use the big needle."

"What else can we say, Willie? 'My, what nice veins you have?'"

"Will it keep me out of the Miss American pageant?"

"It's a fair cut, deep but clean, but you bled very well. I'll freeze if it you want."

"Stitch away, seamstress. I gotta get back out there."

"No way; you're finished for the night."

"Doc, I have the hockey player's macho image to maintain."

"I've only dealt with baseball players before, and they're not great for 'carry on regardless.'"

"Different game, Doc," I say as the needle bites. "You can play hockey with a busted finger but it's tough to throw a slider with one."

He needs only a few minutes to complete the job.

"How many?"

"Two dozen," he says. "He'd make a good butcher."

"That kid will have a shiner and he won't be very kissable for a few days. Will I have a scar?"

"Some swelling for a few days, then a mark for a couple of weeks," he says. "Your ferocity in that fight surprised me but you don't like it, do you?"

"It's distasteful to poke a man in the face with a bare fist and I wish they'd do away with it. But even more, I wish they'd stop shit like sticks in the face. An inch from an eye is too close."

Rooney receives two majors and a gross misconduct for

the head-butt. I draw a major and when I return, wearing a different sweater, the score is the same and I have a minute to serve.

Hartley, who's sitting with the family, comes over to check on my condition. I hold up one hand to indicate five stitches.

"Bullshit but I'll tell 'em," he says. "Still got that sneaky left, eh?"

Pierre Lambert hits on the power play and after an intermission with ice on my cheek, I make it 3-0 early in the second, finishing off a good play by Jimmy.

By placing heat on our defense (Sven isn't dressed), the Leafs tie the score after forty minutes. I get my third goal in the third to send us ahead again when Brooker's shot bounces in off my backside. That's our last sniff and the Leafs score three to win, 6-4.

Jackson, who never asks how I am, plays the hell out of me. Late in the game, I'm simply out of gas and my face is aching and uncomfortable.

Doc Stanley removes the bandage, says "hmmm" three times and gives me some pills in case I can't sleep. He cleans the wound, replaces the bandage and I hustle to meet my family. Clarice lays a major hug on me, tears in her eyes.

"Oh, Willie, I was so worried because it was close to your eye. I don't know if I can watch you play again. It's so violent."

"Oh, that was tame," I say. "I only hit him because he gave me a stick in the face for no reason."

"How bad is it?"

"Just a little cut."

"Don't use your macho on me. I've seen a cut before."

"If you must know, its twenty-four neat little stitches," I say and she gasps.

"I never suspected my youngest had such potential for violence," Big Bertha says. "At least that silly boy will think the next time he has an urge to cut someone's face."

"You like our team?" I say. "Pretty uniforms, eh?"

"The one you used to wear was nicer," Diane says. "But it hasn't hurt the way you play, chum. You were never off the ice."

"I recall we had another center of promise one time but I can't remember what happened to him," I smile.

Hartley is talking with some Leafs. "Willie, he's never been this frustrated," Diane says. "Since the injury, he's really down. He thinks it's all hopeless and if it weren't for you, he'd quit. Is it that bad?"

I shrug; "Can't be too optimistic but it's not all black, either. Hartley will be okay when he starts to play again."

Brooker and Lester drift over. "Still the only true '57 Chevy, eh, old Di?" Lester says.

I introduce them to Big Bertha and Clarice and my mother surprises Brooker with a kiss on the cheek. "I hear good things about you and your family, Brooker," she says. "And how's the Howard Hughes of Saskatchewan?"

Lester is shocked. He also inspects Clarice. "Will, where you find this '57? Didn't think no more of 'em was available?"

"Got 'er cheap, Lester," I say. "A lot of the equipment's not original."

"If I knew what you were babbling about, I'd know if I should be insulted," Clarice says.

Diane sets her straight: "It's the kiddies' secret code to exclude adults from their conversations."

My mates file past on the way to the bus and Clarice, wearing a pale green jump-suit, is well ogled. The Leafs head out, too, and a few nod. Cam Rooney, whose face looks as if it were battered by a two-by-four, drops his head when he spots me.

Big Bertha gives me a rib-cracker and Clarice is misty-eyed when it's time to go. "Watch out for high sticks or you won't be just another pretty face much longer."

"See you next week for the exciting home opener," I say.

After the bus ride to Toronto, Hartley and I take the two back seats on the plane, with Brooker and Lester in front of us. My entire face throbs and when the stew brings me ice and glasses, I pour us each a healthy nip of Scotch. Two nips later, the pain eases.

Hartley, who can sleep standing up in a canoe, dozes off. I

lean back and close my eyes, the glass in my hand. It's removed and I look to see Andy Jackson sniffing it.

"What the fuck is this?" he snarls.

"A glass with some ice and good Scotch in it."

"Mulligan, I thought you were a half-assed pro," he says. "Drinking on a goddam plane! Have you no brains? What the hell kind of an example is this?"

"For god's sake, Andy. My face is cut in half, it hurts like hell, I don't like pills and booze cuts the pain."

"I don't care if your balls were shot off," he replies. "No drinking on planes or buses for my team. We got enough ding-dongs when they're sober, let alone drunk."

"Coach, could I offer a suggestion?" I say. "Isn't it preferable to have beer for the guys who want it than to have them drinking straight sauce out of a coat sleeve? If the players want to drink, they'll drink unless you get twenty sets of handcuffs."

"Think so, asshole? Just fuckin' watch! When I set my rules, we'll see if I can stop it or not. Drink on a plane again and it'll be a thousand bucks."

"Yes, sir!" I say smartly.

"Mulligan, don't use that attitude with me," he says. "Who the fuck do you think you are?"

"I'm a man of twenty-seven, a rational, mature human who will go to hell in a wheelbarrow for anyone who treats me that way," I say softly. "I like a drink after a game, the same as most players I know. My face doesn't hurt now because of the medicinal properties of Scotch."

"My, aren't you brave?" he sneers. "A dinky little nick! When I played, we wouldn't have had it stitched."

"Yeah, and when you played, a broken leg didn't even slow you down, I suppose," Hartley says.

"If there's any shit to stir, you two sure grab paddles," Jackson says. "Well, hot shot, a little pulled muscle wouldn't have kept me out for two weeks."

"Oh shit, Andy, it's no use talking to you about anything," Hartley says. "Keep it down so I can get some sleep."

"I'm sure lucky to have two genius college boys to tell me how to do things," he says.

"Someone needs to tell you something," Hartley mumbles.

Jackson heads up the aisle to his seat.

"Oh, coach," I say.

"What now?"

"Can I have my glass? I wouldn't want you to get caught with booze on a Big Green flight."

In the morning, I have trouble opening my eye. My cheek looks like a bulldozer track but the ache is almost gone.

"The Big Green's first annual cutdown day," Hartley says. "They're naming the roster of nineteen skaters and two goalies to open the season."

I figured maybe I boozed myself to Fort Worth.

The roster is posted when we arrive for practice at noon with few surprises except that Henry and Marc-Luc Radisson are the goalies and the four Europeans are on it.

GOAL: Henry Lamont, Marc-Luc Radisson

DEFENSE: Sven Stinquist, Joel Reid, Pierre Lambert, Lester Franklin, Walter Simpson, Miro Kardek, Marty McNeil.

CENTER: Hartley Laidlaw, Willie Mulligan, Anders Nilsson, Firpo Zybysadoskowski.

LEFT WING: Harry Li, Jimmy Miller, Biff Byers, Sal Mancino.

RIGHT WING: Brooker Duncan, Pete McFatridge, Ilko Mikkolainen, Serge Lapierre.

"It kinda makes a fella think Stanley Cup," Brooker says.

"Or suicide," Hartley adds.

October 12

A hockey-free day and I wish I were: (a) at the farm to pick beech nuts; (b) alone with Clarice; (c) figuring how to spend another Stanley Cup bonus as a Canadien.

Instead, I try and make sense of the Big Green now that the exhibition games are over and the real thing is about to begin.

Against the New York teams, we lost—4-3, to the Islanders in Erie (a good effort), and 6-3, to the Rangers in Hershey. I had three points against the Isles and two assists against the Rangers to finish the eleven games (only Brooker and I played them all) with 11 goals and 14 assists.

Hartley took a full shift against the Rangers, working with Hi Li and Pete The Cheat, which is like Robert Redford dating Phyllis Diller. They're fringe NHLers and even though Hartley was rusty, he had to reduce his speed or he'd be a half-zone ahead of his wingers.

I've been with Brooker and Jimmy and, on quick breaks, I've left Brooker behind. But he's smart in the attacking zone, an excellent cornerman. Often, he gains possession or makes the defender do something dumb to avoid being rammed.

In one game, Brooker headed into the attacking zone with the puck and I caught him. When he gave it to me, the defenseman on his side moved and Brooker headed for the hole. I gave him the puck but the guy cut him off. Back at the bench he said, "Bubba, you horse's ass. Nice that you think of me as a fast, young guy. But in situations like that it's a waste for me to get it. You're a thoroughbred; I'm a beer-wagon horse. Let's work it so I don't get in your way."

Jimmy has seemed in a permanent fog. Occasionally, he's flashed his offensive skill, a magical little deke or a great pass. But he's seventeen and, in many ways, going on twelve, a very young boy in a man's league. When a move doesn't work, he sulks.

Jackson tried everyone he could find with Anders and Ilko before settling on Biff Byers, who gets in their way less than anyone. Their skill level is high in the flow-and-motion game but there's a need for some straight lines, too, in the NHL.

Often, Biff has been a spectator to his linemates' carousel. Biff is thirty-three, a pro for twelve years, and the last expansion gave him enough NHL games for five years in the pension plan. The Philly Flyers got him on waivers from Hamilton last season because of injuries and he was in the playoffs for the first time.

Biff says little, except when he's full of beer. He loves country music and plays the banjo. A bachelor, he's invested in a hardware store in his northern Ontario hometown, in partnership with his brother. Biff's wardrobe is two brown suits, a brown sports jacket and two pairs of brown shoes.

Biff can't give or take a pass too well and because Ilko and Anders do things quickly, he can't really participate. The only time he has the puck is when he gets it himself. But he's content to chug up and down the wing and do the checking for the line.

One night he sat in the room just shaking his head and said, "You know, Willie, if I ever figure out what them fuckin' Germans is doin', I'll have 'er beat."

Firpo is still on the team because there isn't anyone else at center. He has good athletic ability but no grasp of the subtleties yet. Firpo lives at Big John's house and has mastered a few words of English.

Last week Big John asked for help because Hartley's introducing Firpo to the finer things in life has turned the poor boy's head.

"Firpo wants a big car and many new suits to be like you two," John said. "He hasn't got his first pay check yet. What can I do with him?"

What do you tell a nineteen year old who's discovered you don't need government permission to get laid?

"Is he happy here?" Hartley asked as Firpo smiled broadly and nodded his head.

"He loves his new country and the people are good to him, especially you two. He sent pictures you autographed to his mother."

"How does he feel his hockey is going?" I asked.

"He thinks he plays badly but he has much to learn. He wishes the coaches would teach him instead of shouting at him. In Poland, hockey was more like a school. He tries to learn by watching you."

"Is he happy with his life?"

"He likes my wife's cooking. He's from a big family and

my children help him not be homesick. Ask him about women."

The best I could do was: "Does he like the women here?"

Firpo outlined a girl's figure with his big paws. It seems his ideal is built like Brooker on top, Jimmy on bottom. As he made the hand motion he talked fast in Polish, though the occasional English word crept in, including "blow-job."

"Firpo says girls here are very beautiful. He thanks you for introducing him to fine lady but he is tired of her because she never talks to him. He has met other girls, one with Jimmy Miller. Tell him so much thought of women is not good."

"You aren't translating everything he says," I smiled.

Big John looked shocked: "I tell you all."

"Two English words, or one with a hyphen, were in the last outburst and you never mentioned them," I added.

John grinned: "Oh that! He says things that should not be repeated to a gentleman. Tell him he should think more of hockey and less of women."

"John, you're a sophisticated guy," Hartley said. "Tell him what he needs to know and credit it to us."

John talked for what seemed like five minutes and Firpo looked increasingly depressed. When the speech was finished, Firp shook our hands.

"Run that past us," I told John.

"I say his good friends think he pays too much attention to the wrong things. He doesn't have the strength he did at first and women can destroy great athletes. He can be a good player but he must be more dedicated. He's sorry and will change in the future."

"I wish I'd said that," Hartley piped in.

"You must have, pal," I replied. "Because I never would."

We have late breakfast this morning and Hartley is introspective and distant. "Sort of hopeless," he says after a long silence.

"What? My omelet?"

"Not that, dummie. The stupid team."

"You don't see Laidlaw, Li and McFatridge as the new French Connection?"

"Closer to Larry, Moe and Curly."

"Pick two wingers from our splendid collection?" I say.

"Henry and Baby-Joel," he says. "We'd be the Warp Trio."

Hartley isn't the only one who's down on the team. I have a large batch of Sunday papers because most carry their NHL previews. Even Hap Lonsdale's appears today, a nifty little re-write of a handout from the NHL publicity department. The Big Green is covered in a few paragraphs.

Discount the Green's pre-season. Their fair record was against clubs using few regulars. Facing good teams using first-stringers, the hodge-podge line-up had more holes than a Swiss cheese.

The team has quality players in centers Hartley Laidlaw and Willie Mulligan, hockey's labor malcontents. Mulligan was outstanding in the exhibitions but Laidlaw missed much time with a groin injury. However, hockey's only attorney should have some useful seasons left.

Under the iron hand of coach Andy Jackson, who never gave an inch as a player, every ounce of potential will be brought out of the Big Green players.

I read that one to Hartley, who seldom looks at the sports section.

"Nice to know I have some useful seasons," he says.

The other previews give us a paragraph or two, mentioning only me, Hartley and the Warp Brothers' farce at Lake Placid.

Hartley doesn't have a high regard for hockey writers, sports columnists or broadcasters. He had problems with the Toronto writers, who often called him "the Rosedale kid" or "the center born with a silver spoon in his mouth." When Diane opened her first store, there was ample coverage because she was Mrs. Hartley Laidlaw and the publicity didn't hurt business. Later, one guy wrote that Hartley was "playing hockey like a dress designer" and, to this day, he's refused to talk to anyone from that paper.

"The consensus is that the mighty Rangers have built a dynasty of all-stars and Soviets and along with the Canadiens loom as the top contenders," I say. "The Islanders, Philly and Buffalo all have a chance."

"Four hot contenders in our division," Hartley says. "But what do those guys know? They never voted Biff Byers to the all-star team, did they?"

"By the way, a scribe makes an appearance here this afternoon," I say. "Jennifer Brown wants to talk with an NHL seer before she writes her preview for Tuesday so I invited her and her husband over."

"Jennifer could be the exception to my rule that most sportswriters are a pain in the ass," he says. "She stays within her limits and asks tough questions."

"You've been sneak-reading the papers."

"Just keeping track of my mates, toiling in the west. She did a beauty on Brooker about color, his career and its frustrations, fighting and his family."

"She got Brooker to open up," I say. "He told her it could be on the record, then worried about it. He bought her a jug because it was such an honest story. It's a surprise Jackson hasn't barred her from the room."

"Not a word or I'll poison your best heifer," he says. "She slipped into the room in the euphoria at Lake Placid and the next day, Jackson told her that if she came in again, he'd boot her ass out. I heard it and mentioned it to Gee-One Anderson, who knows about publicity. The next day, Jennifer said Jackson snarled that she could be in the room but if she got raped, it wouldn't be his fault."

"Your humanitarianism is amazing as you travel this troubled world, righting wrongs and spreading joy."

"I just don't like to see people get crapped on when there's no good reason for it," he says.

Hartley's statement about reasons for doing things calls up an incident against the Rangers last night. I wouldn't call it "getting even" but that's what I did with Soviet defenseman Valeri Dinkov, who cross-checked me last spring and made my neck smart when I turned my head. He didn't even have a good reason for doing it; I was just waiting in the slot for a pass.

Dinkov probably is the best player in the NHL now, twenty-three, smart, fast, tough, great with the puck and good defensively. The Rangers own the best pure talent in the league and when Dinkov tries a high-skill, creative move, his mates react to it. On the Big Green, rarely do players read and react to a simple give-go-get.

When I thought about giving it to Dinkov, a cheap-shot crossed my mind. But maybe Clarice massaging my neck to correct the damage Dinkov had wrought lessened my vindictiveness. Or maybe I just don't operate that way.

Against the Rangers, I wanted to spear only Jimmy Miller, who screwed up so often Brooker and I started treating him the way Anders and Ilko use Biff Byers.

The Rangers were up by three and my opportunity came by accident. Dinkov and the other Soviet, Sergei Pukov, used a pet crossover move. Pukov carried the puck and Dinkov swung in behind him. Near the blueline, Pukov left it and cut to the boards; Dinkov took it and swung along the line. When the defenseman followed him, Dinkov passed backwards to Pukov, a move that's automatic. Pukov wheeled for the net and Dinkov did too, with a swing up the slot.

This time, they added a variation. Pukov held it when he cut outside, Dinkov went along the line and Pukov tried a pass to his stick from behind. I was hurrying to shut off Dinkov's move into the slot when Jimmy, with the play for once, deflected the pass a little.

Pukov yelled and Dinkov turned and reached back for it. I stepped into his blind spot, braced on my skates, and popped him! My shoulder hit his chest, my hip hit his middle and the comrade hit the ice, all air gone from his body. Had I tossed an elbow into the package, I'd be wanted for manslaughter.

Dinkov, a noted "diver," wasn't playing dead Russian this time. He was flat on the ice, gasping for air, his body heaving a little. He was groggy and when he tried to stand up, his knees buckled. Pukov and the trainer helped him to the bench.

He came back a few shifts later and on a faceoff, ol' Valeri said: "Hey, Villie!" He made a cross-check motion, then placed his hand on his neck. I nodded and said: "We're even!" He smiled and nodded, too.

The drop-in by Jennifer and her husband Hank is an all afternoon session plus a big feed of Italian food and Chianti. Hank paid his way through college playing guitar in rock and cowboy bands. Thus, he and Hartley become friends forever. Hartley has three guitars in the den and he and Hank disappear, leaving Jennifer and me to talk.

Jen has done her homework extremely well. I offer only a few assessments on teams, spots where they could be strong or weak. When we get to the Big Green, I suggest she give me her view first and we can go from there. Her evaluation of our prospects is extremely accurate, although she'll write it somewhat softer than we discuss it.

I ask about her relationship with Jackson and Edmunds. "Their attitude towards me, I suppose, is bemused tolerance," she says. "They've both warned me about digging too hard and said that I should write more about the games, less about the people, and not to believe what players tell me. Edmunds' enlightenment surprises me. We had trouble all summer but lately, he's very friendly. Beady Bascom, who's not dumb, is my pal and tells me a few things."

"My pattern with him is the same," I say. "Is he having trouble with Jackson?"

"Beady says it's a constant hassle between them. You know Jackson got Clive Eye-Vee and Clive-Five half-gunned and talked them into signing him to a contract. Gerald had a bird and Edmunds almost quit over it. Jackson's contract gives him large clout in the operation and, somehow, he has two Anderson's on his side. Edmunds is trying to get as many others on his side as he can for the inevitable showdown.

"Willie, can you tell me why Jackson seems so hopeless in

the job? Doesn't this team need more teaching than coaching?"

"He's a classic anachronism, a man out of his time," I say. "He's from the six-team NHL days and hasn't changed his outlook. He's from an era when, with rare exceptions, players were at least twenty-three before they got big-league jobs. They learned the game in the minors, mostly by osmosis. NHL coaches did little skill-teaching and fear was a motivator because of competition for jobs on most clubs. Besides, no players' association meant management could crap on players any way they wanted.

"He's the classic NHL mistake—a man with no knowledge of the teaching arts placed in coaching, now basically a teaching profession. Young players are apprentices who must be taught the craft. You can't motivate by fear now in hockey or any other field.

"Andy is all hung up in his own macho, too. He was the self-made small man who terrorized the NHL. He just can't understand that everyone doesn't work the way he did. I don't think Jackson is an evil man. He's twenty years late and he simply can't adjust."

"Can I quote you on all this?"

"Wouldn't be wise," I laugh. "If you do, I'll be in Port Huron and you'll be back on the night desk."

~3~
The
Season

October 15

A new hotel downtown has changed Buffalo from a stop few NHL players like to one they tolerate. I don't mind it because of some excellent eating spots and a good jazz joint.

I'm not wild about Memorial Auditorium. The ice surface has a short neutral zone and most games are played in the end zones. That's why the Sabres always have a quick team and a good home record. But it's a major league arena, the first look at one for the Big Green.

Demands on the Coliseum by rock shows and basketball shift our workouts to a small rink in Richfield, a five-minute ride to a good building with a regulation ice surface but colder than a witch's tit.

"This freezer is like your frog pond in February," Hartley says.

We dress at the Coliseum, carry our skates and ride to the little rink in vans. Yesterday, when we returned to the dressing room, Jackson carried a sweater to the center of the room.

"Peter Edmunds, Sammy Sparks and I decided that the first captain of the Big Green will be Brooker Duncan," he rasped.

Brooker looked shocked; Hartley applauded, I cheered and everyone joined in.

"Brooker, here's your sweater with the 'C' on it," Jackson said. "We all respect you, no one works harder at the game and you'll be a good leader."

Brooker took the sweater from Jackson with tears in his eyes: "Nobody ever did anythin' like this before. We all know how big a job starts tomorrow. Let's be men enough to settle any beefs in this room by talkin' 'em out. If there are any, lemme know and I'll see what I can do."

There were handshakes and back-slaps. Hartley said: "Too bad the 'C' doesn't stand for Cardinal and we'd only have to kiss his ring. I knew when we gave 'em the vote, they'd take all the good jobs."

"What's goin' on here?" Brooker said to us. "The captain should be one of you two, not an old cuss who might not have a job at Christmas. Is it part of the shaft to you?"

"Willie, what is this old goat babbling about? Has power snapped his mind?"

"Brooker, you're the man for the job," I told him. "Who else can get Baby-Joel to go to bed?"

"You're full of crap but I'll lean heavy on you in this. Listen, Walt Enright wants to know about our player rep. Which of you dudes is it?"

I shook my head: "After the strike, we took an oath and broke a bottle of Chivas over a D-cup filled with a '46 Ford to support to the death the association but not to hold any office. Brooker, you're it. Firpo won't do it because there's no poon on the executive."

"Then Lester's the man, if that's okay."

Last night the Anderson clan hosted a team dinner in their suite. All three Andersons were there with their wives and families plus a large contingent of friends. The evening opened with cocktails in a room the size of the Mount Everest Arena.

Hartley was reluctant to attend. "If it's just players, fine," he said. "But I don't like owners introducing me to their friends like a trained bear. I won't go unless there's a unicycle for me to ride."

"Come on. If it's dull, Henry will bite Baby-Joel on the leg again for fifty bucks."

Hartley brightened. "Maybe The Cheat will have his new line of watches on sale. By the way, you owe me $150."

"That's interesting," I offered. "Is there a reason?"

"It's that party at Gee-One's palace Friday. Brooker says he won't go because Julianne isn't here. I called her and said airline tickets were one of my tradeout deals and I have some to use soon. She could surprise Brooker by coming for the party and home opener. She said no but I told her the tickets are at the airline in Halifax and she better use them.

"She can come from Toronto with Diane and Clarice. We'll get Brooker to the pad before the party and Julianne will be a little surprise. Your share is one-five-oh."

A strange man, my roomie.

Peter Edmunds was at the door of the suite as greeter. And there was Clive Eye-Vee, a long booze in one hand and a short wife in the other. Clive-Five was with his fifth bride, Inga, an astounding twenty-five-year-old Swedish airline stew with blonde hair to her waist. Lester said he would give a year's salary to walk into one dance in Peterson with Inga on his arm.

Gerald (Gee-One) was with his wife Pauline, their daughter Geraldine (Gerry), who's eighteen and pretty, and son Gerry (Gee-Two), who's fourteen.

Then add two dozen friends and various wives—the rubber man from Akron, the lawyer who arranged the condo, assorted bankers and other dudes for whom no tag days will be needed.

Some players congregated in corners uncomfortably, several ogling Inga, who was involved in a laugh-filled chat in Swedish with Anders Nilsson. Jimmy Miller befriended Gerry Anderson, who seemed quite impressed.

Sven Stinquist, in professorial tweed, discussed U.S. financial policy with a couple of bankers. Brooker and Gee-Two became instant pals and arm-wrestled. Biff Byers talked to a bartender while kayoing a few dozen beers. And Andy Jackson, with Sammy Sparks at his elbow, stayed close to Clive-Five.

Hartley, in an $800 suit, looked more like a millionaire

than the guys who are and had Mrs. Clive Eye-Vee and several ladies tittering away.

I joined the "misfits" (Firpo, Ilko, Baby-Joel, Henry, Miro Kardek and the French-Canadians) in a corner.

"What's this shit got to do with hockey," Baby-Joel said.

"Yeah, me n' Joel n' Marc-Luc was goin' to a porno movie," Henry moaned. "I never saw one before."

"Hold on!" I said, "Most clubs have a dinner before the first game but never this classy. Enjoy it."

"Okay, but why all the phoney-lookin' rich bastards?" Baby-Joel asked.

"Just a minute. The man talking to Sven is president of a bank. The chap with The Cheat and Hi Li is the chief executive of a rubber company. Little Sal is with an investment broker who handles more money in one day than we'll see in our lives. The man with Anders and Inga Anderson is a lawyer. Hire him and it's $1,500 a day plus expenses and he doesn't eat burgers and fries for lunch."

"Big shit deal!" Baby-Joel shot back. "What's it do for me?"

"What am I goin' to do?" Henry said. "Walk up to a bank president and say: 'Hey, buddy, you gettin' much?'"

"Use what's in your head. You're an average Joe, who would never meet people like these. If you want to deal with Bill Cleaves' investment house, you talk to a kid just out of college. But I guarantee because you're a hockey player, if you say: 'Mr. Cleaves. I'm Henry Lamont of the Big Green; I signed my first pro contract and I need financial advice,' he'll say: 'Henry, give me a call and my secretary will arrange an appointment to come in and see me.'"

"You're shittin' us, Willie," Henry said. "That guy wouldn't give me the time of day."

"Okay, I just made it up."

Joel looked a little defensive. "What did these rich guys do for you?"

"I met the rubber company man last summer and he sent me $8,500 worth of tractor tires, which we're testing for him. Hartley met that lawyer, and he arranged our apartment. Hartley will spend time in his office this winter."

"You're a star, Willie," Henry said. "Them guys won't talk to us rookie shits."

"Instead of sulking because you missed a dumb skin flick, mingle a little."

"What can I say to a banker?" Baby-Joel whined.

"Try sticking out your hand and saying: 'Hello, there, sir; I'm Joel Reid. Do you like hockey?'"

"That little creep Miller sure is talkin'," Henry said. "Look at him suck-holin' around the boss's daughter."

"I'd call that a pretty good move."

Joel nodded in Anders' direction. "The Swede has made a better move with Clive-Five's wife. Ain't no wool like her in Red Deer!"

"Imagine how good it is for Anders to find someone who speaks his language. Well, I'm going to talk to a millionaire, preferably one with a daughter."

"Hey, Willie, point out some rich guy I could talk to," Baby-Joel said.

"See the man in the blue blazer with the gold buttons? His family owns a big construction company; your family is big in Red Deer. Maybe you can talk about back-hoes."

As the night wound down, Joel rushed over to me. "That construction guy asked all about Reid Excavating. I'm going to construction sites with him and to see their shops. He even says I can go in and fiddle around because I love to tinker with machinery."

Edmunds knows I have breakfast early and he regularly interrupts my newspapers. Obviously, he needs a friend in the organization, a shoulder to weep on about Jackson.

"Andy thinks pre-scouting is a waste of time," he says when I ask about preparation for the game. "He says it's useless to know how a team forechecks two days before a game and you find out all you need to know in two shifts."

I shake my head: "By the time you find out, you're down by three big ones. It's good to know line combos and try for the right match-ups."

"Matching lines is another thing he poo-poos," Pete says. "His idea is that a player should handle anyone he faces."

"Does James Miller understand that?"

"We'll look at Miller, Lambert, Henry and the European forwards for ten games, then decide to keep them or send them to the minors or junior."

"What about Baby-Joel?" I ask.

"His junior team doesn't want him because he's too much trouble, especially his village idiot family. We can send him to Fort Worth."

Jackson's pre-game speech is brief.

"Let's start it right," he says. "Use the systems I gave you in camp and get on 'em fast in their zone. Don't jack around! Shoot it in and kick some ass in there."

The opening ceremonies seem to take forever and during the anthems, Henry sneaks into the room and up-chucks.

My line starts. I win the faceoff and Jimmy Miller comes within two seconds of the record for the fastest goal in a career. I take the puck, circle in the neutral zone and pass to Brooker. Jimmy flits into the middle, Brooker places it on his stick and Jimmy is between the defensemen before they can react. Twenty feet out, he snaps it and the puck is on the top shelf over the goalie's glove.

The goal is at the seventeen-second mark. The record is fifteen seconds, set by Gus Bodnar of the Maple Leafs back in 1943.

Jimmy dances for several minutes, it seems, and Brooker retrieves the puck for him. Jackson warns the bench to sit tight.

We have a good ten minutes, forechecking well, which seems to unsettle the Sabres, although we don't score on about four good chances.

When the Sabres move, it's trouble for our defense and penalties don't help. Joel gets one for an elbow smash that makes a Sabre wonky. Hartley and I, Lester and Sven kill it. Hartley says before we start: "Standard box and hold your ground."

Hartley and I pursue in the neutral zone, then drop back and set up the box. The Sabre power play relies on movement and quick passes to lure someone out of the defensive formation. When we stand our ground and the puck zips around the outside, the crowd is impatient and boos when they don't get a shot on goal in two minutes.

"Wish they were all that easy," I say.

"Wait till the next one, pal," says Hartley.

Biff Byers hooks a Sabre and this time, they station a large defenseman in front of our net. When he moves in, Henry hacks him with his stick. The Sabres keep the play on Lester's side and Sven has to push the big guy.

Jackson replaces Lester with Baby-Joel and I tell him: "Don't kill him; move him out or tie him up."

The Sabre giant moves in; Joel knocks him flat. Because Joel is occupied, Hartley, Sven and I play a triangle with me in front dogging the points. With ten seconds to kill, we face off in our zone and although my legs are shaky, I say to Sven: "I'm gone."

The NHL coaches annually vote Hartley as the best faceoff man in the league. He slides this one back to Sven, who heads behind the net while I wheel towards the blueline and hesitate, as if setting up the box, to hold the defenseman, then burst up the middle.

I hit the red line, Sven has the puck there and I'm alone in the Sabre half of the ice. The breakaway revives my legs and I go flat out. Hartley, who's deadly on breakaways, has a theory: "Don't slow down. Most guys get all deliberate. I skate faster and make the move that comes open. If you slow down, the odds go to the goalie."

Discuss a hockey play and it sounds as if you have time to compute the possibilities when, really, it's two or three seconds of instinct and reaction.

The goalie is in the middle, balanced and ready to react. On Jimmy's goal, I noted that when Jimmy pulled his stick back, the goalie lifted his body and his stick came off the ice.

Thirty feet out, I raise my stick and up he goes, stick too! I bring my stick down but slow it and use my wrists to shoot along the ice. The puck goes under his stick and between his skates.

"You sneaky bastard!" the goalie hollers.

We take the 2-0 lead to the room. The smokers (Henry, Byers, Lester, Li, McFatridge and Serge Lapierre) go into the shower area. Hartley takes off his skates to rub his feet and I have my cup of black coffee.

When Jackson doesn't appear because he's on television, Sammy says: "Okay, more of the same."

"More of the same what, Sam?" Hartley says.

"Whaddaya mean?" Sparks stutters.

"Do we go after them flat out or moderately or be conservatively defensive?"

"Shit, do what you did to get ahead," Sammy says.

Hartley hollers: "Okay, guys, more breakaways."

The Sabres pour all three forwards in to forecheck and pinch their defensemen up at the points. Only several miracles by little Henry holds them off.

In ten minutes, we freeze or ice the puck at least two dozen times. Jackson uses Hartley on every draw, leading to a run-in with the referee Bill Mathews. The ref waves Hartley off, claiming the Sabres have the last change. Jackson does a semi-berserk and waves the official over.

"What the fuck are you doing to us?" he raves.

"Andy, when it's set you can't change," Mathews says.

"Bullshit! You can't stop me from getting a faceoff man out there."

When another icing is on the way, Jackson takes off two forwards and Hartley and I go on. Because the Sabres can't win many faceoffs from Hartley, they try to get him heaved out.

It's old stuff for Hartley and he stands like a statue until the puck is dropped. Mostly, the Sabre gets the hook but when a linesman throws Hartley out on two in a row, he isn't happy.

"I didn't move a muscle," he says. "How can you toss me?"

When a linesman is slow dropping it and the Sabre jumps, Hartley says: "Drop the fucking thing. Nobody paid twenty bucks to see you hold the puck."

I'm there to take the faceoff if Hartley is tossed. I'm not Laidlaw but I'm fairly good.

The faceoffs stretch the second period to over an hour and the crowd is restless. The stalling breaks the Sabres' tempo and our lead holds through forty minutes, although we're out-shot, 32-11, in that stretch, 18-4 in the second period.

When we go off, Jackson and the NHL's supervisor of officials, Charlie Webb, are nose-to-nose outside our room.

"A referee in the league eight years should know the fuckin' rules about player changes," Andy rants. "A linesman waves Laidlaw out on four faceoffs and he didn't move a fuckin' eyelid. What shit is that?"

"Andy, it's not the seventh game for the Cup," Webb says. "That period took seventy minutes and the TV people don't like it."

"Who runs this fuckin' league? TV assholes?" Jackson shouts. "Those creeps can crawl up my ass and take your dumb-shit officials with them. I'll take four hours to play the third and the TV people can eat shit. Christ, our first game and your referee is screwin' us. He got some young pussy with an 11:30 curfew?"

"Andy, we go back a long time," says Webb, a fine referee for twenty years. "What's all the steam about?"

"Charlie, get the goddam skates on and referee the way it should be done," Andy wheezes. "If you had the whistle, we'd be havin' a cold one now. Instead, we got an arrogant jerk who don't know the rules."

"He's a good ref," Webb says. "Try to speed it up, I can't handle you and the TV guys on my ass."

"So they postpone the eleven o'clock news," Andy says. "There's nothin' on the news in this dump but fires, anyway."

When Jackson comes into the room, Hartley applauds and everyone joins in. The coach smiles, takes a little bow and says: "Told that piss-pot, eh?"

The Sabres stay away from the stalling tactics in the third and go to a puck-control game with quick passes and neutral zone crossovers.

"Don't chase the motion," Jackson pleads.

The Europeans play that game better than they defend against it. Hartley and I split the first five minutes with a variety of wingers, then Jackson uses Anders, Ilko and Biff.

The puck goes from the Sabre zone up to the center and when Anders moves on him, he drops it back to a defenseman, who loses control. When it skids slowly towards the line, Ilko bursts after it and I hear Jackson say: "No, Finn, no!"

The defenseman beats Ilko, banks it off the boards to the center, who has crossed with the left winger, and when Anders hesitates on which man he should cover, the Sabres go on a three-on-two.

The wingers' cross in front of Lambert rivets him to the spot. Sven just misses deflecting the pass that the center sends the right winger for a tip-in from the crease.

We sag, the crowd comes alive and so do the Sabres, forcing Henry to play miracle worker again, diving, flopping, cursing to stop shots. He must be the only goalie who stops shots by calling the puck a sonuvabitch.

When Anders' line is pinned in our zone, Jackson cuts to six forwards—Hartley's line, and Brooker, Biff and me with Miller on the occasional shift.

The Sabres increase the pace when they see the double-shift. Hartley's line is attacking when Hi Li loses the puck and away they go. Hartley gets back, Li and The Cheat don't make it and we're out-numbered in our zone. Henry makes an incredible split save on the first shot but the rebound sails over him and it's tied.

But not for long. Hartley stays on and he's whipped because of inactivity. He wins the draw at center, can't get to the puck and the Sabres take control. A thirty-foot slapper off a drop pass by a defenseman when the center "picks" McNeil beats Henry, who's screened on the shot.

Hartley, Sven and I play the remainder of the game. My roomie wins two faceoffs in their zone with Henry on the bench. The second one goes to Sven, who rings a shot off the post, right to a Sabre, who sends it 175 feet into the empty net.

Henry and I earn stars but he won't take the bow. On my way in, Jackson is surrounded by reporters in the anteroom and I listen briefly.

"If we play that well, we'll beat many teams," he says. "Some players had extra ice but who doesn't use his good ones in key situations? Henry? A little unorthodox but he's nineteen and will learn technique. The ref? I asked if he had a good summer."

I step back to go into the room and Jackson spots me: "Willie, come here! These folks would like to talk to you. I'm damned proud to coach this man."

Andy slaps me on the back like we're old buddies and disappears. I'm stuck with the press and several microphones stuck in my face. The radio guys, whose business is talking, extend their mikes and say nothing. The questions invariably come from the newspaper guys at the back.

There is silence for several seconds and I say: "So much for probing questions." They laugh and away it goes.

The opener is one I know will lead off most interviews this season. "Isn't it a big come-down for a player of your status to go to this bush-league outfit?" says Duke Gage, a Buffalo columnist. Duke is hard-hitting and controversial. Or he thinks he is, anyway.

"The term bush-league can't refer to the Big Green," I say. "It's a first-class operation in every way. No players ever were treated better."

The guy persists: "Yeah, but isn't it a long slide to an expansion team?"

"I'm not as big in the discos on Crescent Street in Montreal," I say. "I'm a farmer and I like green. It's a big slide to Yankee dollars. Let's see, a half-million a season at an exchange of twenty-point-five, that works out to...the numbers are too big for me. But we can get an indoor whizzer on the farm."

They're all writing furiously.

"I'm kidding; it's only $450,000," I smile.

Duke hangs tough: "Is this the most hopeless NHL team ever?"

"What new team was loaded with all-stars?" I say with a little bristle. "We'll be competitive. No team with Hartley Laidlaw on it will be a pushover. We have some NHL and pro experience and some really fine young prospects."

Duke keeps it up: "Your first draft, Mr. Miller, spent most of the night on the bench."

"Duke, he's seventeen. When you were seventeen, was your column running every day?"

The group laughs but Gage rolls on: "If you had known the end result, would you have led the strike?"

"The end result I know is the NHL players have by far the best agreement in pro sport in pension plan, benefit package, the whole thing."

"Is it true there's resentment on the team because a black was named captain?" he says.

"In a career of being dead wrong, you've never been deader or wronger. I've never met a man I respect more than Brooker Duncan and every guy in that room feels the same."

Harry Tatum hollers: "Willie! Roll the wagon!"

"Thanks for your time," I say. "I have to run or the lower berths on our delux bus will be gone."

I whip off my equipment, head for the shower and encounter a rather weird sight. Henry is in a three-piece suit and tie but he wears his helmet and face mask.

"What's with Henry? Hallowe'en isn't for two weeks," I say to Brooker, who's knotting his tie.

"Henry feels he cost us the win so he flipped out," he says. "He tried to kill a toilet with his stick, then swung at me when I suggested the head was already dead. Then he cried like a baby. Tough, because he had his helmet and mask on but Baby-Joel talked to him between sobs. Henry says he gave up a rebound on the tying goal and blew the winner. He showered with his helmet and mask on and says he ain't takin' it off, night or day, until he makes it up to us."

"Jackson talk to him?"

"Saw him in the shower and laughed like hell," Brooker says. "It was a bit hilarious. Charm the press, bubba?"

"Knocked 'em dead. That guy Duke Gage was in top form. He asked about the resentment on the team because a spade is captain."

"What did you tell him?"

"For the home opener, we're wearing white hoods."

Brooker whacks me on the bottom with a towel. "Bubba, two things," he says. "Ain't no one ever played better than you tonight. You're some hell of an athlete. Second, would you try to talk Henry down? Hartley and I got nowhere."

"Thanks and I won't. He looks better with the mask on. What did you think of the game?"

"We're in deeper shit than your heifers in a swamp," he says. "When a team double-shifts me, it's in some trouble."

It's a point.

One should be more serious with the press, I suppose. Two radio guys come on to our bus to see if there are sleeping berths.

Henry, with helmet and mask, is alone in a seat. Just about every guy has a six-pack of Michelob and if Jackson notices, he says nothing. He's in the front seats, telling Edmunds how he restyled the NHL's officiating staff. Sven's ice-pack isn't for a bruised calf and he hands me a stout belt.

Twenty minutes down the road, I sit with Henry. Because of the mask, I can't tell if he's alive or dead. I ramble on with a variety of anecdotes and gradually swing to how players must care about each other (examples from the Canadiens), how we all have great faith in him and how he showed us it's justified against the Sabres, how he made the best save I've ever seen before their second goal, how no goalie who ever lived could stop the winner and how he must show maturity to hold the confidence we have in him.

Thirty seconds later, Henry takes off his mask and helmet and softly sobs. He puts his head on my shoulder, I place my arm around him, and we're both sound asleep that way when the bus reaches Cleveland.

October 17

Julianne Duncan is jittery when the ladies arrive in town and I gather them up at the airport.

"Willie, I wish Brooker knew I was here," she says. "He doesn't want to go to the party."

"We told him that as team captain, he had to appear at the owner's bash," I say. "He agreed to go for an hour. Think he'll be surprised?"

"He'll croak when he sees me and the new dress," Julianne says. "He might spank me because he'll think I paid $500 for it. Oh, why did I take it? These nuts ordered champagne for lunch and we got all giggly. When we went to the store, it was a dream world for me. With seven kids, you don't buy originals. And there was this incredible dress, so new the stitches were hot. When Diane asked if I'd like to try it on, I almost fainted. And when she said it was mine..."

"We had to tie her down to get her into it," Clarice says. "It's sensational."

"She has a figure my models would murder for," Diane says. "If she has seven kids, I'm Harry Li."

"Brooker will be here at seven, moaning all the way," Hartley says at the condo. "Sven and his date are dropping in, too."

"Are the players' wives here now?" Clarice asks.

"Margie Franklin and the kids got here this week," I say. "Only Hartley, Brooker, Lester, Walter Simpson, Harry Li and Marty McNeil are married."

All three ladies are in Diane originals. They are only incredible, especially a physiotherapist I know. Sludge Symons would be so impressed he'd jump into the pond by himself.

Sven Stinquist arrives, tweeds and pipe in place, with a slender, dark-haired girl. Her name is Lia, who teaches at the college where he's taking courses this winter.

When Brooker is on his way up, Hartley puts his surprise in motion, sending Julianne up to the guest room on the second level to wait. We stay in the living room, having a drink, and welcome a very unhappy Brooker to the suite. "I wish

Julianne was here," Brooker says. "I hate these things, anyway, and it will be hell without her."

Then Hartley springs it. "Brooker, it's really presumptuous of me but I arranged a date for you."

"You what?" Brooker says, his face a storm cloud.

"We arranged a date so you won't have to go alone."

"You gone too far this time, bubba. You know I never fool around."

"Oh, Brooker, who mentioned fooling around, although the lady might be willing?" Diane says. "She's my friend, she's gorgeous and she's a big fan of your's."

"Big fan? What bull!" Brooker steams. "I can't believe this. It's gotta be Mulligan's idea."

"Hey, don't blame me," I say. "I told these loonies you wouldn't buy it."

"Well, I sure don't."

"Brooker, the lady's in the guest room," Hartley says. "You go tell her you're not interested."

"What are you doin' to me? I'm not tellin' no lady anythin'."

"Brooker, get up those stairs and tell the lady or I'm going to be very insulted," Diane says.

"What can I say to her?"

"Tell her you think she's an ugly old broad and you wouldn't take her to a pig-fight," Hartley suggests.

"You're as crackers as Henry Lamont."

Brooker climbs the stairs like he's on the way to the gas chamber and taps on the door. When it opens, we can hear him gasp. "Where did you get that dress?" A few minutes later, the Duncans descend the stairs, all smiles. Julianne, tall and svelte, looks like a high fashion model.

"I should've known your taste in ladies is impeccable, Laidlaw."

"She's definitely a fifty-bucker in a downtown bar," I say.

"Yeah?" Brooker says. "Best she does in Halifax is twenty-five."

"What is this party celebrating?" Lia asks.

"Didn't Sven tell you?" Diane says. "It's part of his

research to study the North American male in a state of arrested development. I just hope there are no trees tonight or the boys will be in them."

"Henry will be in the pool as a piranha," Hartley says. "And Baby-Joel will climb the chimney, carrying a girl, while planes strafe him with bullets."

"Are you guys ever serious?" Lia laughs.

"Flip humor to hide their breaking hearts, Lia," Clarice adds.

"If you play for Andy Jackson and don't laugh," Brooker says, "they put you in a home."

Clarice starts a research program of her own. "Sven, tell me what a sophisticated man with a Cambridge background is doing here, playing hockey."

"I wonder myself sometimes," Sven says. "For me hockey was fun but only as a method of physical fitness. As a boy, I played in my hometown and for one year at the small college there. Then I was awarded a scholarship to Cambridge and didn't play for three years, but when I was working on my master's in Oslo, I tried for the Norwegian national team. After a half-season with the second team, I joined the main team for the world championships.

"When Peter Edmunds contacted me, I said no because of my doctoral studies. But he persisted. Professional sport had appeal for me in two ways. I wanted to know if I was a good enough athlete and, as a social scientist, it was a chance to examine a completely new milieu. Before I agreed to come to camp, I wrote to several schools in the area about courses. Lia handled my letter at her college and is now my staff advisor."

"Any regrets?" Clarice says.

"No, the hockey is a big challenge and that I am still here is a surprise. I'm amazed by the status of the athlete here. The team dinner was attended by important people in banking, law, construction, medicine, manufacturing. Most of them really want to play center for the Big Green or quarterback the Browns or play shortstop for the Indians."

"And what do the folks back home think of it?" Julianne asks.

"I guess I'm a bit of a hero, the first Norwegian in the NHL. I receive many calls from reporters in Norway. Next week, two newspapers are sending writers and photographers to do stories. A paper wants me to write every week on my experiences."

"You'll soak up a lot of experiences tonight," I say. "We better roll to the Anderson palace."

"As I asked before old windy got rolling, what is this party all about?" Lia says.

"We can't lead the NHL in wins so we're going for the league record in parties," Hartley replies.

Shaker Heights is a suburb of estates, and Gee-One's residence has the same floor space as our barns on the farm. I could tie maybe 150 head of Jerseys in the family room at the back beside the fifty-foot indoor pool.

The Anderson clan and their pals are out in force, a live band plays for dancing, the food is Big Bertha caliber and there are two bars and three waiters. The lads are on their best behavior.

Jimmy Miller is Gerry Anderson's escort and Gerry has arranged dates for Baby-Joel, Henry and Pierre. When she lines Henry up with a tall girl and Joel with a short one, they trade but Henry says he should get future considerations because the tall one has bigger jugs.

Firpo brings Big John's very shy seventeen-year-old daughter and they provide an exhibition of Polish folk dancing plus four encores.

Pete The Cheat is with a slightly faded bar-fly whom he claims is a fine country singer. With a snootful of gin, she sings "Your Cheatin' Heart" and threatens the crystal. Lester conducts a player poll on the top '57 Chevy, Clarice or Inga Anderson, but I detect a fix when Lester announces that The Cheat's lady wins by a write-in vote.

Biff Byers befriends another bartender and a large amount of Michelob out of a silver stein. I ask him if it improves the taste. "Will, I've drunk 'er out of a bottle, a glass, a glove, and an old oil can and a running shoe and I never met a beer I didn't like."

When the band leaves its instruments for later pick-up, Diane, who peaks at midnight, decides the party isn't over. Gee-Two helps her turn on the band's amplifier, and she wanders over to the microphone: "Ladies and others, we have here tonight great tamounts of alent. I mean trait amounts of gralent. Whatever. The Big Green Ladies Auxiliary presents the first annual Other-Than-Hockey Talent Extravaganza. For our opening act, direct from a standing room only engagement at the Crown Pool Hall in Peterson, Saskatchewan, that brilliant beer-hall pianist, Margie Franklin."

Margie shakes her head and turns bright red, but Diane just says: "Margie, haul your pretty little bum to that Steinway or I'll tell why Lester really missed those games last season."

Wearing her practical Peterson pant suit, Margie walks shyly to the piano, gives a little curtsy and sits down. She plays in an orchestra back home; Lester's father owns the dance hall, of course. Margie makes two false starts, then pours out the "Beer Barrel Polka."

Biff Byers lurches out to his car and returns with his banjo case. He misses the chair and sits on the floor, then tunes up with Margie. Ol' Biff can really pick it.

Henry Lamont, a drummer in his high school band, sits at the drums and while he isn't Max Roach, he brushes them enough to get by. I know Hartley must have a load of Scotch when he takes over the rhythm guitar because he simply refuses to play in front of anyone.

Doc-Jay Stanley can pick a little bass guitar and Lia, Sven's date, tries the band's electric piano. She's classically trained but can swing a little, too.

Then Gerald Anderson disappears and returns with a battered trombone. He hasn't played it since college and says he hopes the others won't mind if he tries to toot along.

When Harry Tatum, a music major in college before switching to physiotherapy, bemoans the lack of a clarinet,

Gee-Two runs to a friend's estate and brings back a kid in T-shirt and pajama bottoms plus his clarinet.

The band has three mainstays—Margie, who knows every song ever written and has a top drawer "and a-one, and a-two, and a-three" that Lawrence Welk could envy, Harry, a good musician, and Biff, who can't suggest a single song but can play everyone's choices.

Margie takes them through some easy stuff and then gives them each a little solo. Hartley does "Wildwood Flower," Harry produces "Memories Of You," Gee-One, who improves the most as the night progresses, does "I'm Getting Sentimental Over You" and Biff delivers a socko "Bye Bye Blues."

Andy Jackson and his wife Dorothy, a lovely, dark-haired lady, stay in the living room area with Clive-Five and the other non-participants. At 2:45, the band is wailing, when The Cheat reappears. He took his lady home when she decided a skinny dip was a good idea. That was just before she locked herself in the john.

"You know, I wish my friend was still here. This band needs a singer," Cheat says. "Should ask Pinhead Jackson's wife to sing."

"If her voice is anything like Andy's, forget it," I say. "You think she can sing?"

"Yeah, pop and jazz," he says. "In Atlanta, 'bout six years ago, her name was Dorothy Lindsay and her old man was a piano player. Had a big band and a super small group plus a jazz club. She sang like an angel with both. Did the anthem at our games a few times. Best ever 'cept for Roger Doucet in Montreal, God rest his soul.

"Two in the a.m. in that club, this great-lookin' lady does 'One More For The Road' or 'In The Wee, Small Hours,' the clarinet soft, everybody droppin' tears in their sauce. Andy had a missus and two kids then but, before long, he's in that club every night. He starts goin', the players stop. Soon, the first missus and the kids haul ass back to Canada and that piano player starts lookin' for a new singer and a new old lady."

"Did she keep on singing?" Diane says.

"When she got together with Pinhead, she stopped. He's 'bout the most jealous mother I ever saw. At a team party, a guy asked Dorothy to dance and Pinhead popped him one."

"Well, it's time ol' Dorothy made a comeback," Diane says. Just then, Jackson goes to the head and Diane says: "Come on, Clarice. Let's ask a lady to sing."

They talk to Dorothy, who shakes her head, but they half carry her to a spot beside the piano. I hear her say: "Andy will be furious."

Diane reassures her: "I'll handle Andy."

Dorothy and Margie talk for a minute and Margie noodles around and starts "You're The Top," not an easy song. Hartley, Lia and Gee-One drop out, leaving Henry, Doc-Jay, Biff and Harry adding support.

A little "one-two-three" and Dorothy starts. She's only magnificent, a full, rich, voice that swings easy. When Jackson hears her voice, he charges across the room but Hartley and I intercept him.

"Hey, coach," Hartley says. "You haven't met our ladies. This is my wife, Diane, and Willie's friend, Clarice."

He rasps a greeting and says: "Who's brilliant idea is this?"

"The party, coach? Gerald Anderson's, I would suspect."

"You know what I mean, Mulligan. My wife singing."

"I take credit for that, Mr. Jackson," Diane says. "She's remarkable. You must be very proud of her."

"Keep it quiet, please," Lester says in a stage whisper. "A big league lady is performin'."

Gee-Two dunks the lights except for the one over the piano. Jackson storms to the living room and when Dorothy finishes her song, the applause is enormous. Harry launches "S'Wonderful" and away Dorothy goes. For an hour, the wistful lady with the gamin haircut, an elbow on the Steinway, a cigarette in her hand, turns everyone into putty.

Finally, at 4:40 a.m., it's time to go. Dorothy closes with "In The Wee, Small Hours" and The Cheat cries like a baby. Dorothy hugs Margie, Hartley, Henry, Doc-Jay, Harry and even Gee-One, who announces another party soon if Margie Franklin and the Big Green All-Stars featuring Dot Jackson will appear. That might not stand when he sees that Jimmy is wearing his daughter's lipstick.

I say to a well-gunned Pete Edmunds: "Should go straight to practice."

"Willie, you old hayseed, to show I'm human, no work-out," Pete slurs. "We needed a party more than another of Jackson's boring practices."

"But what will coach Jackson say?"

"Screw Joke Cackson. I'm the powerful general manager of this team."

Coach Jackson has deep-sixed on rye and ginger in the living room. Brooker, Hartley and I carry him to the car.

"Thanks, you nice people," Dorothy says. "Maybe he'll forget and I won't catch hell tomorrow."

Brooker looks down at the crumpled coach and says softly: "Too bad he don't pass out before games."

October 22

We're in St. Louis after an early flight from Chicago, and I'm rooming with Pete McFatridge. I finally discover where the nickname "The Cheat" comes from.

The contents of his large suitcase resemble garbage— empty tissue boxes, burned-out light bulbs and cardboard centers from toilet paper rolls.

"Never stayed here before so I can give 'em the full treatment," he says. He takes the bulbs out of two lamps and replaces them with burn-outs of the same brand. He removes the toilet paper plus the spare and places a cardboard tube on the roller. Same with the tissue box—full one out, empty one in. Bulbs, toilet paper and tissue go into the suitcase.

"Can't I read, blow my nose or go potty?"

"Oh, sure. Just wait a minute," he says, dialing the phone. "Housekeeping? Mr. McFatridge in 1711. I hate to complain but there's no toilet paper or tissues in this room and two lights have burned out. That's 1711. Right, ma'am, it's difficult to get good help these days."

The Cheat writes in his notebook while the maid replaces the goods.

"My inventory," he says. "Of course, I can't work the same hotel too often."

We lost another "toughie," 6-2, to the Black Hawks last night. The first period was tied at one, then the Hawks discovered our susceptibility to forechecking and it was 5-1 after forty minutes.

I scored the opener, a shot from the slot after Brooker out-muscled two Hawks for the puck. In the third, I set up Brooker for his first NHL goal in three seasons. Hartley had a terrible night and his line was on the ice for three against.

In the paper today, the NHL's scoring list looks like this.

	GP	G	A	PTS	PIM
Mulligan, Clev	3	3	4	7	2
Beaupre, Mont	3	2	5	7	0

"Tugs the heartstrings," Brooker needles. "A boy from the farm achievin' such heights."

The home opener? Jennifer Brown said it all in her lead Monday.

The Montreal Canadiens, the oldest, the quickest, the deepest, the most talented, showed the Cleveland Big Green, the newest, hockey's promised land last night.

Les Habitants were only mighty. The score was 9-4; the shots, 49-17. If Henry Lamont hadn't been Turk Broda and Bill Durnan all in one five-seven package, they would have had twenty. The Canadiens reminded me of our team three seasons ago that had a 61-8-11 won-lost-tied mark, then lost only one game in the playoffs. There were no fringe players on that roster.

Gaston Beaupre, my old pal, had two goals and two assists. I got one plus assists on two goals by Brooker. I only scored because I know a defenseman goes for an outside-inside fake and the goalie is weak low on the stick side.

I was with Clarice outside the ladies' lounge when Alfie

Brisebois, the Canadien coach, came over. "Willie, you still no take de second-best in any-ting," he says when I introduce her. "Clar-eece, if I hab dis guy here still, dey can gib me de Cup right now."

Attendance? Well, 5,632 fans jammed the Coliseum for the game. The Browns, unbeaten in five, were in Los Angeles and the telecast started at 4 p.m., undoubtedly keeping many fans away from our game.

At least, that's what we hope.

October 27

Hartley is gabby at late breakfast today, an off-day for the winless-in-six Big Green. He has obviously been reviewing the situation and is ready to unload.

"I had no use for them around the Leafs but I miss the hangers-on and 'go-fers,'" he says. "I'll have to get my car serviced myself. Last year, I'd phone a garage, drive my old hack to practice, a guy would be at the back door and after practice, the car would be there."

"Maybe we need to learn about the real world."

"Don't tell me the almighty Canadiens had no flock of barnacles to scratch your back."

"In that town, paying full price was tough for a Canadien," I say. "A pack of valets was ready to fill your every whim. A few were dudes with a hustle on, but mostly it was guys who saw it as a big deal to hang around hockey players. A failure with the Canadiens was a guy who paid full price for a three-piecer."

"In Toronto, there was a little guy we called the 'the wives' man,'" Hartley says. "We often chartered out after Saturday night games and the ladies would go for a feed or drink. He'd tag along and in the winter would warm up the cars."

"Wasn't the Leaf highlight those lovely young females at the side door of the Gardens?"

"That was the most depressing part of the scene," he says. "A half dozen were always there — grungy, overweight teenage girls with acne. One never spoke but she'd run up to me with an envelope with pages of crazy fantasies. One day, she and I would be on a tropical island; the next, we'd be skiing in Switzerland."

"How many did Diane give you before you asked her for a date?"

"I was in love with 'cake-girl,'" Hartley says. "That little waif never missed a player's birthday with a decorated cake and card. Somehow she could get players' addresses and phone numbers."

"We made certain our cars were locked when we parked near the Forum," I say. "You left nothing on the seat with your address on it. Gaston Beaupre got a new car and forgot to lock it. After practice, the seats had big chunks cut out of them and kids had pieces of the material for him to autograph. Then some punk sold the chunks at five bucks.

"Once, Gaston heard a ruckus outside his house at 6:30 a.m. after a big snowfall and two kids were fighting over who would clean his drive, swinging at each other with snow shovels. Must have been hell with a profile as high as your's in Toronto."

"I never allowed it to be. A couple of guys did and, to me, their lives were hell. Of course, some think the best thing in life is people at their doors at all hours; folks—and not just kids—staring at the houses for hours, and not going anywhere for dinner without signing autographs until the food is cold."

"How did you stop it?"

"Two exit-door saddies located our house and, for two nights, they stood in the street. When they showed up again, I called a detective I know and he scared the hell out of them. He told them he'd bust them for loitering and if they gave out the address, for invasion of privacy. Then we had three or four good eating spots where we made friends with the owners and they'd keep the pests away."

"Let's run an add in the paper that says: 'Wanted, go-fers for athletes who can't do menial tasks themselves,'" I suggest.

"In this town, you wouldn't get any response." He doesn't even chuckle at his last remark. Instead, he looks even gloomier. "Ever been on a team that lost six in a row?"

"Not since Junior B. The Canadiens lost four once and folks were catatonic. The press screamed for Alfie Brisebois' scalp and trades to shake a crumbling dynasty. We won the next eleven in a row."

"Six wasn't unusual in blue-and-white," he says. "But no matter what, the Gardens was sold out."

"Think we'll ever see a home ice SRO again?"

"Only if the NHL's top scorer does it," he smiles.

"It won't last long so permit me to revel in it while I can," I reply.

It's in the paper this morning and the name looks to be in the proper place.

	GP	G	A	PTS	PIM
Mulligan, Clev	6	8	8	16	10
Beaupre, Mont	5	6	8	14	6
Dinkov, NYR	6	2	11	13	4
Duncan, Clev	6	4	7	11	8

It would mean more if the line in the standings didn't say: Cleveland 6-0-6-0-21-39-0.

"You'd have to look a long way down that list to find 'Laidlaw, Clev,'" Hartley says.

"You're a notorious slow starter."

"Usually, I'm adequate defensively until I get the scoring touch," he continues. "I'm not checking worth a shit because I lose my concentration. Last night, you cut the Kings' lead to 6-5, I screwed up, they went two up and I wanted to throw up."

"Don't blame yourself for that. There were four or five screw-ups. Li and The Cheat stayed too high with Baby-Joel and Kardek on defense, Joel went to a corner where Miro was already and Marc-Luc didn't cover the short side."

"But if I take the center out, nothing happens," he says. "I forced him to pass off and didn't finish the check. I turned for the puck, he was back in the play and his move created the goal."

"You missed most of camp. These six games are a tune-up for you."

"I pulled my groin, not my brain," he says. "Why your fast start, oh mighty farmer?"

"Luck. Everything is bouncing right for me, that's all. Brooker helps, too."

"I don't like superlatives but you're at the top of your game," he says. "You're in majestic condition or you couldn't carry the ice-time load. You're thinking the game beautifully, my good man. B. Duncan is very limited but you make him an asset. J. Miller is dead-weight. But the line is a plus on a club that's oh-and-six, so the center is doing something right."

"Oh, you flatterer! The last time I heard you give anyone a line like that, you had your hand on the inside of her thigh."

"We're very different, thou and I. You are a strong individual and your line works because of it. You harness the bit Brooker has and use Jimmy when he won't get you killed. Brooker is smart enough to be where you need him. The kid is too young to realize that as your caddy, he can score forty."

"So why are we so different, hockey maven?"

"My strength is using the players on the ice," he says. "I rely on them as equals and their abilities augment mine. Li and Cheat can't reach my modest level of sophistication. I've tried, goddamit, I've tried. But I have to hide half my game. I try to play like you but it's a big adjustment. As you may have noted, I'm extremely frustrated."

"Pick two wingers from this motley collection of motleys."

"I would like, given my druthers, to perform on left flank with Swede and Finn," he replies. "Or move Anders left, me at center, and maybe we would have two lines."

"Maybe our coach will have a rye and ginger vision about it."

"I suggested it to him after the Chicago game, and his response was 'mind your own fucking business,'" Hartley says.

At least, the Green loses in different ways.

The St. Louis Blues, undoubtedly fearing our awesome attack, checked us daffy. They scored two early and we had only fifteen shots on goal in losing, 3-1. The Blues matched the best defensive line in the league against us and we did little, although I broke the shutout. Jimmy's fifty-foot pass, lofted a foot off the ice, landed on my blade when I had a step on everyone.

We came home for a three-game stand, a rarity for a team in the east. There were 4,522 spectators Friday when Chicago hung us out, 8-5. We had a 3-0 lead, blew it, then led, 5-3, before the Hawks scored five in the third. I got two goals and two assists but my line was on for two against in the third.

Yesterday, the football Browns monopolized the local scene, with 85,000 at Municipal Stadium for their sixth win. Super Bowl talk abounds. We had 3,782 fans and no Stanley Cup talk when we lost, 9-7, to the Los Angeles Kings.

I scored three and set up two but it was a frustrating night. We were down, 5-1, then cut the lead to 6-5 until the foul-up for which Hartley blames himself. I doubt if I've ever worked harder and Jackson picked last night to unload a five-minute diatribe, an indictment about the size of our testicles, brains and hearts. If I hand't been so low, it probably would have been very funny.

"What are your plans for our wonderful off-day," I say.

"Lunch and a planning conflab with some big-buck legal minds on a gigantic international deal," Hartley says. "Your agenda?"

"I'm joining Sven and several Norwegian scribes for lunch."

"How do you plan to pass your time?" he says. "I'd go nuts were it not for a little law in which to dabble."

"An extension course from Cornell. It's the start of a master's in cows, herd health and dairy nutrition."

"Speaking of dabbling, I forgot that a stew of my acquaintance will be in our fair burg and has a friend who's dying to meet the NHL's leading scorer. Interested?"

"Why not?" I reply. "Just as long as it's not Sven's old friend. That's an act I wouldn't care to follow."

November 1

We play the Maple Leafs tonight and the Toronto newspaper story this morning is a dilly. I read it when Clarice and I breakfast after spending the night apart, as do Hartley and Diane, a point on which Jackson is fanatical.

The writer was in Cleveland for our seventh loss, the worst effort yet in a 5-2 defeat by the Washington Capitals. A promotion tie-in with a supermarket had 10,773 in the seats, and Hartley figured most probably wished they'd taken the alternative to the tickets—stale bread at fifteen cents a loaf.

The game was so dull that Sal Mancino claimed: "Even the quadriplegics walked out."

The Toronto papers spend much money to cover hockey, even though the Leafs have done zilch since the 1960s. Hartley has had many calls from Toronto papers and radio stations and saves fuss and bother by telling Beady Bascom, our PR man, to take the numbers and he'll call them between two and three on Thursday.

Tim Watson, the writer of today's article, should avoid our coach for a few years.

NHL RED-FACED OVER BIG GREEN

Send in the clowns!

The National Hockey league does it tonight at Maple Leaf Gardens when the Cleveland Big Green, named after a trucking company, meets the Maple Leafs.

Seven games is too few to claim the Green is the worst team in NHL history. It is certainly among the dillies.

The NHL stiffed the team with the worst talent ever granted for $8 million. Wouldn't you love to be on a desert island with the Anderson family, the owners of this mess, and have a deck of cards?

They added to it by hiring Pete Edmunds as general manager and Andy Jackson as coach. They've had more flops than Richard Nixon and Spiro Agnew.

To be fair, Edmunds has surprised with his efforts for this team. He tapped a drained European market for four players, notably Sven Stinquist, a dandy Norwegian defenseman.

Young players, potential yet to be determined because they're teenaged children, include the much-publicized Jimmy Miller.

The Big Green doomed itself to the dark ages and 24th place by hiring Jackson. He was a great NHL player but, so far, he's been to coaching what Tab Hunter was to acting. The Green has little talent; it has no system, no discipline. In short: a bad team without a plan.

A practice session this week was a cartoon, the type thinking NHL coaches abandoned 20 years ago —boring repetition of stale drills, antiquated approaches and wasted time. One player remarked sardonically that it was the most creative workout of the season.

The Green lucked into two quality players in centers Hartley Laidlaw, who the Leafs miss like a lost wheel, and Willie Mulligan, who never got the credit he deserved for the Montreal Canadiens' success. They were exiled to Cleveland like lepers when all they did was give the players free agency, the chance to escape the Andy Jackson's of the world.

Laidlaw missed two weeks of camp with a groin injury. Never a quick starter, the lack of wingers with whom he can work his elegant playmaking has curtailed his effectiveness.

A fine player on a great team, Mulligan now is an exceptional player on a lousy team. He leads the NHL scoring, playing on a line with Brooker Duncan, who's somewhere between 30 and 45, and Miller, who's 17.

The story has quotes from Edmunds on his long-range plan, Jackson, about the game still being one of hustle and toughness, and Clive Eye-Vee on their commitment to Cleveland.

"There will be a gut to clean over this."

"From what I've heard since Grenada, the writer's perceptions are very accurate," Clarice says.

"It's one thing for me to tell you things like that but in print, it's something else."

"I like that word exceptional," she smiles. "That's my boy, exceptional Willie. If we had spent the night together, what would Jackson have done?"

"Had me gelded or sent to Fort Worth."

"Which is worse?"

We walk up Yonge Street to the Gardens for our skate and Clarice heads for Diane's where the Mulligan clan is gathering for an early dinner. I need eight tickets because Joey and Marty are seeing their first NHL game.

It's a scramble for tickets in Toronto because most teams have players from the area. Each player receives a pair and tradeouts are in order. I get tickets from Baby-Joel, Henry and Marc-Luc in Toronto and they'll use mine in Alberta, Vancouver and Quebec City.

I pick up coffee at the little shop off the Gardens' lobby, kid with the two friendly ladies who run it and bump into a Toronto sports columnist I've known for years. He asks about the farm, not the Big Green. I tell him his paper should have a reporter and photographer at the Royal Winter Fair when our heifer wins the best in the show. I know it will appear in his notes next week.

Hartley is there, too, after going home to have breakfast with Diane. Harry Tatum says that Edmunds and Jackson want us outside.

"Breakfast with one's bride is against Andy's rules," Hartley says. "Cripes, you did it without a license. It'll probably cost you a grand."

"You see the papers this morning?"

"You know I don't read papers in the a.m.," he says.

"Be ready for anything."

The GM and coach are in the corner of the Gardens' catacombs and Jackson has a paper in his hand.

"Hey, guys, what's up?" I say. "Have a wild night?"

"You see this?" Jackson says, waving the newspaper.

"I read the papers this morning," I say.

"I read a book on criminal law, coach," Hartley says. "Papers are bad for a guy. They get your hands all dirty."

"Well, wise guy, read this. But I have a goddam good idea you know what's in it."

Hartley glances through the article.

"Well?" Jackson says.

"We got some ink in Toronto," Hartley says with a shrug.

"It's not very good ink, Hartley," Edmunds says.

"It's vicious shit and I know where it came from," Jackson rages. "You media darlings gave that guy a real crock of bullshit. Of course, you smell like roses, two great stars forced to associate with inferior beings. Jesus Christ, when I played, being paid bought some loyalty to the people who signed the checks.

"Think my practices are boring? You stars come from teams with talent so great you didn't bother with the basics but we don't have three guys who can skate up and down the fuckin' ice without getting lost. Why did you assholes give a writer this crap and what have you got to say for yourselves?"

I feel myself coming to a boil. "I'll gladly tell you what I have to say. I resent your assumption, Andy, that I had anything to do with this story. Tim Watson was there and, sure, I talked to him. He taped every word of it and I could get it for you to hear. Anything he got from me is inside quotation marks, attributed to me. I'll swear it on anything you want to produce."

"Well, if you're Mr. Clean, then it must be the attorney here who did it."

"Andy, I have a little surprise for you," Hartley says softly. "I never talked to Watson."

"You expect me to believe that?" Jackson shoots back. "A big-wheel writer from a town where you were a hot-shot comes in and you have the balls to say you didn't talk to him? You figure I'm stupid?"

"I haven't talked to him or anyone from that paper for four years."

"Why not?" Jackson snaps.

"A personal thing."

"He shittin' me, Mulligan?" Jackson says.

"If Hartley says something, I stake my life on it," I say.

"Well, that bastard Watson don't talk to me or get in our dressing room," Jackson says to end another classic interview.

Although, as Hartley says, the Maple Leafs haven't stood for anything except the national anthem for many years, Maple Leaf Gardens is a special spot for most of us. We grew up on *Hockey Night In Canada* and the folks at home watching you play on the box is one of the best things about making the NHL.

Tonight's game will be on the national network and Joel Reid, Henry Lamont and Pierre Lambert are excited that their families can watch them. Baby-Joel says his family will be sore if he doesn't get into a fight, so I suggest he and Henry have a little chase in warm-up.

"My wee buddy got a little carried away that night," Joel says. "But under my good influence, he's behavin' himself very well."

After our skate, I notice Hartley standing in the corner with Harry Li and Pete McFatridge, chatting for a long time. Hartley and I walk back to the hotel—three exit-door girls hand him letters—via a sidestreet route where he isn't likely to be recognized.

"Interesting conversation with the brass. It really zapped me that you never talk to Watson."

"After reading that story, I should buy Watson lunch," he says.

"Talking to your wingers about Taiwan?"

"It's my fault but we haven't talked much," he replies. "My darling bride lectured me at breakfast about my attitude. I guess I've been sulking."

"Not at all. You have been moodily introspective. Sounds better. Any conclusions?"

"I asked why they thought our line wasn't doing much," Hartley says. "The Cheat says it's because the center figures he has Rocket Richard and Howie Morenz on his wings. I said it might work better if I forced play more and The Cheat said he didn't care a helluva lot if he never saw the puck. Harry was a little reluctant because he doesn't see himself as slow."

We play our best game to date against the Leafs. We lose, 5-4, but we're in it all the way. Hartley does all he can to get us a win over his old team, which looks shallow at center without him.

Hartley works his buns off and scores two goals, one on a breakaway with Sven's pass. I get another one, a tap-in of a good Miller move, and Baby-Joel scores his first NHL goal, blasting in my passout.

I retrieve the puck on my goal, which befuddles the TV commentators, who can't really figure out the significance. It's simple, really: I promise Marty and Joey the puck if I score.

Baby-Joel dances Swan Lake after his goal to guarantee the TV cameras pick him up so the folks in Red Deer can see him. He also makes a gesture that resembles the thumbing of the nose. "My old man bet me a hunnert I wouldn't score this season and that was for him. My pop and those three crazy asses 'll be dancin' around the house. Bet there ain't a stick of furniture left in one piece."

Hartley is the game's first star and when he skates out for his bow, the quiet Gardens' fans give him a fairly raucous ovation.

My niece Marty breaks Hartley up after the game when she says: "Uncle Willie, why didn't you come out instead of Uncle Hartley? You played better than he did."

"Just what the world needs," Hartley says. "Another smartass Mulligan."

November 7

The Big Green brass blunders this week. We play in New Jersey Wednesday, then have two days in Quebec City. Seclusion might have been wiser.

Quebec is a beautiful, historic old spot, a town that has built the new and modern and retained the old in fine co-existence. To Canadian school kids, the place is vivid from the history books from the Wolfe-Montcalm battle on the Plains of Abraham, though Americans never heard of the place.

"Aren't the planes of Abraham the Israeli air force?" Jennifer Brown says on the bus from the airport.

Quebec City is regarded as the best "wool market" in the NHL. Hartley claims it's appropriate because Quebec was once the center of the fur trade in North America, specializing in beaver. It's nice to know old traditions still exist.

Although the residents are very pro-French, the females don't mind chaps bilingual through English and profanity. There are large numbers of ladies in town and plenty of spots where a young traveler can meet them.

Hap Lonsdale, the vet scribe, started wondering what he could do for three days when he can't speak the language, even though he doesn't do much but drink with Edmunds or Jackson and sleep, no matter what city we're in.

I tell him that if he can't get lucky in Quebec, then a monastery is the only place for him.

"I played here for part of a season in the American League," The Cheat says. "If I had stayed the whole year, I woulda been Henry's size and none of it was from hockey."

The team stays at the wonderful old Château Frontenac on the edge of a small cliff, with the "old city" and the St. Lawrence below it.

Brooker Duncan isn't along. Released from hospital yesterday, he's okay, although there was doubt for a few days. He'll play at home Sunday.

Brooker was speared in the gut last Sunday in Cleveland and the incident has created much controversy. The anti-violence media has kicked the game in the head as if the incident represents everything bad in hockey.

The guy who stuck the captain was Marv Chambliss, the Philly Flyer tough kid. Chambliss won't play for a few weeks and faces league disciplinary action. When the dentists and doctors repaired the damage to his teeth, jaw and cheekbone, his jaw was wired shut. Brooker did that with one right hand shot.

The game, which attracted 13,878 fans because the Flyers are the NHL's best draw, was wild.

In the warm-up, Chambliss worked on Jimmy Miller. Obviously, he wanted a rematch with Brooker and figured to get it by intimidating Jimmy.

"You're going to get it, Miller, you little chickenshit," Chambliss said as he first skated past.

"You're ass is on the line, you little yellow bastard," he said the next time around.

"Where's your bodyguard, Miller?" he hollered on the third circuit.

The next time, Baby-Joel skated with Jimmy and when Chambliss yelled, Joel stopped and waved him over. But Brooker got him moving before anything could happen.

The goals came fast when no one was thinking about defense, and at the end of a tame first period, we were up, 4-3.

In the second period, Pierre rushed, passed off and was flattened by Chambliss' elbow to the head. On his way down, Pierre chopped him a two-hander on the arm with his stick and when he got up, Chambliss was ready and in the fight. Pierre hanged tough but took a pretty fair trouncing. Hartley had to tackle Baby-Joel to prevent his earning a game misconduct as third man in.

The fans liked the speed and action and at the end of the second, the score was 6-6. I had two goals and three assists on two goals by Brooker and one by Jimmy.

With his radar finely tuned to avoid checks, Jimmy made a monkey out of Chambliss on the goal that tied it. Chambliss lunged at him from the blind side but Jimmy stopped suddenly. Chambliss missed and I went into the hole for Jimmy's pass and a goal.

Chambliss and Brooker met in the corner late in the

period, a skirmish from which Brooker skated away. But in the third, Chambliss was determined to fight my winger. The Flyers went ahead, 8-6, and when Brooker went into the corner with him after the puck, Chambliss' stick nicked Brooker over the eye.

"Oh, it's red," Chambliss said. "I thought it would be brown, like shit."

A little tape on the cut and the captain was back at work. Chambliss hollered at him, much of it a combination of colors, black and yellow. Brooker ignored him.

Baby-Joel offered to "get that asshole for you," but Brooker waved him off.

Sven moved us within a goal on a nifty rush but the Flyers scored two more. Hartley got one back to make the score 10-8, with six minutes to go.

Brooker and I were forechecking deep when it happened. Chambliss moved behind the net where the ice was sticky and had trouble controlling the puck. When he looked down, Brooker belted him a honey of a bodycheck, a clean hit with shoulder and hip.

Brooker chased the puck in the corner and when he looked up for a pass-target, Chambliss speared him. I still shudder when I think about it because it was as if he had run a pitchfork into a bale of hay. The tip of the blade was buried in Brooker's side at waist level. I was close enough to hear him grunt and see his face distorted with pain. Brooker dropped to one knee and saw Chambliss coming with his gloves off. I tried to grab Chambliss, but too late. Brooker got to his feet, right glove off, and Chambliss walked into the most fearsome punch I've ever seen. Brooker's right hit him flush in the face and I could hear bones crack.

Brooker bent over in pain, gasping, "I'm hurt bad, bubba," and collapsed on the ice. He had got it in the kidney area.

Harry signaled for the stretcher and Doc Stanley had the ambulance down the ramp when they carried Brooker off. Chambliss, his face a mess, went to the hospital, too. He received a match penalty for deliberately injuring an opponent and Brooker got a fighting major. The game finished tamely, with us losing 10-8.

The media crowded around Jackson after the game.

"The kid asked for it all night," he said. "What he did is the most vicious attempt to injure someone I've ever seen. There was no motivation for it."

"What about the hit Duncan gave him?" a writer asked.

"That was a routine bodycheck, hard but clean. It's no excuse for impaling another man on a hockey stick."

Several of them moved to me, and a Philly writer asked if Brooker did anything to Chambliss to motivate what happened.

"Not that I saw, at least not tonight," I told him.

"What do you mean 'tonight'?"

"You were at the exhibition game in Portland. What happened there?"

"Duncan beat the crap out of Chambliss," the guy said.

"Who started the fight?"

"Chambliss."

"Who was quoted as saying he could beat anyone in the NHL?"

"Chambliss."

"Next question."

"Ever see a harder punch?" asked a radio guy.

"I've never rated them."

In the room Hartley just shook his head. "I wish that goddam phone would ring and they'd say he's fine."

"Chambliss was looking for it all night," said Jennifer. "It wasn't accidental when he clipped Brooker with the stick."

"Jen, Chambliss was shooting off his mouth in the warm-up," Hartley said.

"Was color involved?"

"Yes, but please don't quote me. Brooker wouldn't want that one out of the box. He laughs it off. Come on, Willie, haul your ass. Let's go to the hospital."

Hartley drove like a fiend to the city and we talked our way to the floor where Brooker was located. The doctors were still with him, but after an hour, Doc Stanley appeared, smiling a little.

"He's okay but we need a little time to fix the exact damage because that part of the anatomy has complicated parts," he said. "His vital signs are all strong. He passed blood in his urine but it's stopped. That leads us to believe he had kidney trauma. His stomach is as hard as this floor, and that probably saved him from a really serious injury."

"Is he conscious?" I asked.

"He collapsed more from pain and shock than anything," the Doc added. "He was conscious before we were out of the parking lot. He's really upset about punching that kid. You can see him for a minute."

Brooker's eyes were closed when we went in. I suggested to Hartley that maybe we should have some soft organ music.

"My organ ain't ever soft," Brooker said. "That's why I got seven kids. You pull it out?"

"Your organ? I'm not that strong," Hartley laughed. "No, something new. We lost. How are you, Brook?"

"I can't do sit-ups until Wednesday, but the docs say I'm okay. I got a sore side and peeing bright red scared the hell out of me, but that's cleared up. They're certain there's no damage to anythin' that counts."

"You're such a tough old bugger that bullets would bounce off that belly of your's," I said.

"I feel bad hittin' that kid. It was just a reflex action. Man, I was hurtin' and I just reacted."

"That punk could have killed you or made it so you always pee in a tube," said Hartley. "Maybe he'll think a little next time."

"What are my kids goin' to think? For years they've taken crap about me being a goon. This year, I get a few goals, thanks to Willie, and their friends want autographed pictures, if you can believe it."

"Want us to call Julianne?" I asked.

"Doc Stanley called and I talked to her. She cried, I cried. It's okay. She's a tough lady. But yeah, maybe you could reassure her that ol' Midnight is alive, semi-kickin' and loves her."

What Chambliss got out of it was a broken jaw, a broken cheekbone, four teeth missing and a few more out of line. Brooker's tests were negative and he took thirty bucks from Hartley and me in a hearts' game before we left for New York. We called him Wednesday and he told us that Chambliss was released from hospital and stopped in at his room.

"Kid's got a face like a bag of rocks and he'll be out two months," Brooker said. "He had trouble talking but we had a little chat. He apologized for harpoonin' me and me for cloutin' him. He said he lost his head when I checked him. I suppose I gave him a sermon. Told him I can't understand why a guy with his talent acted like a dumb-ass, hollering at people to show how tough he is. He wanted to know if I didn't fight to try to prove how tough I was. I said I've never been in a fight to prove anythin'."

Serge Lapierre is now right wing on my line. He's as slow as Brooker but half as smart.

I got my twelfth goal against the Islanders when we lost, 3-1, and the next night the Rangers beat us, 6-2. How easily they did it is depressing because it shows where our club is on the NHL spectrum.

After the Islander game, Edmunds announced that all junior-age players would stay with the team.

"It wouldn't be bad if they were getting any coaching here," Hartley said. "But it's gone from being ridiculous to just being sad."

"You know, Hartley," I said, "I'd love to rent ice and have Doc Bradshaw and Brooker run a clinic two hours a day for a couple of weeks. The Doc on fundamentals, Brooker on positioning and playing in your own end."

"I think the kids would go for it," Hartley replied.

"Sure, but Jackson wouldn't. Next week, though, Jimmy and I'll stay out after practice because he realizes he can learn something."

The lads cut loose in Quebec City and, last night, Henry and Baby-Joel were arrested. With Pierre as guide and interpreter, Firpo, Anders and Ilko—Jimmy is smitten by Gerry Anderson and doesn't stray when he's in love—joined the Warps on a pub crawl. About 1 a.m., they were in the square outside the hotel, each with a snootful of sauce and a local lass.

Baby-Joel earned them eviction from two bistros with his loud political views, notably his claims that French-Canadians are assholes, except Pierre, of course, and that Alberta will cut the oil supply until "the frogs learn who the bosses are in Canada."

There were garbage cans on the side of the hotel overlooking the old city and Baby-Joel decided to solve Canada's language problems by heaving the dustbins on the city below. He picked them up over his head, ran across the boardwalk and heaved them over the rail, making an incredible clatter as they hit the roofs below.

After a half-dozen of the cans flew over, two police cars arrived and the Europeans scurried into the hotel with their ladies. Baby-Joel declined advice from "any goddam pepsi fuzz" and when two policemen tried to halt another can-heave, he substituted one of them for the container.

Joel lowered the cop who, Henry tells me, was "yellin' and kickin' up over the Baby's head, sure he was on his way to the old city." Joel figured it was just a little fun but the cops didn't agree and put Baby-Joel under arrest. Of course, Henry told the cops to fuck off and leave decent citizens alone and started into the hotel with the girls.

Henry was no problem, except for a few swings. But when four officers got Baby-Joel to the squad car, he placed his hands on the top of the door and braced his feet.

"Four little cops try to move my buddy," Henry related. "But they can't budge him. Only way they can get him in the car is with a gun."

Hartley and I were in bed when Pierre banged on our door, half-hysterical. We took a cab to the police station where the Warp Brothers were in the cells.

The first plus was that the desk sergeant recognized me. "Ah, Monsieur Mulligan, the Canadiens could use you. But without you, maybe our Nordiques can beat them." He nodded towards the cells. "Your young friends are in serious trouble."

Hartley's legal mien and a large dazzle of words helped to get them out and the charges dropped, and Hartley and I guaranteed no more trouble. We also promised the sergeant six tickets to the next Nordiques' home game against the Canadiens, possibly the toughest ticket in sport, and signed a few autographs before he fetched the prisoners.

"Listen you two shit heads: If you ever get into a mess again, don't call me because I never heard of you," Hartley told them on the way back to the hotel.

"Shoulda dropped that cop over the cliff, Henry," Baby-Joel said. "Be one less pig to bother folks. Hey, did them girls split?"

Tonight, Sven, Hartley and I soak up a little Quebecois culture in that museum with all the flashing lights on the top floor of a big hotel, where Lester is dancing up a storm with a '46 Ford.

"I'm revising the poon-rating a little," Lester says. "Gotta include a French car. The Renault is the best and this year's model is the finest."

Sven's French is an asset and his scholarly look, nifty tweeds and pipe are a magnet. One lady simply drops her room key in his jacket pocket.

My French isn't perfect but it's good enough. Same with my dancing. At least a lovely young nurse with jet-black hair and flashing dark eyes thinks they're just fine.

Hartley claims his French is limited to "la plume de ma tante est sur la table." It gets the job done.

November 10

We lost in Quebec and at home to the Vancouver Canucks for thirteen defeats. I'm still the league's scoring leader with 13 goals and 17 assists but the team's situation is a bad dream.

I'm about to do something to change that dream a little, but I know it will do nothing for my warm relationship with Andy Jackson.

Today's practice is optional but Brooker, who played Sunday although his side still hurts a little, Jimmy Miller and I plus a few others are there. I skip most optionals because a day off isn't a bad idea, but I go often to the rink and work in the training room on the bike and weights plus a sauna.

In New Jersey last week, Jimmy hinted he'd be interested in some help. He was very unhappy when he joined me for breakfast the morning after the Islanders game and told me he couldn't sleep for thinking about the mistakes he made.

"Jim, you played pretty well. Holding the Islanders to three goals was a fair effort."

"Yeah, not bad but I wish they'd send me back to junior."

From any player that would have been a surprising admission; from Jimmy it was a shock.

"Why do you feel that way?"

"I'm learning nothing except how to lose. I see now what I need to be a good NHL player. Maybe in junior I could work on those things. Jackson isn't on my back but he never teaches me anything. All he ever says is: 'Kid, just play your game offensively and don't worry about defense.'"

"How about extra time with Brooker and me? Maybe we could help a little."

"Would you do that?"

"Monday will be an optional and we'll be there," I said. "The coach might not be happy about it, though."

"I'll tell him we're trying to be a better line," Jimmy said.

Jackson runs the optional with nine players. It's mostly three-on-nothing rushes. When he leaves, Jimmy, Brooker, Sven, Lester, Pete The Cheat and I stay on with Marc-Luc, who wants extra work. Brooker and I discuss the instruction.

"He's weakest in his own zone but we won't touch that," I say. "He needs offensive confidence first. He's always been a big scorer and he's not getting many points."

"He's best at free-form stuff but he has to learn some discipline, too," Brooker adds.

We decide that to help him get confidence, we should emphasize what he does well. He's a good passer and we can help him use that skill better by trying to get him to think the game better, so we'll set up a few situations and see how he reacts to them.

Brooker is the professor, a natural teacher. Using Lester, Sven and Pete as opposition, he creates defensive situations and has Jimmy problem-solve them. We run through the plays slowly, then quiz Jimmy on what he should do and why.

"Jimmy, you often hit the line and fade towards the middle," Brooker says, skating the path. "Willie looks after the middle and if you're there, too, it means we're using only half the ice. For a few plays, stay wide."

Our line goes against the defense pair with Pete as Jimmy's checker. Pete crowds him and Jimmy's frustration shows. When his lane is jammed, he eases up.

Short talk by me: "Jim, when your space is reduced, dig in! Don't ease up. Go wide, cut inside, do anything to shake the check. You're quick and smart. What's Pete's weak point?"

"He doesn't turn quick."

"How can you use that?"

"Speed up and make him turn."

Jimmy bursts at the line and leaves Pete cross-legged a few times.

"Jimmy, you wave the white flag when things get clogged up in front of you and I'll boot your tail," Brooker says. "Daylight isn't always available. You have to turn it on yourself."

Jimmy is reluctant to go into the corners, nervous about being hit by bigger, stronger players.

"Little chum, we'd all love it if there was no corners or boards where guys can shit-kick you," Brooker says. "You ain't big enough to go in and kick ass but you can use the corners without gettin' killed. You got super radar to avoid bein' belted. If you can learn to set up in the corners and along the boards behind the net, you'll be murder."

We set up situations where Jimmy has the puck in the pits and show him positioning to avoid hits.

"Sometimes, you gotta take a hit to make a play," I tell him. "It takes balls but if a guy commits himself on you, he's leaving room for us. Don't get rid of it until you can do something constructive with it. You're great at slipping hits. Use it."

Brooker uses "hamburger drills," moving on Jimmy and telling him to hold or pass the puck to either Pete or me, who then try to get open against Sven and Lester.

"Too soon. Hold it a little longer," Brooker says once. "Good play," the next time when he is on top of Jimmy before he passes.

At one point, I see Jackson standing at the end of the rink, so we quietly wind down the practice.

"Thanks, guys, I see some things clearly now," Jimmy says. "Can we do it again tomorrow?"

"Sure, for a few minutes," I say. "But remember, we have a game next night."

November 11

Our main workout today is tough. After a load of line rushes and a long power-play drill with no instruction except curses, Jackson gives us a big skating load. When the coaches depart, only a few players head for the room. Jimmy, Brooker and I plan a short time on the same stuff we did yesterday.

Brooker and I are sitting on the boards by the bench, waiting for the ice to clear, when Jimmy, Sven, Lester, Baby-Joel, Pierre, Anders, Ilko, Firpo, Henry and Pete gather around us.

"You doin' somethin' with Jimmy?" Baby-Joel asks.

"Just our line tryin' some things," Brooker says.

"Jimmy says you taught him good stuff yesterday," Joel says. "Mind if we stick around?"

I look at Brooker, who shrugs. "Sure, but it's no big deal. What are you expecting?"

"Ve like to learn ting 'bout hockey," Anders says. "Ilko and me play like horse's ass and coach Yackson tell us no ting to help play better. You and Villie, Brooker, please tell us vat ve do wrong."

"Gonna be trouble, bubba," Brooker says. "But how can he get sore because we want to work?"

"He'll find a way," I say. "Remember, you're volunteers. What should we work on?"

"We ain't won a fuckin' game so there should be somethin' we can do better," Baby-Joel says and everyone laughs. "I can't pass the puck worth a shit. Can somebody help me?"

"Sven, give Joel and Pierre passing drills to a moving forward. A little technique, too, if you like," Brooker says. "The forwards come with Willie, me and Lester.

It's lively and, after an hour, the players moan when we end it. We show the Europeans about NHL play in the attacking zone, positioning, movement and funneling play to the net.

"Dis can't be real practice," Anders says at one point. "Nobody call me stupid Svedish azz-hole."

Jackson and Sparks are in the exit near the team's offices on the second level and it's no surprise when Harry Tatum says the coach wants me upstairs.

In the room the players show the most life in weeks, laughing and telling each other ideas on how to play. I find Brooker and Firpo, Ilko and Anders, watching a tape, stopping and starting the action.

"Willie showed you this," Brooker points out on the screen. "You crossed well, lots of speed, but you did nothing with the confusion in the defense. You went over the line and tried to cross again. In Europe on the big ice, it works but there's no room here."

"Vat do, Brooker?" Ilko asks.

"Strike on the first cross," Brooker says showing the play again. "When Anders wheels towards the boards and you have the puck in the middle, give it to him there. Anders, turn it on; Ilko, go up the middle towards the net. When the openings come, go like hell for them."

Brooker comes over by the door.

"Jackson wants me upstairs," I say.

"Any idea why?" Brooker smiles.

I nod: "That was the most fun I've had this season."

"Sad part of it is how these kids want to learn. Want me to go with you?"

"Sorry, pal, you weren't invited."

The secretary says the coach is on the phone and will be a minute. Eight minutes later, he hollers: "Get in here, Mulligan!"

"Help yourself to the coffee," he says as he shuffles through some papers. "You know, I've looked everywhere and I can't find where it says William Mulligan is coach of this team. Or Brooker Duncan, either. Tell me what's going on?"

"A few guys stayed out for extra work, nothing other than that."

"I saw two guys, three if I count that Norwegian asshole, doing something that's not their job. I saw three guys coaching this hockey club and unless there's been a big change, that's my job. So what the fuck are you guys doing?"

"I'll tell you exactly," I say, fighting an urge to grab him by the throat. "Jimmy Miller, who plays on a line with Brooker Duncan and myself, asked for some help. Yesterday, we worked on a few plays. Jimmy's seventeen and struggling in big league hockey, so we set up some defensive situations for him to work against. We were going to do it with Jimmy again today, the others stayed, too, and we ran over some basic things. Brooker's been a pro for fourteen years and he knows a little about the game. I like to think I've learned a couple of things, too. If we can pass it along, what's wrong with that?"

"What in hell's wrong is that you're trying to undermine my position and Sammy's, too. A few tips? Bullshit. That was a full-scale practice. I'm surprised genius Laidlaw wasn't there, too."

"Coach, I can't believe this. We've lost thirteen games and either anything that might help is my concern or I've got a warped outlook. No one is trying to undermine your job."

"Well, you coulda fooled me," he says. "I saw three guys doing the coach's job. Think I don't have a plan for this team?

I know how to help Miller develop his talent and you and that jerk Duncan can screw him up. Miller has great natural ability and you don't mess with that. You just let him play any way he wants. I almost puked when I saw Duncan with the kid in the corners."

There's nothing to say. I sip my coffee and stare at the wall.

"Since you have no more revelations, here's how it is," Jackson says. "The coaching career of Mulligan, Duncan and Stinquist is over. No more of that shit I saw the past two days. That's all there is to it.

"I run this team, Sammy is my assistant and if there's any coaching to be done, we'll do it. One of us will stay on the ice until everyone is off. Is that understood? Any questions?"

I just shake my head.

November 17

The Big Green's public relations man, Beady Bascom, thinks he has a brilliant idea today. I can't decide if it is or not.

Beating the drums for a team that has lost all sixteen games must be a barrel of chuckles, although we receive considerable attention. Every week, writers and television crews cover our futility.

After a 7-4 loss to the Calgary Flames last night, Beady asks if he can see me soon. I plan to skip the optional but I tell him he can buy me lunch.

Brooker and I had a difficult time explaining the end of the instructional sessions to the kids. Jimmy came up to me the day after Jackson's veto and said: "How about breakout plays from our zone next?"

When I told him he couldn't do that any more, he looked stunned.

"Willie, what are you saying? I learned so much and guys are really happy to be getting some help."

"Sorry, Brooker and I can't do it."

Jimmy told Baby-Joel, who told Pierre, who told the Europeans and they gathered in front of us.

"Villie, dat true you tell Yimmy?" Anders said. "You can't work on us no more?"

"That's right, Anders. It's just not possible."

"Why not, Willie?" Baby-Joel said. "At least give us a reason."

"Tell 'em straight, bubba," Brooker shrugged.

"Okay, but don't broadcast it. Coach Jackson has ordered Brooker and me to stop trying to coach the team. I'm sorry, but that's it."

They all looked as if they were going to cry.

"Brooker, maybe ve vork with wideotape, hey?" Anders said. "Dat help ven you show us ting."

Brooker just shook his head: "That's out, too. I went to check the tape from the last game and the machine had a padlock on it. You need the coach's permission to use it."

"Let's rent the little rink in the evenings for some work-outs," Jimmy suggests. "We'll pay if you guys will come."

"Guys, understand our situation, please," I said. "We've been ordered not to coach you. We'll pass along what we can but if we sneak sessions, there will be hell to pay."

"How be I have my brothers come down, dig a big ditch and put that stupid bastard Jackson in it?" Baby-Joel offers.

"He's the coach so we do what he says."

"That's great, Brooker," Jimmy said, "except the fuckin' airhead never tells us anything."

The gloom was thick enough to slice for a few days. Anders told me the one thing preventing Ilko's leaving for home is a girl, a Finnish nursing student Doc Stanley discovered at the hospital.

But the lads' spirits were lifted by a party in Detroit the night before a game. Jimmy phoned some junior groupies he knows in Windsor and they crossed the river for a mingle with our youth corps. If nothing else, those kids have learned the best way to handle a downer.

Our workouts now have an unusual feature: Either Jackson or Sparks stays on the ice until the last player is off. That doesn't take long because the players can't get off fast enough since Jackson squelched our sessions.

"You'd think the coaches was afraid we was goin' to pound our pudding after practice," Baby-Joel says.

I have a sauna, hoist weights, ride the bike and drink coffee with Harry Tatum this morning before I see Beady.

"Being our PR man must be like trying to hype the Germans late in the war," I say.

"Creating publicity for the team is not the easiest task," he admits. "But the negative aspects are attracting attention. Our game Wednesday has attracted a large contingent of out-of-town reporters."

"And a small group of in-town spectators," I add.

"Our attendance shows a promising trend. There's a solid increase in the average for eight home games. The team plays entertaining hockey and our fan feedback is producing a positive feeling about the product."

"It must be tough to find a positive base to market us, though."

"It would be easier if the club had won sixteen games," Beady says. "We're attempting to pick the bright spots and the fact you are the leading scorer is a good feature. We're attempting to maximize your excellent play in our marketing program. That's what I want to talk to you about today.

"The players have made appearances and are very popular in the community," Beady drones. "We have requests from charities for our players to be involved and I will call on you for help in that area."

"I prefer to pick one charity and get involved on some sort of meaningful basis," I say. "I've never liked those drop-in-for-five-minutes sort of things."

"Any preferences?"

"In Montreal, I worked with the association for the mentally retarded on fund-raising and floor hockey programs."

"That association would like to have a player involved and I'll notify them of your interest," he says. "But there are some specialized promotions in which I would like to use you."

"What sort of promotions?"

"Well, one might not be agreeable to you and if it isn't, I'll abandon it. But because you are our highest-profile player and a bachelor, I would have a contest in which a female fan would win a date with you, perhaps dinner and a show."

I smile, then laugh: "You took me by surprise. What sort of contest? Maybe the winner could receive a big cake and I'll pop out of it in a loin cloth."

Beady doesn't laugh: "Only the very best of taste. Fans would submit a letter of fifty words or less on why they would like to have a date with you. We would select ten finalists and you would pick the winner."

"What will you call it?" I ask.

"A simple 'Win A Date With Willie!' We'll work with the radio station that carries our games. It has a very big rating among young people. Can I go ahead?"

"Sure, why not?"

Hartley says he's angry it's not him. "Beady has no imagination," he says. "Large numbers of drooling women would fulfill their ultimate fantasy if they could spend a few minutes with me."

"Maybe Beady will have a contest in which the winning couple has dinner with the charming Mr. and Mrs. Laidlaw," I say. "But if you're going into a jealous sulk about it, I'll suggest a 'Win A Hump From Hartley' contest."

"The other guys will want to be in on it, too," he says. "Next would come 'A Bang From Brooker.'"

"How about 'A Roll With Baby-Joel'?" Or 'Show Your Pair To Pierre Lambert.'"

"I can see 'A Maul From Miller' grabbing the teenagers."

"And there's always 'A Fiddle From Firpo.'"

"I've got it, the ultimate contest," he says. "Why not 'The World's End With Sven,' because that's what it would be?"

November 21

Making history has its drawbacks and I hope Lenin, Napoleon and Benedict Arnold had less trouble than the Big Green. At least we picked a good place to do it—Washington, D.C. Or rather, Landover, Maryland, where the Washington Capitals play home games.

No group ever worked harder to avoid making history because losing eighteen consecutive matches is not really a high. When the Caps beat us, 3-2, they shake our hands because that team held the record of seventeen.

Our visit is a major media event, which means it's attended by more writers and broadcasters than there are athletes in the game. When we arrived in the Maryland suburbs yesterday, the hotel was lousy with reporters and a TV camera was set up to film us getting off the bus.

"Should get free rooms because of all the business we bring this dump," Pete McFatridge declared.

"Cheap-turd reporters probably all sleep in their cars," Jackson snorted.

I figure The Cheat may feel justified in hiding a bed in his bag, then telling them something's wrong with his room.

"That TV crew figures we'll fall out of the bus," Hartley said. "Turn your collars up, walk backwards down the steps and go to the other side of the bus."

Pete Edmunds and the coaches were already off when we took Hartley's suggestion. About half uproarious was all it was. I saw us later on the news, coming off the bus backwards, collars up and shoulders hunched, then slinking to the other side. When the reporters moved to that side, we ran to the other side. Even Jackson was laughing. The third time around, I hollered: "Stop and wave your hankies," and twenty guys stood beside a dopey bus, waving white hankies on the national news.

At least ten reporters shook hands and said: "You have a few minutes?" I knew I wouldn't have any peace for the entire evening and Hartley knew a place "where the food and other things make a fella forget he's a loser," so I suggested a group interview in the lobby in twenty minutes.

Hartley was reluctant to be interviewed. "On my way to the gallows, I don't want a guy with a mike asking: 'What's it like out there?' If I wasn't playing half-assed, we wouldn't be in this spot. You can make it funny; I can't."

"I don't know how else to handle it," I said. "This is the most depressing time in my life because it's so hopeless. I almost wish I wasn't leading the NHL because that just attracts attention."

"I'm declining interviews for a while," Hartley said. "The question is always the same: 'If you had known this would happen, would you have led the strike?' If I don't pop some nerd who asks me that it will be a miracle."

After the press conference, where I'm at my wise-ass best, Hartley, Brooker and I went to dinner. Sven was in Washington to break bread with the Norwegian ambassador. Later, Brooker went back to the hotel and we adjourned to the bar, where a jazz trio was making nifty sounds.

The place was well-populated with ladies and two of the finest were at the bar when we pulled up a chunk of rail. They were chatting with Tim Watson, the Toronto writer who's Hartley's long-time enemy.

"Hi, Willie, great interview," Watson said.

"Hello, Timothy, how's life? Glad to help out other tax-payers."

"How are you doing, Tim?" Hartley said, shaking hands. Watson looked like he was in shock. "First-rate piece when we were in Toronto. It must have busted your heart when Jackson booted you from his life and our room."

"Hartley, I appreciate the compliment," Watson replied. "When Jackson told me, I said it's like getting kicked out of the Book-Of-The-Month-Club."

Watson introduced us to his friends and I figured I'd lost my pal for the evening. He needed at least ninety seconds to cut the splendid third wheel out of a small herd. When I was excluded from that conversation, I checked to see if anyone would like to hear about my Jerseys and sure enough, on a nearby bar stool, was a well-assembled young lady.

I smiled, she smiled, and I edged over to deliver a terrific opener: "Do you know the name of that last song? I just can't think of it."

She smiled again: "I'm sure it's 'Our Love Is Here To Stay.' Do you think it is?"

"Do I think that's the song or that our love is here to stay?"

"This is an original approach. I'm Ellen, you're Willie."

"How did you know that?"

"Your friend called you that, you responded to it, so I assumed it was your name."

When I got back to the hotel from Ellen's apartment at one a.m., Hartley wasn't there, rare for him on the night before a game. At 6:30, he's sleeping away.

I'm behind a newspaper at breakfast in the coffee shop when a voice says: "Mind if I sit down and join you?"

"Tim, since you're sitting down, why don't you join me?"

"Make a new friend last evening?" Watson asks. I nod. "Explain something. Hartley ignored me for four years, now we're buddies like before I wrote that silly little dress designer quip. He's a puzzling man but I almost croaked when he talked to me last night."

"I don't try to figure him out," I say. "I play him where he lies. Could be that a spare major leaguer was with you."

"Cripes, he bowled her over in record time," he says. "Ol' Hartley is the best operator I've ever seen, bar none. Of course, it helps when you're that good looking. And who wears clothes like him? When he zeroed in on Chris, I thought she'd be down to the laundry, standing at the bar. We had a great conversation so it couldn't have been just her. He even told me a few things. In fact, I wrote a piece for today's paper."

Watson hands me a printout from his computer terminal. Hartley, indeed, had a dandy chat with Watson. The story is only stronger than Baby-Joel's underwear.

In it Hartley rips the NHL for the "retarded" protected lists of the Big Green's expansion draft, for rushing teenage players into the big league hockey and ruining the junior leagues, for not cracking down on "goon garbage," especially the use of sticks, for not pushing the officials to enforce the rules and for not using free agency.

He zings the Leafs for staying mediocre because of front office "chaos" and for giving up too soon on draft choices.

There's a dilly of a quote: "It was discouraging to see a Leaf Stanley Cup roster, all with other teams."

On stickwork in the NHL, he says: "Two years ago, a recurring dream, night after night, haunted me. I'd get cross-checked from behind and spend the rest of my life with a heavy cast on my shoulders and neck. I woke up in a sweat many times about that one."

Hartley says the sixteen losses are "an embarrassment to me and they should be to the NHL." He admits that he hasn't contributed much to the Green and can't explain his ordinary play.

"I'm not motivated the way Willie Mulligan is," Hartley's quote says. "He's playing the game better than anyone I've seen in years."

He doesn't ignore Jackson. "We have five teenage players who are being taught absolutely nothing by our coaches. A couple of veterans tried some teaching sessions for the kids and Jackson stopped them. We're back in 1928 and if he orders us to wear bearskins, carry spears and appear on the ice, dragging females by the hair, I won't be surprised."

I shake my head: "Tim, I'm not questioning your integrity but did Hartley know you'd quote him when he said these things."

"I don't blame you for asking, Willie, because it's the strongest stuff I've ever had an athlete tell me. But it was on the record and he even checked over the quotes. It's not as bad as he says is it? Hartley seems as frustrated as a guy can get. He told me, off the record, that if it doesn't change, he'll think seriously of getting out."

"It is that bad," I say. "But don't quote me on that. I've got enough problems."

Jackson's pre-game speech is another beauty.

"I have no magic to make it all better for this team," he says. "I've done all I can and I have no more answers. It's up to you to show your balls ain't the size of pinheads. If you have any pride, you'll play the game of your lives. Go out there and stick the assholes."

"So the dumb bastard doesn't have the answers. He doesn't even have the questions," Hartley says when Jackson leaves.

"Some people had a few of both last night," I say. "Interesting interview with Watson."

"Timmy showed you, eh?" he smiles. "What did you think?"

"Oh, it's 'Timmy' now; three weeks ago, it's 'that asshole.' Was it necessary?"

"William, some things had to be said and he's the best outlet. I can't sit still and allow my life and these kids' to be wrecked. We can't tell the Andersons to jump this jerk so maybe that story will sow a seed. Sure, I'm vulnerable and open to criticism because I'm playing so horseshit. But I don't care about that."

"Man, it's your business but won't Jennifer Brown be a tad pissed off that you didn't bare your soul to her?"

"Well, I thought about that. But she has to live with this team. If she wrote that story, this outfit would treat her like a disease."

The Caps, a fast, aggressive team, wind the pace as high as possible. We hang in pretty well and it's fine hockey, solid hits but few penalties, good offense and superior goaltending, especially by Henry.

After a dreadful sulk, Jimmy is alive again, using the corners and the ends of the rink effectively under Brooker's in-private instructions. On our first goal, he sets up in the corner and waits, and waits, until a Cap defenseman moves on him, then calmly slips the puck to me.

Jimmy's play in our zone needs work and he costs us the tying goal by exiting too soon. Sven has to eat the puck but it's pokechecked away from him.

The Caps go ahead in the second but Brooker ties it, tipping in a bang-bang relay from Jimmy and me.

In the third, I have seven shots on goal, enough to win it

by myself. But the Cap goalie stones me three times and stops Hartley on a breakaway.

Really, I cost us the game. Halfway through the period, I'm busting my butt to overtake the Cap center in the neutral zone. When I hook his stick to shake the puck loose, he does a magnificent dive. The ref, our old pal Bill Mathews, calls me for a trip.

"He dove like a duck, Bill," I complain. "I only touched his stick."

"Sure, sure, and I'm Charlie Chan," he says.

Hartley and Ilko, Sven and Lester almost kill it off, but with fifteen seconds to serve, a slap shot from the line hits a stick and goes in our net.

I play every second shift in the last ten minutes and while we place some pressure on the Caps, we go into the history books with eighteen consecutive losses.

The room is like a morgue. Henry has his helmet and mask on, smoking a weed through the wires. I walk to the center of the room: "I apologize for taking a dumb-ass penalty. You deserved a win and because of me, you didn't get it."

A glove whistles past my head. "Sit down, you dumb farmer shit-head," Lester says. "No one sucker gonna take credit for our record, eh, lads?"

Gloves fly at me from all corners of the room.

November 25

I'm alone and lonely in my luxury condo. Hartley calls from Fort Worth, Texas, to say he was only four over par this afternoon. He's been there since Sunday with the Fort Worth Texans of the Central Hockey League and he scored four goals last night in his first ever game in the minors.

He seems thrilled to learn there's a hockey team that has fun playing the game.

Sunday morning, the phone rang when we were getting dressed to prepare for the New York Rangers.

"Mulligan, gimme Laidlaw," Peter Edmunds said.

Hartley didn't say much: "Peter, what can I do for you?... I what?...Cleared waivers. Right....To Dallas. At two o'clock.... First class or steerage?... Tied to the fucking wing.... Peter, my attitude hasn't changed in twenty-eight years; don't hold your breath.... Good luck to you, too."

The look on his face was one of relief: "Guess what? I cleared NHL waivers and I'm off to Fort Worth this afternoon."

"Some joke! We're going to be late."

"You'll be late," he corrected. "Our GM has assigned me to Fort Worth until my attitude changes or hell freezes over, whichever comes first."

I was in a state of semi-shock: "You couldn't clear NHL waivers. You'll refuse to report. I'll get Walter Enright and we'll blow the lid off this mess."

"Simmer down, old pal. A ticket to Dallas is at the airport with my name on it."

"Are you nuts? This is a Catch-22. It really isn't happening."

"William, have a coffee," he said, motioning for me to calm down. "Peter says I'm a negative factor on the team and the Toronto story was the last straw. I was placed on waivers to twenty-three NHL clubs and no claim was made. We know why. Thus, I'm assigned for an indefinite period to the farm. I have two choices: go or not. In the latter case, I'm suspended without pay and I will never see Fort Worth and all the other spas in the CHL. Peter also tried unsuccessfuly to suspend me for conduct detrimental to the team and the game, I presume for the Watson yarn."

"You won't go, of course."

"Of course, I'll go. Of course. I need this year and the next on this contract for my investments and the loan Diane has for the stores. I don't care where I earn the money. Ah, the benefits of the one-way contract! They can't cut my salary and I have no NHL bonuses. I have no family to move. I'll pack two suitcases; Edmunds is sending my skates and equipment by cab."

I could only sit there, speechless.

"Look, Willie, this cartoon has screwed up my head and that I allowed it to happen really bugs me. Just looking at

Jackson almost makes me (a) puke and (b) cry. I need a change of scenery to sort myself out."

"At least you'll be on a winner."

"Glad you mentioned it. I know nothing about the Fort Worth team. How is the team doing and who is the GM and coach?"

"The coach is a young guy named Dave Berman, out of Tier Two junior in Alberta. He was at camp—a tall, skinny guy, but Jackson never had him on the ice with us. They don't have a GM because Edmunds runs things from here. The Texans have fourteen wins and two ties in their first twenty games and are leading the league. Harry Tatum talks to the trainer there and he says Berman is a really fine coach."

"Is there anyone on the team I know?"

"Don't you pay any attention to the wonderful world of hockey? Barf Badgly and Red-Light Regan are the goalies, which should be fun. Quite a few expansion draftees are there —J-P Marcotte, George Johnson, Rejean Labroche, Hector Ankorn on defense; Rene Racine, Guy Lacombe, Jimmy Sanders and Shorty Long up front. And, to conduct a tour of America's fleshpots, the lovely Al (Red) Barnes plus some kids."

"I'll fit right in," he said. "Gotta make tracks. Keep the home fires burning. I should be back soon."

At the rink, Jackson made a speech: "Fellows, Hartley Laidlaw won't be with us for a while. He's having trouble getting his game together and asked if he could go to Fort Worth to try to get things going. We agreed and he left today. Now, it's a big loss but if he gets rolling, it will help us in the long haul. Firpo will take his spot with Li and McFatridge."

When Jackson left, everyone talked at once. Brooker spoke up the loudest: "Load of shit, ain't it? No way that dude goin' to ask for the sticks."

"Edmunds called this morning and told him he had cleared waivers."

"I'm surprised he didn't quit and start bein' a lawyer," Brooker added. "How did he take it?"

"Brook, he was relieved. He says he needs a change of scene or he's going to go nuts."

"You think he gave that story to force 'em to do somethin'?"

"I wonder. He told me some things had to be said and it was the time to do it."

The players crowded around me.

"They whipped a big ass to keep the little ones in line," Lester remarked. "Jim Sanders, who's leadin' that league, is happy as hell there and hopes he don't get called up here. Says that young Berman's a fine coach. Maybe when Hart comes back he'll bring that coach with him. Jimmy says the town's heavy on '46 Fords, too, so Hart ain't goin' to be lonely."

Brooker left me with a thought that hadn't occurred to me. "Now Hartley's gone, you gonna get the shit checked out of you. They had to pay some attention to him."

The Rangers assign their best offensive center to me. Wally Merizzi, a big, fast guy, has remarkable quickness for a man his size. He seldom fouls his check but stays between the victim and where he wants to go.

On the opening faceoff before a crowd of 12,000 to see the champs, I say to him: "Wally, go bother someone else and leave a poor kid trying to make a living alone."

"If there's anyone else worth covering, point him out and I'll switch," he smiles.

When I think I've lost him in our zone, I cross center and he's cruising beside me. He talks more than any player I know. "Willie, you little sneak, don't leave me alone."

"I'll give you the phone numbers for two '48 Mercs if you'll go away, Wally." I reply. He was Lester's mate last season.

"Jimmy, you and Brooker go in there like hell, get it and set up," I say. "I'll hang out and try to shake him for a move on the net."

There's a flaw in my idea. The Ranger breakouts are

gorgeous because their defensemen, especially my Soviet pal Valeri Dinkov, move the puck so well. Ol' Val saves himself the bother of a pass by lugging it himself. Often, when we're on our way in, he's on the way out with the puck.

Dinkov creates two goals and they're a joy to behold. On the first, he works a give-go-get around Baby-Joel and scores himself. Then his pass from behind the goal-line hits his comrade, Sergei Pukov, right at center for a breakaway.

Jimmy, using the corners better all the time, feeds Brooker for our first goal in the second. I'm forty feet away, Merizzi at my elbow.

Anders and Ilko are trying to combine circles and straight lines. They produce the tying goal with a cross in the neutral zone and a quick pass to Anders for a dance around a defense-man.

We actually get the lead five minutes into the third, my eighteenth of the season. Jimmy works the puck in and has it in the corner while I'm wrestling with Merizzi in front. The contest is strength, not guile, and I push Wally towards the net when Dinkov forces Jimmy to pass. I shove my stick between Merizzi's leg and deflect it into the net.

"Willie, you do that again I'm going to be all pissed off at you," Merizzi smiles.

The Rangers have a quality we had with the Canadiens: the ability to score goals in bunches. They bag three in two minutes for a 5-3 win.

The writers crowd around Jackson, who holds his press chat in the dressing room, not out in the hall like normal coaches. Of course, the first question is about Hartley.

"I'll make one statement about Mr. Laidlaw," he snarls. "He asked to be sent to Fort Worth because his game wasn't together and he wants to play a great deal and sort himself out."

"Mr. Laidlaw says he was assigned to Fort Worth by the team and did not request it," Jennifer Brown counters.

"Are you calling me a liar, Mrs. Brown?"

"No, just telling you what Hartley told me at the airport today."

"Well, that's interesting," Jackson says. "Your puzzle is which one of us to believe. In your case, I know goddam well the one it will be."

"Did the Toronto newspaper story have any influence on the fact that he's in Fort Worth?" a New York guy asks.

"What could have been in a paper that would inspire Laidlaw to ask for a demotion?"

"How long will he be there, Andy?" Hap Lonsdale asks.

"Hap, that will be up to Mr. Laidlaw. He'll be back when he can be a fully productive member of the Big Green."

Jennifer sits in Hartley's spot between Brooker and me. "Our Andy is wonderful, isn't he?"

"You saw Hartley at the airport?"

"He called to tell me about his request to be sent to Fort Worth and I met him there," she smiles. "I can't get over how peaceful he was."

"Incredible how he reacted," I say. "He claims he's all screwed up and time away will help. What did Edmunds say about it?"

"The same words as Hitler's Kid," Jennifer says. "You think there's any chance Null and Void got together on what they would say?"

"What an awful thing to suggest about our leaders."

Edmunds is talking with some people near the wives' room and he turns his back when he spots me, but I wait at the bottom of the ramp, the route he takes to his office.

"Willie, great effort the past couple of games," he says as he tries to walk quickly past me.

"Hold on. What's the story on Hartley, Pete?"

"What story, Willie? He's gone to Fort Worth to get himself straightened out."

"Straightened out where, on or off the ice?"

"What are you driving at? He just hasn't been the player we thought we had and maybe a change will get him rolling."

"Peter, why are you saying he asked to be demoted? Can't you be honest about it? You know he will be."

"Willie, we do what's best for the team," Edmunds says. "Besides, if he can tell lies in the papers, then why can't we?"

"Is what he said about the coach lies?"

"Come on, Willie, Andy isn't bad. But that's not the issue. Laidlaw has no right to sound off in public. Who the hell does he think he is? Do you think Andy Jackson is as bad a coach as Laidlaw seems to?"

"No, he's worse. In fact, he's the worst. When are you going to do something? It gets more hopeless by the day. Our kids are slipping backwards."

"That makes horse racing, old pal," Edmunds says. "We think the club is making good progress, especially the young guys. With a break we would have won the past two games. Look at the way Andy has Jimmy Miller working the corners. And Anders and Ilko are getting the hang of NHL hockey. See how they set up that goal tonight? Motion outside the line, then a move to take advantage of it."

I find it hard to resist grabbing ol' Pete by the throat. There's a rage growing by the second. "Jackson had fuck all to do with the kids learning those things, and you know it. What you just talked about—Jimmy in the corners and the Europeans moving in straight lines—is all stuff Brooker and I taught them in those two little sessions before Jackson went berserk."

"Willie, you must be cracking up," Edmunds oozes. "Trying to take credit for improvement in the play of our young players? Good heavens, man!"

"Peter, what the hell is going on? Not long ago we talked about the hard time Jackson was giving you and the lousy job he's doing?"

"You are going daffy," he says. "I don't remember any talk like that."

Hartley and I talk for a half hour tonight and I tell him about the chat with the GM. Hartley fills in some of the details in the Edmunds-Jackson saga as he's heard them from one of the scouts.

Apparently, Edmunds tried hard to dump the coach but Clive Eye-Vee and Clive-Five blocked it strongly so he changed his tune. The Andersons told him that the GM's job was in jeopardy, not the coach's, and Edmunds figured if he couldn't fight him, he'd join him. The scout reported that Jackson was trying to convince the Andersons that he should handle both jobs.

"So what's this golf stuff?" I say.

"Quite a few guys play every day here. I haven't bought cowboy boots yet, but I had chicken fried steak and it was great."

"You got four?"

"Yep, got four against Salt Lake Golden Eagles and we won, 8-2," he says. "I'm on a line with Shorty Long and a pepsi kid, Alain Houle, a tenth-round draft pick. The team isn't too fast but it has experience and discipline."

"Anyone there who could help us?"

"I don't know yet. Jim Sanders is going well but he's twenty-nine and has failed with two NHL clubs. He's smart and that works in a young league. Some kids—Houle, who's twenty—and maybe three others have potential.

"One guy who would work wonders in Cleveland is the coach, Dave Berman. Remember that name! He's going places and it's a big surprise Edmunds ever hired him. He's only thirty-two but he seems to know the game inside out. He's spent a fortune going to every coaching clinic he could find. He'd scouted Salt Lake's game in Dallas Saturday and had a written report on them. He bought a videotape unit himself and uses it as a teaching aid.

"Runs the best workout I've seen in years, creative and organized. Kept some kids out and worked on specific skills. He asked me to help two young centers on faceoffs. Then we had lunch and talked hockey for three hours. He wants me to tell him and the kids anything that will help."

"It sounds like heaven. Any '46 Fords around?"

"I haven't had time to check but Red Barnes, Red-Light, Barf and me are going honky-tonking tonight. This is country music country."

"I tried to call Diane to offer my condolence, but no answer."

"She's in Paris on a buying trip," he says. "I got her today.

Talk about equality. She's in Paris; I'm in Fort Worth."

"How long you going to be there?"

"No idea," he replies. "We've got a road trip to Wichita, Oklahoma City, Indianapolis and Salt Lake and I'll be a Texan through that, at least. By then, I might be the same as most guys here. They're worried they'll be called up to the Green because they know what a zoo it is. They don't want Jackson and all the bullshit when they can play for an adult like Dave Berman. They're happy here."

"You guys should learn that happiness isn't everything," I say. "Get your ass back here."

"You know they want me to call with my hat in my hand, apologize for being naughty and promise to be a good boy," he says. "My attitude seems to be consistent. Fuck 'em. My best to all and tell Midnight to get sent down because I need a caddy."

I'm at loose ends, trying to figure out what to do with myself. I've started my college courses but I can't settle down to study tonight. The telephone rings and it's like an air hammer.

"Willie, it's Darlene," the now familiar voice says.

"Hey, what's doing?"

"I just landed. Is your roomie around?"

"No, he's not, Darlene. He's in Fort Worth for a few games. It's a long, complicated story."

"Why don't you tell it to me?" she says. "Like to get together for a drink or something?"

"Terrific idea! Want to come here?"

"Terrific idea, too. I'll be there in a half hour. One more thing, Willie! I have an early flight so could we have coffee early in the morning?"

"I'll load the pot right now."

Funny thing! We never get around to talking about a guy I used to know named Laidlaw and why he's in Fort Worth.

November 29

The fans in the Montreal Forum applaud and cheer for one minute, forty seconds. A French writer always times such things. The ovation is for me when I'm introduced for tonight's game against the Canadiens and the tears show when they holler "Will-ee, Will-ee," the way they did a few times when I stood on that other blueline.

My return receives a large amount of publicity and the French papers, with several hockey pages, and the one English daily have big Mulligan yarns today. That I lead Gaston Beaupre by two points in the NHL scoring race is a big deal.

But I don't quite return in triumph. Twenty-one consecutive defeats hardly merit a parade.

I took Gaston and his wife to St. Amable last night for dinner.

Gaston and I have a special relationship—draft picks the same year, a season in Halifax and the same boarding house, then a spot with the big club and, as rookies, linemates on spot duty. The only time we were not together in six years was when he had a knee injury. I was best man when he married the luscious Giselle, and I'm a god-parent to their son, Jean-Guy. We were roomies and he helped me speak French with some proficiency while I polished his English.

We had several right wingers for two years until the club drafted Real Ladouceur, a cocky kid from Chicoutimi and the fastest skater in the NHL. Alfie Brisebois placed Real with us and it was, as Alfie said, "de marriage made in de heaven."

Alfie never knew the trouble we had with Real on and off the ice at first. He thought every woman was in love with him, and he kept going offside because he said we didn't get the puck to him fast enough. He had no idea how quick he was.

"Willie, my man misses you dreadfully on the ice but more as a friend," Giselle said at dinner.

"It's just a bad dream, Giselle. I keep thinking I'll wake up in a Canadiens' sweater, Gaston will burst in and yell 'Willie' and we'll ride down Ste. Catherine on a nice day in May with the Stanley Cup. It's funny how close you get to people in this game. For five years, I spent more nights in a bedroom with this bozo than you did."

"On that subject, Gaston tells me of your friend Clarice and how very beautiful she is. Don't tell me you're settling down?"

"I'm closer to thinking about it with Clarice than I ever have before."

"Is it bad to be with a team that hasn't won a game? Gaston hears such bad things."

"It's discouraging even though I knew the team wouldn't be very good," I said. "It's all a bit weird. We didn't get normal, solid citizens. They'll never build a new zoo in Cleveland; they'll just put a high wire fence around our team. Strange things happen."

"What sorts of things?" Gaston asked.

So I told them about my week.

SUNDAY. Hartley goes to the minors where he gets nine goals and four assists in three games. Edmunds tells me he won't be recalled until he apologizes to Andy Jackson for his remarks about the coach and agrees not be interviewed.

TUESDAY. Mar-Luc Radisson is a devotee of science fiction and the occult. When he told me he'd been a Protestant, a Muslim, a Jew and a Catholic, I didn't understand. This week I find out.

Marc-Luc is into reincarnation. He drew a big laugh when he said he understands Baby-Joel Reid well because he was a caveman himself in a previous life.

Tuesday, Marc-Luc limps into the trainers' room and Harry Tatum emerges shaking his head: "I just don't believe it."

"What don't you believe, Harry?" Jackson says.

"Marc-Luc says he has a bad leg. Coach, go hear it yourself or you'll have me committed."

"Marc-Luc, what's wrong?" Jackson says.

"My leg hurt me like son-of-bitch."

"When did you hurt it?"

"About a hundred years ago."

"Don't be an asshole, Radishes (Jackson's nickname for him)," the coach says.

"In another life, I was a soldier in the Civil War and I was shot in the leg," Marc-Luc says seriously. "Every so often, the wound gives me pain. I have one from the Russian Revolution but it never bothers me."

"You crazy little bastard!" Jackson snorts.

"Reincarnation is no joke; it's a serious science," M-L says. "Everyone has had previous lives on earth. What were you when you were here before, coach?"

"If I ever come back to this world, I sure won't be a hockey coach," Jackson says. "Listen, we can't have an injured goalie. Maybe a little stretch in Port Huron will get your leg back in shape."

"Coach, it's not too bad," M-L says. "I'll try it today. Okay?"

"Okay, we'll see how it holds up."

Jackson comes out of the room, shaking his head. "Are there no sane people here?"

"What's the trouble, coach?" Brooker says.

"Loonies! Nothing here but loonies!"

"Hey, Brooker, what were you in your previous lives?" I say.

"The Queen of England and Babe Ruth."

"I hear Jackson was a soldier in the Civil War, too," I say. "But he fought for the west."

WEDNESDAY. For the first time, Jackson is on the ice for our game-day skate against the Quebec Nordiques. He says the team is in lousy condition and something must be done about it.

A game-day skate is a way to get the troops up in the a.m. Some teams don't have them, especially in the second half of the season. But Jackson stages a full-scale workout with line rushes, shots at both goalies (usually the starter doesn't appear) and a full skating drill at the end.

In the game we have our best forty minutes of the season and lead the Nords, 5-2. I have two goals and an assist, Jimmy a pair and Brooker three assists. But late in the second period, there's no life in my legs or anyone else's.

In the third, we're out of juice, although the guys try hard because we feel we can win. But players like me, Jimmy, Sven, Brooker, Lester and Anders, who work a great deal, have nothing left. The Nordiques, who saw our morning ordeal, wind up the pace and in the middle ten minutes they score five goals to win 7-5.

Lester is hurt because he's exhausted on a long shift in the third period. He has the puck in the corner and two Nordiques are on him. He sidesteps the first one but he just has no strength to avoid the second man, who bangs him into the boards on his shoulder. At first, it appears to be a separation, then Doc Stanley says it's a severe bruise and he'll be out at least two weeks.

When Jackson asks about the injury, Lester pops off: "A two-week holiday, thanks to you, Jackson."

"What are you talking about?" Jackson snaps.

"The strength I needed to miss that check I didn't have because I lost it, doin' stops and starts in the mornin', you dumb shit."

"What horseshit!" Jackson says. "You guys blame everyone but yourselves. Tonight's game proves you're not in shape. You had nothing left because you're lazy and out of shape."

"Andy, you can't even add up one and fuckin' one," Lester says. "We ran out of gas because you skated it out of us. A retarded baboon could figure that out."

"I've been too soft," Jackson hisses. "That's over. I'm going to whip asses now."

THURSDAY. Boston is one of my favorite towns but when we charter in, the plane is like a meat-wagon going to the morgue. Brooker says that if Jackson has a heavy workout in the morning, he'll suggest a boycott of it, and I agree to back him up.

Jackson saves us from a confrontation, and Brooker and I spend the morning in Quincy Market and The Common.

The Boston Garden ice surface has a short center zone and the Bruins have big, musular wingers who forecheck your buns off. The building, an old duck-blind, has character and the fans with their New England accents are a delight. I've always gone over well there because a name like mine never hurts a guy in Beantown. An old usher always says to me: "Mulligan, me boy, you were wasted playing anywhere but in Baw-ston."

The Bruins play a simple game at home: Forecheck with the big wingers until you think you're in a phone booth with a gorilla. To have a chance, our wingers must interfere with their's outside the blueline to give our defense time to move the puck. Brooker tells the team that when Jackson doesn't give one word of preparation.

The game is tough, grinding, no-nonsense big league hockey with excellent open-ice hitting. The crowd loves it. Firpo scores in the first, the Bruins tie it in the second, and in the third period close checking heats tempers up a bit. Baby-Joel gets the crowd on his case when he belts Peter O'Leary, the local favorite, of course, into the boards.

Halfway through the period, O'Leary roars into our zone and belts Ilko a clean check. When Ilko get up, he misses a spear at O'Leary, who drops his gloves and goes after the Finn, who's never fought in his life.

Jackson slaps Brooker on the back quickly and says: "Go and look after the kid."

Brooker shakes his head and says: "No way I'm going off the bench."

By then, Baby-Joel is in the middle of it. After O'Leary takes a couple of swings at Ilko, Joel grabs him, spins him around and drills him.

Jackson goes at Brooker again: "You stupid old shit. Get on that ice and help that kid."

"Fuck off, Andy. Joel's got it under control," Brooker says.

The fight is a dandy, if there is such a thing. Joel is bigger than O'Leary but the Bruin is good at it. No clutching or holding, just free swinging, and they each land a dozen good ones. Eventually, Joel's size and strength tip it his way and he has that look of glee on his face.

O'Leary pushes a linesman trying to get at Joel to even the penalties—majors and game misconducts.

Jackson spits at Brooker: "You're finished on this hockey team."

So our best player on the night, Brooker, sits on the bench. He's replaced by Sal Mancino, who immediately gives away the winning goal by passing to a Bruin in the slot when pressured in our zone. They wrap up a 3-1 win into an empty net.

"Duncan, you're suspended," Jackson says in the room. "You refused an order and I can't have that. I know you didn't want to fight O'Leary because you're damned careful with your tough-guy reputation. Tough guy? Shit! I could clean your ass."

"Andy, nothing would be better than to pound you," Brooker says. "But what would it prove? You know you can't suspend me for not leaving the bench. If Baby-Joel hadn't been there, I would have gone. But if I'd listened to you I would have been suspended for nothing. Let's just forget it and we'll save a mess."

"You think I can't suspend you?" Jackson says. "Just fuckin' wait and see."

He storms out and Brooker says to the players: "Guys, don't breath a word of this, especially to the writers. I'm certain they can't suspend me but if they do, there's going to be a big stink. Ilko, if Baby-Joel or someone else hadn't helped you, you know I would've come runnin'."

Brooker and I locate Edmunds.

"Am I suspended?" Brooker says.

"Yes, for refusing a coach's order."

"You know goddam well you can't do it," I say.

"Willie, it's none of your business."

"Pete, can I see you in an hour?" Brooker says. "I want to cool off before I talk about it."

"There's nothing to talk about, Brooker," he says. "But I'll see you, alone, in my room in an hour."

I call Walter Enright, the executive-director of the NHL Players' Association, from the lobby. He promises to call the NHL president right away. He assures us they can't suspend Brooker and that if they try, the association will raise hell.

Brooker and I walk back to the hotel. He's really down. "Can't take much more, bubba. I need the money but this madhouse ain't worth it. I was close to givin' it to Jackson but they would have had a real excuse to do it to me."

Brooker has just left for Edmunds' room when the phone rings. "Willie, Brooker can relax," Enright says. "The president is sore but he's not very wild about anything in Cleveland. If Edmunds and Jackson try to suspend Brooker, he'll suspend and fine them. He said he was calling them immediately."

Brooker is back in five minutes: "Can't believe it. Edmunds gives me a snort of Scotch, cheap junk, by the way, and says let's forget it. Jackson doesn't apologize but says he'd appreciate it if I'd just pretend it never happened. I couldn't get away from those crazy people fast enough."

"And that, dear friends," I said to Gaston and Giselle, "is a week in the life of the wonderful Big Green."

Too bad the cheering ends because it means the game against the Canadiens has to start. They have sixteen wins, three ties and only two losses and are four points in front of the Rangers in overall standings.

Jean-Paul Couteau, a spot center for two seasons, has replaced me between Gaston and Real, the fastest line in the NHL. Jackson uses Ilko, Anders and Sal Mancino, instead of Biff, against them.

Minus Hartley and Lester, our line-up is as shallow as an Andy Jackson smile. The Canadiens always have great ability to "counter-punch," to go from defense to offense in one move. That quickness is murder on our lack of speed and discipline.

The final is 7-2. I have an assist on a power-play goal by Sven, but Gaston has two goals and an assist. When I leave Montreal tonight, I'm tied for the scoring lead with my old chum.

December 1

I miss today's optional after playing thirty-five minutes in four games in five nights. I don't feel at all guilty. After lunch, I'm grappling with the subtleties of vitamin digestion by mature dairy cattle when the phone rings.

"Willie, it's Jennifer Brown. Edmunds made his first trade. Thought you might like to know."

"Terrific. Who did he get for me?"

"No such luck," she says. "Could you evaluate the deal?"

"I would if I knew what it was."

"The Green sends Rollie Regan, Sal Mancino and Harry Li to the Winnipeg Jets for Geoff Peters."

"Peters for Red-Light, Little Sal and Hi Li?" I ponder. "Not a bad trade."

"Tell me about Peters."

"He's about twenty-six. He's from Toronto, played at Northern Michigan U. and was All-American twice. Four years with the Jets, who signed him as a free agent. Solid, defensive type who handles the puck well. He'll help us back there."

"Why would the Jets make the deal?"

"A goalie is hurt and they need an experienced guy," I explain. "Hartley tells me Red-Light is playing super in the CHL. He's the key. The Jets are weak on left wing and Sal has speed and might be able to score a little with a good team. Hi is a throw-in."

"Will Peters be the best defenseman here?"

"No, Sven is playing very well. But Peters will help because he's good defensively. He and Lester, when he's sound, can kill penalties and free Sven for offense."

"How's Hartley?"

"Too happy!" I say. "In four games, he has twelve goals and six assists and he says he's never had more fun playing the game or been to as many country music joints. He and Dave Berman talk hockey for hours. Hartley's a top hockey mind, both technically and on how the NHL works. A young dude like Berman can learn a lot from him."

"When are these nuts going to get him back here."

"They have a funny idea they can teach Hartley some humility or change his attitude down there. They want him to apologize for being a bad boy and beg forgiveness. Well, that won't happen. They'll have to call and beg him to come back. He's got no fuss or bother, which he likes. He plays golf every day, which he loves. And Berman has made him an unofficial assistant coach, working with the kids."

Jen clears her throat and I sense something in the works. "Edmunds had another biggie."

"I shudder to ask."

"On January 6, the Big Green hosts the national team of the Soviet Union at the Coliseum," she says. I start to chuckle, then laugh uproariously.

"What's so funny?" she asks.

"The greatest team in the world," I say. "Migawd, why would Edmunds book a game with them?"

"The Soviets want six games and the NHL could get only five teams to play them—the Islanders, Canadiens, Nordiques, the Oilers and the Winnipeg Jets," she says. "The Rangers wanted them but the Russians refused because of Dinkov and Pukov."

"Maybe when they see us, they'll laugh so hard we can beat them."

It takes me a few minutes to get the smile off my face before I can call Li and Mancino to wish them luck.

"It's a break," Harry says. "I feel sorry for the guys left behind. Willie, it's been an honor to be your mate. Don't know how you keep doing it the way you have."

"Appreciate it, Willie," Little Sal says. "Except for one guy, this coulda been great. You're the best, man, and don't let the bastards grind you down."

December 10

Today, we're checking into the hotel in Vancouver, where, of course, it's raining, when across the lobby comes the sight of the year: Hartley, with Jimmy Sanders.

"The prodigal has returned," he says.

The best part of the handshaking and general jacking

around is Andy Jackson's scowl. "Did we find a cure for cancer or call up a couple of minor leaguers?" he snorts.

"You're the ugliest sum'bitch ever but am I glad to see you," Brooker says, giving Hartley a hug.

"You didn't know we were coming?"

"Are you kidding?" I say. "That would mean telling the troops something they should know."

"Dave Berman called at midnight and we were on a flight from Dallas to Seattle at 8 a.m."

"Bubba, do we need you guys!" Brooker says. "They play Willie any more, he'll be Henry's size."

"Can't be hurting him much," Sanders says. "See you're still leading the old NHL, brother."

I figured when Gaston Beaupre passed me last week, that would be it for me on top. But today, I'm three points in front with 54 points—26 goals and 28 assists in 27 games (all defeats).

Because Lester is still out, Geoff Peters is a good addition, a solid type who fits in well with Sven. He's a jazz nut, splendid because I'm surrounded by country and rock fans.

We have sixteen skaters, one under the limit, for two games. Saturday in Los Angeles, Ilko Mikkolainen stretched a ligament in his knee and went east for treatment, so Jackson moved Pierre Lambert to the wing.

Hartley, Sanders, Brooker, Sven and I move to a bar.

"So, you apologized for all the nasty things you said about the dynamic duo and promised not to be naughty again," Brooker says.

Hartley chuckles: "Yep, three times. I was so humble they didn't believe it was me. Funny, I heard no more about that. I tried to talk to Jackson in the lobby and struck out. He just asked me if I caught a dose down there. How's it been?"

"Our record shows that we only needed to get rid of one troublecauser to turn it around," I say.

"Jackson is in a strange shell," Sven adds. "He seems to have given up completely. He hasn't called me a chickenshit European for ten days. There is an unusual atmosphere because everyone seems to be waiting for a big happening."

"Laidlaw treat you guys okay?" Brooker says to Sanders.

"Brook, he devoured the Central League," Sanders said. "Nineteen goals and 13 assists in ten games. Taught the kids two things they should know: how to win faceoffs and how to impress chicks."

"That guy Berman's good eh?" Brooker says.

"He's the best coach I've had in fifteen years in this game," Sanders declares. "The team's got a batch of sour old pros and kids from well down the draft. The first day after the roster was picked he says: 'It'll be a long winter if we don't do something worthwhile. The easiest way to have a little fun is to win a few hockey games.' He takes no bull but too many coaches don't realize that if you give out no bull, you don't get much back. He's as straight-up as any dude I know. The kids on that team have improved like you can't believe."

"Can he coach up here?" Brooker asks.

"Do ducks go barefoot?"

December 14

The loss string hits thirty tonight, the NHL record of the Winnipeg Jets, who at least had seven ties. A 5-4 loss really hurts because we should have won. The Calgary Flames are ripe to be plucked.

Why should their engines be revved? We haven't won a game, are at the end of an eleven-day road trip and have a long injury list. We're missing Lester and Ilko, Sven, who took a shot on the ankle in Vancouver, and Baby-Joel.

After looking very pale for a week, Joel passed out in the dressing room in Edmonton. He just folded in a pile on the floor and the Oilers' doctors figured it was a virus.

Henry disagreed: "It ain't the flu. He's been draggin' for a month. He wasn't right in Van. Wanted to grab a couple of good-lookin' hooks and he wasn't interested."

Indeed a sign that Baby-Joel is off his feed.

The Reid family took Joel home to Red Deer and will have him in Calgary Monday for the trip east. Edmunds is happy the Red Deer Munsters left town before he had to post bail again.

We face the Flames with fifteen skaters but the guys give a big effort. Hartley hasn't been hurt by his time away. He scored on his first shift in Vancouver and bagged two more in Edmonton. Tonight he's hounding the puck in top form. But mistakes that should have been corrected two months ago cost us the game.

On this trip, I'm fighting hard with my attitude about my situation, the team and its record and, especially, Andy Jackson.

Am I just a bitcher, the same as a grade three student, who automatically sees the teacher as a bad person who makes me do things I don't want to do?

I've been monitoring Jackson all week, looking for any sign that he knows his stuff as a coach. Our two practices were the same as all others — no teaching, no re-creation of trouble situations and no work on specialty teams.

In San Francisco, Brooker and I sat in the sun on Fisherman's Wharf, overlooking the bay, and I presented my conclusions.

"Bubba, I've scrapped with my attitude, too," he said. "For the first time, I play every shift and I have a dozen goals and thirty points, more than in any full season I've played. Maybe I should thank Jackson for using me as a hockey player when others saw me as a goon.

"But, Willie, a coach has such an influence on your life and I can't find one redeeming feature in that man. A half dozen games could've been won if the kids were coached at all or if the vets had any sort of system. Biff Byers asks him about something and Jackson rants that he gave us his system in camp and how many times do we have to be told?"

"I've figured a few times I was cracking up," I confessed. "And not only in wondering if I've made Jackson my personal scapegoat to blame for everything that's wrong. Sometimes I think that if we had a good coach, we'd be a .500 team. Hardly realistic."

"Great minds think alike," Brooker said. "I called Julianne and she started laughin' and said: 'You're a beauty, dear husband. You call long distance to tell me what a jerk Jackson is.' I've blocked him out of my dome since. Julianne says I should redefine my world and see it as you, Jimmy and me on an island. That's helped."

"My only contact with the man who's a big influence on my life is when he tells me to go on the ice."

Brooker grinned. "You talk to him twice as much as I do then. Ah, Willie, aren't you feelin' worn down?"

"I'm feeling good but some nights I don't have much snap. At least we've both been lucky. You had those wrestlers and I had Doc Bradshaw to teach us about stamina-building conditioning programs. I've been at it long enough that it's paid off."

Our talk turned to more humorous, if not less depressing areas.

"Ever hear a bigger joke than us playin' the Russian national team?" Brooker laughed.

"If we hadn't taken the game, the tour would have been off."

"Always wanted to play those guys," Brooker said. "I've admired them as athletes and wanted to see for myself how strong they are."

The sound of cheering and the vision of me in *bleu-blanc-rouge* filled my mind: "The Canadiens played their best club team, Central Red Army, three times. Two were on New Year's Eve at the Forum, great nights in a hockey rink. The pace of those games was the fastest I've ever seen."

"We'll show them dudes a pace they ain't ever seen before," Brooker smiled. "But not because of the speed."

We're up, 4-2, on the Flames in the third because we show some discipline. I have a pair, Brooker one and Hartley, his fourth in three games.

But as has happened so often in the third period, they place pressure on our zone, where we're a mess without Sven, Lester and Baby-Joel, although Geoff Peters gives it a big try. Tactical mistakes hand the Flames three goals to win it.

Brooker, Hartley and I sit in our underwear until everyone else is gone.

"Tonight, my friends, I am tired," I say.

"That game makes me wonder why I bother," Brooker adds. "Each mistake could have been fixed in the first month of the season."

Riding back to the hotel, we see a half dozen hookers on the street although the temperature is thirty below.

"Should make a deal and get the price down by offering a warm spot," I suggest.

"Yeah," Hartley says. "But when it's twenty-below, you have to be careful what you do with one who has an IUD."

December 18

Another bonus day as the NHL's leading scorer! We've played three more games than most clubs and the gunners group up behind me, ready to shove the upstart aside.

Since last night, we are the unchallenged NHL flower of futility. We lost, 9-6, to the Hamilton Steelers for our thirty-first consecutive defeat. I popped in three scores, making it 31 for the season. I have 32 assists, too.

When a radio guy asked me if I could maintain a goal-a-game pace over the schedule, I said: "It might be easier to maintain a loss-a-game pace."

The surprise was that 14,934 spectators were there.

"We're comforting for them," The Cheat commented. "Nice to know somebody's having worse luck than you."

Hap Lonsdale's paper has run a contest that's drawn a large response: "When Will The Big Green Win?" The prize for predicting our first triumph is two weeks in Hawaii.

"What if we don't win all season?" I said to Hap. "Do you get the prize for dedication?"

Today is different because (a) Baby-Joel has the strangest ailment in hockey history; (b) it's Win A Date With Willie night, and (c) Hartley unveils a scheme that convinces me he's bonkers.

Baby-Joel is hospitalized, pale, weak and lifeless, after a rough trip home from Calgary. Last night, Doc-Jay Stanley said they were having problems diagnosing his illness. He has lost twelve pounds in three weeks. They are testing for mono-nucleosis and diabetes but with no conclusive results. Doc-Jay figures there must be a valid reason why a big, strong kid of nineteen loses weight and stamina.

Tonight, Hartley hosts the "Big Green Pre-Christmas Shitkicker Music Festival." Margie Franklin leads the band at the $30,000 Steinway in the den. Henry brings his drums (he's been taking lessons), Harry Tatum brings his clarinet, Doc-Jay is on bass guitar, Hartley on rhythm guitar, and Biff on banjo and Michelob. An added picker is Hank Brown. Hartley recruits Brooker and The Cheat as bartender and doorman and arranges for Chinese food at 10:30. He also regrets that I can't stay since I'm "booby-prizing the poor broad who won the contest."

Doc Stanley is the first arrival and, of course, we want to know about Baby-Joel.

"You won't believe it," he says. "He's okay, but I might boot his ass when he's sound. When six heavyweight specialists nailed down what's wrong with him, we felt like dummies. It's malnutrition."

"Malnutrition?" Hartley says. "You're kidding?"

"Isn't it something in this day and age," he says, shaking his head.

"Doc, I've seen him inhale four hot dogs in an airport a dozen times."

"That's his trouble, Willie," the Doc says. "In junior hockey, he boarded where he ate well but here, he took an apartment alone in Richfield. He has never cooked. Since the start of camp, he's lived on junk food—hamburgers, hot dogs, french fries and pizza—a terrible diet for a physical profession. It lacks protein, minerals and vitamins. He never drinks milk, only pop. Henry says on the road, it's the same. Over almost three months, he has had very few balanced meals. Lack of proper nutrition wore him down."

"So what's the treatment?" Hartley asks.

"A balanced diet. In four days in hospital, he gained strength on intravenous. He's still weak but he's going home for a week over Christmas to load up on his mother's cooking.

When he comes back, he'll live with a doctor's aunt who will feed him properly."

"Doc, there's another little potential problem in that area," Hartley says.

"What's that?"

"Willie appears to be living on Scotch whisky. That's not a balanced diet, is it?"

"Pour a sizeable amount of his brand over some rocks and I'll check its nutritional properties."

Three days ago I judged the contest. Beady Bascom was excited because it attracted close to 2,000 entries. A few were hard-core porno; one started: "Dear Willie. Do you like whips and chains?"

Beady cut the field to ten finalists and from those, I selected the winner. A couple were from twelve-year olds, all gushy about how great a date with a hockey star would be. I read them all and one stood out, as we say in Mount Everest, "like a fart in church." It was written in crisp longhand.

Dear William:

I am a long-time sports fan through television and the occasional visit to a live event. I admire the artistry of the great sports performer because, to me, that's what it is, art, the same as ballet or opera.

Some friends took me to see the Big Green's game against the Los Angeles Kings. You scored three goals and had two assists that night when you were, indeed, an artist.

You appear to be a man of sensitivity, wit and style. I'm certain that a date with you would be a fine experience.

People tell me I'm a good-looking lady and I'm not overweight, oversexed or over-eager. I would welcome the opportunity to meet a fine athlete in person.

"This is it, Barry, number seven," I said.

"Good, I liked that one best myself," he replied. "The

winner's name is Agnes Burke. (To guarantee impartiality from the judge, Beady removed the names from the entries.) I'll call her and set the date for Thursday. We have a limo and driver and you'll pick her up at eight."

The Big Green All-Stars are tuning up when the limo driver buzzes the condo. The place is semi-crowded as most players are there as well as a few ladies attracted by the band's reputation.

"May never see you again if this set-up turns out to be anythin' above a '56 T-Bird," Lester says.

The Burke residence at 550 Shady Lane Drive is in a neighborhood of neat, medium-sized houses. I have a few butterflies as I ring the bell and a trim, elderly lady answers it.

"Agnes Burke, please."

"I'm Agnes. And you're Willie," she says simply. "Come in."

If Big Bertha walks out of the kitchen, I won't be surprised because it's her kind of place.

"You're really Agnes Burke, who wrote that terrific letter?"

"Are you disappointed, Willie?" she says. "Were you expecting a blonde twenty year old with big bazooms."

"Agnes, I didn't know what to expect. But you and I are going to get along just fine."

"I never had my doubts that we would. Like a little nip before we leave?"

"Why not? Got any Scotch?"

"I only have Chivas, if that's okay?"

"Now I have absolutely no doubt that we will get along just famously."

Agnes is seventy-two, has three sons, seven grandchildren and a garden. We chat like old buddies over a Swingo's dinner, and she grills me about my family, my lady, the farm, hockey and what it's like to be a pro athlete. She invites us to dinner when Clarice is in Cleveland.

Agnes gives me a peck on the cheek at her door, explaining: "I never fool around on the first date." I promise to call about that dinner. I'll do it, too.

When I return to the condo, most of the suspects have departed, including the band.

"The band was terrific," Hartley says. "Hank Brown adds a lot. Great fun! How was your night?"

"Only fanstastic!"

"How old was the chick?"

"Seventy-two."

"You're kidding," he laughs. "What did you ever talk to an old doll like that about?"

"Okay, my mother is sixty-eight. You ever have trouble talking to her?"

"Big Bertha? Are you kidding?"

"This was Big Bertha's twin sister."

Hartley, Brooker, Sven and I are having a nightcap when my roomie hints at a brilliant scheme.

"How be we break our losing streak against the national team of the Soviet Union?" Hartley says matter-of-factly.

"It would have to be on a day when the sun rises in the west, you vow celibacy and Brooker joins the klan," I say.

"Are you guys willing to try to win it?"

"The Green tries to win every game," Brooker says. "That's why we're feared all over the world."

"I'm serious and I have a plan on how to do it," Hartley says. "I can't tell it all to you now but are you with me?"

We all agree that we might be crazy to agree, but then we'd definitely be crazy not too.

"Just the four of us will be in on it for now," he says. "The first thing is that we'll scout their early games—Willie and Sven in Montreal, Brooker and me on Long Island."

"They are the best team in the world, we are the worst," Sven says. "What possible plan could you have?"

"Sven, you must have faith."

When Brooker and Sven depart, Hartley says to me: "You willing to spend a few hundred to have some fun."

"My kingdom for a giggle. Count me in but I haven't any idea what in hell you're up to."

"Of all people, William. Don't tell me you have no faith either?"

December 25

A good word for the Big Green with an assist to the players'
association: I'm home for Christmas. Of course, it's a struggle
but what isn't for Big Greens?

But I make it, the first time in seven years I can relax at
Shoot-The-Puck Farm. With the Canadiens, I got here but
usually for no more than twenty-four hours. One year, a
snowstorm kept me in Montreal. It was a lonely time.

We played on Dec. 23 at home and don't play again until
the 27th in Toronto. We figured to be off between games and
assemble in Toronto Saturday morning. Guys like Brooker
could make the long trip home. Henry had plane tickets to
Vernon, B.C., for a month.

We get itineraries for two weeks with a practice listed for
Boxing Day at the Coliseum at 9 a.m. Our agreement states
that "where possible" no game or club activity shall be scheduled on December 24, 25 and 26.

"Gotta be a mistake," Brooker said. "Not even Jackson
could do that."

I went to his little office and asked if he had a minute.
"Coach, is there a practice on the 26th?"

"What's your itinerary say?"

"One is scheduled but it's very tough on the guys who
want to go home for Christmas."

"Isn't that too bad!" Jackson sneered. "They are being
well paid to play hockey. We have a game Saturday and it's
normal to practice the day before a game. Miss it and there will
be a large fine or a suspension."

"Andy, I appeal to you as a human being," I pleaded.
"Things are bad enough but if these guys can't get home, it will
be worse."

"Mulligan, quit snivelling. This team hasn't won a fucking
game and all you want are favors. When I played, we often
had games Christmas Eve."

I just shook my head and walked out. My face said it all to
the others in the room.

"Don't panic for a minute," Hartley said and left the
room. He was smiling when he returned and said: "Give it an
hour."

After the workout, Edmunds appeared: "A change in plans. Friday's practice is cancelled. Be in Toronto Friday night if you can."

Jackson walked past me and muttered: "You son-of-a-bitch!"

"Yeah, you bastard, Mulligan!" Hartley laughed. "I want to kill Santa Claus and you get in the way."

"This is one of your machinations I'll gladly take the blame for," I smiled. "But how?"

"Called on a heavyweight connection," Hartley said. "Wallace Morgan, the lawyer, is on the board of this team. I told him about grinch-time, he said he'd call Gee-One Anderson, who undoubtedly called Edmunds and talked some sense into his thick skull."

It would have been heartening to celebrate Christmas with a win but the best we could do was a noble effort against the Rangers.

"Let's open it up crazy-wide," I suggested before the game.

"We play tight and there's no chance," Brooker agreed.

When we tramped three forwards into their zone, they were surprised and confused. The Ranger coach was hollering "check, check," but they obviously thought it would be fun to play shootout. They were better at it and beat us, 8-6.

I scored two, making it thirty-four for the season. The next one is worth a $10,000 bonus. Brooker and Hartley also got two each and Jimmy had four assists.

"This isn't a bad hockey team," Hartley said. "A half hour a week on our zone and breakouts, we'd win a few."

"Let's hope that Santa brings Andrew Jackson some enlightenment."

Yesterday's early flight to Toronto carried eleven Big Green, who connected there with flights for all parts of Canada. Clarice was at the airport with my agent's four-wheel drive because Mount Everest is under large amounts of snow.

Christmas is idyllic. The frog pond is in fine shape and on Christmas Eve we had a family skating party—Sandy and

Ralph; Little Charlie, Nadine and the girls; Millie and Doc Bradshaw, Clarice and I.

Big Bertha had a roaring blaze in the big stone fireplace and large amounts of cocoa (only city folks call it hot chocolate). Made with fresh Jersey milk, it's right up there with Chivas among beverages. Then came big bowls of vegetable beef soup and stacks of homemade bread.

Today, Big B does her number on a turkey the size of a linebacker and her pudding with brandy sauce that's one-two with a four-goal game.

Obviously, a family concern is my gift to Clarice and when Little Charlie and crew arrive, Marty and Joey give it away. Quickly, they're on Clarice's knee, examining her hands.

"Where is it, Clarice?" Marty says.

"Where's what, sweetie?"

"Your 'gagement ring from Uncle Willie," Joey says.

"I guess he just plumb forgot," Clarice says.

"Uncle Willie's stupid then," Marty comments sagely.

"I'll vote for that," says Big Bertha.

December 30

Sven and I are in the Montreal Forum and I can't quite figure out what we're doing here. Oh, I know the purpose of the trip: We were assigned by Hartley (Boris) Laidlaw to scout the USSR national team against the Canadiens.

He is obsessed with our game against the Soviets and I've never seen him as buoyantly enthusiastic about anything. We were given our orders and schedules yesterday following our workout. We are to fly to Montreal through Toronto, watch the game, then grab the first connection to Cleveland for our skate prior to a New Year's Eve game against the Edmonton Oilers.

"This is madness," I said. "If anything is a minute late, we won't make it."

Hartley brushed it off. "The long-range weather forecast guarantees success."

D-Day was sloppy planning compared to Hartley's scheme.

He then handed me a folder with a list of USSR tactics to check and the charts on which to do it.

"Willie, cover their breakouts, forechecking, what they do in the neutral zone, power plays and penalty-killing. I want Sven, who has played these guys, to list individual weaknesses and tendencies."

"How do we get to Long Island?" Brooker asked. "We're in Philly the next night."

"The Soviet games are televised in Canada and I know some TV guys. I suggested that Duncan and Laidlaw be guest commentators and they cleared it with Edmunds. They'll pay our expenses and drive us to Philly after the game and we get tapes of all Soviet games instead of a fee — I've already got the tape of the tour opener." (A 5-0 victory over the Quebec Nordiques.)

"And we got a break," Hartley added. "I asked Jackson what he thinks of playing them; he said it's a waste of time so he's turning things over to Sammy Sparks for the game. With that dope in charge, we can do what we want.

"I've rented the little rink for two practices, late afternoon on New Year's Day and the evening of the fifth. Harry will sneak the equipment over for us."

"If Null and Void find out, it's a firing squad," I remarked.

"They won't," Hartley said. "That's all for now, I'll reveal the rest of the plan soon."

When Sven and I hit the hotel this afternoon, the Soviet team is in the lobby. Several players recognize Sven and some shake my hand. Sven has a lively conversation with the players and coaches.

"You speak Russian?" I ask.

"Yes, fairly well," he says, introducing me to several players. The comrades know much about the NHL. At least, they know we haven't won a game.

When they head to the bus, Viacheslav Sanisov calls Sven aside. Sanisov is one of the world's best half dozen players, a tall, handsome left winger.

"What was that all about?" I ask.

"He's an anthropology student, too, and I've talked with him several times," Sven says. "He made a very unusual request."

"A clinical report on Baby-Joel's hockey philosophy for his thesis?"

"Not quite," he laughs. "He wonders if there's any chance of me introducing a few players to females when they are in Cleveland for three days."

"Hockey players are the same the world over," I say. "That information better be in our report to coach Laidlaw."

A game like this in the Forum is no ordinary occasion and the pre-game noise is very loud. Reporters flock around us, wanting to know why we're there. We tell them Sven is researching a hockey instruction book.

The game is superb with a pace sustained at an incredible level. I react as a fan and must concentrate to analyze the Soviets.

"Head-to-head with big lines," I say at the opening faceoff.

The Canadiens use Gaston Beaupre, J-P Couteau and Real Ladouceur against the troika that has led the Soviets for seven years, Boris Vikulov between Sanisov and Vladimir Snych.

The Canadiens' approach is strong forechecking, forcing the Soviet to ice the puck five times in three minutes.

"In Europe, no team would forecheck them that way on the big ice because their quick-break plays would trap players there," Sven says.

"Alfie Brisebois feels if you stay back and concede them the neutral zone, you hand them the strength of their game on a platter," I say. "We forechecked them and they had trouble with it."

It pays off in the Canadiens' first goal. Couteau's quickness forces a bad pass, Ladouceur intercepts. Zip to Gaston! Bang, a wrister on the top shelf and the Forum goes crazy.

"I see what you mean," Sven says. "But our team doesn't have the speed to get on them that quickly."

"That's up to Boris Laidlaw."

A two-minute, three-goal burst early in the third is the Soviet edge in a 6-4 win. Gaston and Sanisov each score three goals.

"No one will ask for his money back after that one," I say.

"The best hockey game I have ever seen," Sven says.

"You just haven't seen the Big Green in action against them pussycats."

"If I don't like that game, can I get my money back?" Sven says.

In the hotel, I discover that we have voluminous notes. We make out a scouting report, including a fake page about Sanisov's request to Sven. We're ready for bed when the Soviets filter in.

Sanisov and Vikulov chat for a minute, Sanisov talking seriously to Sven, again asking about women in Cleveland.

I keep wondering what Agnes Burke is doing that night?

December 31

Sven and I arrive on time for the skate with the tapes of the Soviets against the Canadiens from the TV people. Hartley dives into the scouting report at lunch.

"Is this a joke?" he says, holding up the gag page.

"It is but he wasn't joking when he said it."

"Fantastic! How did you talk to him?"

"I speak Russian, Hartley," Sven says. "I studied it in school."

Hartley shakes Sven's hand: "Yow-ee and Harry Li! Great news!"

I find this over-reaction curious. "Tell us why Sven speaking Russian and the comrades wanting some poon is such a big deal."

"Okay, here's the master plan, although you'll have me in a strait-jacket," Hartley says. "The reds could spot us ten goals and beat the spread. Scouting, preparation and the best game we'll ever play won't change that. So we have to throw them off their game, to make them sub-par by quite a bit."

"If you're thinking what I think you're thinking, we'll all end up in jail," I smile.

Hartley has the diabolical look as if he's got a scheme to rob a bank: "We'll do it and it will work."

"Can I hear the joke?" Brooker says.

"Brooker, what's the downfall of more hockey players than anything else?"

"Booze and tail, I guess, if your knees are good."

"Correct!" Hartley says. "To bring the commies to the level of normal folks, we'll supply large amounts of both."

"How you goin' to get past the coaches, officials and secret police who are always with them?" Brooker asks.

"Here's my plan," Hartley says, a gleeful look on his face. "The night before the game, the Green is having a dinner for both teams at a big hotel that should finish by 9:30. Clive-Five will then have a reception at his home for the officials of the two teams, which takes care of some Soviet watchdogs.

"I've rented the presidential suite on the top floor, a five-room layout. We'll invite the Soviet players to a party and advertise that female companionship is available. Our guys are included."

"You plan an orgy, right?" Brooker says. "It'll tucker our guys more than them, the shape they're in."

"No Big Green will indulge in anything, no booze, no wool. We'll be in our beds, alone, by midnight. The Soviets, or what's left of them, hopefully will see the sunrise."

"How will you arrange company for the Russians?" Sven asks.

"It's all set. Cutting the candidates down to workable numbers is the problem."

"Did you recruit in every dive in town?"

"You think I would do anything like that?" Hartley says. "These high-class athletes on a cultural exchange deserve only the best."

"Okay," I ask, "where did you find the poon?"

"Easy as a slap shot. Remember the chick Red Barnes found here? The one I introduced to Firpo? She's a remarkable lady who thinks there's nothing better than athletes' bodies. I gave her a proposal and she will coordinate the project. She has recruited several friends and they're excited about meeting the great Soviets."

"Will the Soviets go for anything this loony?" I say.

"I wondered until I saw that joke note. Viacheslav Sanisov isn't spoiled borscht and if he wants to get his rocks off, it's legitimate. The Soviets trained hard and had no contact with their wives or chicks for a month before this tour. Unless they nailed some hooks in Quebec or Montreal, which is tough the way they're watched, they should be keen. Sanisov's request shows they're eager. Sven can outline what's in store for them and they'll paw the ground.

"I'll have plenty of booze, including top-drawer Russian vodka, plus food that makes you feel like the bottom of a bird cage next day—raw oysters, shrimp, marinated herring. I'll coach the waiters who will serve so our guys'll only get soft drinks. When a Soviet glass is empty, a waiter will fill it and there will be plenty of toasts. Our guys will fake being gunned a little and some chicks will leave with them. The Soviets will think we're doing the same things they are.

"If it works, they'll be so pussy-whipped and hungover that they won't play at their peak. If we wear them down and are well prepared ourselves, they won't beat us by twenty goals. You with me on it?"

"You're nuts, but I wouldn't miss it," Brooker says. "Who's paying for this?"

"The project has private backers."

Sven smiles: "I have little affection for the Soviets. I'll help any way I can. What about the watch-dogs?"

"If the Soviets know what's upstairs, they'll find a way to get there."

"How much is this going to cost the private backers?" I say on the way home.

"Just a few hundred."

"Could have kept costs down by bringing in Sheila Symons-Dawes to look after them by herself."

"Our only problem," Hartley says, "is to make certain Sven doesn't take his pants off or none of the wool will want any Soviet."

He spends the afternoon breaking down the tapes of the two games on a video unit. Tonight, he plays his best game of the season, scoring four against the Winnipeg Jets. I get one but it's not enough. The Jets beat us, 8-6.

We have a small New Year's Eve party at a restaurant in Richfield. I call Clarice and tell her I hope next year is as good as the past one.

"I'm staying away from Grenada, though," she says. "You meet weird people down there."

I buy the champagne at midnight and Hartley proposes the toast: "A better year for us all. And may a pregnant rhinoceros break water over Andy Jackson's bed."

January 5

"No, no, Ilko," Hartley barks. "Don't chase the motion in their zone."

We're at the little rink this afternoon for our second pre-Soviet workout. Andy Jackson gave us a break last night on the way back from Philadelphia, where we lost our thirty-ninth, 3-2, to the Flyers. "No optional," he announced. "There's a skate Tuesday before we play the fuckin' Russians. Sammy is in charge of that waste of time so do what he tells you."

Hartley is a tough taskmaster. At one point, the players gather in a corner and holler in unison: "We want Andy." He's been a man possessed in this project and his intensity has rubbed off on everyone. He's spent hours analyzing the video-tapes of the Soviet games and he and Brooker watched them beat the Islanders, 4-2, on Saturday.

Hartley's approach is simple and he's a good teacher. Today, he runs through the Soviet systems in slow motion and works out how we can counter-act them.

"The Soviets remember that hockey is a simple game," he says. "They complicate it in skill-teaching and conditioning. Their execution is impeccable and we must play the most alert game of our lives to make this work. My plan might be a little strange but I'm open to a better idea."

In the room, Hartley delivers another lecture. "Tomorrow night, don't pay attention to what Sparks says. Willie, Brooker and I will make the changes. Everyone plays but in short shifts—twenty seconds, then get off. The bench has to be alert. I've gone over tonight with each of you so no slip-ups, eh? It would be nice to do something with this season and we have the chance tomorrow."

The Soviets practice early this morning, then Sven lunches with Viacheslav Sanisov, his brother scholar. Sven reports back that word of the party, and of the women, has spread among the Soviets. Sanisov assured him they'll think of a way to make it.

Big Gracie, Hartley's "talent coordinator," drops in this afternoon to go over the arrangements. She's a tall, red-haired, zesty broad of thirty-two (she claims) with an awesome configuration.

"When word got around my circle there was a bash on, I could have had enough ladies to handle the Red Army, not just their hockey team," she says. "I've never done it with a commie. Wonder if they know what's going on?"

"Gracie, all I care about is that those Russians' asses are whipped," Hartley says.

"I guarantee it," she declares. "I've found a few man-eaters so those reds will discover the joys of capitalism." She departs in a swirl of fur for a lavish dinner at our expense with her pals.

"Is she a hooker, Hartley?"

"She's a school teacher, if you can believe it. She says she's thirty-two and she just likes young, strong bodies. She screws her friends and she doesn't have an enemy. Her honesty about it is a bit much for many people. I'm turning her loose on Sanisov tonight."

"Who are the other ladies?" I ask.

"See what great shape she's in? Well, she works out at a health club every day and so do a few others—teachers, divorcées, various and sundry ladies. There won't be a pro there. She has about thirty of them, divided into two catego‑ ries: those who leave with our guys to set the Soviets up and those who will make the comrades think they're the greatest thing since Sputnik. And she guarantees there won't be one that cute Willie Mulligan wouldn't take home to his mother."

Hartley leaves for the hotel early for a last-minute check.
I wander over at 6:30 for cocktails before the dinner. The
Anderson family is out in force and Gee-One tells me the
game is a sellout.

"I'd love to kidnap about six of those guys," Pete
Edmunds says, looking at the Soviet players.

Sven and I mingle with the Soviets, all in three-piece suits.
Firpo finds a USSR winger who speaks a little Polish and they
laugh away. I hope he's extolling Gracie's talents.

Boris Vikulov, the great little Soviet center, nods me over
to where he stands. "You like it here?" he says in flawless
English.

I've always suspected that the Soviets speak more English
than they reveal.

"It's not the Canadiens but in the NHL, nothing is," I say.
"I didn't know you spoke English."

"I studied it in school. After hockey, I will try for the
diplomatic corps and I need English for that." His eyes do a
quick scan of the vicinity. "Viacheslav tells me there's a party
later."

"Yes, he has the details. Can you make it?"

"If our plans work out," he smiles. "Unusual, isn't it, that
grown men must resort to devious means to find some relaxa-
tion? There will be women there?"

"Yes, a few."

"But no wives or girlfriends?"

"No. We decided on a party because our team has been
under much stress."

"I have read about your women but have never observed
them closely," he says.

I give him a smile and a pat on the arm. "You'll find them
very interesting."

The dinner is the usual baloney (the speeches, not the
menu)—a welcome by a city councillor, a few words from
Clive-Five and the head of the Soviet delegation. At nine, the
brass leaves for Clive-Five's house. Four dour, older men
remain with the Soviet players.

"How will they get away from those tough-looking

dudes?" I say. "They'll probably string barbed wire around the exits."

"Sanisov says they have a plan," Sven replies. "They should be up within a half hour. They scouted their route today."

The Big Green and the ladies are there when Sven and I arrive. Hartley's staging is magnificent. The suite has a huge, two-level living room with a dance floor, a stereo playing soft rock, a bar and waiters, and plenty of easy chairs. It's like an expensive club. Around the room are Big Gracie and her corps. Hartley was right· There's nothing below a '56 T-Bird in the lot.

In twenty minutes, the Soviets start to appear in small groups — six, then four more, a few minutes later, another half dozen. Vikulov and Sanisov come ten minutes later.

"They think we are in our rooms because the television sets are on," Vikulov says. "Viacheslav and I distracted them while the others escaped."

"What will happen if they find out?" I ask.

"Oh, we'll all be shot," he laughs.

The Soviets are awestruck by the scene. They stare at the ladies, who stare back, and Hartley, with Sven as interpreter, makes a welcome speech as the Soviets all have a drink. Our players are belting down the soft drinks and Baby-Joel, healthy from his mother's cooking, is acting half-gunned.

"As one group of athletes, we welcome the excellent hockey players from the Soviet Union," Hartley says. "Fellowship among friends is a great thing, so please enjoy yourselves."

The comrades raise their glasses in the first of many toasts. Gracie asks Sanisov to dance and quickly, the floor is packed. Booze flows like the Volga River because the Soviets see us tucking away our liquid and keep pace with vodka.

It is a night to remember! Six Soviets do a Cossack dance in a squat, kicking out their feet, and try to teach Gracie and five ladies the same step. The result is a wrestle that Henry says reminds him of Red-Light Regan's game "goal-mouth pile-up."

A little blonde with a handful of diamonds decides Boris Vikulov is a cute little devil. They dance, then disappear into a bedroom.

"He a good player?" Gracie asks.

"One of the best," I reply.

"Well, when Judy gets through with him, his career might be over. Hey, Willie, that Vichyssoise Hartley wants me to look after is a good-looking guy. I'll enjoy this assignment."

Our guys deliver a superb performance. Baby-Joel and Henry fake a drunk routine in which the Baby holds Henry above his head. Hartley is squeezing several ladies at once and even Sven does a little easy-chair wrestling.

Vikulov reappears, in a towel, to recharge his glass.

"Are North American women interesting?" I ask.

"Extremely," he says. "Soviet education is lacking."

At 11:30, on cue, the "drunken" Green, most of them with a lady in tow, depart. Even Brooker runs a little fake.

Hartley, Sven, The Cheat, Lester and I stay around, dancing, laughing and generally carrying on. Sanisov, who has visited the bedroom at least three times, is well hammered. He and Sven chat briefly.

"He wants to know where our players have gone," Sven says. "I told him some have rooms and have gone there with their ladies, others who are afraid of their wives have gone home. He says some things are the same in America and the USSR."

"I almost forgot," Hartley says, pulling a batch of room keys from his pocket. "Tell Viacheslav I have rooms one floor down they can use. Tell them to grab a bottle and go camping."

The rooms are very popular and a dozen comrades depart with a jug in their hand and one of Gracie's fleet on their arm. Sanisov, the greedy pig, has a crock of vodka, one of wine, and both Gracie and Judy. Another Soviet who tries a doubleheader is Veniamin Kovin, their brilliant goalie, who has caused more frustration among NHL shooters than trying to find a '48 Merc on a Monday night in Hartford.

Before long, only the Big Green stragglers remain.

"Coach," I say to Hartley, "do you think it would be hypocritical of us to have a small nightcap?"

"One short one," he says, laughing uproariously.

"A toast to a great man of history, Hartley Laidlaw," Sven announces. "The United Nations should name him to handle the Soviets."

"He's not such a hot guy," Lester says. "He throws a party, invites me and a bunch of Russians, I see a commie heading out with two '48 Mercs and I get to ride home with Pete The Cheat."

January 6

I'm resting this morning and when I leave for the Coliseum at 8:30, Hartley surfaces, but barely.

"How much will last night cost us?" I say. "An absolutely brilliant effort, by the way."

"Imagine the mess those suckers will be in when their brass find out," he grins. "I have good news, chum. No charge for the party."

"We agreed to split it."

"We had a sponsor. My attorney friend loves to raise a little hell. I told him of our scheme and he liked it so well, he volunteered to pay for it. It's tax deductible and he owns a piece of the hotel."

At the rink, Peter Edmunds runs down the ramp, looking distraught and muttering, "goddam Russians!"

I'm struck with a terrible fear that we've been discovered. "Peter, what's the trouble?"

"I wish I knew what the hell went on last night," he steams. "The Soviets' head man, so friendly last night, called this morning and said they won't play the game. I got on the phone with the NHL president, he got the Russians and there was a big argument."

"Are they going to play?"

"Yes, after he told them they wouldn't get their $35,000 a game or expenses and that they'd have to pay their way back to Siberia."

"What happened?" I innocently ask.

"The commie told the prez their players got into bad trouble last night and he figures they had outside help. You know anything about it?"

"Pete, what could I know?" I say. "I can't even talk to them."

"What a mess if they'd pulled out. We got a full house! I'd have had to leave town."

"Sure glad the game is on," I say, heading for the room.

"Must have been some party," Harry Tatum says. "The Russians cancelled their workout this morning."

"Harry," I say, pouring a coffee, "they'll be lucky to find six guys who can stand up."

Hartley arrives at 10:30, full of exuberance. "Gracie called and thanked me for a truly memorable night. She thinks those Soviets are okay guys, not bad in the rack. But they were a pretty grim bunch this morning when they realized there was music to face. Gracie says if we can't beat them now, then we can't beat a team of hairdressers."

I drive back to town, have lunch, get dressed in a suit and drive back to the Coliseum. I'm there at 2:30 for a game at eight. I walk every inch of corridor in the building, drink a pot of coffee and play checkers with Hannigan, the old trainer.

The gate man calls me when the Soviets' bus arrives at 5:15. Curiosity makes it a must to meet them by accident to see how they look.

They're coming down the ramp when I emerge from the room. Most who spot me look away, although Vikulov winks and Sanisov has a weak smile. I've never seen so many bloodshot eyes in my life. I hear a "psst" and see Boris Vikulov around a corner from their room. I point to the wives' room.

In a few minutes, we meet there and he shakes my hand. "Thank you for an evening we won't forget."

"It was a good party," I reply.

"We have big trouble when our leaders discover we have broken training. They found our goaltender in bed with two women, too drunk to stand up. They questioned us but no one said you were kind enough to have a party for us."

"Thanks for that," I say. "How do you feel?"

"Very bad because of, how do you say it in English, a hangover. I cannot eat today. How do you look so rested?"

"We do things like that often and are conditioned to it."

"No wonder you do not win," he replies. "We are fortunate not to be playing a good team."

"Very fortunate," I say. "Good luck, Boris."

"Good luck, William. Thanks again. I have many new things to show my mistress at home."

Before the game, Sammy decides to play coach.

"I've always figured these commies was overrated so there's no reason why we can't beat 'em. They're chickenshit bastards who don't like heavy goin'. Let's stick the assholes."

Henry throws up a record four times and Hartley has Baby-Joel at the blackboard in the room. Hartley's pre-game speech is only brilliant: "You sacrificed a great deal in that suite. Be a shame to waste it."

It's an incredible sight to see more than 18,000 spectators in the Coliseum and when we appear for the warm-up, they give us a loud ovation. There's a huge boo when the Soviets speed around.

They look lively to me, and I wonder if even Gracie and her barracudas can't slow them up.

Our only hope is to stay close to them for two periods, then hope they run out of juice.

We make the traditional gift exchange, our gold pins for their crummy pennants, then line up for the opening faceoff. My line starts against the Vikulov line and, immediately, Hartley's advice pays off. The puck goes back to their zone and the Soviets do a whirly-gig routine back and forth across the ice.

But we stand outside their line and watch, not taking the lure. The Soviets complete sixteen passes and don't gain an inch. They move back behind their net to form an attack. The defenseman brings the puck, Sanisov and Snych do a crossover before they hit their own line and Brooker makes a key move. Hartley's analysis revealed a tendency that when the right defenseman carries the puck and wingers cross, the puck goes to Snych. Brooker cruises in from the side just as Snych gets the puck and destroys him with a bodycheck.

The Soviet bench screams for a penalty when Jimmy grabs the loose puck and legs it past the defenseman who carried it. I swing in behind him up the slot, he skates at the other defenseman and drops it. I gun it low, past the screen, and hit a corner of the net.

The Coliseum goes berserk while the Soviets storm after the referee, old pal Bill Mathews. Snych skates to the bench, doubled over.

Our bench is a strange place. Sammy paces up and down, saying: "See, I told you to stick 'em."

A Soviet strength is consistency. They have a plan and stick to it, whether they're five ahead or five behind. Sammy sends out Hartley's line but one Hartley has created goes instead — Firpo at center with Anders and Ilko.

"What's goin' on here?" Sammy says.

Hartley waves him over. "Sam, that European line has played 'em before. Keep them on against the Russians' least experienced line. My line will go against their third line because it has the least speed and our big line will go against their's."

"Hartley's line up next," Sammy hollers.

The Sanisov-Vikulov-Snych line, together for seven years, has faced a few situations. This time, they go straight up and down like a standard NHL line, except their passing is beautiful. In about three seconds, they set up shop in our zone.

Again, the scouting pays off and Sanisov suffers. He's a gorgeous player, a long-strider with great speed. Vikulov, Snych and a defenseman play with the puck while Sanisov sneaks to a spot just off the post. He uses his reach to deflect shots and he distracts the goalie, who can't move out on the shooters with him there.

Hartley has Baby-Joel clued in on a move. He's on

defense with Geoff Peters and when the quick passing starts, Joel glances at Sanisov, wheeling down the boards towards the net. When Sanisov moves through the corner, Baby-Joel moves quickly and nails him to the fence. Sanisov jumps to avoid the hit and Joel's shoulder slams into his stomach.

Baby-Joel skates to the penalty box while Sanisov goes to the bench. Hartley and Lester kill the penalty with Geoff and me.

"Basic box and don't get sucked out," Hartley calls.

The puck zips around the outside of our formation as they try to draw one of us out of position. We ice it once, freeze it twice and they have only a soft shot on goal in two minutes.

We escape the first period with a one-goal lead in a strange game, which I think befuddles the Soviets. We initiate little on our own but react to what they do.

Sparks confronts Hartley in the room: "Laidlaw, what's going on? I'm the coach."

"Sam, you want to be a hero, the only coach to beat the Russians? If you do, keep quiet, lead the cheers behind the bench and don't think about the team. We won't tell anyone you didn't call the shots, not even Jackson. Now fuck off out in the hall and pace up and down like you're thinking up strategy."

Before the second, Hartley says: "They're going to come at us. Stick to basic positional hockey. Dump, dump, dump the puck over the blueline. Make them skate bcause if we survive this period, last night might catch up to them."

The Soviets come at us like they're starving and we're raw meat. Henry stops two sure goals early and they pour it on. To dump the puck out, we need possession of it and that isn't easy to get. Their speed forces us into two penalties. We kill the first and most of the second. But a defenseman unloads a slapper, and Snych darts in behind Lester and deflects it home.

"Not to worry," Hartley says. "Open up a little bit. Each line try a shift of forechecking."

We move in on them but it's risky because the puck is up to a moving forward quickly. A great defensive effort by Sven foils a two-on-one and Henry makes three more big saves.

Halfway through the period, the Soviets go in front on a play they've used for years. The forward line moves in, the puck zinging around until Anders and Baby-Joel move towards the middle. The defenseman moves in, a quick pass and Henry has no chance on his shot.

"They use the late-man play often," Hartley says. "Don't bunch up in our zone."

We're down one when the second period ends.

But back in the room, Hartley's just flying: "We got 'em. We got the bastards."

"I hate to rain on the parade," Brooker says softly. "But they got two, we got one."

"They were short-shifting late in the period. They're out of gas," Hartley says. "Gracie's sweeties are going to do it."

Hartley uses the board before the third: "They'll try to put us away quickly so we have to ride out the first five minutes. Give them the five-man wall, then we'll go to work."

The Soviet plan has worked often against NHL clubs. Just when you're close to them, they wind the pace up to a very high point and kill you with a quick burst.

When the Soviets light the jets through the neutral zone, Sven, Baby-Joel, Sanders and Pete are at the blueline with Hartley in behind them. When they shoot the puck in, he ices it.

Hartley wins the draw and Sven banks it off the boards. The Soviets launch a rush and hit the four-man wall again. Instead of shooting it in, the man with the puck goes back to his own zone.

For five minutes, it resembles a game we used to play at Mount Everest Public School called "red rover," where a kid would try to run through a line of other kids. The Soviets skate miles, wheeling up the ice to meet the wall at our line.

On the bench, Hartley's jumping. "They're getting frustrated. They're skating the shit out of themselves. Come on, Gracie, do your stuff."

The Soviets are famous for their "pick" plays that NHL people call interference. Vikulov's line tries one to penetrate the wall and it backfires. Three attackers move towards Jimmy at our line and I move to that side to back him up. The defenseman drops the puck to Snych and when he tries to block Jimmy out of the play, he knocks Jimmy down. Mathews calls a penalty.

We don't score but the penalty discourages pick plays. At the halfway point of the period, the pace of their play is falling off noticeably.

"Okay, open it up but not until late in a shift," Hartley says. "Their asses are dragging; let's take advantage of it."

The man scores the tying goal himself. Mathews won't allow the Soviets to change lines for a faceoff in our zone. Hartley slides it to Sven and takes off straight up the middle. We haven't used a breakout like it all night and it catches the Soviets flat-footed. He breezes past the defensemen, who are up at our line. Sven's pass hits him near center and who's better on a break that Hartley? Kovin is moving out when the puck goes behind him into a high corner, where Hartley figures the Soviet goalie is weak.

The Coliseum isn't even quiet from that goal when Brooker gives us the lead. Vikulov's line, especially Sanisov, has been losing its pep and for the first twenty seconds of a shift, they skate a great deal in their zone. It's a play Hartley suggested. When a defenseman moves the puck, I'm to back off the line and, nine times out of ten, the videotapes showed us that the defenseman passes to his right when he has room. There's a flash of Green when Sven goes past me and intercepts. The Soviet backliner—probably the drunkest last night —curses in Russian and falls down. Sven swings wide on the other defenseman and dumps a little pass to Brooker, who picks a low corner and dives into the net for the puck in one motion.

Six minutes to go, a long time against a great team for a club with no experience in sitting on a lead, and old Firpo supplies the comrade-killer.

The Soviets clear the puck into our zone and a full-court press shapes up. But the Polish Prince, who does not have predictability as his strong point, picks a fine time to be unpredictable. The plan is to dump the puck out and revert to the wall. But when Firpo is the first man back, he takes off up the ice with it.

It's only totally ridiculous. He roars past the forwards moving in to forecheck and jets between the defensemen. The legs the Soviets need to catch him are in a hotel downtown.

Firpo has the Soviet half of the ice to himself and subtlety isn't part of his style, either. Twenty feet from Kovin, he rears back and slaps the puck. It's a dead heat across the line—the rubber and Firpo—when he falls down.

The crowd yells "Fir-po, Fir-po" in unison almost to the game's end. We have a handshake with the Soviets, then stand at the bluelines for the winner's national anthem. We leave the ice three times in all because the crowd keeps cheering us back.

In the room, Hartley tells Harry: "No one in, I don't care who, for two minutes." He bangs his stick on a table until there's quiet. Tears are running down his face. Mine, too, and just about everyone else's.

"We all know how we did it," he says. "We used the dirtiest, sneakiest tricks that could be thought up. We used every gimmick ever invented and we probably couldn't win another game that way in a hundred years. Now, let's enjoy every stinking, goddam minute of it."

The room is pandemonium for two hours. Andy Jackson, however, is nowhere to be seen, a fact noted in every story on the game.

January 26

All players attend today's ninety-minute optional workout. A two-game winning streak indeed inspires devotion.

Correct! Two consecutive victories, a 3-1 clout of the Red Wings at Detroit and 5-4 whipping of the St. Louis Blues at home. "I've never used heroin," Hartley said after the Blues win. "But I imagine the jolt is like what you get from two in a row."

We're perched on the boards by the bench when Dave Berman rests an elbow on the fence.

"There's nothing in the coach's manual on how to get guys off the ice when they don't want to go," Berman says. "When I re-write it, I'll have to cover the subject."

"Tell 'em a guy with the initials A.J. is a guest coach and they'll depart fast," I suggest.

Berman is six-foot-three and no more than 155 pounds, but he's so relaxed he'd make Valium look tense. He's been our head coach for ten days and this morning, Baby-Joel breaks us up when he says: "Dave is the antithesis of that other son-of-a-bitch, ain't he?"

"The what of who, Baby?" Hartley says.

Baby-Joel gets a look on his face as if Hartley couldn't understand "hello." "The antithesis," he says. "Ain't you got no knowledge of the English language?"

"Where did you learn that word?" I ask. "Henry, did you teach him a dirty word?"

"Don't blame me," Henry says. "I had a tough time teaching him to eat with a knife and fork."

"What are you laughing for?" Baby-Joel says, offended. "The Norwegian uses the word and no one laughs. Did I use it wrong? Ain't Berman the antithesis of the other guy?"

"Baby," I tell him, "your usage is impeccable."

Berman watches Jimmy Miller control the puck in a game of "hog" with five players. "I hate to be poetic about it," he smiles. "But I wonder how many men have worked a lifetime and never had one of the greatly gifted like that kid to coach."

As Berman said in his first talk to the team: "I'm a few months out of Tier Two junior in an Alberta dog-patch. Don't despair if I have a look of bewilderment at being here."

To date, we haven't spotted any bewilderment in Berman. Mostly, we've found, in the immortal words of our new philosopher, the antithesis of how it was.

Our triumph over the Soviets, as the political writers say, "sent shock waves through the nation." That Andy Jackson divorced himself completely from the game received wide publicity, and two days after, Jennifer Brown wrote a long story on it quoting "a source close the Big Green." The source was me.

The yarn included a detailed explanation of our preparation for the game, the scouting, the secret workouts and Jackson's attitude. It didn't mention the party.

The party now is the most-discussed underground story in the NHL. Of course, the fable has expanded. On-ice chats reveal that we (a) drugged the Soviets; (b) fed them spoiled booze to induce illness; (c) lined them up with carriers and the needles produced a weak condition.

A day after the Soviet game, we played the Chicago Black Hawks and came down so far from the high that they beat us, 8-3. Jackson was there in body but looked very grim.

The next morning, Peter Edmunds invited (ordered is a better word) Hartley and me to appear at the home of Clive Anderson IV for dinner that night.

Definitely a summit. No wives, just we two, three Andersons, Edmunds and Wallace Morgan, the attorney. I hardly recognized Clive Eye-Vee without a long booze.

Gerald did the talking and he didn't jack around. "When we have trouble with a division of our transport company, we don't have the truck drivers in for a conference. But we've made an exception this time."

Hartley looked as if he was ready to storm out.

"A bit harsh I know," Gee-One added. "But what has happened is serious stuff. My father, my brother and I got involved in hockey to have some fun and make a buck, if we could. But we've made serious mistakes. We're successful truckers because we've been good businessmen. When we got a hockey team, we forgot about good business. But we've been jolted to our senses this week.

"What's said remains in this room. So let's be frank. First, we congratulate you on the win over the Soviets. Don't try any bullshit about how you did it or why. We know the whole story and it was brilliant.

"It accomplished what you wanted it to do. Andy Jackson is finished as our head coach. Hiring him was a mistake, made because of our lack of hockey smarts and a mix-up in our operation. From now on, the hockey decisions will be made by Peter Edmunds. Believe that. And no tricks on your part will force us to replace him. Our stubborn backing of Jackson forced Peter into a, well, strained relationship with you. We've cleared that up and hope you can, too.

"We want viewpoints on a new coach from you, although it's probably bad business to allow the workers to have any say in picking their boss. Hartley, you were in Fort Worth. Is Dave Berman ready to coach in the NHL?"

"Yes, no doubt about it. He's young, bright, creative and innovative, handles people well and knows the game inside out. He's an excellent teacher, works hard and is a secure man who doesn't allow anyone to take advantage of his easy-going nature."

"Is he the man for the Big Green job?"

"Absolutely."

"Why?"

"In Fort Worth, he got old pros to produce and helped young kids make good progress. We have the same combination here."

Gee-One nodded: "Good. I was hoping you'd say that. Because Pete wants to make a new start with Berman as head coach. He'll be under no pressure to produce quickly, although we won't get upset if the club shows an improvement. It will be a long-range plan. One other thing: Any ideas on an assistant coach?"

That was the question I'd been waiting for: "Brooker Duncan."

"Brooker?" Gee-One said in an astonished tone. "Are you serious?"

"He knows how to play maybe better than anyone I've ever seen," I replied. "He's great with kids and he can really teach. He's also one of the best people I've ever met."

So Jackson was fired, Sammy Sparks, too, and left town immediately. There were no quotes from Andy in the press. He didn't even call us up and say goodbye.

Berman arrived and the team held a low-key press conference for him. He then had a low-key meeting with us.

"I need time to get to know you and how you play," he said. "I'm easy to get along with, I think. I don't rant and rave; it wastes energy. I like players who make suggestions, so do it. I lean to basic hockey because if you don't play it well, you can't do the other stuff.

"I'll have some help, and these guys hate me because they figured they were doing enough. Harry Tatum is in charge of all areas of our conditioning program. Brooker will be my playing assistant for the rest of the season and I'm very happy about that. Guys with a particular skill will work with you in those areas—Hartley on faceoffs, Sven on passing and Mulligan on milking cows.

"Don't expect miracles. The best way I've found to have fun is to win a few. Remember, though, that Jimmy Miller is a grizzled NHL veteran compared to me."

It would be nice to relate that we executed a quick turnaround, but it doesn't work that way. In our first game under Berman, we were so up-tight we tripped over the blueline and lost to Hartford. We lost to Toronto and New Jersey, too, but slowly, Berman's gentle efforts to improve the club showed.

Our workouts are now lively and productive because there's a purpose to everything he and Brooker do. Often, he has to chase us off the ice after two hours. On a road trip to Minnesota and Winnipeg, we played two fine games and earned our first point of the season, a tie with the Jets.

Then came the win at Detroit when Berman had the team well prepared and the Red Wings scouted thoroughly. We executed a simple plan well.

And we'll do it again. Sure, we won't bag a berth in the Stanley Cup playoffs, but even that has its good side.

For the first time in years I'll be home in April, helping Little Charlie get ready for the spring planting and the operation ready for the season that matters most. Maybe I'll even drop in at Wally Kelly's hardware store during the Cup final telecasts to add a little personal color commentary for the old timers who have assembled there for years to watch the big one. Of course, for the last few years they've been there to cheer on the old river skater as he led the Canadiens to another great parade down the rue Ste. Catherine. So maybe the boys will be quieter this year.

By April, too, my house will be ready to move into. It'll cost me my goal scoring bonuses to get the workmen to put on some speed, especially in the winter, but by March some smart-ass woman now known as Clarice Mulligan wants to start decorating the place.

The night of the magnificent win over the Soviets I talked to her on the phone, babbling away almost incoherently. And as soon as I asked her to marry me I figured it must be the euphoria, the champagne, anything, that finally made me do it.

But when I had to call her back the next day, and the next, to see if she'd thought it over enough, I knew it was more than booze or beating the Russians. On those days I was seriously sober. If I didn't know her so well, I would have thought that she'd been coached by the Big B to play hard to get.

The thought strikes me tonight that life might not be as much fun, having settled down and all. But I'm still playing the greatest game in the world, even if it is for an outfit in Cleveland, of all places. And the way the kids have been improving, we'll be in the playoffs next year, given luck and a good draft.

As for the fun. Well, last night Hartley and I were driving back to town. He was deep in thought for most of the journey, then finally he said: "Hey, Willie, want to spend a hundred and have a little fun?"

"I shudder to ask how."

"Well," he said. "We play the New York Rangers on Wednesday night and I have this little scheme on how we might win that game."